PITCHFORK

THE POMEGRANATE SERIES
BOOK II

PITCHFORK

NICOLE SCARANO

Copyright © 2019 by Nicole Scarano

All rights reserved.

No part of this book may be reproduced in any form or by any electronic or mechanical means, including information storage and retrieval systems, without written permission from the author, except for the use of brief quotations in a book review.

Cover Designed by Fay Lane
Formatting by Nicole Scarano Formatting & Design

*No generative AI was used in the writing or design of this book.

CONTENTS

Prologue	1
I	3
II	13
III	21
IV	31
V	43
VI	57
VII	75
VIII	81
IX	89
X	97
XI	111
XII	123
XIII	137
XIV	153
XV	159
XVI	169
XVII	183
XVIII	193
XIX	203
XX	215
XXI	223
XXII	229
XXIII	237
XXIV	245
XXV	253
XXVI	261
XXVII	269
XXVIII	283
XXIX	291
XXX	305
XXXI	319
XXXII	329
XXXIII	337

XXXIV	343
XXXV	349
XXXVI	355
Epilogue	363
Also by Nicole Scarano	365
About the Author	367

*For My Dog, China.
She is my Kerberos.*

PROLOGUE

The Oracle of Delphi's eyes rolled back into her skull; their whites an eerie beacon in the night's inky black; her growling voice suddenly silenced by her body's violent spasms. She shook uncontrollably on the cold stone floor, her fingers bloody. Fingernails cracked and splintered. Then as abruptly as the convulsions seized her, they ceased, and with the thud of her skull, the Oracle sprawled to the floor. Eyes flickering in her head, she lay impossibly still, unconscious.

Her handmaiden hovered in the doorway, feet cemented to the cold ground in consuming terror. She should go to her mistress, should lift her cracked head from the floor, but the handmaiden could not peel the soles of her feet from the icy tiles. So there she stood, paralyzed in silence.

The handmaiden had been in the Oracle's service for as long as she could remember. She loved this woman and was honored to serve the almighty gods by serving the prophet, but here in the dark, she could not bring herself to help. She had seen prophecies, seen the Oracle convey the gods' commandments since childhood, but this trance was the likes of which she had never seen before. This was different. The evil bleeding through the room from the Oracle's body was palpable.

Without warning, the Oracle bolted upright, eyes wide and understanding. She had returned her own mind, and frantically she searched the darkened chamber. She knew not where she was, nor why her fingers burned in pain as she stared at the indecipherable symbols her blood had traced on the cold stone. The Oracle's gaze shot to the handmaiden, but the girl offered no explanation save the expression of fear marring her face, and the Oracle knew. She had prophesied, yet that was not why the maid stood frozen in the doorway. The Oracle understood, and dread crept from the maiden's eyes into her own heart.

"What did I say?" The Oracle whispered, her bloody fingers shaking. When the handmaiden failed to respond, she shifted to her knees and stared at the crude etchings carved into the floor. Her body grew cold, gooseflesh disfiguring her skin. "Tell me!" she screamed into the darkness. "By the gods, what did I say?"

|

"Wife?" The deep gravel voice intruded her sleep, rousing her to the land of the living.

"Hmm," Hades mumbled and stretched out a hand, blindly groping around the bed until it brushed against rough stubble. "Quiet." She clamped her fingers over Alkaios' lips, all the while refusing to open her eyes. Alkaios smiled, lips dragging across her skin at the movement, and kissed her palm before peeling it from his mouth.

"Wife," he repeated, tugging gently on her hand. "Your dog…"

"Is something wrong?" Hades bolted upright in search of the beast. Alkaios rolled his eyes. Like a mother, Hades babied the three-headed monstrosity, and he was convinced nothing motivated her like the love of that god-killer.

Hades blinked the sleep from her eyelids, and Kerberos' sitting form came into focus at the foot of their bed, all six black eyes staring daggers at Alkaios. She shifted her gaze between her husband and dog and rolled her eyes, flopping back to the comfort of the pillows.

"Hades!" Alkaios groaned as he nudged her reclined figure.

"Please make Kerberos move. It is unnerving when he hovers over me in the night." In response, Kerberos' left snout's lips twitched slightly, baring massive fangs only to yawn wide and dramatically when Hades peeked through heavy eyelids to glimpse him. Innocence peppered his eyes as if he could not possibly be guilty of midnight terrors.

"Oh, great King of the Underworld!" Hades mocked with outstretched palms beckoning her pet. "You are the keeper of Hell, yet the god-killer terrifies you."

"I may be king now," Alkaios said as Kerberos padded to his mother's touch. "But that dog cares for only you. All of Hell seems to care for only you. I am a god, but you, my Queen, are the ruler."

Hades shifted and clasped Kerberos' middle head in her hands, drawing his devil's face to hers. "My darling, I am glad I am your favorite." With a smile, she pressed a kiss to the dog's leathery hide before releasing him.

Hades straightened with the realization her husband's paranoia was the end of her sleep, but as she sat up, a vicious wave of nausea crashed through her. Her stomach roiled and heaved, and it was all Hades could do to lunge over the bed before its contents spewed to the floor. She retched, coughing as her torso dangled in mid-air. Both Alkaios and Kerberos froze, and for a long moment neither dared to even breathe as alarm coursed through them. Tentatively, Alkaios reached out and placed a rough palm on the flat of his wife's back. Hades' muscles spasmed beneath his touch, and he could feel her ribs shudder within her skin.

"Hades?" Kerberos's left head looked at Alkaios, disdain replaced by concern, yet Alkaios only stared back, eyes wide and confused as Hades' body shook.

"Hades? Are you all right?"

Hades convulsed and with a ragged cough, pulled herself to sit on the bed.

"I do not know." She wiped the back of her hand across her mouth. "I have not been nauseous like that since I was mortal."

HADES LOST the contents of her stomach twice more before drifting into an exhausted sleep. Alkaios sat in the stillness, chin resting in his palms as he watched the soft even breaths fall from her ruby lips. Kerberos crowded his giant mass against the mattress, all three heads leaning on the bed in apprehension, his warm breath caressing Hades' skin.

Alkaios looked from the dog to his wife. This new world differed drastically from the life he had been born into, and sitting in the Underworld, concern consumed him. They had been married barely a year, but it was a year of both bliss and worry. Hades had sacrificed her birthright to save him from the Touch of the Gods; abandoned her Underworld's throne without hesitation, and the Universe had headed her plea. Her request judged selfless, Alkaios rose from farmer to King in a heartbeat, his body consuming power that was once Hades', but that was not what worried him. No, what plagued his thoughts was how the loss of divinity affected the woman he cherished. Stripped of what was rightfully hers, Hades had been deprived of the power that ran through her veins. It was not legitimately Alkaios' to wield, and the Underworld knew it. The beasts and the land bowed to him, but not in the way they submitted to Hades. She was what they desired, what they needed. Hence why the massive god-killer, who hovered at the edge of the bed, loved and respected his wife more than him. The whole of the Underworld craved Hades, taking her words as law. Even the Pitchfork, the divine weapon of the Underworld, still responded to her. One weapon with two masters was unheard of, especially when one master was no longer a god. Yet the pitchfork and all its might obeyed her commands. Alkaios understood why the beasts idolized Hades, perhaps even understood why the pitchfork deferred to her, but when the throne room shifted and groaned, all were astounded and shocked. Since the dawn of time, the throne stood solitary in the darkness. The Titan Cronus, the first great god the world ever worshipped, had reigned on that seat, and when Hades severed the Underworld's seal, it became hers. The single ruler destined to grace the thrones between Tartarus – the perpetual and winding staircase of torture where vile shades of cruel and evil mortals were punished for all eternity - and Elysium - the vibrant and gorgeous fields of heaven where the pure of heart were granted eternal blessings. For thousands of years, it remained stoically unchanged and alone, a figure of singular reign, but the moment Hades gifted Alkaios her power, the chamber transformed. From the ancient living citadel, a second throne grew beside the original, for the day Hades bequeathed him her divinity, even the Titan Fortress protested. The stone evolved as if to say it accepted Alkaios, but Hades was, and would always be, theirs.

Watching Hades' nausea this morning unsettled Alkaios. He was no fool. It was not his place to rule, and it terrified him that losing her power was affecting her. Hades had forgone her birthright, who she was at her core, and Alkaios worried the sacrifice was destroying her.

A knock at the door jerked Alkaios from his thoughts, and both his and Kerberos' eyes flicked upward, landing upon the lovely brunette peeking in.

"Alkaios?" Keres whispered softly as to not wake Hades. "You both should come. They are here."

HADES WAS first to round the corner and enter Charon the ferryman's bedroom, Alkaios and Keres hard on her heels, and the moment they saw them, all three of them, they froze in reverent silence.

"By all that is holy, they are beautiful," Hades murmured, gliding across the floor toward the bed where Ioanna reclined. Two, tiny golden-hair infants were cradled in her arms, their faces angelic in sleep. Charon perched beside her on the sheets with a third blonde babe dozing against his chest. Hades reached out, instinctively craving to hold one of the newborns, and Charon hauled himself to his feet and placed his child in her grasp. The moment her arms grew heavy with the small weight, Hades lifted the baby's silken head to her nose. She breathed deep the scent of new life and pressed a soft kiss on the lily-white skin.

"Three girls," Charon beamed through a wide smile. "The gods are good."

"Our god is good," Ioanna corrected, and it was not lost on Alkaios that she looked to Hades and not him.

"Come," Ioanna commanded Alkaios and Keres. "Hold them. I am now a mother of three, and my arms already need rest." A soft laugh escaped Keres' lips as she rushed to the bed and settled beside her friend. With gentle care, she lifted a babe. Alkaios followed suit, scooping up the third triplet, and the women smiled at the sight of the massive King of the Underworld cradling one of the smallest infants they had ever seen.

"You will need a bigger home," Alkaios observed, eyes examining the room. Charon and Ioanna's two-room boathouse grew from the River Styx, born from a piece of the ferryman's boat. After Charon's resurrection, Hades had severed a chunk from his ferry and plunged it into the river that separated earth from Hell; a body of water so poisonous that it would flay the skin of god and man alike all save for the shades – the souls of the departed traveling to their afterlife. The souls of the dead could pass through the Styx unharmed, although the journey was treacherous until Hades' rule.

The detached piece of wood came alive and rose, forming fiber-by-fiber, branch by intertwining branch, until a single plank of rotted timber became a living house hovering over the water. This home was comfortable for the ferryman and his wife, made cozy by Ioanna's touch, but as Alkaios looked around, he realized that with triplets, two rooms would not suffice. With a nod of his head, one wall began to un-grow. The wood shrank and retracted in on itself until a gaping hole tore through the bedroom, allowing the thick mist to rush in and envelope them. The infant in Hades' arms squirmed at her first taste of the river that would be her eternal home, the river her father ferried the dead across.

In a matter of moments, the tear in the wall changed directions as the wood extended farther over the current. Roots plunged down deep into the riverbed, and another room formed next to the bedroom. The expansion did not stop there, though. The walls continued their growth, and the house rose higher still until a second floor evolved into existence. Three rooms for three girls. Then as suddenly as it began, the timber gave one last shudder and returned to its solid state, and Alkaios turned back to the new parents.

"I can change it however you like, but a larger home will serve your family better," he said, surprised the power he associated with his wife was his to wield. Alkaios was a farmer, a man who survived off of endless work and despair. This power was not natural. It was Hades who coaxed the greatest responses with merely a nod of her head, not him.

"It is perfect." Ioanna gestured for him to come closer with a grateful smile. Alkaios obeyed and settled carefully on the mattress, and Ioanna leaned toward his cheek and pressed a kiss to his warm skin.

"Thank you." Charon clapped Alkaios' back as he walked past to settle behind Hades. His strong and calloused hands smoothed her shoulders, and he peered over her to gaze lovingly at his daughter cradled snuggly in the queen's arms. Her tiny eyes were clenched shut in peaceful slumber, and her soft cheek pressed comfortably against Hades' chest. The queen's heartbeat thundered a rhythmic lullaby against the child's ear, and the serene beauty on her chubby face defied the Underworld to its core.

"What are their names?" Hades asked as she twisted to glimpse her ferryman's profile. Charon's appearances were that of a young man, but the Titan was thousands of years older than she, and while the birth of his daughters made him a true father, Hades felt he had become one the day she resurrected him. His counsel and love guided her, and Hades trusted him enough to keep him hidden and safe from Zeus' vengeance. For if Zeus knew Charon lived, he would execute Charon like he did the rest of his Titan brethren.

"You hold the firstborn," Charon answered. "Her name is Clotho. Alkaios holds the second, and she is Lachesis. Keres holds Atropos, the youngest of our triplets."

Hades nodded, turning her head back to the golden infant she cradled. "Such fates these three are for you. The ending you both deserve after hundreds of years of separation. They are your Moirai, your fates - one to spin, one to measure, one to cut."

AFTER AN HOUR, the infants grew inconsolable. Their tiny lungs forced breath out in shrill screams. Their miniscule fists beat the air. The visitors took their leave with soft kisses and promises of return visits, and as Ioanna settled the babes to sleep, the walkway extended from the dock toward the dark shore. Hades moved gracefully to the sand where Kerberos and Chimera hauled themselves up from where they laid in restful waiting. Their paws, large and gruesome, padded after her to flank their mother with loving protection. Alkaios smirked as his wife and beasts continued ahead, and as his soles landed on the riverbank, the plank shriveled back on itself to return the boathouse to isolation.

"You should give up hope they will ever love you best," Keres grinned, sidling beside him to slip her arm through his. They watched with amusement as Hades reached out to rest her palms on each of her beasts' massive skulls. "She is their mother, a bond that cannot be usurped."

"I would not dare try," Alkaios laughed, placing his calloused hand over Keres' small fingers, but as suddenly as the sound burst from his lips, his laugh froze, voice strangled in the oppressive air. The hairs on the back of his neck rose, skin prickling warily, and his eyes shot to Kerberos. The god-killer had felt it too, his scarred, leathery hide riddled with gooseflesh.

"Who is it?" Alkaios asked, dropping Keres' arm. The dog twisted his necks, three sets of glaring eyes regarding the king, but beneath his surly demeanor, something lingered behind his irises. It was a protectiveness Alkaios had never seen the hound direct toward him before, and as Alkaios' long strides drew him beside his wife, Kerberos angled his neck protectively around the new king.

"It is he." Hades lifted her face to the air, feeling the presence born on the breeze, and Alkaios stiffened. He knew whom she meant. The one who bore the message; the one who had betrayed them. Hades had allowed the messenger access to her Underworld, the only god of Olympus permitted past the hellhound, and Zeus had known it. Zeus was the master behind the Touch of the Gods, but it was he who had delivered the eternal death by his fingers.

"Hermes!" Alkaios spat, voice echoing throughout the ever-changing terrain of the Underworld. In a shimmer of power, the messenger god appeared, far from the god-killers' reach.

"I am sorry," Hermes intoned, unable to meet Alkaios' burning stare. "I…"

"What is it you need," Alkaios interrupted harshly. He knew that Zeus had forced Hermes to carry the soul-shredding Touch of the Gods to the Underworld. He knew he should let the messenger apologize; that deep down, Hermes was not his enemy, but a man caught between what was right and what was all-powerful. His wife cared for the messenger god, and Alkaios would eventually forgive him of his sins, just not today.

"Zeus," Hermes quivered. "He has called an emergency council of the gods, and that demands you, Hades." Hades stepped forward past her beasts, and Hermes' eyes shot up to meet hers before flicking to her husband's. "He requires the god of the Underworld," he clarified, gazing fully at Alkaios' hulking frame for the first time since he had arrived. "He needs you."

II

The colossal council chamber doors swung wide with such violence they nearly wrenched from their hinges, and Alkaios strode through with thundering steps, the clang of the pitchfork striking the stone floor punctuating his footfalls. Dark head raised in confidence, his long stride bore down and propelled him into the center of the circular chamber, his hand outstretched behind him. Hades' smaller frame followed with equally regal force as her fingers lifted to slip into Alkaios' waiting palm. The same ferocity colored her eyes now as it did the time she discovered the council chamber had birthed a new throne, a throne destined for the third great god of might, Zeus' left hand. The trinity above the rest, their thrones reigned higher than the others. There was only one difference from the last time Hades had sat in on a council. That seat was now no longer hers.

The double doors thudded shut as the king and queen of death drifted through. The waiting gods startled in their seats at the slamming force, and Alkaios climbed the few steps to his throne, leading his raven-haired queen by their intertwined fingers. An uncomfortable noise escaped Hera's throat, which ignited a small smile on Hades' lips. Hera had tried desperately to separate Hades from Zeus, yet the universe saw fit to grace the throne between her and Zeus to the god of the Underworld.

"This is a council of the gods," Zeus said to Alkaios by way of greeting.

"And so I am here," Alkaios grunted as he settled into his seat and released Hades' hand. She slipped effortlessly behind him to lean on the stone back, black dress whispering about her ankles.

"Yet she is not." Zeus nodded to Hades without raising his eye to look at her. He had been unable to meet her gaze since his attempt to destroy Alkaios' soul with the Touch of the Gods. Zeus had expected the mortal's destruction to put an end to her, but her salvation of the man she loved infuriated him. Adding insult to injury, the mortal had publicly assumed the name Hades, god of the Underworld. To Zeus, Alkaios would never be more than the vile human Hades had used to embarrass him, but by transferring her power to her new husband, Alkaios was now Zeus' equal.

"Your wife is on the council," Alkaios responded, laying the pitchfork across his knees. "If your wife is present, then so shall mine."

"Hera is divine," Zeus said with bitter venom. "Hades is nothing after she so foolishly sacrificed her birthright for your life."

"Your wife, even as a god, has only a fraction of the power Hades holds," Alkaios snarled, the color in his eyes draining to solid and terrifying black, and with cold precision, he turned them on Zeus. "This pitchfork, the weapon of the Underworld, still answers to her. The Underworld still does her bidding. The great throne that your Titan father sat upon was a solitary figure since the beginning of time. The fortress never saw fit to grant your mother one, yet the moment Hades transferred her power, a second throne formed from the old stone. There now sits two, one for a king and another for his queen. She rules as I do, and so Hades stays. I make no decision without her."

Zeus twitched, but Poseidon's slender fingers clamped around his brother's bicep in a vice-like grip, holding him in place. With an almost imperceptible shake of his head, Poseidon sent a silent warning to his brother. The last time they challenged the god of death, an exacting price had been paid to stop her, and just because the players differed now, did not mean the power did.

"She stays," Poseidon said with a nod at Hades, "but only as an observer."

"Very well," Alkaios responded as he reached behind him. In response, Hades slipped her hand over his broad shoulder, and he covered her knuckles with his encompassing palm. The caring gesture was not lost on Zeus, and a pang of jealousy raged deep in his stomach.

"What is it that warrants this council?" Alkaios asked, looking around the room. He still had trouble believing that he, the lowly farmer, was in the divine's presence as an equal.

"A prophecy," Zeus answered, shaking off his irritation and standing. He walked to the floor of the chamber, removing a piece of parchment from his robes, and placed it on a stone pedestal in the middle of the room for all to witness. "The Oracle of Delphi's prayer called out in the dark hours this morning. I could hear the fear in her pleading, the urgency. I wasted no time in answering her. The Oracle was distraught and in pain, a deep terror in her eyes, for she had prophesied during the night."

"Why would a prophecy terrify her?" asked Ares. "The Oracle is anointed with a direct connection to the gods. She prophesies for us with regularity."

"Because," Zeus said, annoyed at the interruption. "She claims to have no knowledge of who spoke through her, nor does she have any memory of the prophecy. If it were not for her handmaiden witnessing it, she would have woken on the cold floor without an inkling of what had happened."

"How is that possible?" Poseidon asked. "She knows us well enough to recognize our presence. We never possess her in secret. She would have known whose message she spoke."

"She knows all, save one," Zeus twisted his eyes accusingly toward Alkaios with intent.

"This is why you summoned me," Alkaios spat, leaning forward in his seat. "The dark and evil god of the Underworld, who else would have possessed and terrified the Oracle?" Alkaios laughed, the sound harsh as it echoed about the room. "It was neither my wife nor I. We have had no need of the Oracle, and if we did, believe me, she would know for whom she spoke."

"In truth, I hoped it was you." Zeus stared at Alkaios, rubbing his fist over his mouth. His chest deflated in obvious concern. "I had hoped it was the dark god."

"Why?" Poseidon asked as he shifted forward in his throne.

"Because," Zeus exhaled, running his fingers through his short, golden-blonde hair. "She knew not who spoke through her. The king of death is the only god she is not acquainted with, and if it was not him, then who? Pray tell me, if anyone in this room prophesied through the Oracle last night and hid your identity from her, speak now."

"It was none of us," Ares answered as Zeus searched their faces with pleading eyes, but the Olympians only murmured their agreements with Ares.

"If it was not I nor any of the others, then who inspired the prophecy?" Alkaios asked, but Zeus just stared at him, rubbing his hand over his mouth once again with a furrowed brow.

"I do not know, and that concerns me. The Oracles are blessed with a divine connection to the supernatural hence why we speak through her with such ease. Anything of power should be able to use their prophetic voices, but if it was not the gods nor anyone from the Underworld, who then possesses the strength to not only enslave her but to cause her memory to fail?" The whole room fell silent, staring at one another, the gravity of Zeus' words sinking in.

"If something or someone can do this to her, we need to know," Zeus continued. "If there is a power besides us prophesying, this could bode ill."

"How do we know she is not lying?" Alkaios asked, and at his words, the gods burned scowling glances into his skin.

"The Oracle does not lie," Poseidon said. "Chosen at birth, the Oracles are women with divine connections to all things spiritual. They are born pure of heart to speak our messages to the masses, a requirement to become vessels of the gods. She would never lie on principle alone, but even if tempted to, she would refrain out of fear. It never ends well for those found lying."

"You did not see her," Zeus added. "One cannot fake the terror I saw in her soul, not to mention her fingers. She had dug them raw and bloody into the stone floor, her nails ripped and jagged. Something drove her to do that to herself. It was not of her own accord."

"What was the prophecy?" Alkaios stood and made his way down the steps toward Zeus.

"She could not tell me. It seems she carved the prophecy into the ground with her blood without knowing what she wrote." Zeus gestured to the parchment. "I attempted to see past her words, but whoever spoke through her is cloaked from me. I only know what little her handmaid witnessed."

"What did she hear?" Poseidon asked as he followed Alkaios' lead in making his way down the steps toward his brother.

"The first have come," Zeus answered. "The first have come, and they seek the last."

"The first?" came Ares' voice above the room's murmurs. "What does that mean?"

"I am at as much a loss as you," Zeus replied. "I assume the prophecy is written in full on that parchment. The Oracle copied her blood writing in ink for me to study."

"What language is this?" Alkaios asked, picking up the parchment from its resting place. Crude symbols were hastily etched across the surface. They resembled no normal letters, and despite the Oracle's penmanship, the runes were raw and primitive.

"I have never seen it," Zeus admitted.

"Nor have I," Poseidon agreed, and as the room burst into rumbling murmurs, Alkaios set the writing back on the pedestal and looked to his wife. She no longer stood behind his throne but was walking toward the parchment, eyes narrowed on the symbols. The gods jostled, vying for a sight of the strange words, and not a soul besides Alkaios bothered to notice Hades as she slunk through the chaos.

"This is not a language of our time or our father's." Zeus raised his voice above the din of the crowd. "Its crudeness hints of ancient origins, but there is an evil to these symbols. It bled through the Oracle's home, permeating from her blood, and I am concerned what dark power could cause this? I need all on this council to go to your realms and search. We must discover for whom the Oracle spoke."

As the crowd jostled, Alkaios noticed Hades pass him, inching toward the unattended parchment. He stepped in behind her only to be elbowed harshly in the ribs by a wildly gesturing Athena.

"I have seen these before," Hades murmured under her breath, her voice drowned in the conversation's confusion. Alkaios watched her drift, seamlessly parting the sea of bodies, and sidestepping Athena, he rubbed his stinging skin and drove through the crowd after his wife. He closed the distance with a few long strides and reached for her elbow just as she grabbed for the prophecy.

"I know these..." but Hades never finished her sentence, for the moment her fingers connected with the parchment, her eyes twisted violently into her skull, and her body convulsed in heaving spasms. Her head snapped backward at an unnatural angle, her neck twisting like a broken doll, and Hades crashed to the floor. Alkaios shot forward, arms outstretched to catch her falling figure, but she plummeted with such a force, his fingertips merely brushed her cold skin as she slipped through his grasp. The room fell into sudden silence at the crack of Hades' skull against the stone. Not a single word escaped the gaping mouths save for Alkaios' desperate voice calling Hades' name as she writhed on the ground, eyes rolled so far back that only the whites could be seen.

III

"I have never seen these symbols," Charon said as he and Alkaios made their way through the fire-lit fortress. The crumbling fixture had once been home to the Titans before the Great War's destruction condemned it to rot in solitude between Tartarus and Elysium. "If this language ever existed, it predates the Titan."

"It was worth asking," Alkaios sighed with disappointment, taking the parchment back from his friend. "Zeus has never seen this writing, but I hoped since you are older you might have."

"I wish I could help, but this is beyond me."

"But what I do not understand is why it affected Hades and no one else?" Alkaios said. "It was instant. She touched it and was convulsing on the floor. She thrashed about, her body refusing to calm, and when she stilled, she remained locked in unconsciousness and has yet to wake. Zeus said this was only a copy of what the Oracle had carved in blood. How could ink and parchment curse her?"

"It makes little sense," Charon answered as they turned the corner toward the ancient throne room. "Simple ink should not carry a curse, but we know not what is written here. The Oracle is human, and she wrote it, so it does not seem to affect mortals. Nor does it affect us, the gods. Perhaps because Hades is now immortal, but that seems improbable. There is a small chance, yet also unlikely, that this message is meant for her. Hades has seemed unwell as of late. I see you try to hide it, but do not forget I am still a god in my own right. Perhaps the loss of power is causing her troubles, but these are only guesses. Until you find the meaning behind these symbols, we will not know for sure."

As they entered the throne room, a black figure huddled on the second throne drew their gaze. Bare feet rested on Kerberos' giant ribcage, rising and falling with his deep breaths.

"Hades?" Alkaios' voice echoed off the cavernous walls, and his wife turned her head. She gave him a weak smile, and the dark circles under her eyes took Alkaios aback. They spread heavy over her pallid skin like black ink smudged from dirty fingertips.

"How do you feel?" Charon asked as he stepped over the three-headed dog and captured Hades' face in his palms, examining her sluggish features.

"My vision is blurry," she whispered. Her lilted words passed through her lips with unusual difficulty.

"Why did you get up?" Alkaios asked as he sunk to a crouch beside the ferryman.

"Looking for you." Hades gripped her husband's fingers. "But I cannot see through the pain in my head. I waited for you to find me instead."

Both men grimaced at her words, and Alkaios stood, careful to avoid crushing the reclining dog, and scooped Hades to his chest. Kerberos bolted upright, his incredible height allowing one of his heads to nudge his mother's limp and hanging arm until it rested across her belly.

"Thank you," Alkaios nodded to Charon and carried his wife into the darkness, concerned god-killer in tow.

Blood streamed down the walls, pooling on the floor and causing Hades' bare feet to slip and stumble over the slick stone as she fled. Death engulfed her, the smell permeating her nose. Decay clung thick to her hair. She knew not where she was nor why she was running, only that she must escape. This massacre knew no bounds, and the bodies sprawled on the ground begged her to join them in their cold slumber.

Hades skidded around a sharp corner, feet sliding over the sticky surface. Her shoulder smashed into the wall with such savage impact, pain exploded in her bones, and her stumble plummeted her racing form to the foul ground. Yet she did not stop. She could not stop, and so Hades crawled, hands slapping before knees, fingers slipping in the red puddles. Her black dress grew heavy with crimson as it dragged over the carnage, the wet weight slowing her flee. She struggled to stand, but her toes grappled in the slickness, and her panicked body crashed to the floor. Her cheek slapped the pooling blood, splashing blindness into her irises, coating her hair. When Hades blinked the thickness away, the eyes of death stared back. Wide, unblinking eyes.

Hades' heart vomited into her throat. Pure and unadulterated panic snuck boney fingers chokingly about her heart. Deaf and blind with terror, Hades vaulted over the unearthly corpse, but salvation was not to be had, for the shadow was now ahead of her, its dark mass falling on the stone as it rounded the corner. The horns poised to shred flesh from living bone.

"Hades!" a distant, urgent voice reverberated off the haunted halls. "Hades!" With a sudden violent pitch, the corridor heaved. The hallways shuddered, threatening to open wide the mouth of Hell and swallow her whole, yet she ran, desperate to remain on her feet. "Hades?"

Hades bolted upright violently and heard the crack of a nose breaking before the pain of the impact split her forehead, but that did not stop her escape. She leapt from the bed and ran, tripping over yet another body sprawled in death.

Kerberos grunted as his mother stumbled forcibly over him in her haste and looked to Alkaios. The dog stared in wide-eyed bewilderment as Alkaios snapped his crooked nose back into place with a sick crunch. For a moment their eyes held one another's gaze, uncertainty coloring their faces, and then as if of a single mind, they simultaneously surged after her into the blackness.

Hades burst from the bedroom and stumbled over Chimera, who failed to flatten himself against the wall in time to evade her wild flee. One of Hades' god-killers, the massive lion with the tail of a snake appeared as a large goat to his prey until their fate was sealed. Only then would they see his true form, but here in the Underworld, Chimera preferred to remain in his vicious feline state and slept faithfully each night in Hades' doorway. Most nights his mass was a comfort to his mother, but tonight as she crashed over his body, heels crushing his ribs, Hades' only acknowledgment of him was her stumbling. The sprawling lion roared at his panicked mother, but Hades was deaf to his cries. Her feet carried her with thundering power farther into the night. Chimera shifted his beastly head to watch Alkaios and Kerberos vault from the doorway before hauling himself forward in pursuit of his queen.

"Hades?" Keres mumbled. The pounding commotion woke her, and at first, she thought it merely a dream, but at Chimera's familiar snarl, she pushed her legs from the warmth of the blankets. The cold floor pricked her feet as she shuffled toward the door, but the moment she crossed the threshold, her body was shoved viciously backward. Hades' powerful fist forced her to crash against the doorframe. Keres' arms flailed, grasping for a fingerhold to halt her fall, but it was of no use. Her skull cracked against the stone.

"Are you all right?" Alkaios called as he sprinted past, not slowing to help the crumbled woman.

"Fine," Keres murmured as she watched god and beast disappear down the hall. Her palms drifted behind her and pushed her from the wall, and with absentminded strokes, she rubbed the painful welt swelling on her head. Hades had never raised a hand in violence to her. Not once, not ever, and Keres knew something had to be wrong. She should follow her mistress, but she hovered in the darkness too concerned to move.

Alkaios chased his wife through the fortress. He had never witnessed Hades move with such speed, and despite the raw strength coursing through his legs, he failed to gain on her. It was as if Tartarus itself clawed at her heels, the look in her eyes that of a crazed and cornered animal.

"Hades!" Alkaios called, and in a twisting mass of black inky smoke, he disappeared only to materialize seconds later outside the door to the Underworld. Hades screamed at the vision of his bulk barring the door, eyes wide with terror as she dug in her heels. Her feet skidded, desperate to stop, but her speed propelled her forcibly careening through the door. With a bone-jarring impact, she collided with Alkaios' solid chest. The force sent them sprawling to the ground in a pile of intertwined limbs, and as fast as a bolt of Zeus' lightning, Hades scrambled over his prone body. Before she could escape, Alkaios shot out his fist and caught her ankle. Hades wrenched her foot, but his iron hold refused release, and Hades careened forward. Her face slammed into the dirt, grit flooding her mouth as she heaved in anxious breaths. A scream ripped from her lungs, and her nails clawed the dirt. Hades spit the dust from her tongue as she thrashed, frantic to free herself from Alkaios' fist.

"Hades!" Alkaios bellowed. "Wake up!" He yanked her ankle, hauling his wife across the ground. "My love, wake up." He seized her waist with a thick bicep and with a groaning heave, pinned her beneath his hulking weight. When mortal,

Alkaios had been powerful for a man, but the day Hades gifted him her power, his mass grew in strength. He was imposing and massive, yet as she thrashed in screaming terror, his wife was almost impossible to contain. Despite Hades' smaller stature, her strength rivaled his with ferocious brutality.

"Hades," Alkaios called over her protests, voice softening. "Hades, please." At his soothing tone, her struggling calmed, and her gaze slowly settling on his handsome face. The blood from his broken nose dripped down his skin, and Hades' breath jerked from her ragged and terrified.

"They are dead," Hades sobbed. "They are all dead."

"No one is dead, my love," Alkaios whispered, pulling his weight off her and lifting her frame into his lap. "You were having a nightmare."

"They are!" Hades insisted through desperate tears. "They are all dead. Their blood... I'm wearing it!" She glanced down as if to prove her words only to have confusion cloud her eyes when she saw only dirt stained her palms. Hades looked back to her husband, the blood dried on his lips the proof she searched for. "See." Her fingertips ghosted gently down Alkaios' cheek to find the flaking rusty drops. "All are dead. It is their blood we wear."

"Hades, you did this when you bolted from bed. You broke my nose. This is my blood, and mine alone."

"Could I really have been dreaming?" Hades sobbed, clutching at his chest for comfort. "It felt real. I could have sworn the bodies were real."

ALKAIOS WOKE HOURS LATER. In the early morning, he had finally calmed Hades enough for her to speak the blood-soaked dream. He had listened in the dark with his fingers clamped around her hands, and when her racing heart slowed to its normal rhythm, he had fallen asleep, cradling his wife flush against his chest.

Alkaios shifted in the sheets and found Hades long gone, her pillow abandoned and cold. Alkaios exhaled, the air a rush as it escaped his lungs, and shoved the blankets from his legs. His spine no longer cracked and groaned with the burden of mortality, but he still stretched out of habit as he wandered into the silent hallway. The air felt empty on his skin, telling him he was alone, and Alkaios disappeared in tentacles of black smoke.

Moments later he stood on Charon's boathouse. Mist shrouded the Ferryman as his boat pierced the River, but Alkaios could vaguely see the outlines of the souls he bore to their judgment. Ioanna rocked her sleeping daughters' lazily on the dock as she watched her husband's skilled form slice through the Styx.

"I think they like the babes," Ioanna called over her shoulder. Confused, Alkaios opened his mouth to question her, but Keres chose that moment to exit the house. She smiled at the king and nodded toward the dark shore before shuffling to Ioanna. Alkaios shifted his eyes to where she indicated and was surprised to find both Kerberos and Chimera lounging lazily in the sand.

"I should let them meet the girls once they grow older," Ioanna continued with a tired but blissful smile as Alkaios settled behind her. "They seem almost protective of my daughters."

"So it is only me the dog takes offense with?" Alkaios laughed.

"The dog holds no one but his mother in high regard," Keres smiled. "He tolerates us. The lion is slightly better, but it appears not even the monsters of Hell can resist the charms of baby girls." She scooped one of the sleeping infants into her cradling arms and kissed her silky head, savoring the scent all newborns wear upon their skin. Alkaios' lips turned up in agreement and with tender care, lifted the child's impossibly tiny fist into his palm.

"Is Hades here?" Alkaios asked as he rubbed the soft knuckles. The child's skin was perfectly smooth, and Alkaios felt he could be content to simply sit here on this dock with her small hand in his. "Or is she with Charon?"

"I have not seen her this morning," Ioanna answered.

"Not since last night," Keres chimed in foreseeing his question as she absentmindedly rubbed the back of her sore head.

"Hmm," Alkaios mumbled and left before either woman could ask if there was reason for concern. "Come!" he commanded as he passed Kerberos and Chimera, and without challenge, both hauled themselves off the sand. Monsters in tow, Alkaios returned to the fortress, delved deep within his own mind. He searched for Hades' presence, and when he felt her like the sun on his skin, the three of them vanished in tentacles of inky smoke.

"Alkaios!" Hades blurted, bolting to her feet. Her limbs shook violently as she closed the distance in two strides, and Alkaios enveloped her in his strong arms. He crushed her to his heart hard enough to break her bones, but her strength withstood his fierce embrace as Hades clung to his chest.

"What are you doing here?" Alkaios asked as Kerberos and Chimera circled Hades to rub their skulls against her legs. They had found Hades huddled in a section of the fortress' rubble none of them had set their sights on before. Alkaios knew this ancient home of the Titans was extensive. Rooms and corridors were shrouded in dust, unseen for centuries and destined never to have eyes view them again, and finding Hades so far from all they knew concerned him.

"I am not sure," Hades answered as she pulled back to look into his mud-blue eyes. "I woke up deep in the fortress and did not recognize my surroundings. I wandered for hours but only succeeded in confusing my directions. Eventually, I sat knowing you would come for me."

Unsure how to respond, Alkaios clung to his wife. Hades was not a woman who lost her way in her own realm. She was not a woman to sit and wait to be rescued. Something was wrong with the woman he loved, and an ugly fear churned Alkaios' stomach as he brought her back to the familiar rooms they called home.

IV

"This is not Hades," Alkaios said, voice carrying through the mist. "This is not the woman I married." He sat on Charon's boat as the ferryman shoved his pole deep into the riverbed. The thick fog clung to their skin, only parting long enough for the vessel to slice through before enveloping the water once again with its heavy curtain.

"She is the rock our Underworld was built upon," he continued, meeting Charon's gaze. "She may have times of uncertainty, but she is the one we pray to… not a woman who loses herself in her own home."

"I wish I knew the words to help you," Charon said. He drew the pole from the resisting mud and let the ferry drift through the rippled current. "Her transfer of power is unprecedented. No god has ever gifted their divinity to another, especially a mortal. Zeus transferred Olympian divinity to Hades when he so-called created her, but that had no bearing on Hades' rise. No man-made god could possess the strength required to shatter the seal to the Underworld like she did. This realm was hers since time began. If you had asked me, I would have told you that transferring such power was impossible, but the universe saw fit to grant her request. You became Hades, but I do not think you were meant to. Hades was destined to be our god. Her control of the depths was absolute, and against all odds, remains so. The darkness still craves her, still bows to her. The fortress birthed a second throne so your reign would not usurp hers. If your fate was to ultimately seize power, she would have been merely a placeholder; a figurehead destined to fade once you rose to the throne, yet our domain has refused to allow that. She rules the darkness despite her stripped title. I believe Hades, deep in her soul, is our god, but her sacrifice caused a gap between her reality and her destiny. Perhaps her mind cannot handle the fragmentation."

"So this is my fault," Alkaios sighed, running a hand through his hair. His body deflated like sails being purged of their wind, and he felt small amidst the endless fog that blanketed the river.

"No." Charon sank to a seat. "You are not to blame. Hades made a choice, and perhaps I am mistaken. Perhaps her actions were preordained. Only, the pitchfork prefers to answer to her. Kerberos loves her only, and Chimera chooses her before you. Keres and I serve you loyally, but we are your family. We differ from the beasts, but we bow to Hades. That will never change. Power is not something to abuse. You cannot treat it carelessly without repercussions. This is the only explanation I can see, but by the gods, I hope I am wrong."

Keres sat with Ioanna and Hydra in the boathouse, eating pomegranate seeds and watching the triplets sleep. Alkaios and Charon had disappeared into the mist a while ago and had yet to emerge.

"Hades should join us," Ioanna said, wiping red juice from her fingers. "I have three daughters and three friends. She should come help so I do not have to hold any children when you all visit."

"Motherhood tiring you already?" Keres laughed.

"Yes," Ioanna said with a teasing smile. "I was so happy when I discovered I was with child, but triplets! Someone is always hungry."

"In time they will be grown, and you will wish they were home with you instead of trying to ride demon horses or chasing Hydra's snakes."

"I know most mothers would balk at that statement, but if they want to chase Hydra and not me, then I will be thankful for the respite." Ioanna laughed with raised eyebrows at the snake-eyed woman.

"Speaking of Hades, where is she?" asked Hydra, her white-blue eyes glinting in the mist that crept its way into the house. The third god-killer of the Underworld, Hydra resembled an exotic woman until the deadly snakes of Tartarus slipped from her veins. For every one you killed two more were born until all was consumed in death and poison.

"Not sure," Keres answered not making eye contact.

"Keres," Hydra interrupted. "We aren't fools. We know something is not right. I can feel it in my bones, something is shifting in her, cracking her. Besides, I scent the blood in your hair."

Keres fingers flew to her skull and feathered over the lump from the night before, a result of Hades barreling into her.

"She did that to you didn't she?" Hydra pressed.

"Yes," Keres blurted in frustration, "but this is no time to come against her."

"We are not coming against her," Ioanna insisted. "I owe my life and happiness to that woman. I love my husband and daughters more than anything in this world, except for her. Hades possesses a spot deep within me no one can replace."

"We want to help," Hydra added. "I know Hades and you

have a bond that is unbreakable. You were the first to find her, and she holds you in high regard. I had just hoped you knew what the turmoil below her surface was."

"I do not wish to speak about this any longer," Keres said, standing to leave. "It feels like blasphemy." And with that, she left.

KERES WANDERED through the fortress in search of Hades, but as her slight figure drifted from room to room, all she encountered was empty silence in the flickering torchlight. Hades was nowhere to be found, and standing at the edge of the light's reach, Keres realized she would have to venture into the dark decay. Returning to the clean and lit sections they had transformed from destruction to a home, Keres settled into the doorway of Hades' bedroom to find Chimera sleeping on his mother's bed.

"Take me to her, darling," she said as his fangs yawned large in a lazy complaint. Chimera blinked his wide eyes and with a rumbling purr, slid from the mattress. Hades called her monsters darling, and Keres found herself repeating the term of endearment with more frequency. She was not sure when the shift in her perception of them had occurred, but as Chimera padded down the hall, a small surge of affection for the graceful creature thawed Keres' heart.

Following the lion through the dark rubble, they came upon the second doorway of the fortress. Hades had broken the sealed door that led to Tartarus and the Underworld, but this one opened to the rolling fields of Elysium. The scent of fresh grass wafted on the warm breeze as Keres closed the distance, and in the cheery light that spilled into the citadel from the heavenly fields huddled Hades and Kerberos.

"Hades?" Keres called, but no sooner did her voice leave her mouth, Hades bolted upright and screamed. She scrambled across the stone floor in panic, leaving Kerberos to watch dumbstruck.

"Get away from me, demon," Hades spat, backing into the shadows. She was feral, a cornered animal.

"Hades?" Keres inched forward but froze in her tracks when Hades flinched in terror. "It is me, Keres."

"Stay away from me!"

"Hades, please..." Keres reached her hands out in a placating gesture, but Hades lashed out, slapping her hard across the face. Keres sprawled to the floor with a thud, a red flush blooming over her cheek.

"Keres?" Hades questioned, suddenly recognizing the woman before her. She pushed off the wall and scrambled to lift her friend from the ground. "Is that you?"

"Hades, what is happening to you?"

"I do not know." A hitched sigh escaped Hades lips as she sank against the doorframe, the cold stone contrasting with Elysium's spring breeze. "I saw you, but to my eyes, you appeared as a monster. I did not recognize you." A small tear escaped Hades' eye and traced a slow path down her skin, and Keres' heart broke. She shifted her weight and settled beside her queen, wrapping an arm around Hades' shoulders. For long moments they sat side by side in comforting silence, Kerberos and Chimera curled on the floor before them.

"I see what is not there?" Hades whispered leaning her head against Keres'. "I fear I am losing my mind."

ALKAIOS WOKE with a start as the bed pitched beneath him. He did not remember falling asleep. He had been laying beside Hades, their fingers entwined between them as they faced the ceiling deep in conversation. She had become nauseous during the evening meal they shared with their surrogate family, and despite her best efforts to conceal it, Alkaios had noticed Hades' discomfort radiating through the air. Excusing himself, he had scooped her into his arms and carried her to their bedroom, her laughter bouncing off the walls as Keres and Hydra smirked at the antics of the newlyweds. It was not until they disappeared from sight that Hades sagged against her husband's thundering heart. The fight seeped from her skin, and her temple rested on Alkaios' collarbone in exhaustion.

Both Kerberos and Chimera meandered behind them, their ever-watchful eyes protecting their mother as Alkaios crawled over their lavish blankets to settle his wife among the cushions. They laid content in the silence, their breathing the only sound filling the space, and long moments passed where Hades had not moved save to place a hand on her roiling stomach. Alkaios left her in peace, unsure if touching her would cause further discomfort, but eventually, her fingers crawled across the mattress to seize his. Hades smiled into the air and recounted a story of Charon's triplets that brought light to her beautiful eyes.

The conversation flowed from their lips with tumbling speed after that, and as the night turned to morning, they felt almost normal; their troubles forgotten in their unending words. They talked about everything and nothing, and it reminded Alkaios of the nights they had spent together in their early days when a farmer and a woman named Persephone were desperate to learn all they could about one another.

"Hades!" Alkaios' heart leapt into his throat as Kerberos lunged with snarling fangs. His massive chest collided with the bed frame, the peace shattered by teeth shredding the air.

"Hades, what is wrong with him?" Alkaios mumbled as he rolled to find cold, empty sheets as the dog crashed around the foot of the bed to shove his middle snout against her pillow. Kerberos' outer heads stared poignantly through the night while his concerned eyes bore into Alkaios.

"Where is she?" Alkaios asked, and Kerberos growled in response, snapping his teeth against Alkaios' skin before lumbering anxiously toward the door. Alkaios flung the sheets from his legs and swung his feet to the stone. The moment his soles connected with the floor, the dog bolted for the doorway with the king hard on his heels, and together they plunged into the darkness, weaving through battered hallways no life had seen in centuries.

The rooms in between the two great doors where they dwelled were in decay, but through Hades' and Keres' tireless work, it had transformed into something almost homey. Their home was nothing like the devastation they found here. These distant sections of the fortress no longer resembled the structure it once was. Walls had deteriorated to dust, doors wrenched in half, and debris littered the floor in blankets of carnage, baring their path with nearly impenetrable obstructions. The ancient ceiling had long ago collapsed, the air above nothing but a vast, eternal blackness.

Their descent into the depths was endless, the twists and turns the wreckage forced them to take confusing Alkaios' sense of direction, and when they passed a scorched wall, déjà vu washed over him. His fingers brushed over the scoured stone. Its pattern struck him as familiar, and Alkaios' eyes shot to the flanks of the beast before him. Was the dog lost, or was he leading them in circles on purpose?

"Kerberos?" Alkaios started, but the words caught in his throat and the god-killer froze, massive paw hovering mid-step. They felt it before they heard it. The air shifted causing gooseflesh to rear its ugly head over their skin. Something darker than this pitch-black night was manifesting here, creeping through the corridors, its icy fingers clawing the air for something to latch on to. A guttural woman's voice stalked through the corridors. Harsh and primitive, it was unlike any language Alkaios had ever heard, but the voice that uttered it... that voice he would recognize even if he had not heard it in centuries.

Both god and beast bolted, vaulting over the debris toward the sound. Their feet stumbled over the crumbling stone at a breakneck speed, but despite his raw power, Alkaios strained to keep pace with the hellhound's bulging thighs. Kerberos surged over the fallen walls, refusing to slow for his king, and with surging muscles, the god bounded after him. The voice beckoned them, a demonic siren in the night, and they plunged onward until they came to a remarkably preserved room. A dead end that forced them to a skidding halt.

"Hades?" Alkaios whispered. She stood before him, undisturbed by their sudden entrance. She faced the wall, only her back visible. Her hands flew with furious purpose, although what they were doing, he could not tell. "Hades?" he repeated a little louder as he crept forward, but Hades continued her shaking movements. Her body gave no sign she heard him, her actions that of a woman who believed she was alone.

"Wife?" But Alkaios' words died on his lips. He saw with sudden clarity what she was doing. Bile rose in his throat. It threatened to spew from his lips, and despite his desperation to look away and erase the sight before him, his mud-blue eyes remain locked on her moving figure. Alkaios sensed Kerberos freeze, and the dog's alarm crackled over his skin like a stream freezing solid in the dead of winter. For there Hades stood, muttering in an archaic tongue, carving those cursed prophecy symbols into the stone... with her own bloody fingers.

Hades' nails ripped from her fingers, and even in the darkness, Alkaios could see the deep red blood running down her perfect skin and over the wall. She carved in a frenzy as her voice escaped in low demonic tones. Bloody fingertips traced and retraced the symbols, her body deaf and blind to all but her crazed mind. Alkaios closed his eyes, desperate to keep the vomit from heaving itself onto the floor.

"Hades?" Alkaios ventured slowly, reaching a calloused hand toward her. He was afraid to touch her but could not watch her carve her fingers down to stumps. "Hades?" he brushed a tentative palm over her shoulder.

With alarming speed, Hades turned, the force shoving him off balance. The whites of her eyes bore down on him. Her irises rolled into her skull. Dirt and blood streaked her face and chest, and her palms reached for Alkaios with clawing fingers. Her unintelligible words grew aggressive, and before Alkaios could stop her, Hades clutched his throat in a vice grip. Iron fist constricting, Alkaios' trachea began to collapse in an explosion of pain. Her strength always rivaled his, but in this moment she was stronger as she crushed him in her bloody palm. Her blank eyes twitched, voice thundering through the fortress, and as black consumed Alkaios' vision, Kerberos let out an unearthly snarl and lunged for Hades. Shock rippled through his addled brain, and Alkaios watched through clouded sight as Kerberos surged to protect him. The dog' massive shoulder blade barreled into Hades' hip, and the jarring impact wrenched her hand from her husband's throat before cracking her head against the wall. The harsh sound reverberated throughout the stone, and Hades' collapsed in a boneless heap.

Choking for air, Alkaios doubled over and stumbled to his crumbled wife. Kerberos beat him to her and with tentative care, nudged Hades toward her coughing husband. Through the gagging pain, Alkaios fell to his knees, ignoring the sting the impact shot through his bones, and scooped Hades into his arms. A groan escaped her lips, and with fluttering eyelids, she blinked slowly as he enveloped her in his embrace.

"Alkaios? Why am I on the floor?" Hades looked around, but the effort it took to move her eyes burned through her skull, and she clenched them shut, collapsing against his broad chest.

"Do you remember anything?"

"Where are we?" Hades ignored Alkaios' question and

reached a hand out to Kerberos. His three heads eyed her with wariness, but his love propelled him to her side, an unseen tether woven into the fabric of his heart. His lumbering limbs collapsed beneath him the moment Hades' fingers landed on his leathery hide, and Kerberos curled his hulking frame around the couple to envelop them in his warmth.

"You remember nothing?" Alkaios asked.

"I remember going to bed... then bloodshed and chaos? There was a massacre," Hades whispered. "It felt real. I could smell the blood and taste the death and then nothing. Only blackness." Her gaze swept up to meet her husband's, and she saw the concern hovering in his face. "What did I do?"

Alkaios shifted his eyes to the bloodstained wall, and Hades followed his gaze. The color drained from her face at the site of the gruesome letters, and suddenly the thudding ache in her fingers registered in her brain

"What is happening?" she whispered, voice stumbling in panic. "I have no control over my mind. Every time I close my eyes, I see the same massacre. I wake in places I did not fall asleep in... and now this. Why this prophecy?"

"I think we might have to consider telling Zeus," Alkaios said, cringing at the idea even as the words left his mouth.

"Absolutely not," Hades insisted as she unstably pushed herself to her feet. Kerberos, seeing her teeter, shoved his side against the back of her legs for support, and Hades clutched his spikes, thankful for the aid. "We cannot tell him."

"Hades," Alkaios interrupted. "Something is happening, and neither of us knows what. Perhaps he can help."

"He can help?" Hades asked incredulously. "Alkaios, he tried to kill you, to destroy your soul. Is that who you truly wish to turn to?"

"Of course not." Alkaios rose from the floor to return her stare. "I do not want his aid nor his advice, but I cannot help you. Hades, this is killing me. When we met, I was mortal, and you always came to my aid, but now I am a god. I am supposed to be all-powerful, yet the one person in this entire world I would move mountains for is struggling, and I can do nothing. You are not the same. No one is ever truly fearless, but to me you were. Now there is fear in your eyes, and it terrifies me."

"I do not know what is happening," Hades said, voice softening. She took Alkaios' face in her bloody hands and looked deep into his mud-blue eyes, eyes she loved. "But we must not tell him. We cannot give him anything to hold over us. If Zeus finds out, imagine how he could use this against us. I almost lost you when he forced Hermes to curse you with the Touch of the Gods. What else is he capable of?"

"Very well," Alkaios said, leaning in and kissing her lips with a love so deep the air shifted, the oppressive evil lifting. "We will not tell him. I only wish to help." He gathered her into his arms and pulled her against his chest, and Hades could feel the thundering beat of his heart beneath his skin. "I love you more than I know how to admit."

Hades smiled against his broad chest, Alkaios' bare flesh hot against her lips.

"I love you."

"If you will not tell Zeus, there is another we might speak to," Alkaios murmured into her hair. "I think it is time we paid the Oracle a visit."

V

"I wondered when the king of death would grace my halls," the Oracle crooned, her back turned to what had been an empty room only moments before. "That is a darkness I have yet to feel." She swiveled on her stool before standing to greet her visitors. "Hades, god of the Underworld, and his queen Persephone… I had heard you were more beautiful than Aphrodite herself," The Oracle said, body drifting toward the raven-haired guest, "I thought it could only be blasphemy, but as you stand before me, queen of Hell, I must agree. You are exquisite."

The Oracle of Delphi was neither young nor old, ageless with her silver hair yet perfect skin. She was tall and lean, and her legs appeared to drift over the ground rather than walk. Her eyes were impossibly light, and the dark marks inked beneath her flesh showed through the sheer cloth of her dress.

"What is it I can do for you, god of death?" The Oracle asked, turning her gaze upon Alkaios.

"We are here about the prophecy," Alkaios answered, pitchfork in one hand, Hades' fingers in the other. At his words, the Oracle's eyes darkened.

"There is nothing I can tell you that I have not already told

Zeus." She backed away, a flicker of fear rippling across her face. "I do not know who spoke through me, and I have no memory of that night. If it were not for my blood on the floor and my handmaid's account, I would have never known I prophesied."

"We have not come to question you about it," Alkaios said, dropping Hades' hand and moving closer to the Oracle. "We came to ask for help."

"Help?"

"For my wife, Persephone," he explained stumbling over the name. Alkaios had not called Hades by the name Persephone since they first met years ago when he believed her to be merely a mortal woman in need of aid. "Zeus told us that the parchment you gave him was ink and paper."

"That is the truth."

"Ink and paper hold no power, yet the moment my wife touched it something happened," Alkaios continued. "It is as if a curse descended upon her. A violent insanity has taken over her sleep, and I do not know how to help."

"My ink would not have caused that," the Oracle said defensively, "and as for the words I wrote, who knows what power they hold."

"I understand…"

"Then how is it you think I can help?" Her eyes flicking to Hades as if for an explanation.

"All Oracles have divine sight, a connection to the supernatural," Alkaios answered. "Perhaps you might see something in Persephone I cannot."

"You want me to do a reading for your wife?" The Oracle asked, raising her eyebrows. "What could I possibly perceive that a god cannot?"

"It is not about what he cannot detect," Hades said, speaking for the first time since their arrival. "Rather what is out of place. My husband knows me. We need fresh sight. Someone who can distinguish from his darkness and my own, and being that you and I seem to be the only ones this prophecy affected, it would appear you are our best hope."

"Very well, I will do this." The Oracle stepped toward Hades. "May I take your hands?" Hades reached out her palms in agreement, and the Oracle took a deep breath before shutting her eyes and pressing her skin against Hades'.

"Who are you?" the Oracle demanded, her voice colored with alarm as she snatched her arms back with the speed of a woman scorched by burning coals. Her eyes grew wide with terror, and she leapt backward, placing distance between herself and the Underworld's Queen. "Who are you?"

"I am Persephone…" Hades started

"Do not lie to me," the Oracle spat. "There is a dark power within you that a mere immortal would not possess, even one of the Underworld." Hades and Alkaios shared a look, and it was if an entire conversation passed between their eyes. After a moment, Alkaios sighed and nodded slightly; an answer to his wife's unspoken question.

"I am Hades."

"I thought he was the god of the Underworld?" The Oracle's head swiveled rapidly between her guests.

"He is now," Hades explained, "but was not always. My name is Hades. It is the name I was born with. I am the one who broke the seal and tamed the evil trapped behind that door. My husband is Alkaios. He was a mortal when we met, but there was turmoil between the gods of Olympus and myself, and Alkaios paid the price for it. They cursed him with the Touch of the Gods. You have heard of that I assume?" The Oracle nodded, and Hades continued. "No man nor beast can survive it, only a god. So I did the only thing I could think of. I transferred my power and made him god of the Underworld. He assumed my place. I could endure the loss of power, but I refused to lose him." Hades turned to Alkaios, and the Oracle saw the fierce love between them. A twinge of both joy and jealousy stung her heart as she watched Alkaios reach out to grip Hades' fingers.

"He adopted your name?"

"By that time, earth had already acknowledged the arrival of a new god, a god of the Underworld named Hades. Many believed Hades to be a woman, but many had also seen Alkaios and I in public together. Zeus had tried to convince mortals to kill Alkaios, cementing in their minds his importance to me. When I pulled a child's shade from the Underworld, returning life to her, Alkaios stood beside me. It was not difficult to persuade earth he was a god, and I was merely his queen. It would have been a greater challenge to change the name people prayed to than the god's gender. Publicly, he is now Hades, and I am his immortal wife, Persephone. In the privacy of our lives, though, I am the true Hades, and he is Alkaios."

"She retains a residual of her power," Alkaios added. "The pitchfork and the beasts of Hell still answer to her."

"Most children prefer their mother." The Oracle blinked as she looked back and forth between her guests. "That would explain what I witnessed. I understand your deception, but if you come to me for help, please do not lie. You forget I recognize more than most." She raised her eyebrows. "Shall we try again then?" Hades nodded and stretched out her palms, pressing them against the Oracle's.

The Oracle's eyelids drifted shut, fingers gripping Hades' hands in tight fists. After a few silent moments, a grimace plagued her face, yet she remained rooted in place. Her mind began to hum, and with a sudden viciousness, the Oracle recoiled as if an unseen hand had struck her cheek. Her grimace deepened, the humming rattling her brain with increasing madness, and as her eyelids clenched harshly, she flinched again. Pain emanated from her figure. Her breath jerked in ragged huffs, and then without warning, The Oracle's body wrenched backward, the demand of the jolt forcing her to drop Hades' hands.

"There is a great darkness lurking beneath your surface," the Oracle finally shuddered, eyes haunted. "Some of it is remnant from your position as god of the Underworld, but there is something else fighting to emerge from the depths. It feels violent and powerful, the likes of which I have never felt before. It is subtle at the moment but will not remain so for long. It is chomping at the bit, begging to surge and grow. Whatever is within you, Hades, is not like anything I have ever experienced. I can neither say what is happening to you nor how it connects to the prophecy, but I will say this. Both the prophecy and what awakens within you are strong, dark, and ancient."

"What could that be?" Alkaios asked, turning to Hades, concern lacing his voice.

"I have no idea."

"I am sorry," the Oracle said. "There is something simmering beneath your surface, but truthfully, I have no answers. I realize it is not much, but in my limited ability, it is all I can see."

"Thank you," Hades said. "It's more than we knew when we came today."

"Of course." The Oracle turned to Alkaios. "I am here to serve the gods."

"Thank you. We will not take up any more of your day." Tentacles of inky smoke began to twist and grow from Alkaios' body, the curling darkness weaving around Hades like a starving snake. Fascinated, the Oracle watched before working up the courage to reach out and plunge her fingers into a strand of the black vapor that ensnared Hades' arm. The contact sent an electric jolt burning through her body, and her eyes locked with the queens with wide-eyed revelation.

"Wait." She seized Hades' wrist to halt their departure. "There is something else... a woman of snakes. I cannot explain it, but I believe she is somehow tied to you."

"A woman of snakes?" Hades said sharing a look with her husband. "Hydra?"

"Who is Hydra?" The Oracle asked.

"She is one of the Underworld's three god-killers," Alkaios said.

"No." The Oracle' words dripped from her mouth with slow consideration. "It would be no one you know. If it were, you would have had no reason to seek my counsel. No, this woman is something far older than you or I."

"A woman of snakes who has come before us?" Alkaios asked looking from the Oracle to his wife. "Who could that be?"

"I do not know," both Hades and the Oracle answered in unison, but Hades' voice trailed off halfway through her words. Her eyes went wide, and she stared at Alkaios, disbelief leaking from her pores.

"No." Hades shook her head. "No… it cannot be her."

"Medusa?" Alkaios asked. "Who is Medusa?"

"A myth," Hades answered, pacing back and forth over the planks of the boathouse. Both Charon and Alkaios leaned against the wall, tracking her movements with flickering eyes while Keres, Ioanna, and Hydra sat around the room watching the exchange. "Or at least she is believed to be a myth. She is a bedtime story, something to frighten children with so they behave. Even the Olympians believe her to only exist in lore."

"I have never heard of her," Alkaios said.

"Legend has it," Hades started, "that Medusa was the most beautiful woman to walk the earth. Men were enamored with her, and it was said her hair was her crowning glory. Medusa, growing accustomed to men falling at her feet to grant her every wish, began to use her beauty for her own gain. She turned first to the most handsome, and once she had them eating out of her palm, she progressed upward to rich merchants. They were helpless against Medusa' spells and gave all she desired, but her appetite was insatiable. She next fixed the leaders of her city in her sights, and when she grew bored with the limited authority they held, Medusa aimed higher. Her charm used and then discarded men, leaving behind a trail of broken hearts and emptied coin purses. Royal courts and the desires of princes' were conquered, but it was still not enough, and so her desire lusted after the king. The unfortunate man was powerless to resist her seduction, his status bringing her joy. The most powerful figure in the land bowed to Medusa's whim. She had risen to the heights of honor, but one fateful day the king prayed to the gods for aid.

"When Medusa saw the Olympians, her heart hardened toward the king. His mortal reign no longer satisfied her voracious hunger, and Olympus was to be her newest conquest. Her allure ensured all the gods clamored over themselves, turning on each other to capture her affection. Poseidon's obsession ignited into a consuming flame. He fell deeply in love, pursuing her with ardent vigor, and for a time she was content to have him. But alas, Medusa's greed would not allow her to settle for second best, and she harshly turned her back on him. Zeus became the object of her ambition, the ultimate prize. So cruel was her dismissal of Poseidon that his broken heart prohibited him to release her. He refused to be a pawn in this selfish rise to power, and so he hunted Medusa.

"Terrified for her life, she fled, but not a soul offered her sanctuary. She had jilted many men, caused too many to pass over their loved ones in favor of the great beauty for any woman to offer aid. Utterly abandoned in her desperation, Medusa sought refuge in a temple of Athena. She begged the goddess for salvation, but Athena was no fool. She had witnessed the games Medusa played, how her callous beauty served to fulfill her hunger, and Athena refused to help.

Poseidon found her alone and unprotected in the sanctuary and unleashed his rage. He took her on the altar. When finished, Poseidon was so repulsed he discarded her without a backward glance.

"The desecration of her shrine sickened the god of warfare, driving Athena to unleash a horrid punishment on Medusa. Disgusted by how she drove men to insanity with beauty, Athena cursed her pride and joy, and Medusa's glorious head of hair transformed into a mass of tiny snakes. Yet Athena's torture was not complete, and she condemned the mortal woman with the sight of stone. No longer could Medusa gaze upon men and have them yearn to do her bidding, for now a single glimpse of her eyes would turn the viewer to stone. Unable to look at the once holy shrine, Athena sealed the temple. It had been desecrated, no longer a house of worship but an eternal prison damned to darkness and bitter solitude. Athena hid it from the world, allowing only men inside, never women, for she considered them to be the only innocents in this travesty. All who ventured within turned to statues, punishment for their foolish lust of a shallow and selfish woman, and those who venture to seek Medusa out have never returned."

"That is a story for children?" Alkaios asked incredulously when Hades finished speaking.

"It serves to teach men not to shallowly love only beauty and women not to become vain."

"And the gods allow the spreading of this myth? It paints Poseidon in a cruel and foolish light."

"Both Athena and he deny its truth, but it spreads, never dying. Perhaps they permit it for its message, but one would think Poseidon would put an end to it. Yet here we are, telling it."

"This tale has been told for longer than you realize." Charon interrupted the couple and pushed off from the wall.

"How do you mean?" Hades shifted her weight to look at the ferryman.

"The Titans, too, had a story about Medusa."

"How?" Alkaios asked. "Poseidon and Athena..."

"... were not in our version," Charon answered before Alkaios could finish. "We had a myth about a woman named Medusa long before Cronus and Rhea gave birth to their sons. It began similarly to Hades' tale. Medusa, an unearthly beauty with hair of pure seduction, was vain and greedy, always searching for ways to remain young and beautiful. She used men's lust to her advantage, spitting them out when they had served their purpose. This is where our tales differ, though," Charon continued as one of his daughters loosed a small fuss from tiny lips. He strode to her cradle and lifted the blonde infant into his muscular arms. "Our legend tells that in Medusa's search for infinite beauty she met a witch who promised to turn her into a sight to behold. She assured that one look from Medusa would freeze men where they stood. Too arrogant to question it, Medusa offered all she had for the magic, but the witch's words were a curse, not a blessing; a punishment for her vanity and cruelty to those who had loved her blindly. True to her word, the witch turned Medusa into a great sight, one that froze men in their tracks. Her glorious hair transformed into snakes. A single glance from her eyes transformed flesh into stone. Horrified by the transformation, Medusa fled to the mountains never to be seen again, for all who sought her out never returned."

"How is it possible that two different generations of gods have two contrasting stories about the same woman?" Alkaios asked, looking from Charon to Hades.

"I am not sure," Charon answered as he returned his daughter to her cradle. "It seems unlikely that she would be merely a fantasy. The similarities are too coincidental. It is possible a real woman once existed that served as a muse for the legends."

"That still does not account for Poseidon," Alkaios said.

"Whether it is a simple fable or an exaggerated truth, I doubt the king of the seas would allow tales of his monstrosity to spread so salaciously."

"The only other possibility I can fathom, however unlikely and alarming, is that Medusa is not a legend but a truth," Charon said, "a being of such cunning and power that even the gods have been fooled."

"What kind of person or creature would have the power to do that?" Keres asked, speaking for the first time since they had entered the boathouse. "Hades' version of the story directly involves the gods. What god would allow the spread of that tale if it was not true?"

"None I know," Alkaios answered, his hand snatching Hades' as she passed before him. Slipping a solid arm around her waist, he folded her into his side to calm her rapid pacing.

"That is my point," Keres said. "Both versions cannot be true, either one is and not the other, but then how did there come to be two interpretations? Are they both lies? But no god, especially Poseidon, would let those falsehoods spread." There was urgency in her voice. "If Medusa is real and her stories true, then she has been changing the legend to fit her needs… who has the power to do that?"

"Someone who wishes to remain hidden," Charon answered, "and likely someone I would not wish to cross paths with. Whoever possesses the skill to fool generations of gods is a dangerous person."

"Could such an individual exist?" Alkaios asked incredulously.

"This morning I would have said no, but what other woman of snakes is there besides Hydra?" Charon asked gesturing to Hydra. "What kind of woman requires two myths to hid behind? If Medusa is real, why does my tale differ from yours? Why the need for a new lie to protect herself?"

"Is it possible that when the Olympians took power from the Titans she needed a different identity?" Hades asked.

"That is a valid argument," Charon said. "The Titans were dead, killed by their own children. Do you think these new gods would fear a creature cursed by a witch?"

"No," Hades said, pausing to consider, "but they would fear one cursed by the god of war."

"How do we find her?" Keres asked.

"I do not know if we should," answered Charon as he sat down beside Ioanna, who slipped her fingers into his large hand. Absentmindedly, he lifted her hand to his lips and kissed her knuckles as if it was second nature, an automatic reaction to her loving touch.

"I may not have a choice," Hades said, separating herself from Alkaios. "You know something has changed within me, and I have no answers. This is my only clue. My nightmares grow more vivid, and sometimes my mind cannot distinguish between what is real and what is madness. I cannot keep waking up lost in this fortress with no memory of how I got there or how to get back."

"If you must find her, we will help you," Keres said. "But how?"

Hades opened her mouth to answer, but only air and hope rushed out of her lungs. She had no answers. How does one find a myth?

SHE DWELLED in the darkness once again, the dim light casting only shadows on the carnage. Hades ran through the hallways, bare heels slick with warm blood. Her feet slid, but she had no time to falter. Her shoulder crashed into the wall, and using it as leverage, Hades propelled herself around the corner despite the shattering pain. The dark shadow loomed behind her growing ever closer, and Hades' heart pounded in fear so intense, she was sure it would fail at any moment. Her chest ached, and lungs burned hot as she rounded the next corner, and Hades careened into a solid figure barring her way with a jarring impact. Her body ricocheted off the mass and slammed to the floor, and her skin convulsed in pain as the stone tore at her soft flesh.

"Alkaios!" Hades screamed bolting up in bed, her arm flinging out to smack her husband's face. Alkaios grunted and leapt up, weapon in hand, ready to protect his family. Kerberos, whose heads had been hanging off the mattress in slumber, jerked so violently he crashed to the floor, jaws cracking on the stone. His roar shook the walls, and Kerberos was on his feet in a flash, the growl in his throats strangled by a mass barreling into his ribs. The dog faltered, claws gouging the ground to steady himself as Chimera's shoulder cracked his ribcage as he bolted into the room. Kerberos snarled at the lion, sinking his teeth into the monstrous cat's fur, but Chimera's retaliation was swift, a massive paw swiped across the god-killer's snout. Three gouges blossomed crimson. Blood drops rained to the tiles, and rage simmered in Kerberos' eyes as he prepared his vengeance.

"Stop!" Hades bellowed, throwing herself between the beasts and shoving them violently apart, yet Kerberos snarled at her and lunged for Chimera. "I said stop!" Hades slammed a palm into his broad chest to force him to a halt. "Get back on the bed!" Kerberos obeyed with fangs bared, but Hades ignored his defiance and shoved his snout aside to angle the claw marks to her gaze. With a sigh, Hades released her dark power, and the tentacles of black smoke drifted from her fingers to delve beneath his hide. When the skin had knit together, she seized Chimera's mane, healing the bite the dog had inflicted.

"By the gods, Hades," Alkaios breathed, leaning the pitchfork back against the wall. He sank to the mattress, hair mussed and tangled by sleep. "Are you trying to kill me?"

"I am sorry. Her hand reached and rested with comforting

weight against his chiseled chest before her fingers lifted to calm his wayward curls.

"Was it one of those dreams?" Alkaios took her palm from his hair and returned it to his chest. His heart beat strong beneath his skin, and Alkaios cradled her fist to the organ that thundered only for her. Hades nodded in response, and Alkaios pulled her into his arms. "It is not real," he whispered soothingly into her dark locks. "I am though, so wake to me, for I love you."

"That's just it," Hades said, craning her neck to gaze into her husband's eyes. "I think they might be real, and they are telling me where we can find her."

VI

Keres' back dropped hard to the earth, only to have Hydra plummet onto her stomach seconds later. The force choked the air from her lungs as the oppressive weight of another's body bore crushingly on her internal organs. Hydra groaned and rolled off Keres' chest, only for both of them to almost be crushed as Chimera collapsed on his side, a hair's breadth from their heads. A cloud of dust catapulted about the lion's heaving body, the dirt imprinted where he lay, and both women scrambled backward just as Kerberos landed with a vicious roar exactly where they had been lying. His massive claws dug gouges in the soil as he shook himself with angered disorientation.

The air cracked, and Hades and Alkaios slammed into the ground with an echoing thud. They landed on their feet, but the impact of the crash jarred the bones in their spines together with grinding shock.

"Alkaios?" Keres groaned as she stood, lungs struggling to recover their breath. "What was that?"

"I did not do this," Alkaios answered with confusion, the

inky tentacles of smoke still writhing about his frame. "Something is blocking our movement further up the mountain."

Hades tentatively reached her hand out in front of her and brushed her fingers through the empty air, and when nothing resisted her, she stepped forward. She paused for a moment and waited for ill will to befall her, but whatever had barred their way, no longer resisted her.

"But it seems we can walk," Hades said as she took another step. "The mountain blocks our movement as gods. We cannot travel directly to the top like we planned, but we can continue on foot." She carefully placed one toe in front of the other.

"If we cannot use our power to pass this point, that explains why the gods have never accidentally stumbled upon her temple," Alkaios said, following his wife.

"Why is our entrance blocked when we travel as gods, but we are allowed passage if we walk?" Keres asked, hesitantly stepping forward.

"I believe whatever protects this mountain wants us to ascend on foot as mortals," Hades called over her shoulder as she pulled herself up a jagged rock. "A secret this well-kept would be virtually impossible to find."

"Why does it want us to travel on foot?" Hydra asked as she began her climb after Keres, the massive beasts following on their heels.

"Because it is a trap," Hades said, "forcing all who come in search to walk into it on equal ground, and I guarantee you, whoever is lying in wait for us already knows we are here."

THE GROUP FOLLOWED Hades up the mountain which offered no resistance other than the treacherous and grueling climb. Sweat dripped down Hades' skin as her fingers clung to sharp and serrated rocks. Her arms shook with fatigue, yet she continued to haul herself with agonizing effort up the perilous cliff face, eyes ever searching for both handholds within the stone's crevasses and traps bent on ill will. Kerberos and Chimera shadowed their mother's heels, their brute force shoving Hades' body over the jagged edges when her limbs faltered. Keres and Hydra climbed behind the beasts using their tails as ropes, while Alkaios brought up the rear, wielding the pitchfork as a climbing axe, burrowing it deep into the rock's fissures for leverage. Every pebble their feet dislodged, each whisper of the wind, spiked panic in Alkaios' thundering heart. With every inch gained, he expected an assault to rain down on their heads, yet the eerie stillness held.

The sun rose high into the sky, beating down on them as they climbed, but the farther they ascended the cooler the air blew. Hades, dirt streaked through her sweat, thanked the heavens for the breeze, for the sun refused to relent. It strode across the sky with punishing cruelty, offering the travelers no aid save to tell them that time had swiftly passed. It was not until the sun was at its zenith, the pilgrims having struggled for hours, that Hades finally hauled herself over the final ledge. She crawled over the level ground with weak limbs as they fought to bear her exhausted weight. Her lungs screamed with grueling fire as they sucked in the cool mountain air, and the earth rumbled beside her with the impact of the collapsing god-killers. Hades shifted and watched Kerberos hoard breath with three snouts while Chimera's ribs shook in relief. With dirt-crusted fingers, she reached out and smoothed the lion's mane, and Kerberos offered her one of his heads to heave her to her feet.

A woman's hand flung over the edge, clawing at the grass for purchase, and Hydra heaved herself to safety. Her body rolled across the ground where she lay panting, refusing to stand. She closed her eyelids to shield her irises from the sun and was oblivious to the fact that Hades stood frozen above her, eyes transfixed on the distance. The queen's gaze was not lost on Keres, though, as she struggled to conquer the mountain. Her eyes traveled to where Hades looked but saw nothing, for the moment Keres glanced up, her foot slipped from its precarious hold. Her fingers tore from their grip, and her chest scraped over razor-sharp rocks. Her heart halted its beating in panic. Keres frantically clawed for any crevasse to save herself upon, but her nails only ripped from their anchored beds. The image of her shattered body dashed against the boulders below flickered through her thoughts. Keres plummeted earthward, destined for an anguished end, except Alkaios' unearthly speed launched himself forward.

"Keres!" he grunted as her back slammed into his chest. He gritted his teeth, holding the pitchfork with sweating palms, and heaved forward. "I got you." A steadying arm wrapped around her waist. Alkaios could feel her shaking beneath his touch, and for a moment Keres did not move, only leaned against his broad mass in panic. "Are you all right?" he asked, straining his already fatigued body to hold her up.

"Thank you," Keres exhaled and slowly extended her arms back toward the ledge above. Alkaios shoved her with all his strength, and together they vaulted over the edge and landed with a thud on the grass. Keres sputtered on the ground, but Alkaios forwent rest and dragged himself up to stand beside his rigid wife.

"What is it?" Alkaios asked, sensing Hades' wariness, but her silence was his only answer.

"By the gods," Keres gasped. Her mouth fell open as she pushed herself to a seat. "She is real."

This was not the pinnacle of the mountain as they had hoped. Instead, it was a massive plateau that stretched deep into the clouds until it collided with another upward expanse, its peak hidden in the heavens. Ancient walls covered the plateau, crumbling from an eternity of decay. Enormous boulders lay cracked and scattered amidst the sectioned walls, and untamed bushes grew in a maze around the stone, obscuring any path that may have once lain there. But it was not the overgrown maze that halted their breath. It was the men... stone men.

"By the gods," Alkaios muttered, eyes flicking from statue to statue until the overgrowth swallowed their ancient figures. If this many were visible at the mouth of the labyrinth, how many more awaited them in hiding?

"How far is her reach?" Alkaios asked lifting his view to the mountain summit shrouded in the distant mist. If Medusa's temple was on this ridge, then that is where he assumed it would be, yet men frozen in horror haunted this field; a distance seemingly too vast for one woman's gaze to pierce. If this truly was home to Medusa, how far did her savage power extend?

"Keep your eyes down," Hades said, stepping forward. "If you see her, by the gods, do not look into her eyes." And with that, Hades descended into the chaos. The beasts clung close on her heels, as did Keres and Hydra, but Alkaios hung back for a moment. Power seeped into the pitchfork, darkness overtaking both man and metal. He would allow no witch to turn his family to stone, and with one last glimpse of the silent grave of frozen men, he plunged into the fray. But as the group disappeared into the claws of branches and brittle walls, not one thought to cast a backward glance. For if they had, they would have seen the stone man standing guard at the entrance twist his head ever so slightly, his blank, hollow eye sockets watching as the bushes swallowed them alive.

THE SILENCE HELD as they ventured deeper into the maze, and despite the men being mere stone and the only footsteps heard theirs, uneasiness gripped Alkaios' soul. Yet Hades plowed forward, leading them onward as he brought up the rear, no trap unleashing itself.

"Do you smell it?" a female voice suddenly crooned from

nowhere and everywhere. It was rusty as if it had not spoken in ages, vile and cruel. "Fresh meat…"

"Hades?" Keres whispered as her eye searched for the voice's origin.

"I hear it."

"We have not smelled fresh meat in so long," a second voice groaned, the words sounding as if they were being dragged over gravel.

"And one scent is different," the first hissed. "I have not breathed that before."

"I want that one!" A third voice blurted in sharp graveled hisses. "Gives it to me…"

"Where are those voices coming from?" Keres whispered.

"I cannot tell," Alkaios said as his eyes peered through the twists of impenetrable vegetation.

"They are in our heads," Hades answered. "They are speaking directly into our minds."

"No," the first voice spat out harshly as if in answer to Hades' discovery. "That one is mine… mine to eat… mine to kill-llll," she crowed, dragging out the last word.

"I do not like this," Hydra thrust her arms out to her side. The veins beneath her pale skin began to writhe and bubble as the snakes of Tartarus clambered to break free. "Alkaios, can you locate them?"

"Hades?" Alkaios said slowly, his voice stern as he ignored Hydra's request.

"I am trying to find them," Hades answered.

"Hades!" Alkaios' harsh word cut her off, his tone a rumble not to be argued with. Hades flicked her eyes over her shoulder surprised by his sudden aggression, but the moment they met his, the realization that Alkaios was not looking at her but at something beyond felt like a fist seizing her gut. He parted his lips to breathe a warning, but Hades knew. The alarm in his eyes told her.

PITCHFORK

Hades slowly swiveled on her heels, and there, far down the aisle of branches, stood a woman. She shuffled toward them with an unnatural gate, and Kerberos moved closer to the stranger, loosing a deep, guttural growl past three sets of massive fangs. Yet the woman continued her halting movement. She was thin, all angles and harsh lines, her body ageless. She was naked except for thick streaks of mud plastered to her frame and down her talon fingers. It matted her dark hair and face, yet that was not what caused Hades' lungs to inhale a sharp breath.

The mud obscured the grotesque disfigurement, but the closer she hobbled, toes dragging trails in the dirt, the clearer Hades could see. Both of the woman's eyes were sewn shut with thick, coarse thread, rendering her blind, yet she seemed to know precisely where the intruders stood. Her mouth, too, was stitched together, the dark cord cutting bloodily into swollen lips.

"Their scent is delicious," she hissed despite her unmoving mouth as she hobbled forward, the words clear in their heads.

"Alkaios," Hades whispered, reaching her hand back. "Give me the pitchfork."

But before her husband could react, a strangled scream ripped from Keres' throat. Hades whirled around in time to watch a second mud-clad woman surge from the hedges and tackle Keres. The bushes swallowed them whole as they barreled through the cracking branches. Hades' heart barely had the chance to leap into her throat before she was moving, racing forward to plunge into the foliage after Keres. But a flash of movement ricocheted through the corner of her eye, and Hades slid to a halt, toes scraping over the uneven ground.

"Alkaios," she whispered, "behind you." Alkaios turned to the sight of a third blind woman crawling toward him with alarming speed, her fingers clawing at the dirt foreshadowing their intent for Alkaios' flesh.

"Go!" Alkaios commanded, shoving Hydra into the bushes. Hades and the beasts tore through the thick after her, Alka-

63

ios hard on their heels just as the crawling witch leapt through the air in an assault.

"Keres!" Hades screamed, branches whipping her face like starving fingers. A muffled cry seeped through the hedges, and a maniacal laugh of sadistic pleasure at Keres' distress broke into their minds. Keres' terrified gasps flooded Hades' skin and sank into her chest with oppressive weight, and the dark queen batted thick thorns and dying leaves from her path is if her brutality against them could push the panic from her lungs.

"Get out of the maze," Alkaios commanded his wife. "I will find Keres." Without breaking stride, he angled toward the screams, the third witch hard on his heels. Hades paused for a moment, desperate to remain at Alkaios' side and rescue her friend from the clutches of madness, but Hydra seized her hand with a frantic grasp and hauled her in the opposite direction, the first witch thundering through the brush after them.

"Chimera!" Hades screamed. "Go with him!" The lion surged after Alkaios, the intertwining vines snapping across his chest, unable to hold his sheer power.

The branches stung Hades' and Hydra's faces as they plunged through, but Kerberos pushed them onward, his three skulls forcing them through the whipping onslaught. With a sudden jerk, Hades lunged to her right, yanking Hydra harshly behind her, and the two women burst onto the virtually non-existent path, their cheeks blooming with scarlet lashes. Their footfalls pounded the ground as they careened into the open air, but inexplicably the first witch barred their way, running toward them with a limping gate. Hades skidded to a halt with such force that Hydra collided with her spine. Her anguished gasp washed hot over Hades' ear; the impact almost tearing Hades from her feet, but Kerberos was before his mother with a deafening roar. He slammed his ribcage into Hades' thighs, urging her away from the charging witch, and Hades shoved Hydra's wheezing chest as she scrambled to obey the dog.

"How do they find us?" Hydra screamed, releasing a black snake of Tartarus from her vein. It dropped to the ground and slithered toward the blind pursuer. Its body heaved and rippled as its mass grew. Hades dared not glance over her shoulder, but the vicious crack that echoed through the maze told her all she needed to know. The witch had crushed the snake's head with her bare heel, knowing exactly where it slithered despite her sewn eyes.

"I have no idea," Hades panted as Hydra screamed at the loss of her babe, and her skin rippled and churned, birthing two more snakes. For every one killed, two took its place.

Suddenly Hydra was ripped from Hades' grasp, body thundering as she crashed to the ground. Her face slapped the dirt with striking force, her cry of pain suffocated by the lack of air in her lungs.

"Hades!" she wheezed, and Hades stumbled to a halt, nearly toppling at the force of Hydra's plummeting form, and bent to tow her friend back into a run. She heaved, but Hydra cried out in agony as her body refused to budge.

"My ankle," Hydra gasped, and Hades flicked her gaze down her friend's ivory legs. She lay sprawled on her stomach, a stone man frozen in time at her feet... her ankle in its hand. Hydra kicked and twisted, desperate to wrench free as the witch bore down on them, and Hades watched in horror as three more statues moved their hands to grasp her friend. Hydra's skin turned blue as the statue's fingers choked her circulation. Two snakes, surging in size, coiled around the status' forearms and attempted to shatter their wrists, but to no avail. The sculptures, immobile save their arms, scooped the writhing beast into their unforgiving palms and crushed their skulls.

"Hades!" Hydra cried as four more god-killers ripped through her flesh, and Hades summoned her darkness to the surface. Black smoke wove from her skin, enveloping her in their powerful embrace, and with a bellow that shook the mountain, Hades gripped the stone men. Her fists constricted with unnatural strength, shattering them to dust. Limbless, the statues bucked toward their prey, but Hades seized Hydra and heaved her bruised limbs as Kerberos shoved his snout against his fellow god-killer, launching Hydra to her feet.

Whack! Hades' vision blurred, and the breath abandoned her chest as she plummeted to the earth. The witch's impact sent ravenous fire curling up her spine, and as Hades gulped air into her empty lungs, the crushing weight of the blind witch caved in her rib cage. The witch's claws drew blood as they raked through Hades' pure skin, but just as the crazed woman lifted a hand for a devastating blow, her body shot through the air like a blade of grass on the wind and slammed against the stone wall, the curve of the pitchfork's prongs encircling her throat. Alkaios was above Hades in a flash, hauling her to her feet as Keres helped Hydra, and the six of them bolted past the witch, pitchfork still embedded in the wall trapping her neck.

"I want that one!" the witch screeched into their minds as she struggled against the weapon, her tongue licking Hades' blood off her talons through corded lips. "Gives it to meeeee!"

Her two wailing sisters rounded the corner and were on her like sharks in blood-infested water. The travelers took advantage of their distraction and charged onward as Alkaios reached out to the pitchfork, summoning it to his fist.

Blood seeped from her cheek, but Hades wiped it away as she raced through the rubble. A cluster of effigies littered their path, and as the group drew closer, their stoic heads shifted rigidly toward the onslaught of pounding footfalls.

"Hades!" Alkaios bellowed from the rear. "The statues..."

"We know!" both Hades and Hydra interrupted as they barreled forward, closing in on the waiting stone hands.

"Come back!" One of the witches sped around the debris, her pace alarmingly fast. "Come back!" Hades glanced over her shoulder as the witch clambered for Alkaios, and with a surge of the inky tentacles, she lowered her head. The stone men groped for her, but Hades surged through with a deafening crash. Their bodies shattered, crashing to the floor just as the witch launched herself at Alkaios, but with a single mighty swing, he raised the pitchfork and collided it with her skull. The crack clanged like a rung bell as her lithe body catapulted through the air, and he dove through the falling dust, all that remained of his wife's stone victims.

"Alkaios!" Hades called, and as he burst through the particle-laden air, he saw a witch bearing down on his wife. Without hesitating, Alkaios launched the pitchfork, and with a grace only a true queen of death could wield, Hades snatched the weapon from the air and crashed it into the witch's skull. The hideous creature screamed, her voice an invasion of their minds, and plunged into the bushes. No sooner did she fall, her sister collided with Hades' chest with such violence they both tumbled into the brush. The force wrenched the pitchfork from Hades' grasp, and her hands flailed unsuccessfully to retrieve it as the sharp branches lashed her face. The witch clawed at Hades' eyes, talons dug viscously into soft skin. What evil were these blind monsters that they could tear Hades' flesh so?

The tangled women slammed to a jarring stop as they crashed into the base of a statue. They rolled over the earth, arms and legs clamoring for purchase. With a harsh elbow, Hades cracked the witch's jaw. The bones crunched as her head snapped backward, and using the momentary freedom, Hades disappeared in dark smoke only to appear above the witch a heartbeat later. Her eyes searched wildly for her companions, but this path was an entirely different section of the maze. She opened her mouth to call to Alkaios, but the witch's talons ensnared her ankle with an unyielding grip, barring the blood passage through her veins, and yanked. Before Hades could brace herself, her feet were snatched from beneath her, and the queen's spine landed in the dust with an unforgiving thud.

"We wants a taste!" the witch's voice hissed as she clawed up Hades' body, but Hades kicked. Her heel savagely connected with a blind eye, and a soft pop rang out as one of the stitches snapped. Yet the witch progressed unaffected as her talons dug deeper into Hades' calf muscle. Hades' teeth punctured her lip as she bit down in pain. Blood ran hot down her scratched and dusty skin, and she twisted her torso, fingers braced to seize the attacking witch by the hair.

"Hades?" Alkaios erupted from the bushes, leaves exploding about his body. In one fell swoop, the king kicked the witch in the face, and her head snapped backward with neck shattering force. Without breaking stride, he bent and seized his wife by the arm and hoisted her off the ground and down the path just as the second witch burst after him. She stumbled over her fallen sister, and in a tangle of limbs, they scrambled to regain their footing.

"Where are the others?" Hades panted as Alkaios pulled her behind him, damaged leg limping.

"I do not know. The third witch separated us when I came after you." Alkaios saw the panic in her eyes. "They will be fine. Kerberos is with them, but I have to get you out of the labyrinth." He dropped her arm like a hot coal and whirled around. He lifted the pitchfork and slammed it across their pursuer's head, but the creature merely stumbled at the impact, her pursuit unrelenting.

"How do they continually locate us?" Alkaios huffed between gulps of air as a witch bolted out of the maze to bar their escape. Alkaios raised the bident aiming it at her heart, but Hades suddenly snatched it from his grasp and brought it down hard on a group of stone men reaching out from the overgrowth. Their lifeless, grasping hands clattered to the soil as she shoved the weapon back to her husband, and as the witch leapt through the air, Alkaios plunged the two-pronged metal forward, driving their attacker into the ground.

"I am not sure!" Hades glanced over her shoulder. "I know not what they are nor why they will not stay down."

Alkaios reached out and seized his wife's hand, and together they shot a torrent of dark tentacles backward. The inky smoke twisted around the witches, forcing them back as both god and queen of the Underworld burst through yet another wall of stone statues.

Hades choked on the dust and coughed violently as Alkaios dragged her along. Her eyes watered with debris, eyelids blinking rapidly to clear her vision as she looked behind them, anticipating a pursuer chomping at their heels, but they had vanished. The queen whipped her sight back to the path before them expecting it to be blocked, yet no obstacle barricaded their flight.

Sudden laughter ripped through their head. Their eyes roamed through the overgrown debris for any sign of their predators, yet not a bush moved, not a single whisper of wind.

"Where..." Alkaios began.

"Alkaios," Hades interrupted, squeezing his hand, but he knew. He had already seen it. There in the distance, suspended high in the air at the middle of the maze, was a towering stone pillar. The hovering clouds had concealed it, but as their feet thundered, carrying them deeper into the labyrinth, the post rose for all to see. Its height loomed, watching the chaos below unravel, but it was not its sheer size that captivated their attention. It was what perched atop it, full and unblinking.

"An eye," Alkaios said with sudden realization. "That is how they are finding us." As if in answer to his discovery, a witch surged from the maze before them, unleashing a curdling scream into their brains. Hades winced in pain, the sound exploding within her skull, and she fumbled for Alkaios. Her fingers clutched his massive bicep as her body shifted trajectory. Their forms plunged into bushes, but a hidden wall behind the vegetation rose before them to deny their escape. Hades and Alkaios' eyes met for a split second, the same thought passing between them, and heads down they barreled headlong into the barrier. Its archaic strength no match for death and his queen, it crumbled upon impact.

"We have to get the eye!" Hades' pace did not slow as she brushed debris from her face. "But these paths will not lead us there," she said, as they closed in on another wall. "What better trap than a maze that leads nowhere?"

Alkaios shot out his hand and braced his broad palm across the small of her back. With a powerful force, he launched Hades through the air, and she landed hard on the wall's ledge. In a flash, Alkaios was beside her, and both witches chasing them snapped their heads upward, their sealed eyes tracking their movements.

"I think you are right," he agreed as they surveyed the winding maze. Not one of the haphazard paths led remotely close to the pillar, confirming their suspicions.

"Alkaios!" Hades' voice caught in her throat as she plummeted off the wall. Her fingers clawed at his body for aid, her stomach punched by the wall's sharp ledge. The impact forced the air from her lungs, and her breath wheezed as pain dug into her abdomen. With divine speed, Alkaios grabbed Hades' arm, jerking her to a halt as the witches dragged her down. Their talons ribboned her calves, the scent of crimson blood pitching them into a frenzy.

"Let us eat her!" they cried in unison. "Let us taste!"

Hades grit her teeth and pulled her legs up. Her knees grated against the jagged walls, but a wave of strength washed through her veins. She refused to be consumed by venomous monsters, refused to allow her blood to bathe the swollen lips of the demons below. Warmth flooded her as Alkaios pushed his power through her skin. Her muscles began to knit together, and Hades clutched his straining forearms as he hauled her to his side. Blood pooled around her toes. Its slickness threatened to slip her from her purchase, but Alkaios did not hesitate. He launched their bodies at the wall across the path not waiting for Hades' flesh to fully heal. The ancient stone crumbled beneath their feet with each thundered landing, but they leapt from one wall's ledge to the next, never slowing.

Reaching the pillar, they dropped from atop the walls, and without pausing, Alkaios raced to the base and hunched his back.

"Go!" he commanded, and Hades bolted forward. With a mighty leap, her foot slammed into Alkaios' shoulder blades and vaulted her through the air, arms straining for the eye.

Wham! Her spine screamed at the impact, and Hades plummeted toward earth. Her body hit the ground with a resounding thud as a screaming witch landed on top of her.

"I want this one," she crooned as Hades heaved beneath her, breath harsh and jagged. "She smells different. Gives her to meeeee!"

Hades watched in horror as the witch drew a taloned finger to her lips and ripped the stitching out thread by thread, freeing her mouth. The stench of death bathed Hades' face as a blackened tongue slid past the swollen lips. The coarse threads hung in swinging deformity as Hades struggled to throw the witch off, but the demon's claws only dug in deeper, refusing to release her prey. Her putrid mouth grinned with savage hunger, revealing a row of filed fangs.

"Why does this one smell different?" she hissed. Foul breath washed over Hades, the witch's voice no longer in their minds but echoing clear in the air.

Hades wrenched her arm free and punched the witch, but the mud-clothed woman merely flinched at the blow and retaliated by clutching the queen's throat and slamming her head violently into a stone. Hades' eyesight blurred, and she could feel the witch's rough tongue drag across her cheek, tasting her sweat-bathed flesh.

"Alkaios!" Hades yelled, bucking her hips in an attempt to dislodge the witch. "Get the eye!"

Alkaios paused only for a moment, caught between aiding the woman he loved and obeying her command. His stomach clenched in nausea's fist at the sight of the dark, oozing tongue savoring Hades' cheek. His hesitation would cost Hades' her flesh, and as the naked form peeled back rancid lips, he backed further into the clearing and bent his legs. The muscles in his thighs curled with tension, and loosing his fury, Alkaios vaulted up the pillar. He crashed into the pedestal and dug his hands into the unforgiving surface. His fingers burrowed deep, dislodging dust and pebbles as he raced to the eye.

"This meat is so sweet," the witch crooned below, and opening her jaw wide with a loathsome roar, she lunged for Hades' face. Hades pitched sideways, but it was of little use. The witch's talons were tethered in the queen's flesh, and Hades knew she could not escape the razor fangs, so she recoiled into the dirt, pooling dark power in her chest. It churned and festered, begging for release. It yearned for the puncturing of flesh so it could flood this filth-clad monster with the poison of death, but just as her filed teeth grazed Hades' throat, a hulking mass barreled through a shattering wall and collided with the witch's bare skin. She screamed as Kerberos slammed into her, and with a crazed evil in his six eyes, he clamped all three of his massive jaws around the witch and pulled. With a sickening tear and a sudden muted scream, Kerberos tore her body into pieces. Blood dripped in sticky streams from his mouth, and he turned to stare at his mother. The witch's head hung from one jaw, her torso in the middle, and her cleaved legs dangled from his third. Screams of anguish ripped through their skulls, and Kerberos spat the severed frame onto reddened mud. Carnage oozed down his necks to pool at his feet, and Kerberos loosed a roar in response to the demon's mourning wails.

The remaining witches barreled out of the maze and with a

swift slit of their stitching, shredded the coarse twine binding their lips. They wailed, brandishing their fangs as they bore down on the offenders, but Kerberos leapt forward. His massive paws landed protectively on either side of Hades' torso. The blood of the dead witch stained his hide in a warning. A warning they refused to heed.

"Gives it back! Gives it back!" they both screamed suddenly as they skidded blindly to a halt. Their arms flailed. Their legs stiffened as their world was plunged into bitter darkness. "We have not had meat in so long."

"Silence!" Alkaios boomed. He had captured the eye in a solid fist, denying them their sight. Careful not to move his finger and let an ounce of light grace their eye, he extended his hand over the edge of the pillar where only jagged debris would cushion its fall. "Take one more step, and I will crush your sight."

"No! Gives it to us!"

"No," Alkaios said as Keres, Hydra, and Chimera suddenly burst into the clearing. "You will grant us safe passage through this maze now and once again when we leave. Only then will I return your eye, but if you attempt to kill or harm any of us, by the gods, I will crush it."

"Very well," the witches spat. "We will allow you to pass, but you must gives us the eye when you are gone from our labyrinth."

"So be it," Alkaios agreed and looked down at his wife. His heart finally slowed its frantic pace, and peace overtook him at the sight of her loving eyes peering up at him. With Keres' help, Hades had stood to her feet, her body beginning the healing process, and all panic trickled from Alkaios' veins as her skin fused together. "Hades, Medusa turns men to stone, so you, Keres, and Hydra have a better chance in that temple than I. Take the pitchfork and go. Find what you need so we can be rid of this place. The beasts and I will keep watch over these witches.

Kerberos will eat them if they so much as move." At that, the witches cried, their voices whining through the air, but a single growl from the hellhound silenced them.

"Watch over him," Hades said to Kerberos and Chimera as she bent and snatched the discarded weapon from the dust. Keres and Hydra followed as she began the trek toward the shrouded mountaintop.

"Hades!" Alkaios called before she disappeared back into the maze, and Hades turned over her shoulder to look at her husband. "Be careful, my love."

VII

Hades stood flanked by Keres and Hydra at the base of an ancient and massive temple. Battered and bruised by unkind centuries, the sanctuary loomed above them, its top disappearing into the clouds. The barren and harsh soil lay undisturbed before their feet, grey and bleak as far as the eye could see. The silence was desolate and eerie, an eternal graveyard reverent of the horror this place housed. Unlike the witch's maze, this land was void of stone men. Empty and alone, the temple towered above them, its crumbling features hunched like a proud man bent under the weight of age.

"I go alone from here," Hades said into the stillness, gripping the pitchfork with white knuckles.

"Absolutely not," Keres hissed. "You will need us. If those witches were her guard dogs, how much more dangerous will Medusa be?"

"That is why you cannot follow me," Hades answered. "It is I who needs her answers. I will not risk your lives."

"We are with you always," Hydra said, stepping forward to place her hand on Hades' arm.

"I know," Hades replied, "but this is for me to do, and me

alone. Whatever darkness I am about to face in there is somehow tied to me. I cannot allow my concern for you to distract me from this evil."

"We will wait here then," Keres said, "but only if you promise to call upon us should you require our help."

"If I need you, I will call," Hades promised as she separated from her companions. Her heels padded softly up the cracked steps toward the shadowed mouth, gaping to swallow her whole, and she entered the temple that until that moment had been nothing more than a myth.

HADES SLIPPED SILENTLY into the dark, eyes well-adjusted to the blackness of the crumbling structure. To her surprise, there were no statues within these walls, mimicking the barren land she had left Keres and Hydra to watch over. Perhaps all who stumbled upon this gods forsaken mountaintop never survived long enough to make it into the belly of the beast.

Hades ventured further into the depths until all signs of the sun disappeared. Her feet made no noise on the archaic stone. Her senses remained peeled for any sign of life in this vast temple, but only oppressive silence greeted her. The absence of light would have rendered most intruders blind, but darkness was Hades' home and no match for her. As the impenetrable blackness oppressed her vision, the heavy air turned suffocating, and Hades could feel an ancient presence brush against her skin. The beast was here. She was closing on the monster laying in wait for blinded prey. Pity the Underworld was darker, and Hades' eyes were all seeing. Medusa would be cheated of an easy kill.

And then there it was, ever so faint. Hades halted, ears hunting for the noise. It came again, the sound of a slithering snake. A body so impressive, its scales engulfed the vast hallways. Hades gripped the pitchfork, her skin electric. Medusa was here.

Hades lowered her eyes to the floor and cocked her head sideways, staring down her arm to the dark stone. From this moment on, her sight must remain cast down. It seemed no one ever made it into the temple to be petrified, and Hades would not be the first. Her body quieted to listen for the slithering as she held her breath. It came again, growing closer, tickling Hades' right ear.

Whack! Something whipped out from the dark silence to her left. Instinctively, Hades raised her eyes but forced their focus back to the ground as she lunged out of the way. That small glimpse, though, was all she needed to see a massive tail crash with a viciously crushing purpose. Hades swung the pitchfork faster than the tail could retract and plunged the dual prongs into the scales. She thrust with such demand; they pierced clear through the flesh and drove against the stone tiles. In the obscurity of the hidden hallways, Medusa sucked in a breath of pain. Her first mistake. Hades now knew where she was, and like Hydra, the beast's head would be her weakness.

Hades bolted through the darkness. Her feet slapped the floor with an uncanny silence, and within moments, she slid around a pillar. Launching into the air, Hades curled her knee and felt the sickening blow reverberate through her bones. Medusa cried out as Hades' kneecap cracked her face. The beast plummeted backward, but her speed was alarming for a creature of such mass. Before Hades' heels could reconnect with the ground, Medusa's massive tail barreled through the corridor and into Hades' back. The impact hurtled the queen of death forward, and Hades tumbled through the air before slamming face first on the cold, hard stone. No sooner did she hit the floor, she rolled to her feet just as the tip of a spear pierced the space where her heart had been. A solitary breath barely had time to escape Hades' lips when the air whistled a second warning. In a flash, Hades lifted her hand and caught the careening spear. With a single snap of her wrist, her iron fist shattered the wooden handle into splinters, the broken pieces clattering to the tiles with little ceremony.

    A sudden slithering rushed behind her, and Hades leapt into the air just as the tail thrashed beneath her and landed lightly on the massive scaled body. With deft speed, she bolted up the tail, feet slapping the icy scales. Gracefully, Hades vaulted over the beast's head and wrapped her legs around a neck seething with snakes. With a jerk, she pitched forward, sending both of them diving for ground, but Hades caught herself at the last moment and used her thighs to force Medusa's face into the stone. The woman let out a scream of pain as her nose shattered, and Hades took advantage of the monster's averted gaze to flick her eyes to Medusa's downcast skull. The tiny snakes that composed her hair seethed in fury. Their miniscule faces challenged the dark queen, but she ignored their taunts and hoisted the pitchfork above their bodies. The weapon plummeted, its aim true and harsh, but just as metal was about to strike skin, Medusa reared her tail and drove it against Hades' ribs. The raven-haired beauty balked and tumbled to the floor. In a fraction of a second, the serpent slithered forward and grabbed Hades' ankles, dragging her onto her back. Hades slammed her eyes shut as Medusa loomed above her, the snakes licking the scent of flesh off the air.

    Hades bucked, and Medusa beat her spine into the stone with jarring strength. In her blindness, Hades could hear a spear drag across the tiles. Panic reared its ugly venom in her chest, but Hades smothered it, and before Medusa could react, she slammed the pitchfork into her attacker. The snakes screamed their pain, but Hades did not stop. She crushed the metal against Medusa's skull repeatedly, blood splattering her fist, and when she felt the serpent's grip loosen, she drove her head into Medusa's, sending the monster sprawling.

    Hades panted with exertion and scrambled to her feet. Eyes

trained on the floor, she cracked her eyelids to slits, and watched the impossibly large body slither away before it doubled back on itself. Through her lashes, Hades saw Medusa's torso lunge, human hands reaching down to seize a spear in each.

Refusing to allow the beast the upper hand, Hades launched herself at her opponent. Pitchfork raised. Eyes pitched down. Medusa swung both spears and blocked the assault with bone-jarring force, yet Hades simply sidestepped the assaulting tail and drove her bident down. The razor prongs pierced Medusa's scales. The scream that ripped from Medusa's lungs was the only warning she gave before plunging the spear at her intruder, but it was all the warning Hades needed. The queen whirled on her heels and caught the pike as its tip grazed her forehead. With a groan, Hades heaved the spear free and flung it to the ground. Without wasting a single breath, Medusa aimed her second spear, but the clang of metal echoed through the temple as the pitchfork deflected it.

"Look at me!" Medusa demanded; their weapons locked in electric resistance. Hades' only response was a wicked punch to Medusa's mouth. The beast staggered, spitting blood, and Hades' coiled her foot and kicked Medusa savagely in the gut. The snakes screamed, tiny voices piercing the echoes, but Hades refused to relent. She drove her knee into the beast's belly as she fell upon the scaled body and punched Medusa. Her aim was true as ribs cracked beneath her knuckles. From behind, Hades sensed the serpent's tail and swung the pitchfork, slicing the flesh. The pain-filled scream was all she needed to pinpoint the monster's head, and in a flash, the pitchfork hurtled through the air. The sound of its metal curve strangling vocal cords echoed in the vast space followed closely by the ringing clash of the dual prongs burying into the stone wall.

Hades paused, Medusa's grappling with the bident in an attempt to escape the only movement in the empty space. But it was no use. Only Hades could free her now.

Eyes still downcast, Hades maneuvered around the serpent's writhing body and seized the end of the pitchfork. With a massive heave, she yanked it from Medusa's neck and raised it for the final blow, but just as she lifted her arm, a hand clutched her wrist in a desperate hold.

"There is only one person who can wield this pitchfork like you do," Medusa hissed. "And I have been waiting for you for a very long time."

VIII

"Yes, my dear," Medusa hissed. "I have been waiting for you for a long time… Hades."

Hades froze, the pitchfork's blow halted midair. She stared down at the human fingers that gripped her free wrist and the immense serpent that coiled behind her.

"How do you know who I am?" Hades whispered into the darkness.

"Because… I have been watching you." At her words, her body began to shrivel. Inch by inch, foot by foot it shrank until the colossal mass dissipated. In the colossal serpent's place stood two very human feet peeking from beneath a tattered skirt. "I always knew the day you found me would come too soon."

"Why did the Oracle send me in search of you?" Hades asked, eyes still trained on the ground.

"Because I hold the answers you seek," Medusa answered, her voice no longer a hiss. "And I have something to show you. Come, you may raise your eyes."

"I am no fool. I will not be added to your stone collection."

"My dear," Medusa laughed, "I have no desire to turn you to stone. I know the fate that awaits me should I curse you. The

Olympian god of death waits outside for you, and I saw how that dog of yours shredded the witch. I do not wish to anger such opponents. Come, you may look up. I assure you my eyes hold no power now."

Hades lowered her weapon but made no move to lift her gaze. Medusa's assurances of safety could be a cornered animal's desperate attempt to save itself from a superior predator, and for a breath, Hades' desire for truth battled with her better judgment. Medusa remained silent, allowing the queen of death to weigh her decision, but curiosity conquered Hades' urge for preservation. With careful dignity, she leveled her gaze at the beast trapped before her. For the first time in centuries, eyes fell on Medusa's face without consequence, and Hades sucked air into her lungs. An impossibly beautiful woman stood before her with eyes slit like a snake's and hair composed of small green-scaled snakes. The pulsating mass hung docile at the moment, coiled around each other to form a long braid.

"By the gods," Hades muttered, "I cannot believe you are real."

"I have spent lifetimes ensuring all think me merely a myth," Medusa answered. "My eyes," she added when she noticed the queen staring at them in disbelief, "they are not a curse but a weapon, a blessing. I control my power, enabling it only when I choose."

"So, the rumors about you hold no merit?" Hades asked. She was struggling to reconcile the tales her mortal parents had told her while she was a child with the exotic and ferocious creature before her. She had lived among the gods, was the mother of god-killers, and yet shock rippled through her veins that the story her human father had once told to elicit good behavior was here in the flesh.

"None," Medusa answered. "I needed to keep two generations of gods at bay, but I also needed you to know of me. I could have hidden without a trace, but one day you had to find me, and so the myths were born."

"Who are you, that you convinced the most powerful of men into believing a lie?"

"That is a long story, my dear," Medusa said, turning to walk off into the darkness. "Come, I must show you, and it is best I start at the beginning." She disappeared into a black hallway without a backward glance, and shoving down her surprise, Hades unglued her feet from the tiles and followed Medusa into the depths.

"At the dawn of time, the first gods were born," Medusa started. "The Titans were not the first. The originals came before them. Their race was unnamed for they were the beginning, and unlike those who followed, the Old Ones' power was absolute. Divine power like theirs has never been seen since, nor will it likely ever be again. Unlike their successors, these Old Ones did not reside in the realm of earth. Olympus and the Titan fortress are connected to the land of the living, but the Old Ones dwelled in another dimension. They accessed earth through an ancient door, but they had no direct contact, nor were they restricted by a need for devoted prayer. Their power was theirs alone, and prayer held no concern. Therefore, they lived wholly detached from their subjects. Not needing love, worship, or even fear, the Old Ones were free to behave as they saw fit, and humanity was destined to live or die by their hands with no rhyme or reason. Some were cruel, and some were benevolent. Their moods dictated their whims, and mankind could do nothing to prevent it, but when you do not require mortals or their devotion why bless them?"

Medusa navigated the labyrinth with memorized ease, and

when they happened upon a fork in the corridor, her lithe fingers swept across Hades' spine in guidance.

"Some of the first were kind," she continued as they descended into the coolness. "A few even took lovers among the humans. Their offspring were not demi-gods, though, their divinity far too aggressive for mortality to resist. A child birthed of a human-god union was born fully god, adding to their ranks. For centuries, an uneasy peace held, but one day the Old Ones' King found himself drawn to a mortal's wife, and he claimed her for himself. The mortal, a man previously blessed by godly favor, was so enraged he blasphemed the gods. Screaming his rage, the foulness of his tongue spread throughout the land like a plague, but the King did not allow this heresy to go unpunished. It was his birthright to take what he wanted, and this blasphemy was unforgivable. Death was too merciful a punishment for the afterlife awaited all mortals. This man had to be made an example of. So, the King gathered his brethren, and together they created the Touch of the Gods."

Hades sucked in a sharp breath and halted in her tracks.

"A curse you are well acquainted with," Medusa said with a soft smile as she gestured for the wide-eyed Hades to follow. "A curse so powerful that it requires all or at least most of the gods to perform it. One touch shreds the victims' souls. No afterlife, no eternity. They cease to exist. The King cursed that mortal with the Touch, erasing him from the face of the earth. Proud with their show of absolute sovereignty, the Old Ones were unaware of the cost owed for introducing this punishment. If used too often, the Touch of the Gods destroys the sanity of the users and gruesomely mutates their flesh, but as it was the Touch's birth, the King knew not the floodgate he had released. Evil is all-consuming. Its use creates intense cravings. It wants to be unleashed again, and a battle of wills must always be fought to keep it in check. Zeus should be thankful your sacrifice of power halted the Touch he gave your husband. The price of craving the dark insanity he would have had to pay would be eternal."

Medusa paused and turned her slitted eyes to Hades, but when the queen merely watched her with wary caution, she continued. "The Old Ones were content for a time, but the appetite was always there, lurking in the shadows. At first, they used it sparingly on the wicked and the sinners, but as the decades passed, the craving multiplied. Each time they fed it, the yearning reared its monstrous head until resistance was impossible. They began to use the Touch of the Gods at their every whim, and no mortal was safe. Mankind took to hiding, hoping without hope they would be spared the gods' insanity, yet their madness only increased. By the end, the gods had become so crazed they no longer resembled themselves. The evil in their souls manifested visually in their bodies, morphing them into monstrosities. Heads of beasts atop bodies of animals, eyes grown together, massive horns sprouting from their heads. Such cruelty could no longer be hidden within, and their forms became the outward appearance of their inner depravity. They grew hideously deformed, pale shadows of a once perfect beauty, and their hysteria drove them to turn on each other. On that fateful day, the Old Ones' home collapsed into war. A massacre broke out, not to end until all were slaughtered."

"My dreams?" Hades interrupted with a hint of questioning lacing her voice. "They are not dreams, are they? The blood in the hallways? The horns casting shadows? I am seeing the past."

"Yes," Medusa answered. "You are remembering their downfall. The day the first gods went extinct. But before they perished, a god and his pregnant wife were awakened from their insanity. The babe in her womb was in turmoil because of the anguish, and its kicking woke its mother. The babe's innocence saved its parents' sanity. They knew they had to protect their unborn child from certain death, but the father's wounds were fatal. He would not survive. So, he dragged his wife through the carnage and cast both her and his weapon to earth. Slamming the ancient door to their dimension shut, he sealed it with his blood, locking them away forever. He died against it, his blood spilling over his seal to confine them to their deadly eternity, for his blood seal could only be broken by the life that ran through his veins. The moment the door closed, his wife became mortal, but she had more pressing issues, for as her body crashed to the ground, her labor began. She birthed a human daughter alone in the dirt, the weapon long lost to her and her children in the fall. Behind the door, though, the King's mother saw the infant as a way for their kind to endure. With her dying blood, she carved a prophecy into the stone. 'When the last of our kind reunites with the last weapon, the Old Ones will rise again to rule'."

"The first have come," Hades said, color draining from her face. "The first have come, and they seek the last…" she trailed off looking at the pitchfork. "This is it… the weapon he cast out?"

"It is."

"So that makes me…"

"The last." Medusa finished for her. "I have been watching over your bloodline since the beginning. Always a daughter, always an only child, and always raven-haired… until you. You were born with red hair. The blood of your father. It was you the king's mother prophesied about. I knew the moment I saw your hair you would find the pitchfork and wake the Old Ones. You are the first reincarnated."

"I am an Old One?" Hades whispered, unable to move.

"Yes. You are one of the originals, the most powerful of them all. How else do you think you broke the seal of the Underworld? No Titan or Olympian could, but you did. There is a reason the Underworld still bows to you, why the beasts answer to you. It is the same reason the pitchfork remains loyal. You gave your husband your power, but there is more to you than that sliver of Olympian deity Zeus transferred to you. When you found that pitchfork the Old One within awoke, and it grows in strength every day."

"Her prophecy foretold that when I reunited with the weapon, they would wake. Have they?" Hades asked.

"Yes," Medusa said gravely. "The moment you took hold of it, they awoke in their realm. The stronger you grow, the stronger they become and vice versa. It is why you are not all-powerful yet. They are not at full strength and will never be... unless that is opened." Medusa gestured as they rounded a corner, and there it, stood solemn and alone in the darkness at the end of the hall. A massive door carved with the same symbols the Oracle had etched in blood beckoned to Hades like a long-forgotten memory. She drifted through the light barren corridor toward it. An unseen pull forced her feet, and unable to stop herself, she pressed a palm against its cool smoothness. A violent jolt of energy and longing shot through her body at the contact, and Hades jerked backward like a child stung by an angered bee.

"The door to their dimension," Medusa said. "If opened, their power will return in full. If that happens, the world stands no chance."

"Is that why I feel I am going insane? Am I inheriting their madness?"

"I am afraid so," Medusa answered with a hesitant sigh. "And it will only worsen as you grow stronger."

"My father? Will he break the seal?"

"I fear he has most likely been destroyed," Medusa said, voice low and sorrowful. "His mind was freed from insanity, and I believe he would have refused to grant them freedom from his eternal prison. He also relinquished his hold on the pitchfork, bequeathing it to his heir. A god's weapon is his direct channel to his power, and by passing it on to you, his divinity is forfeit. His soul and power are reincarnated within you, and if his resurrection were possible, they would have spilled your father's blood again in an attempt to open this gate. It will not work. It must be broken by his hand." Medusa drifted off. She fell silent in the darkness, and Hades turned to gaze upon the beautiful beast.

Uneasiness lingered in Medusa's eyes, and Hades stared at the slits for a long moment before the realization hit her, caving in her chest.

"It can only be opened by his blood... and by his hand," Hades said. "As his descendant and heir, I possess both. That is why the madness is overtaking me. The prophecy... she cursed me with their insanity so I might one day break the seal?"

"And that can never happen," Medusa said firmly, confirming Hades' horrifying realization. "I allowed you passage to tell you your truth, but next time I will turn you to stone. It is my sacred duty to protect this door, even from you."

"How do you know all of this?" Hades' head swam.

"I was there," she answered. "I am a Gorgon, the last of my kind. We were an ancient race of women, charged with protecting this door. My sisters tried to stop the bloodshed that fateful day, but they all perished. I would have too, except your father tasked me to stand watch for all eternity. When he sealed that gateway those symbols were not there, but when all fell silent inside, they burned into the stone. I read what the king's mother had prophesied. Your father had sacrificed his life to save his unborn daughter, but through this prophecy, her reincarnation would return to open the door, and it would fall upon my head to kill the last great god that walks this earth."

IX

Hades stumbled backward until her spine pressed against the cool wall and sank to the floor. With a deep exhale she lowered her head between her knees, white-knuckling the pitchfork. Her chest constricted, fighting the gulps of air she forced into them. Panic pricked her skin with razor needles, and her clenched eyes were the only things slowing the spinning room. The two women remained silent together in the shadows, letting time slip past unchecked.

"So, if I open that door, I destroy the world?" Hades asked, her voice soft in the darkness as she broke the silence. She forced her gaze to meet Medusa's and watched as the Gorgon nodded with somber confirmation. "And I am truly one of them?"

"The last of the greatest," Medusa answered.

"How is one supposed to react to this?" Hades hauled herself to her feet, eyes glazed over. "I need air," she muttered, wandering down the corridor retracing their steps.

"I have called off the witches," Medusa said to her back. "Call your husband. I must speak to him."

"I do not know how to respond to this," Alkaios said, perched atop ancient debris. He rubbed his mouth with a large hand and let out an uneven breath, shifting his gaze from Medusa to the temple's entrance where Hades sprawled on the steps. Her spine leaned against Kerberos and Chimera, their muscled bodies a throne around her. Medusa had just concluded a shortened version of what she had told Hades, and Alkaios felt the air rip from his chest. He understood now why Hades had exited the temple with all the color drained from her cheeks, her sickened expression distracting him from the myth in flesh that awaited him.

"I always knew that woman was extraordinary," Alkaios said, turning his eyes back to the Gorgon. "The greatest of us all... how am I supposed to contain that?"

"By any means necessary," Medusa answered as she perched beside him on the debris. The tiny green snakes gently writhed in their braid. Their forked tongues flicked from their mouth to taste Alkaios' scent on the breeze. "If you do not keep her from here, I will be forced to turn her to stone. I cannot allow her to open that door."

"And you think you are strong enough to stop her?" he asked, gesturing to the welts on her skin from Hades' brutality.

"I have to be," Medusa whispered, voice grave. "Because if you cannot keep her from me, I am the last hope this world has."

"That pitchfork came from the gods before us," Charon said, rubbing his head in disbelief. "I cannot believe my assumption from when Hades found it on your farm was right. Gods only pass their weapons on to their children..." He trailed off, the gravity of his words unbelievable. Charon looked around the room to his wife, Keres, and Hydra who each cradled one of his daughters before he shifted his gaze to Alkaios. The god-killers flanked their king, and despite Charon's aversion to the beasts being this close to his infants, Alkaios had insisted for this meeting.

"How is Hades taking this?" Ioanna asked.

"I do not know," Alkaios sighed, his eyes heavy and body slumped. "She has said little, although I can guess. How does one swallow that kind of shock? The last descendant of the most powerful gods this universe has ever seen. A descendant of madness whose single growing desire is to unleash them, an action that will destroy us all. It is a burden Hades will bear for all eternity... one that will only grow worse."

"How do we help her?" Ioanna asked softly, and Alkaios raised his eyes to hers, a tortured pain spread across his handsome features. He held her eyes for a long while before answering.

"We keep her from Medusa's temple."

Ioanna tilted her head in response. "You mean for us to trap her?" she muttered in horror. "You want us to watch her and prevent her from leaving the Underworld? How could you expect that of us? How can you expect us to keep Hades prisoner in the realm she rules?"

"What choice do I have?" Alkaios bolted from his slouched position against the wall with such force Ioanna jumped. The child cradled in her arms burst into a distressed wail, and Charon almost imperceptibly shifted his weight to block his wife. When Alkaios saw his friend move, he shifted backward horrified by his own aggression. "Ioanna, what choice do we have? If she opens that door, we all could die. We cannot let that happen. The name of Hades may mean the god of death, but I will not put that on her. I will not condemn her to the fate of living up to her name, and if Medusa tells the truth, Hades' madness will only grow. If she breaks that seal and joins them, I lose her." Alkaios choked, combating the tears threatening his eyes, and the room fell silent as he struggled to regain composure.

"Medusa might not be right," Ioanna said. "Until this morning she was only a myth. Who knows if she can be trusted?"

"She tells the truth," Keres interjected when the king did not speak. "Hades' nightmares are visions of the past, of what Medusa has explained. Hades believes her."

"I will lose her," Alkaios finally whispered, "if she opens that door. She will be fully Old One. Their insanity and blood lust will be her own. Her love for us will vanish, and Hades will seek nothing but our deaths. If it comes to that, then I will lose my life because I cannot raise a hand against her. I would rather die than kill her... even if she becomes a monster." Alkaios broke off and buried his eyes in his palm, his lips contorted into a grimace.

"Ahhhh!" he screamed, startling the group, and slammed his fist brutally against the wall, cracking the wood. The whole room froze. Even the babes knew to be silent. No one moved, save the wall as the living timber knit itself back together.

"So please, do what you must to keep her here," Alkaios choked. "Do whatever is necessary to save my wife."

ALKAIOS RAN a rough palm over his hair, exhaustion descending over him in a debilitating wave. He felt drained as he strode through the ever-changing terrain of the Underworld. He wanted life to return to normal, where his wife was the strong woman he loved, free in her own realm. How could he bring himself to imprison the cornerstone of his life and power, the woman who saved him?

A sudden sound of retching jerked him from his thoughts. Alkaios bolted forward to find Hades hunched over in the great doorway to the fortress. She was gagging and heaving over the dirt, oblivious to her approaching husband.

"Hades?" Alkaios cast the pitchfork against the wall with irreverent haste. She jumped at his voice and whipped her head around. Her startled eyes softened when they met his, and Hades wiped her mouth with the back of her hand before rising on unsteady feet.

"I was looking for you," Hades said softly, leaning on the old stone for support, "but nausea overtook me."

"Are you all right?" Alkaios asked, concern clouding his eyes. He reached out and enveloped her smaller frame in his hulking one.

"I do not know..." Hades murmured into his warm and comforting chest. "No. I feel ill and cannot fathom how to digest Medusa's words. How can I be what she says I am? How do I live a life where my sanity slips day by day until I am no longer Hades of the Underworld, but Hades the Old One, daughter of insanity? I could single-handedly destroy the world by opening one door."

"I will not let that happen." Alkaios kissed her soft hair, inhaling her sweet and familiar scent. "You gave all you had for my safety; I will do the same for you."

"And I love you for it," she murmured, "but I fear eventually not even you will be able to stop me."

Alkaios opened his mouth, but before the syllables departed from his lips, Hades jerked backward, hurling herself from him, and heaved onto the ground. Alkaios stepped to her and held her hair with gentle concern. Aching helplessness sunk into his gut as he rubbed her back, but what else could he do?

BACK AT THE BOATHOUSE, Ioanna waited until Hydra and Keres had left and were long out of earshot before she whirled on her husband.

"How are we supposed to cage her?" she demanded visibly shaken, her voice faltering between sorrow and anger. "We owe Hades our lives… our daughters' lives, and yet we are to turn on her and treat her like a tortured soul destined never to leave Tartarus?"

"Ioanna…"

"She returned you to me," she sobbed, clasping Charon's face in her palms. "I had lost you, and Hades brought you back. We owe her our loyalty. She is our true god. I love Alkaios, but he is not Hades. She is still my king, and I cannot cage her like an animal."

"Ioanna," Charon repeated, "it is because we love her that we have to do this. Hades will never forgive herself if she opens that door. Our god of death does not kill cruelly, and if her ancestors force her to, the last shred of the woman we care for will disappear. We are indebted to her for everything, and we owe it to her to keep her safe… even if it means caging her."

"I know you are right." Ioanna curled herself against his chest, "but I feel if I play a part in imprisoning her, then I am ungratefully throwing her goodness back into her face."

Ioanna's voice carried softly over what she thought was an empty River Styx, but her words fell heavy on a pair of ears. Keres hugged her knees as she hid on the dock, her small form concealed in the river's mist. She leaned against the wall and listened to Ioanna and Charon's conversation drift through the night, her heart sinking. She knew Charon was right. Hades could not break that seal, but she understood Ioanna's heartbreak. How do you watch the person you love most descend into madness? How do you imprison pure and absolute power?

Suddenly sure of what she had to do, Keres stood softly in

the fog. She would do what had to be done. She would cage Hades so Ioanna would not have to. Keres was the first to lay eyes on Hades when she broke the seal to the Underworld, and she would be the person to chain her there.

X

"Spirit of violent death," Hephaestus said, slamming his hammer down on a scalding piece of metal as sweat poured from his brow. "What is it I can do for you?"

"I have come to ask for your help," Keres said tentatively as she drifted into the forge. A maze of workshops and storage rooms, Hephaestus' forge was almost impossible to find, but Keres had refused to give up the hunt until she was standing in the scalding room with the blacksmith of the gods.

"What is it you require?" he asked without so much as a glance at his intruder.

"It is a task of great difficulty," Keres began, "and you will not like it." At her words, Hephaestus' hammer froze mid-air, and his gaze leveled at her as if he saw past her eyes into her soul. Keres swallowed with dread and shut her eyelids, letting the darkness blind her.

"I need you to build a cage," she finally said, opening her eyes to return his stare, "… for Hades."

"Which Hades? The man we now call god or the true Hades who broke the seal?"

"My Queen."

"And what kind of cage do you require?" he said bitterly, voice full of scorn, "for the woman who gave you everything?"

"You do not understand." Keres rushed to him, fingers clutching his massive forearm. "You must do this for me. I cannot tell you why, but you have to trust me."

"You expect me to trust you when, without reason, you ask me to cage the Queen of the Underworld? Unless I hear from the King himself, I will do no such thing."

"Hephaestus, please," Keres begged. "I cannot explain why; Hades would not want me to, but you know how I love her. I would not ask for a thing so vile if it were unnecessary. Please listen to me. Something is coming. Something we may not be able to stop. Hades cannot be allowed to leave the Underworld."

Hephaestus cocked his head inquisitively and opened his mouth.

"I cannot explain," Keres interrupted before he could speak. "No one can know... I have already said too much and should not even be here, but you must understand, I love Hades. I need her safe... I need you to do this for me. Please, build me a cage, a way to lock her in the Underworld before it is too late."

Hephaestus gazed down at Keres, realizing with a growing dread in the pit of his stomach that she spoke the truth. She begged with desperation, and he saw fear hovering thick in her eyes like a dark parasitic passenger. Whatever caused the spirit of violent death to feel terror was something he did not wish to meet face to face.

"Very well," Hephaestus sighed despite the sickening knot gripping his gut. "I will build you a cage to lock your beloved queen behind; one she will never escape, and the Underworld will truly become the prison Zeus, Poseidon, and Hera meant it to be. But I have one condition. I refuse to imprison Hades without the King's consent. You have requested its building, but only Alkaios will convince me to unleash it. I refuse to be responsible for the King of death's rage if I were to foolishly imprison his wife. It must be his decision and his alone."

"I understand," Keres said. "But by the gods, hurry... before it is too late."

THE MIST ROLLED thick over the River Styx, obscuring the small boat slicing through the poison waters. It was the dead of night, but when a coin was tossed into Charon's hands, he must heed the call. So, he plunged his pole through the dark water, ferrying the shade of an elderly man who had passed in his sleep. Survived by his wife and son, they knew the commands of Hades and had placed coins over his eyes, ensuring his safe passage to the afterlife.

The boat slid against the shore with a soft bump, and Charon offered the passenger his hand. Most who crossed the dark river were too afraid to accept help from the ferryman, but the elderly shade simply smiled and accepted the support. Charon guided his fare to the safety of the riverbank where the judges waited to weigh his soul. Charon watched as they found the shade pure of heart, who with a peaceful smile, passed on to Elysium.

With the shade's departure, the judges vanished as swiftly as they had appeared, leaving Charon alone in the midnight silence. The ferryman speared the riverbed with his pole and pushed back into the water, eager to rejoin Ioanna in their bed, but just as the shore disappeared behind the gloom, a shadow caught his eye. Charon strained to glimpse the shifting shape through the wall of mist. Whispers of black fluttered in the wind, and instantly he knew who it was. Repositioning the rod, he shoved toward the sand. Her outline grew clearer as his boat sliced through the Styx until Charon could see the paleness of her skin against the grey fog.

"Hades?" Charon called softly, but she did not move. Frozen

on the shore, her toes buried beneath the murky water, Hades remained unaware she was being observed. Charon drifted closer and opened his mouth when he saw her eyes. Glazed over, they were open but unseeing. She was oblivious to her surroundings, utterly blind to his presence.

Gently, as not to startle her, Charon extended his palm toward her arm, but Hades snapped her head, drilling him with a haunting and unseeing gaze. He grunted in surprise, and his stomach dropped at the lack of recognition painted on her face. Instead, her cold, glassy eyes bore straight into his soul with terrifying ferocity. But before he could recover his surprise, the tentacles of inky black smoke smothered her, and Hades was gone.

"Alkaios," Charon called into the stillness, and the words were barely uttered before his friend materialized in a dissipating cloud of dark smoke. Sleep lingered in Alkaios' eyes, and his hair spiked where the pillow had crushed it.

"Hades left," Charon said by way of greeting. "I do not think she was awake." Alkaios sighed and ran a hand over his mouth as his mind's eye followed her trail.

"I found her," he said after a moment's silence. "Thank you." Alkaios clapped Charon on the shoulder before he disappeared just as his wife had a moment before.

On earth, the sun still hid, allowing the moon to reign supreme. Alkaios surveyed the ground in the pale light. Despite the years, his farm looked no different than it had when he was mortal. Hades had preserved the land he had once hated until a woman named Persephone stumbled into his life. Alkaios walked through the crops, observing how everything grew and bore great fruit regardless of the nearly barren soil untended by hands to strangle life from the dirt. Its consecrated fields had become a destination of fruitfulness to anyone in need, and all who braved a pilgrimage to Alkaios' farm were blessed with abundance. It was not a widespread truth, but those who prayed desperately in the night only to have their needs ignored by the gods would wake to find their feet drawn along a path that ended in this eternally growing bounty.

Alkaios walked through the peace toward his old home and smiled at the sight of recently harvested grain. New shoots pushed up through the dirt trying frantically to overtake and replace the shorn stalks. Someone had been here and had reaped the benefits of the ever-growing harvest, and as Alkaios caught sight of Hades sitting on the bench that stretched before the weather-beaten house with her head rested against the wall, lids blanketing her eyes, he was thankful that someone in need had been blessed by his wife's foresight.

"I am not sure how I got here," she said, feeling her husband's presence press against her skin. "I was trapped in blood and pain, and when I awoke, I was here. I must have been searching for peace." Alkaios crossed the distance between them and sat, leaning his head on the wall beside hers. He shifted to study her moonlit face, watching her lashes flicker open.

"Do you miss living here?" Hades asked. "A simple and peaceful life under the sun and moon, no darkness, no death?"

"You, my love, have a different memory of this place than I do. Your presence brought a blessing to this land, but before you, only heartache and exhaustion comforted me at night. I choose to forever live in darkness because you are my light."

"I miss it," Hades said. A soft smile played on her lips at his words. "We had our obstacles then, but compared to now…" Her voice trailed off for a moment. "This farm is simple… peaceful… and I miss the goat."

"The goat?" Alkaios murmured with a laugh. "He bit everything and made caring for him difficult. How can you miss him? Or more importantly, how could you subject the good and pure souls of Elysium to his misbehavior? They earned the reward of the afterlife, yet you plagued them with him."

"They love him," Hades said, slapping her husband playfully in the stomach.

"No, you love him." Alkaios trapped her fingers against his abdomen, and the pressure in Hades' chest eased slightly at the sound of his chuckle. She adored the way his deep voice rumbled when he laughed. It sounded as if all his joy stemmed from her, and Hades could not imagine having ever loved anyone but Alkaios.

"He was yours," Hades explained. "I could not let any animal of yours be cast aside and forgotten after you left this farm. I had to grant them eternal life as thanks for their service to the new god of the Underworld. Besides, I enjoy visiting him. He is so small and soft to hold. Nothing like the spiked bed hog that insists on sleeping next to me every night." She smiled, referring to Kerberos, which despite her joking words, Alkaios knew to be her true favorite.

"You are a better god than I," Alkaios said, voice drifting off into the quiet midnight. A comfortable stillness settled between them, and Alkaios clutched her hand. His rough thumb smoothed the soft skin of her knuckles as if he was trying to memorize every crease and fold of her beloved skin. After long moments, Hades gripped his fingers and drew his palm to her lips. She pressed a reverent kiss to his palm, and an overwhelming heat flushed his skin at the gentle caress her lips painted across his flesh.

"How long was I gone before you noticed?" Hades asked, breaking the silence.

"Moments. Charon saw you leave."

"At least I came here."

"Hades." Alkaios captured her free hand in his and pulled until her back parted from the wall and her torso twisted toward him. "You will not go there. You will not open the door. I know it."

"You do not." Desperation peppered her eyes. "It is in my

blood - who I am. I was prophesied to break that seal, and I am afraid it is only a matter of time before I truly become the god of death."

"I will not let that happen."

"I left the Underworld tonight without you realizing," Hades argued, voice heavy. "What happens next time when Charon is not there to witness my departure? What if none of the others see me leave? How far do I get before you even know to come after me?"

"I will not give up." Alkaios brought both of her hands to his lips, kissing one palm and then the next just as she had done. His mouth lingered against her skin with each kiss as if his determination could seep into her hands by his love alone. "I will stand by you no matter what, and I will not let you near that door. We have seen worse and survived… this will be no different."

"That is just it," Hades interrupted, bolting to her feet so fast her hands ripped from his grip. "We have not faced worse. If Medusa is right, and I know she is because I can feel them inside of me, then Zeus' anger and the price I paid to save you are child's play compared to the Old Ones. Their power is absolute, and they have carved their moral compass from their hearts with their genocide. If they rise, even the three greats of the Olympians may not be able to stop them, and I will no longer be myself. Consumed by their madness, I will be gone."

"I do not care what some dying, crazed god prophesied over you," Alkaios said as he leapt to his feet. His body towered over Hades as his harsh eyes bore into her soul. "You are not like them. Look at my farm. You have turned it into the answer for those who seek help, for those who starve. You return children to their parents. You gave Ioanna and Charon a second chance full of love and daughters. That god prophesied about someone completely different from you. You say if that door opens and earth is destroyed, then you will truly be the god of death, but Hades, you already are. Just not in the way you think. You care for the dead and made the river safe to cross so that all who pass may receive fair judgment. You even granted that goat a happiness I would never have thought to give him. You were destined to wake the first gods, that I am sure of, but when they spoke about the last all those centuries ago, they were not expecting... you. If anyone can take the darkness and make it home, it is you. They were not expecting the woman you are, and because of that, I know no matter what, you will never be the monster they prophesied to come."

"I hope you are right," Hades sighed, collapsing against his chest. "I cannot be responsible for destroying the world." Alkaios wrapped his arms around her shoulders and planted a kiss on the top of her head, burying his nose in her raven hair.

HADES WOKE TO THE SUNSHINE, her sleep free of nightmares. Maybe Alkaios was right. Perhaps she was the person he believed her to be, and their love would tether her soul to her own mind and not the minds of those who had once seen fit to kill their own family.

Alkaios still lay asleep on the bed beside her. They had slept on earth, their bodies intertwined as the fresh air bathed their skin. Hades pressed her lips to Alkaios' temple and wormed out from beneath his heavy arm. She wandered to the creek in the early sun, soaking in the foreign warmth and washed her face with the clear water. Drinking her fill, Hades sat back against a rock and slipped her feet into the bright current so different from her own malicious waters. The stream cooled her skin as the sunlight beat down on her dark hair.

Hunger nagged at her stomach, and despite the bounty of the crops behind her, Hades unfurled a fist. In a swirl of inky smoke, a pomegranate appeared in her palm, and she ripped it open, red juice bleeding down her wrist as the vibrant seeds were plucked from its cream flesh. Hades ate in peace, mind falling empty as she enjoyed the sunshine her realm so desperately missed.

Back inside the house, Alkaios woke with a start, an internal warning electrifying his body. He rolled over and found the cause for the jarring awakening. Hades' side of the bed was absent her form, and as Alkaios bolted from the mattress, his fingers caressed the indent her body had left. The sheets still retained her warmth, and relief eased Alkaios' chest knowing she was not long gone.

Seizing the pitchfork from its resting place, Alkaios burst into the new day's light and blinked rapidly at the rays stinging his eyes. He had dwelled in darkness for so long with the woman he loved that he had almost forgotten how blinding an unobstructed sunrise was. Eventually his pupils adjusted, and Alkaios scanned the crops for any sign of Hades. The search was complete in an instant as his gaze landed on a gloriously dark stain at the creek bed. Hades sat alone in the morning bliss eating a pomegranate, dress hiked high up on her thighs. Her flawless skin soaked up the warm rays, and despite the scar on her arm where Charon had to stitch the flesh wounded in one of Athena's attacks during Hades' rise to power, Hades appeared a portrait of perfection.

Alkaios' heart slowed in relief at finding her and then sped up at the sight of Hades' beauty. Her bare legs kicked softly, dragging her ankles through the crystal water, and Alkaios watched in a trance. Turmoil had claimed their lives as of late, but he never forgot the way he felt the first time he saw his wife. A woman named Persephone had come limping to him from the very spot where she now sat, and Hades still took his breath away. An overwhelming urge to have her body pressed against him devoured his soul, and Alkaios surged toward the river.

He was behind Hades in a heartbeat, and the pitchfork clattered to the dirt as it fell from his hand. Alkaios sank to a seat and pulled her spine flush against his chest. A small gasp of surprise vibrated her ribs beneath his palm as their bodies collided, and while one arm welded Hades to his heart, the other brushed her sun warmed locks from the back of her neck. Alkaios kissed the soft skin blanketing her spine, and Hades' ribcage shook his encasing forearm with laughter.

Hades lifted a hand and laced her fingers through Alkaios' hair. Together they sat in the warmth for long, silent moments. Alkaios' lips lingered against her neck, Hades' fingers caressing his hair. Love expanded his heart, and Alkaios was sure Hades felt it pounding through his skin. He loved this woman increasingly with each passing day, and the swelling in his heart was almost painful. Alkaios could not lose Hades; he refused to. He craved an eternity with this raven-haired beauty, one filled with laughter and children. Even tears and arguments were welcomed if it meant Hades never abandoned him for the madness of these foreign gods. Alkaios could almost picture them sitting here hand in hand by the water, their future sons or daughters splashing in the shallow current. Kerberos and Chimera would be here, keeping guard over their little bodies, and a sudden flash of how beautiful a mother Hades would be played out before his eyes. Alkaios would do anything to keep her insanity at bay so that perhaps one day she would mother his children.

As if sensing his trepidations, Hades peeled her back from his thundering chest and shifted to face him. Her lips were on his before Alkaios could inhale a breath, and her arms were about his neck in a desperate hold. Alkaios felt both her fear and reassurance in the kiss, and he drank all of it in. He would steal all of her pain and anxiety if he could, curse his own soul to free hers, and as they kissed, Alkaios felt the tension in Hades' body release. The kiss was fierce and passionate, full of a love so vast that words could not express it. Alkaios collapsed to the grass, dragging Hades on top of him. A small gasp escaped her full lips before she pushed herself against his solid chest. Their kiss grew deeper, and Alkaios wrapped Hades in an embrace so strong it would have pained a mortal woman, but it only inspired more passion from his queen. Darkness and prophecies could wait. For now, only Hades ,and Alkaios' love for her, existed.

HADES AND ALKAIOS vanished from earth and appeared moments later on the banks of the River Styx. With the setting of the sun, reality had come crashing around their blissful forms. They could no longer hide from the pressing matters at hand, locked away in their passionate cocoon. The hours on earth had brought them both an iota of peace though, and with kisses peppered across his wife's face, Alkaios could not stop the smile that broke through his lips. Hades' spirit was exuberant from a day that had consisted of nothing but Alkaios' love, and as they returned to their true home, her fingers could not be parted from his skin.

Still clutching her husband's hand, Hades bent and scooped up a pebble, but by the time her back straightened, it was no longer a stone but a coin. With a flick of her wrist, she launched it over the water, the fog's dark greed swallowing its whistling flight. The Styx fell still, broken only by Charon's boat slicing through the current.

Not bothering to wait for the ferryman to reach the shore, Hades plunged into the poison waters and climbed into the boat. She twisted her ladened skirt over the side of the ferry while she waited for Alkaios. The rung droplets hastened to rejoin the river until the damp cloth was safe to lower into the boat. The Styx had devoured Charon once before, and Hades refused to threaten his safety even if it was just a single drop slipping from her skin.

Charon swung the ferry along the riverbank, and Alkaios pulled himself up beside his wife. The king was the only living soul besides Hades who could touch the river of death unscathed, but unlike her, he preferred not to wade headlong into the water and test fate.

"Thank you for watching over me earlier," Hades whispered in Charon's ear.

"Anything for you." Charon planted a kiss on her temple as he pushed off from the shore.

"I think," Alkaios said as they thrust deep into the obscuring fog, "it is time we told Zeus…"

"No!" Charon and Hades both said in unison, a cold firmness in their combined voices.

"I know you do not trust him," Alkaios said with exasperation, "but he is the king of all the gods. He brought the prophecy to us and deserves to know what is at stake. If anyone can help, it would be him."

"He will help by killing her," Charon answered. "Look at the lengths Zeus went to eliminate you, and you were only a mortal. Do you think he will allow Hades to survive once he finds out her truth?"

"He loved her," Alkaios argued. "Whether he still does, he did once. Deep down he has to remember she is somewhere in his heart. How could he bring himself to kill her in cold blood?"

"Because," Hades answered, "I am a threat to everything Zeus holds dear. His reign, his family. If he discovers I can destroy the world with power he has only ever dreamed of, he will not hesitate. Alkaios, I understand it is difficult to disregard Zeus after a lifetime spent praying to him, but I know him. When loving me almost cost him a fraction of his control over Olympus, he banished me to the depths. He did not know I would break the seal. He believed he was sending the so-called love of his life to eternal darkness and isolation. Then when he thought I might grow strong enough to take his throne, he tried to obliterate your soul. If Zeus learns the truth, my death at his hands will be swift. He will not let me survive long enough to come close to that door. If it comes to that… comes to my death being earth's only salvation, then it will not be at his hands. I cannot die at Zeus' hand."

"You will not die," Alkaios spat, his tone full of harsh pain. The Underworld's shore peeked through the fog, and when he saw Keres and Kerberos lingering on the sand, he lowered his voice. "I will not let you leave me or allow anyone to lay a finger on you. He might refuse to come to our aid, but perhaps another god? There must be someone willing to help, but the king of the gods and his brother would be the strongest choices. We are the three greats of Olympus, the most powerful of them all. Who better to protect you than us?" Alkaios fell quiet waiting for a response, but only the cold, silent mist brushing against his skin answered.

"Hades?" Alkaios stepped forward and caressed her shoulder with his fingers. She stood frozen under his touch, but after an agonizingly long moment, Hades slowly twisted her head. Her neck turned with an unnatural movement until her face lighted upon his. Alkaios jerked back with a grunt and snatched his hand from her skin, horror seething through his veins.

"It does not matter who you seek for help," Hades snarled. Her voice was low and gravely, not at all her own. Not a single voice, but that of many broke past her lips in a demonic lilt, and her dark blue eyes had vanished, replaced by glazed over black slits. "He cannot help you," the demons' voices continued, echoing harshly over the water in growled insistence. "She has awoken us... she will free us. You cannot stop this... no one can."

As soon as the words left her tongue, the blackness drained from her eyes, and the dark blue seeped back into her irises. Hades blinked at Alkaios and then Charon in dazed horror, and her hand flew to her mouth almost as if she were trying to catch the words that had already fled. The boat was the only thing that moved as it drifted aimlessly through the water until it wedged itself in the shallow sand with a soft thud. Hades faltered at the slight bump. Without thinking, Alkaios shot out his hand to steady her, but with a harsh jerk, she waved him off. In a panic, Hades scrambled over the side of the ferry, plunging hard into the river before she stumbled onto the shore. No one attempted to follow her as she rushed over the ever-changing terrain, their feet lead beneath them.

After a long and oppressive silence, only Keres found her feet, and with silent footsteps, she backed away until the mist swallowed her alive. In her solitude, she vanished.

"Hephaestus!" she tore through the endless forge, her steps slapping a vicious staccato on the tile. "Hephaestus!" Keres burst through the archway that led to the heart of his workshop where the fire ran eternally ablaze. The god shot his eyes upward at her entrance, a piece of molten metal clasped in his bare hands.

"Keres…"

"You must work faster!" Keres cut him off. "I beg you… by all that is holy, finish that cage. We are running out of time… we may already be too late."

XI

THE DAYS that followed were the unbearably obsessive silence before a vicious storm. The whole of the Underworld held its breath, afraid that if even a whisper of air passed through their lungs, the unstable peace would shatter. Hades withdrew within herself, and a sense of overwhelming helplessness pained Alkaios as he watched her presence shrivel. She was a shell of her normal self, fear of her potential fate crushing her, and if he was honest, it was strangling his bleeding heart. Alkaios never let Hades far from his sight, and it killed him to chaperone the woman who had broken the seal. It was her divine right to watch over them, not to be guarded like a debased soul of Tartarus. Alkaios was god now, but he felt it was mostly in name. He commanded great power, but Hades was the true god of death, and following her as if she were a toddler teetering too close to a cliff's edge drained his soul.

All within the Underworld slept with one eye open, guarding Hades' every movement, praying she was in control of her own mind. There was no peace during the long nights as all who dwelled in the depths rotated watch. Hydra even deployed the snakes of Tartarus to all corners of the realm, and they whispered Hades' every action back to their mother.

Despite the uneasiness of the dark air, Hades had not once slipped from the Underworld. Charon caught her sleepwalking one night on the riverbank, but she merely stood, toes in the sand, and stared out into the mist before returning to bed. Kerberos slept with his massive tail coiled around her so that if she rose, the yank on his tail would wake him. Chimera rested each night in her doorway, his immense frame blocking any escape. Hades managed to sneak past both beasts once, but Keres had seized her before she could leave the fortress. On two different occasions, Alkaios woke from a dead sleep to the sight of black smoke encircling Hades, but his restraining speed had tethered her to his body, rendering it impossible for her to vanish.

It was heartbreaking for all to watch and humiliating for Hades, but the peace held. Not once did she escape, and after a week of fragile calm, the Underworld dared to believe she was safe under their watchful eyes. Keres checked unnecessarily often on Hephaestus, but the cage for Hades was slow turning from idea to creation. Keres' hope flickered dim in her chest as the progress fought Hephaestus' molding hand, but still, she clung to faith. Alkaios would hate it, but she knew Hades. Hades would agree. That seal could never be broken, no matter the cost, and Keres was certain Hades would prefer an iron prison to call home than the ever-present eyes hunting her every move, even if it was to only shift her weight. No, this would work… it had to. They had to hold out a while longer, and then Hades would be safe. The door would never open, and their worry would be over.

THE NIGHTMARES WORSENED, drowning Hades in paralyzing fear. She tore through the bloody corridors; the images so palpable, she felt the dead beneath her heels and scented the decay in her nostrils. The shadow of horns loomed massive on the walls as she tripped over the corpse-littered hallways. Slipping in a pool of slick blood, Hades' bare feet shot out from under her, and she slammed savagely into the floor, cheek slapping the ground. Her vision blurred as a searing pain burned through her skull, and she huddled aching on the cold floor, willing her eyes to focus.

When her sight returned, Hades wished it had not. Before her was the face of an elderly woman, eyes open and blank in death as blood dripped from her lips. Hades balked and scrambled away from those empty irises, but her finger slid in the slickness causing her palms to scrape across the stone. Her hand jerked from the smear and froze. She had not smeared a pool of blood, but instead hastily scrawled symbols. Hades shot a glance to the aged corpse and then back to the stained prophecy. This was the king's mother, the woman responsible for ensuring the return of the Old Ones. This was it, Hades' beginning.

Hades' eyes snapped open in the darkness. The tentacles of inky black swarmed around her, clawing at the air. Not a sound echoed in the old fortress; not a soul stirred in their slumber as she sat up in a slow, deliberate movement and slipped her foot unnoticed from Kerberos' circled tail. Silently her bare feet connected with the stone floor and, and the smoke that ensnared her black hair and dress rendered her invisible in the obsidian of the night. Hades stepped over Kerberos with soundless grace and rounded the bed to where Alkaios had laid the pitchfork to rest. Grasping it firmly in her fist, she turned and crossed to the doorway where her faithful lion slept. Skirt hitched above her knees, Hades crept over Chimera; the beast utterly unaware she had left.

An unearthly silence engulfed the hallways as Hades invisibly slipped through the fortress. She passed Keres' and Hydra's rooms without alerting the sleeping women despite their open doors. Hydra's snakes roamed free from their mother to watch as sentries, but Hades simply waited for them to turn their heads and snuck past the beasts. Her power was growing. Not even the god-killers of Tartarus detected the vibrations of her footsteps or tasted her scent in the air. By the time their ever-watchful gazes turned back to sweep the halls, she was gone, a ghost at midnight. In a matter of seconds, Hades had escaped the fortress, not a soul disturbed from their slumber.

Unnatural darkness glazed over her eyes as she surveyed the changing terrain of the Underworld. Her four dark horses watched alert in the night, but their hellish eyes did not notice her slip through the gloom; their nostrils failed to scent their master. Even the furies who littered the shadows, wandering with their halting gaits, missed Hades as she slipped past. It was almost too easy. Yes, her power was growing.

At the river's edge, Hades halted just shy of the venomous waters and turned her gaze to the shrouded boathouse, listening to those sleeping within. One of the babes let out a soft cry, and Hades could hear Ioanna shuffling through the night to comfort her. It seemed only the child sensed her presence. The innocence of infancy could feel the evil ripple from Hades' body, but the rest of the Underworld was blind to her. Satisfied that she was truly alone, Hades waded into the River Styx. The poison water lapped at her skin. It clung to her flesh as it clawed at her infernal power. Tentacles of black smoke began to ebb and flow through the water, growing ominous as they absorbed the Styx's energy, and with a flash of hellish eyes, Hades vanished.

A moment later she appeared in darkness and fury at the base of the mountain. Her dress dripped poisoned water onto the ground, and where the droplets landed, the living green shriveled and died. Hades inhaled a sharp breath and looked heavenward. The mountain stretched upward into the onyx sky. Its invisible shield bared her entrance to the temple, forcing her to mortally climb past the remaining two witches. Hades grimaced, and smoke once again extended from her form. Perspiration beaded on her forehead as her body strained against the resistance.

Imbued with the evil of the river, the smoke grew wide and long, stretching farther from her than it ever had before. Hades' muscles convulsed as her power pushed against that of the invisible barrier.

A shimmer formed as the two forces collided, one malevolent and one unseen. The air burned electric, and with a scream ripping from her lungs, Hades thrust her power forward in a crushing assault. The surrounding air shattered with a bone-jarring crack, and Hades disappeared, leaving behind only scorched earth and a cloud of ash. She had broken through the imperceptible wall, the barrier that forced all to enter as mortals, and in an instant, she appeared in the doorway to the temple. The tentacles of smoke rippled around her body and pitchfork; her eyes glowed impossibly dark in the night, and Hades gripped the metal weapon of days passed in her hand until her knuckles whitened with blood loss. One obstacle destroyed. One more to go.

THE CRACK SPLIT THE AIR, and Medusa knew. She had dreaded this moment; prayed it would never see the light of day, but at the sound of the barrier's destruction, she knew the last had come. Medusa rose to her feet with a fortifying breath and contemplated summoning the witches but dismissed it just as quickly as she had considered it. They were deadly in the maze with their all-seeing eye perched atop the column to watch unobstructed, but in here among the debris and twisted halls, they would be blind fools. No, they were only useful in stopping those who climbed up the mountain. Medusa knew by the cracking, Hades had destroyed the barrier that kept the gods from materializing at her doorstep. Hades would be here in seconds if she were not already. The witches would be little use now. No, this was a fight Medusa would have to wage herself.

With a blink of her eyes, Medusa's legs melded together. Once flesh, her body transformed to scales, and the massive tail began to grow from her limbs until she was no longer in human form. Her monstrosity of a tail swelled and thickened until it filled the room with fleshy coils. She reached back and loosened the cord that held the snakes in their braid. The tiny creatures that composed her hair burst loose as she shook them out, the scaly bodies slithering over her shoulders. Medusa inhaled with a breath of finality, and a grayish film grew over her irises. All who saw her would be turned to stone, and Medusa prayed to anyone who would listen that Hades came alone. She did not wish to curse any to eternity as a statue besides the one she must kill. And kill the last she must. One of them would have to die tonight, and Medusa knew if she did not turn the queen of death to stone, then it would be her own blood that would pave the way for the Old Ones' return.

HADES HOISTED the pitchfork and strode over the threshold of the temple. Malevolent purpose drove her steps. The temple's eerie silence hung in the air as a warning that not all was well within these walls, but Hades slipped through the darkness, ignoring the uncanny quiet. Not a single flame lit the halls, leaving the temple in bitter blackness, but Hades' feet knew the way, her shadowed eye seeing the unseen. Her mind was of a singular task, and she would not be stopped.

Thwack! Hades head whiplashed, her face exploding in pain as she stumbled. The sound of a slithering mass' flee echoed in her ringing ears, but before she regained her balance, the air swished around through the room. Her legs were knocked from beneath her, and Hades slammed to the ground with a thud. Her skull's impact spider-webbed the tile, and an involuntary roar sliced through her lips as an excruciating knife of torture carved into her brain. Fueled by anger and a red haze of blinding agony, Hades flung herself backward, using the momentum of the fall to roll over her shoulder and back to her feet. So, the monster was here to stop her? Hades grinned wickedly and cast her eyes down. Let it try. She would paint the walls with its blood.

Hades bolted into a run, heels slapping her anger on the floor. It mattered not that the beast could hear her movement. She wanted it to. It would draw the Gorgon out, and Hades would accept the creature's violent death as an offering of blood and torment.

Hades noticed the whisper of air to her right a moment before Medusa hurled herself through a side-branching hallway. Hades slid to a halt almost too late, but almost was all the warning she needed to slow as Medusa careened before her, barely missing the raven-haired beauty. Twisting the pitchfork, Hades speared the scaled tail and vaulted over the mass, disappearing into the darkness. Medusa let out a blood-curdling scream as she was left behind in the emptiness. The Gorgon would have to try harder than that.

The beast faded into the labyrinth, but the gooseflesh marring Hades' skin spurred her forward, the hair at the base of her neck a sign of her body's exhilaration at being hunted. Hades burst into an open room of echoing vastness, but this time the whisper of air hit her ears too late, and Medusa's torso slammed into hers. The women plummeted to the floor, and Hades clenched her eyelids as her body clashed with the stone. In her blindness, the queen of death lashed out, but Medusa wasted no time in her assault. In a heartbeat, her massive tail curled around Hades. The tighter it constricted, the more air it forced from her crushed lungs, and Hades gasped for breath, desperate to cool the burning in her chest. Her ribs strained beneath the suffocating pressure. If she did not free herself, her ribcage would crack like a walnut's shell under the force. With a growl from deep within her soul, Hades summoned the tentacles of smoke and heaved. Medusa's tail floundered like a dead fish and slapped the ground with a heavy thud. Air flooded Hades' lungs with searing relief, and she choked, the soreness on her flesh already threatening to turn purple. She could not allow the beast to confine her again, and seizing the fallen pitchfork, Hades hurled. The prongs flew true, and the clang of the metal heralded them hitting their mark. Medusa screamed in the darkness, her serpentine form writhing over the tiles. Eyes glazed dark, Hades extended a palm, and the pitchfork ripped itself from Medusa's flesh and returned to her hand. The Gorgon's heaving breaths rushed franticly from her lips, and Hades could tell by the panting that she had struck the serpent well.

Eyes still downcast, Hades strode forward until the tail thickened to a torso at her feet. Thick crimson coated the floor as it dripped down the monster's scale. Sensing where Medusa's body hovered, Hades lifted her fist and slammed it down. It exploded with a sickening crunch against Medusa's nose. Hades smiled with wicked pleasure at the sound of the bones giving way beneath her hand, and using the pitchfork to pin the beast, she coiled for another savage blow. Medusa cried out as her jaw cracked under Hades' knuckles, but the queen refused to relent and raised her fist again. With a final weak effort, Medusa flung her hair as Hades' hand broke across her face. The myriad of slender snakes latched onto their attacker's wrist and bit down with burning fury. Hades yanked her arm back with soundless force and glimpsed down at the countless welts puckering red on her skin. The pain was excruciating as the blood began to flow down her mottled forearm, but Hades only stared at it as if it was not her own limb but that of a stranger. She paused for a moment to watch the deep crimson run from her veins and drip to the floor before she hoisted the pitchfork into the air and whipped it across Medusa's face. With a thud, the Gorgon's mass plummeted to the ground. Through downcast lids, Hades studied the massive bloody body, but the Gorgon failed to move. This monster was no match for the queen of the Underworld. Hades was the true monster, and stepping over the Gorgon, she disappeared into the darkness of the temple.

———

FEET PULLING HER FORWARD, body unable to fight the drawing force, Hades came to the door. Sealed. Solid. Hades settled before it, frozen in silence. Outwardly she was a stoic figure with eyes of cold resolve, but somewhere deep inside, she was fighting. Her stillness before the gate was the only challenge Hades could manage, but the part of her that struggled was pushed deep within her soul. It was too little too late, and with a shove, the darkness snuffed it out. Hades stepped forward and lifting a bloody palm, smeared red over the seal just as her ancestor before her had. The door lurched at her blood, and power surged at her fingertips like an explosion's recoil before detonation. Hades opened her mouth to speak…

"I cannot let you do that," came a weak and garbled voice. Hades snapped her hand back and almost looked into Medusa's eyes before she realized and cast them to the serpent's torso. The monster's stomach was bleeding from the pitchfork wound, and blood dripped down her throat as a result of Hades' beating.

"As long as I still draw breath, I cannot allow you to open that," Medusa heaved as she slithered closer. For a weighted moment, the two women stood facing each other, and Medusa prayed the true Hades had woken from this stupor, that she had pushed the madness from her mind. But without warning, Hades raised her head, and Medusa shrieked. The queen locked her stare with the Gorgon's, and Medusa saw Hades' eyes were black. Not a single speck of white shone through. She did not turn to stone as she looked upon the Gorgon, and Medusa knew. This was her end. The Old Ones' were feeding Hades power through the door, their evil brimming as a protective curtain over their salvation's gaze. They had her blood. They were one now, and no matter how hard Medusa tried, the onyx eyes looking at her were not Hades'. Medusa could not curse her to an eternal statue.

"Then I will take away your breath," Hades spat, but it was not her voice. It was the voice of the horde speaking through her, and with that, Hades shot a hand out. Smoke erupted from her fingers and engulfed the serpent. The Gorgon struggled to free herself, but the blackness twisted and writhed around her until she was trapped. Hades smiled an evil grin and clenched her fist tight in mid-air. Instantly, the inky tentacles constricted Medusa's body like a suffocating snake. The harder Hades squeezed, the more force choked her ribcage until Medusa cried a gasping panic, but the prison only drew tighter. Her vision blurred, and breathing shallowed. A crack reverberated off the walls as one of her ribs snapped like a twig beneath the pressure. Fire coursed through her lungs as they starved for air. Bruising pain rippled from her chest until all of her flesh screamed for mercy. Medusa gasped, trying to maintain consciousness, but it was no use. A ring of bruises choked a brutal necklace about her throat. She heaved, coughing blood as the view of the dark queen faded to black.

"The first have come," the voices spoke through Hades. "The first have come, and they seek the last." And with those words, Medusa crumbled to the floor.

Releasing the beast's bruised body from the tentacles of power, Hades turned back to the door. She wiped her blood on the prongs of the pitchfork and then drove the metal into the seal. Through her mouth, the Old Ones uttered a language Hades did not know or understand, yet she thrust further. The seal began to splinter, slightly at first, but the cracks grew, and with an unearthly scream, Hades shoved the pitchfork with all of her unnatural strength. The cracking that shot through the stone was deafening, not a single inch of the earth remained still with its violent shattering. With a jarring burst of air, the seal shattered. Hades' head snapped backward, caught in the escaping current. Her skull collided with the wall with a volley of blood, and she crumpled almost lifelessly next to Medusa, their bodies unmoving as the whole of the earth convulsed.

XII

"Alkaios!" Keres jolted upright in bed. Her eyes had barely opened before she was standing on earth, looking at the sky. Her feet touched the dirt only a second before Alkaios' did, and his eyesight followed her gaze heavenward.

"By the gods," he exclaimed, taking a step backward and bumping into Hydra who had just appeared. Her hands reached out to catch him, but the heavens captured her attention, freezing Hydra in cold terror.

"No!" Keres screamed, covering her mouth. "No, Alkaios do something!" She fell to her knees. Alkaios stood in shock as Keres dissolved into a panic on the ground, but he was too late. He could do nothing.

"Alkaios," Keres begged with a distraught tone, and Hydra moved forward to envelop her friend in her comforting arms. The sky had turned a violent color in the early morning light. The clouds burned like flowing red lava, and those circling on the outskirts were black with the ash of destruction. Beneath the eye of the storm, stood a distant mountain that had never been visible before. Medusa's mountain. The barrier had been broken;

that which had hidden the door since the beginning of their time gone.

Alkaios' body went numb, and nausea roiled in his belly. He had not felt Hades leave, but seeing the burning tempest consuming the sky, he knew. Hades had been right. He could not stop her. He had promised his wife salvation from the prophecy but had failed. The first finally found the last.

"By all that is holy," came a deep voice behind them, and all three heads whipped around. When Keres saw who stood there, she launched herself at him.

"You are too late!" she screamed, slamming her fists against Hephaestus' chest. "I told you to hurry, but you are too late..." she repeated over and over, a hysterical mantra. It took all of Hydra's strength to rip Keres away from beating the smith to a mottled pulp.

"What is happening?" the blacksmith asked, looking to Alkaios, but when the god of the Underworld did not answer, he continued, "Is this what you feared Hades would do?"

"How do you know about this?" Alkaios asked in bewilderment.

"I know little." Hephaestus nodded at Keres. "But the spirit of violent death requested I build a cage to imprison your wife in the Underworld. Is this why?" he urged, gazing in horror at the burning clouds.

"Yes," Hydra's panic laced voice answered when Alkaios failed to respond. "By the gods, yes, but it is too late now."

"What has she done?" Hephaestus asked, fear creeping through his body like burrowing worms, but before anyone answered, the air shimmered, and a battered woman appeared cradling Hades' broken form.

"Eyes down!" Hydra screamed, and the four of them slammed their eyelids shut.

"It is all right!" Medusa groaned, straining under Hades' weight. Alkaios opened his eyes first and lunged forward just in time to catch his wife as her crippled body fell from the Gorgon's arms. Alkaios sunk to the ground cradling the woman he loved most, horrified by her shredded arm and hand, her broken nose, and bleeding skull. His questing eyes shifted to Medusa with pleading urgency, but seeing her dawned a terrible realization. Medusa had transformed back to her human form, the living snakes for hair the only hint at what she was. Alkaios' sight roamed over her damaged face, bruised neck, and punctured stomach, and he understood.

"I failed," Medusa said as she collapsed in exhaustion and agony, her figure slick with both her own and Hades' blood. "I tried to stop her, but she is too strong." Her voice caught, and she fell silent, clutching her bleeding abdomen. The five of them sat in horror, gazing at the unconscious Hades. Her breath was shallow and labored, and Alkaios clung to her body, afraid to move. What should he do? What could he do?

"A god comes," Medusa whispered, breaking the silence, and before any of them could respond, she disappeared without a trace.

"By the gods," came Poseidon's voice, and Alkaios shifted to see the two brothers gaping at the sky.

"What happened?" Zeus demanded, his cold eyes staring down at Alkaios and his almost lifeless wife. "What have you done?"

"Call the council," Alkaios said softly, the demand in his statement not missed.

"You do not..." Zeus began.

"Call the council," Alkaios commanded. His features hardened with rage and power as he challenged the king of the gods. "Now."

"You knew all this time what the prophecy meant, and yet you did not warn us?" Zeus asked, his expression full of icy malice. He was the first to break the silence after Alkaios' words. "You knew and kept silent?" His voice was low and even, a far more terrifying sound than his screams. "You let this happen."

"Your solution would have been to kill her," Alkaios said. His bones felt weary beneath his flesh as he stood at the center of the council chamber. His recount of the Old Ones and the door had left him heavy and defeated.

"Of course I would kill her," Zeus spat. "If sacrificing Hades guaranteed the safety of the world, I would have driven my bolt through her heart."

"You will not touch her!" Alkaios' grip tightened on the pitchfork as he leaned forward, ready to strike if Zeus so much as looked at Hades.

"Your weakness," Zeus snarled as he slowly rose from his throne, "your unwillingness to sacrifice one person has killed us all."

"How can we be sure what he says is truth?" Hera blurted before the gods could come to blows. "That this is not a play for the throne, for your power, Zeus? Hades has been known to unleash darkness on earth for her own purposes. Is this any different? Gods before the Titans? Do you expect any of us to believe this?"

"He speaks the truth," Hades mumbled, speaking for the first time to cut off her husband whose mouth was parted in an almost response. All eyes turned to her as she sat slumped on the throne to Zeus' left, and she settled uncomfortably under the oppressive gaze of the gods. She could barely keep her eyelids open or her body upright, and the crusted blood on her skin made her look as if death would claim her at any moment.

"As if I would ever believe a word from your mouth..." Hera spat with venom only a jealous woman could muster, but before her sentence could finish, Hades shifted unnaturally in her seat.

Gone was the pain and exhaustion as she pinned Hera with a dark gaze. The whole chamber froze, watching in horror as Hades' eyes bore down on Hera's rigid body. Power rippled off the queen of the Underworld's skin and penetrated the air as she stared. The gods held their breath, afraid the savage inside Hades would strike. Those who had doubted moments before knew now that Alkaios' horrifying tale was true. The energy had shifted, and all sensed it. Zeus was no longer the most powerful among them.

"You do not have to take our word for it," Hades said, breaking her hold over the room and returning to her hunched state. The entire chamber visibly relaxed, thankful she had chosen not to strike. "You can take hers." Hades nodded toward the massive double doors.

On cue, they swung open, creaking on their hinges, and Medusa strode through with as much dignity as her battered body allowed. Her snake hair hung loose and writhing over her shoulders. The council watched her warily, but it was Poseidon who first recognized the beast entering their holy midst.

"Eyes down!" His command bounced off the circular walls. Heads shot down in unison, eyelids clenching shut, hands seizing weapons.

"I come in peace," Medusa said as she joined Alkaios in the center of the room. "I will turn no one to stone."

"Medusa's power is a weapon, not a curse," Hades explained, "She can control it and means no harm."

"Do not believe her," Hera ordered through clenched teeth. "She wants us to open our eyes to turn us all to statues. This is part of her plan to assassinate us, to take my husband's throne." Hera emphasized husband as a jab at the fallen queen, a reminder she had won, that she still held some power over the woman Zeus used to love.

"She is not here to kill you," Hades said with exasperation.

"We do not know that!"

"Open your eyes," Hades commanded her voice suddenly cold and harsh. "Medusa is here to help." She paused for a moment but when no one moved, continued, "Besides, Hera, if I wanted you dead do you really think I would need Medusa to do it for me? You… you, I could kill with my bare hands, and not a god in this room could stop me. Now open your eyes. She is not our enemy, and with the apocalypse at our threshold, we do not have time for foolishness."

The chamber fell silent, terrified after Hades' menacing words, and then with halting movements, Poseidon lifted his gaze and turned his eyes upon the Gorgon. The gods held their breath as they watched from the corner of their eyes.

"I cannot believe you are real," Poseidon said, and the room audibly sighed when he remained flesh and blood.

"Hello, Poseidon," Medusa said with a soft smile as the rest lifted their heads.

"I have no memory of ever meeting you," the king of the seas said, studying her face. "How could I have turned you into this?" He gestured to her head of snakes.

"You did not do this," she said kindly to him. "I was born this way. I am a Gorgon, an ancient race of warriors."

"The myth?"

"Is just a myth. I have been guarding the door long before the Titans rose to power. I know how to manipulate belief. I needed to remain hidden, known only in stories. If I stayed concealed, so did the door, but my name needed to pass down through the generations in case this ever came to pass. I am the only one who was there when it was sealed and may be the only person who can help you."

"Well, you failed in your protection," Hera sneered, and both her husband and brother shot her a warning look. Her unchecked mouth could damn them all.

"I was never supposed to guard it alone," Medusa explained, unfazed by Hera's disrespect. "In the beginning, the Gorgons were plentiful. A race of female warriors, we guarded the gate, but not from the Old Ones. We defended their domain from earth. Their realm is not meant for those of this world. We were not created to oppose an Old One, and on the day the first gods committed genocide, my kindred were slaughtered in their attempt to stop the bloodshed. I would have perished alongside my sisters if Hades' ancestor had not tasked me with safeguarding the door. When he cast his wife and unborn child to earth, he did not know of the prophecy. He died before it carved its words into the stone and believed I would protect his seal from both mortals and the gods who came after. Not his own flesh and blood. Not his equal. That is why I failed. Hades is one of the first… she is stronger than us all."

"So, that is it?" Zeus asked after a long and heavy silence. He looked around at those he called friends and brothers and saw the beginning signs of fear etched on their faces. "They have returned, greater than we will ever be. Our reign has come to an end."

"Perhaps," Medusa said hesitantly, "but all might not be lost yet." Medusa flicked her eyes to Hades and then to the pitchfork in Alkaios' hand. "The prophecy said when the last of their kind reunited with the lost weapon, the Old Ones would rise to power once again. Hades came to possess that pitchfork some time ago, yet the words they spoke through the Oracle of Delphi were just prophesied. Hades woke them from a centuries-long death, but they took time to manifest themselves. They are not gaining power quickly, which means we may still have time. Their strength is tied to Hades, and when she found the pitchfork, the dormant god within her woke. It has always been there, though. It is the reason the seal of the Underworld broke before her, but it was dormant all the same. The weapon awoke it, and her strength has grown ever since. It is why Hell still obeys her. It recognizes her greater power. Fighting Hades this morning told me she is stronger than she was a few weeks ago when we first clashed. She is not at full strength, and I believe it is because the door to her realm was shut. Her ancestors' power grows from hers, but hers also from them. While sealed, neither can reach their true potential, so while Hades surpasses us, she is not yet fully Old One. Now that it is broken, her power will increase at a rapid pace, as will theirs, but we have a small window where they remain weakened by separation. There is a chance that if we all work together and use Hades while she is in control of her mind, we may push them back into their own dimension and cage them once again."

"Why not kill them?" interrupted Zeus. "If these gods are as terrible as you say, then we should destroy them instead of caging them in the hopes they are never unleashed again."

"I do not think we can," Medusa answered, a note of defeat in her voice. "Just because they are not at full strength does not mean they will be easy to kill."

"But we are the greats," Poseidon interjected. "Surely Zeus, Alkaios, and I can stand against them."

"We might destroy a few, but we could never eradicate them all, and once they recover from their first death, they will be nearly impossible for us to slay. If you do not believe me, try ending Hades right here and now," Medusa said, looking to the bruised and bloody form of the Underworld's queen. "Even in her weakened state, it will take all three of you to subdue her. Imagine confronting a host of them. It will be our genocide if we face them, and once they fully rise to power, Hades is the only one strong enough to challenge them head-on. But by that point, I doubt she will remain the woman we know. I do not believe war is an option."

"We must listen to her," Alkaios spoke into the room. "She is the only person left alive who knows the Old Ones."

"If they are so great we cannot stand against them, how are we supposed to trap them?" Poseidon asked.

"We have one advantage," Medusa answered. "The last

time these gods were free, they slaughtered each other. Generations of death will have done nothing to ease their animosity. If being massacred by your own family was your final memory, your waking thoughts would be of revenge, especially if the Touch of the God's had driven your mind to insanity. They were not gods who worked together; they never had to with their absolute power. Centuries of genocide have most likely made it worse. There will be chaos among them, but if we work collectively, we may catch them unaware. They know not of the Olympians; their concern will be for their own conflict. It will take all of us, but we can strike while they are off guard. Trap them with Hades as bait; use their blind hatred against them."

"You believe that could work?" Zeus' eyebrows raised incredulously.

"I am not sure," Medusa said wearily, "but little else is an option."

"I will act as bait," Hades said decidedly. "We will find them and trap them. We will do this together," she said pointedly at Zeus and Poseidon, "or we die alone."

"Once trapped," Alkaios interjected, "the Olympians will seal the door. When Hades saved me, she transferred the Olympian in her. I am now the Olympian god of the Underworld, while she is the Old One of the Underworld. If we seal the gate, she cannot open it, not if it is a blood seal."

"But he will," Medusa said with heaviness, and the entire chamber turned their raised eyebrows to her. Medusa peered at the questioning faces and understanding washed over her. "You do not know, do you?" she asked softly, looking to Hades and then to Alkaios. When both of them stared at her blankly, she twisted to Hera, who was the only one not wearing a confused expression. "But you do." Medusa's eyes bore down on the high queen. "You sensed it… god of motherhood?"

The entire council went rigid, and Alkaios' eyes flew to

Hades before flicking to Hera. Hera sighed uncomfortably under the expectant stares and gave an almost imperceptible nod.

"Hades is with child," Hera whispered into the silent room. "It is a son."

"The sickness Hades has endured these past weeks has nothing to do with the prophecy," Medusa continued. "It was nature telling her of he who is to come."

Alkaios stared at Hades' battered form curled on his throne. Before he realized he was moving, he was up the stairs, his body drawn to her, unable to resist. The room watched in a trance as Alkaios forgot his audience and took Hades' bruised face in his hands and knelt before his wife.

"A son," Alkaios whispered as he leaned his forehead against hers, "we are going to have a son." At his words, Hades burst into tears and enveloped her husband's neck in her arms. For a moment, the terror on their doorstep faded away as joy seeped into the room.

"He will be Olympian," came Medusa's wavering voice, breaking the spell that had fallen over the chamber. Alkaios peeled his forehead from Hades' and twisted his gaze to the Gorgon. Darkness passed over his eyes, and he gripped his wife with possessiveness only a husband could conjure.

"The child will be half Olympian," Medusa continued, the heartbreak marring her features not halting her words. "Therefore, he could break your seal. But he will also be Old One. The madness growing in his mother, the hysteria of his ancestors, will pass to him, granting him both the means and the desire to open the door. They will use the boy to free themselves again, and unlike this time, they will not be weakened."

"What are you saying?" Alkaios asked, rising to his full height and settling himself protectively before Hades.

"That even if we manage to lock them back whence they came, Hades is one of them," Medusa said, the fear of her words plain on her face. "It would be unwise to let one of their monsters roam this earth. Even a single creature of absolute power, with a mind of violent insanity, could bring this world to its knees. We are not safe, not while Hades remains free. You cannot seal the door with the blood of an Old One for Hades will break it again, but the boy could shatter any Olympian bond this council creates. Just like his mother, it will draw him. He will not resist, and despite the fact they will consider him a half-bred, an abomination, they would use him as the means to their freedom." Medusa took a deep breath and surveyed the room before landing on Hades. "The only way this works, the only way we are safe, is if we imprison you in their dimension with them."

"You best not be serious, monster," Alkaios erupted, thundering down the few steps until he stood before the Gorgon. The entire chamber detonated, and Zeus leapt to his feet, bolt tightly gripped in hand, prepared in case Alkaios struck Medusa. "Because I will never let you lock her up with them. I will not allow you to take her from me so they can rip out our son and sacrifice him to their madness!"

"She is no longer your wife!" Medusa said in frustration, "she is one of them! Look at what Hades did last night! None of us stopped her, but it is the child I am most concerned about. If he opens that door, their power will be absolute and the carnage worldwide. Even if we left his mother to roam our earth, we do not have the luxury of time to wait for his birth. We must act swiftly, and we cannot allow Hades to remain free."

"That is not an option!" Black smoke leaked from Alkaios' body as a manifestation of his rage. "You find another way, Gorgon, for if anyone so much lays a hand on my wife's head, I will drag them to Tartarus myself."

"And while you are searching for another way, the world will collapse in fire and blood," Medusa said.

"Stop!" Hades yelled into the room, her voice a booming interruption as Alkaios opened his mouth to spew more fury. "Please stop," she said softer, looking deep into her beloved husband's mud-blue eyes. Rage burned fierce in them, but the smoke encircling his body dissipated at her request.

"Is there perhaps another way?" she asked Medusa, sorrow flooding her question. To hear in one breath she was carrying the child of the man she loved and then in the next to learn his fate was that of destruction made her sick, and the arguing banged around the walls of her skull like a possessed hammer. She felt exhausted and hallow, and her injured form on the throne was small and shrunken.

"I do not know," Medusa said, her face mirroring the exhaustion and pain in Hades'. "You are gods. Perhaps you can see a way I cannot, but I would not harbor hope. I have witnessed that evil that comes. You will be playing with fire."

"But there could be a way?" Desperation oozed from Alkaios' pores.

"This is a time where I do not believe having faith is wise," Medusa said. "Hope could kill us all."

"Do not take hope away from him," Hades whispered. "It is all he has right now… it is all I have." Tears flooded her eyes, and as they fell, the entire chamber of gods sat rooted to their seats, their hearts breaking. There may not be a great love between them and Hades, but watching her fight the sorrow was too much to bear. Aphrodite was the first to shed a tear, and before long, others joined the raven-haired beauty's despair.

"I brought this evil into this world," Hades continued, wiping tears from her eyes only for new ones to replace them. "If this is to be my fate, I accept it. I will not let the world burn for my failure, but allow my husband to hope. Let him try to save me… to save us." Hades stood stiffly and made her way to the middle of the room and took Alkaios' hand. "Let him try," she cried, studying the face she loved dearly.

"I will find a way," Alkaios whispered, tears brimming in his eyes as he brushed hers from her lips.

"But I understand there might not be another path." Hades

looked to Medusa. "I am aware we do not have time to waste on my salvation." She turned around to Zeus whose face was etched with a strange combination of horror and sorrow.

"So, Zeus," Hades sobbed, "Alkaios will never stop trying to save me, but at some point, it might be too late. He will not admit it, but it will be. I need you, king of the gods, to recognize when time has run out. I need you to make that hard choice because it will kill my husband to do so. Please do this for me. When all is lost, I want you to lock me behind that door with them."

"I will," Zeus promised solemnly as a single tear trailed down his perfect cheek.

"No!" Alkaios blurted through his tears. "Do not trust him with this. He wished you dead before. Who is to say he will not lock you in there unnecessarily?"

"Have some faith in me, god of death," Zeus shot back. "I may have wanted her dead, but do you think so little of me to believe I want this? How could you think I would revel in condemning her and her unborn son to an eternity of torture? I do not want this any more than you." Another tear wandered down his cheek as he turned to Hades. "I swear by my throne. I hope your husband finds a way, but if he cannot, I vow I will not make him do it."

"Thank you," Hades mouthed and wiped her eyes. "It is decided." She stepped closer to Alkaios and grasped his arm, clinging to him as if he was the only thing keeping her standing. "We will search the earth for them, and when we find them, we will send them back to where they came from. And if it is my fate, I will join them… now please excuse me, I would like to go home while I still have a home to go to."

At her words, fresh tears burst from her eyes, and Alkaios enveloped her in his strong arms before they vanished in tentacles of black smoke. Medusa, nodding to both Zeus and Poseidon, withdrew her presence, and after a long and heavy silence, the god trickled out of the room.

"How could this all be true?" Poseidon asked, heaviness coloring his voice.

"I do not know." Zeus placed his hand on his brother's shoulder. "But I think we must believe it. If we do not, and the monster is right, it will be too late."

"I understand. I just hope they are wrong, and not so much for our sake, but for Hades'. I do not care what has happened between us, I do not want that to happen to a new mother."

All Zeus could do in response was shake his head as another tear threatened to shed from his eyes. He turned away from his brother and saw a heartbroken Artemis still collapsed on her throne. She and Hades had been friends decades ago when Hades won his immortality. Hades, a mere human, had helped bring down the Titan demi-god rebellion along with a mortal that Artemis loved, but in the end, Hades was brought to Olympus a hero, and Orion's lifeless body was added to the stars. Zeus remembered those beginning days when the grief of the two women who loved Orion the most bonded their hearts.

"Artemis," Zeus said. At his words, the goddess of the hunt jerked to swipe her streaked face. Zeus looked sympathetically at her and then opened his palm. One of her arrows, simple wood inlaid with vines of gold, appeared in his hand.

"If it comes to that," Zeus said, handing her the arrow, "I want you to be ready. I may have to lock her behind that door, but by the gods, may I be struck dead if I let her suffer for eternity with them. If I cage her, I need your aim to be true. As that gate shuts, do not miss. I would rather Hades die than be ripped to shreds."

"My aim is always true," Artemis sobbed as she took the arrow from Zeus. "I will strike her in the heart. Her end will be swift. I will not miss."

XIII

The soft footsteps at the door woke Alkaios from his thoughts, and he shifted his eyes in the darkened room to see whom they heralded.

"Hello," Keres whispered, leaning against the doorframe, and Alkaios stood from his chair to join her in the doorway. "How is she?" Keres nodded toward Hades who slept curled against Kerberos' protective belly. Alkaios shook his head softly in the pale light of the hallway's torches. He looked distraught and haggard, and Keres forced her eyes from him, unable to watch as he ran a hand over his hair in a defeated motion.

"Hephaestus is here." Keres shifted her weight to peer at Hades. "It is possible he can help."

"You built her a cage?" Alkaios asked after Hephaestus explained the prison Keres had begged him to build.

"I started to, but I never would have deployed it without your approval."

"Would it have worked?" Hades interrupted. She sat

slouched on the old throne, feet propped up on the warm hide of Kerberos' back.

"I am not sure," the smith answered, "but I am inclined to say no. I built this cage for you, Hades, as Persephone the Queen of the Underworld. No prison created for her would ever hold you, Hades, who perhaps is the true god of death despite the power you gave your husband."

"Why bring this to us now?" Hades asked, fatigue lacing her voice. "It is too late."

"Because I could not stop you from breaking that seal, but perhaps I can keep you from being locked behind that door."

"You can do that?" Alkaios leaned forward as if he was trying to catch the hope carried on the smith's words.

"Perhaps," Hephaestus repeated lifting his soot-stained hand in a calming gesture. "Before, this would not have held Hades. I did not know who she truly was, but now that I know her truth, maybe I can tailor this prison for her and her unborn child. I will attempt to create a maze in the Underworld that will keep her and her son lost here for eternity while granting all others the freedom to leave. If we manage to imprison the Old Ones back from whence they came, perhaps Hades can be imprisoned here instead."

"Do it." Alkaios bolted to his feet. "Whatever you need, I grant you freedom over this realm to construct it, but by the gods, hurry."

"I do not know if I can finish it in time…" Hephaestus started.

"Try," Alkaios interrupted.

"Or if it is even possible," finished Hephaestus with a pointed look at the king of the Underworld. "I am attempting to restrain a god, the likes we have never seen before."

"My father's blood sealed that door for lifetimes," Hades said, standing from the throne. She lifted a palm and slid it over the tip of the pitchfork's broken prong. The metal sliced her soft flesh, and red bloomed across her skin. Cupping the pooling crimson, she moved to Hephaestus and smeared it on the hammer hanging at his waist. "May my blood strengthen whatever you forge."

"Thank you," Hephaestus nodded, "I will do my best to help you, but if I build my maze, there is another thing to consider. The reason Medusa believes Hades needs to be locked with the Old Ones is that as her sanity deteriorates, her freedom will wreak havoc on earth. A creature of absolute power with a driving bloodlust, she could blot out the sun with the smoke of her carnage. My prison will cage all of that power and destruction here with you."

"I do not care," Alkaios said with resolve. "If it saves her from their fate, then I do not care."

"You say that now," Hephaestus said, "but have you considered what that would mean? I do not wish to be insensitive, but you could be locked here with a monster, one who is far more dangerous than that hellhound. She could turn the Underworld into a desolate realm in a matter of days if she follows in her ancestors' footsteps. This maze might be a death sentence for all who abide here."

"But we must try. I cannot bear a life apart from her… a life where I never meet my son…" at that, Alkaios' words broke off, and his voice fumbled. He turned and finding Hades, reached out a broad hand and enveloped hers in his.

"Then I will try," Hephaestus said somberly. "I only wanted you to be aware that I make no promises. I may fail, and it will cost you, or I may succeed, and you might still pay the price."

"Nevertheless, thank you," Hades nodded as she clung to her husband, and the smith dipped his chin in response as he turned to leave.

"Hephaestus?" Hades called out before he faded from the Underworld. He twisted his head back and caught the dark blue eyes of the raven-haired beauty. "Do not tell Zeus about your maze of a prison," she said, and when he raised his eyebrows, continued, "I asked him to imprison me behind that seal if it must be done. Unless we have proof this will work, I do not want to give him a reason to hesitate on his promise. Unless there is truly a way to save me, I need him to believe there is no hope; that he must trap me in their realm. If Zeus knows there is a possible salvation, however futile, he may pause. With gods this powerful, all it takes is a single moment, and we will be destroyed. He cannot hesitate."

"Zeus will know nothing," Hephaestus promised, and with that, he vanished back to his forge.

"Hades?" Alkaios called as he pushed through the field of his mortal farm on earth.

"The sky grows steadily darker," drifted her voice through the wheat stalks. Alkaios moved toward the sound to find her motionless amidst the grain, eyes cast heavenward.

"You should be resting," Alkaios said as he settled in behind her. She was right. The darkness was spreading like a cancer. Its origin point hovered over Medusa's mountain, a savage stain on the graying clouds.

"A storm is coming," Hades answered not bothering to look at her husband. "The heavens turn to ash, and the whole of the earth will die. I do not have time to rest. It has already begun." Her eyes narrowed on a grain stalk next to her. Alkaios watched as she raised a hand and grasped the wheat. It crumbled between her fingers, black and rotten.

"How is this possible?" Alkaios asked in shock as he reached out to take hold of the wheat beside him, but it too was diseased with death. "We blessed this grain to grow eternal, to give hope to those who need its blessing. The grass and trees are green." His furrowed brow surveyed the land to assure himself that he was right, that color still sprung from the earth.

"It is because of me," Hades said with sorrow in her tone as she finally turned to face Alkaios. "I am tainted. This land was blessed in part by me, and therefore, it is the first to turn. I am the weed that chokes out the garden, but the rest of the land will eventually follow. Here is only the beginning."

"Hades," Alkaios said, voice soft yet firm as he reached out and grasped her hand. The warmth of his fingers spread over her skin. "We will stop this," he continued with a certainty he did not feel as he drew her to his heart, enveloping her with his strength.

"I cannot find them," Hades said, voice broken and muffled by Alkaios' massive chest. She took a shaky breath to steady herself and pulled back to look her husband in his beautiful mud-blue eyes. "I cannot find them." She sounded unsure of herself. "I should... I should be able to feel them, to know where they are, but I cannot. It is as if they are shielding themselves from me, as if they know I cannot be trusted, that I am still too much yours."

"Hades," Alkaios breathed, taking her face in his hands and looking deep into her eyes. "You will always be mine." He leaned down, and his lips crashed against hers, melding her into his body. He clung to Hades, deepening the kiss until he could not breathe, his lungs thrashing for air, and then he held on longer. When Alkaios finally pulled away, breath surged to fill his chest, and he watched his wife desperately swallow air. Her beautiful face was flushed as she clutched him, unwilling to be parted.

"Always mine," Alkaios repeated, brushing Hades' hair behind her ears before claiming her mouth again in a kiss that made her believe him.

ZEUS STOOD ON THE SAND, watching the waves violently pound the beach. The water was a grey that matched the sky, the beautiful blue faded as if the sea itself was dying. The white bubbling of the tide slammed against the dismal sand as if trying to climb onto the soil and spread its poison. Zeus regarded the swells in their agitated state, and after what seemed like endless moments of waiting, a head broke through the waves. A pair of piercing eyes crested the surface, and Poseidon strode from the ocean toward his brother. Water dripped down his perfect skin, making him appear more handsome than he ever did on land. The sea was his realm, the water his home. Any mortal observing Poseidon stride from the surf would have been overwhelmed by the beauty of the god, but the only soul lingering on the shore was Zeus, and his face wore a mask of anxious concern.

"No sign of them," Poseidon said, shaking his head. He speared the base of his rusting trident into the sand and reached his hands up to brush the wet locks of hair from his eyes. Zeus watched with dismay and sighed heavily, the weight of the world crushing the air out of his lungs.

"There is no sign of them on earth." Zeus ran a broad hand over his mouth. "And now you find no trace of them in the sea."

"Hades?" Poseidon asked, hoisting his trident back from the sand.

"She cannot locate them either."

"But she is one of them?" Poseidon raised a perfectly sculpted eyebrow.

"Her soul remains tethered to that husband of hers," Zeus said with a hint of bitterness at the reference to Alkaios. "She may yet remain too much one of us for them to reveal themselves to her."

"The earth is fading… so are the depths," Poseidon said, surveying the beach. "Something is here, and its reach is wide. I admit I was doubtful, but Medusa was right. Someone is coming, but where are they?"

Zeus opened his mouth to answer his brother, but no words came, rendering him a gaping, dying fish out of water. He had no answers. He was the king of them all, the god of gods, the almighty on high, and yet he did not know… and it terrified him.

Hades appeared in black smoke on Medusa's mountain. She knew the Gorgon would sense the shift in power, so she settled on a slab of debris at the temple's entrance to wait. In a matter of moments, Medusa emerged in human form, the snakes at her crown braided loosely down her back.

"We cannot find them," Hades admitted, turning her head in greeting. "I cannot find them." Medusa nodded and sat next to the dark god. Both women bore the faded bruises of their fight, but they looked significantly less horrifying.

"So, let us see if they will find me," Hades said and with that stood up. She lifted the pitchfork slightly off the ground and with a deafening crack, slammed it deep into the dirt. Black smoke shot from its uneven prongs and rocketed with lightning speed into the ashen stain that burned through the sky above. Hades' fist released the weapon; its embedded base holding it erect as her fingers relinquished their hold. She turned her eyes heavenward and watched the unending onyx stream spew from the bident into the raging storm.

"And if they come?" Medusa asked.

"Alkaios, Zeus, and Poseidon are lying in wait. If they come, we will open a portal to the door. I am the entrance of that portal." Hades reached out and touched Medusa's chest. An electric jolt shot from her fingers through Medusa's breast so suddenly, the Gorgon stumbled backward, feet clambering for a hold.

"And now you are the exit," Hades said. "Go guard the door. If they come, hopefully, we can trap them."

"And you?" Medusa asked with meaning.

"And me," Hades' answered with both strength and sorrow in her voice. The dark god held the Gorgon's gaze for a long moment before Medusa nodded her head solemnly.

Hades let out a trembling breath and faced the emptiness of the mountain as the darkness of the temple swallowed the Gorgon. Hades' hand slipped up and deftly swiped at the solitary tear that snuck from her eye. She knew Alkaios could not see her face from where he hid, but she felt him all the same. He would know what her finger wiped away even if he could not see it, so Hades turned her back to him. She refused to allow that errant tear to be the last of her Alkaios remembered.

And there she stood, under the watchful yet hidden eyes of the three greats, and waited. Nothing happened as the sun passed overhead, the subtly shifting shadows the only hint it still existed behind the blackening sky. The pitchfork poured a steady stream of darkness into the heavens, a deadly beacon calling out, yet the only gods drawing breath on this mountain were the three she arrived with. Hades sighed and leaned back against the debris. They must know it was a trap; they could probably smell the weaker gods laying in wait.

When most of the day had passed uneventfully, Hades pulled herself from her perch and accepted defeat. A movement teased the corner of her eye, and she whipped her head just in time to see what appeared to be a strand of dark hair flutter behind the far side of the temple. With unearthly speed, Hades had the pitchfork in hand and bolted after the teasing sight. She rounded the temple corner and skidded to a halt. Her eyes darted back and forth, seeing nothing but crumbling walls and wind lashed dirt. Nothing moved among the debris, and Hades swallowed a shaky breath. Had she imagined the movement, or were the shadows playing tricks on her eyes? She should return to Alkaios before madness took over her senses.

And there it flashed again, a blurred shape darting through

the rubble. The fluttering of dark hair bolted from behind a collapsed wall before disappearing behind the temple. Wasting no time, Hades disappeared in tentacles of black smoke only to appear a fraction of a second later in the dirt to bar the fleeing shadow's escape. She dug in her heels, bracing for impact, yet none came. The crumbling space was empty save for centuries of decay and an impenetrable pass that ascended the final peak of the mountain at the rear the sanctuary. Hades had wondered why the witches only guarded the maze at the front of Medusa's hidden lair, but seeing the deadly peak that surged into the storm, she realized that no one on foot would have ever survived the climb up the sheerness at the rear of the temple.

A nagging bloomed in the back of her mind at the sight of the impenetrable pass. Whoever the figure was had climbed that treachery. Hades could feel it. Taking a fortifying breath, she drew her dress above her knees and knotted the fabric. Her bared legs strode unencumbered toward the pass, and with the pitchfork firmly in hand, Hades plunged against the jagged cliff side and began the climb. Within seconds, she realized the climb was even more impossible than it appeared, and with shins and knees grating over serrated protrusions, she hauled herself upward one painful fingertip hold after another.

Before long the pallid clouds obscured her vision, rendering even her divine eyesight useless. The razor mountainside abraded her palms as Hades fumbled heavenward on touch alone. Her fingers gouged into the stone, making crevices when her grip failed to find a hold in her blindness. Grit and pebbles fell from where her hands and feet dug in, and the shifting soot threatened to give way and send her body to a shattering death.

Crack! The splitting of stone echoed above her, and with barely enough time to register what she was doing, Hades flung herself sideways. Aching fingers dug desperately into the cliff to save her from careening to the jagged earth below just as a massive boulder plummeted down the ledge. Its lurching mass barely missed Hades' skull, an impact that would have painted the rock with her cranial fluid, and she sucked in a breath trying to steady her erratically thundering heart. Hades felt it. She was gaining on them, and with a surge of power, she shoved herself up. The force of the movement caused the stone to crack where she landed.

Her body scaled the rock with unnatural speed, and Hades felt the top rather than saw it in a matter of moments. Hauling her body over the edge, she stood on the peak of this mountain. The mountain that held the entrance to her kind's realm, and in that moment, she knew she stood higher than Olympus ever would.

Hades squinted in the impenetrable clouds, and her eyes caught on a shadow ahead. Gripping the pitchfork, the queen moved through the blackness toward the figure, the thrashing of the dark hair the only detail she could make out. Gaining on the motionless image, Hades sped up and burst through the fog, but she stopped short as her body obliterated what was merely a shadow. Her toes slid off the edge of the peak, and not a soul accompanied her atop the height. Hades looked down and saw the plummet was a straight drop to earth, not a single ledge or crevice jutted out to break the sheerness. A fall from here would end devastatingly on the ground far below. There was no way the figure had jumped off this peak.

A crunch of stone came behind her, and Hades whirled around. *Whack*! Something slammed into her, and the dark queen stumbled to catch her footing, but there was no hold for her feet to find purchase on. Her balance teetered before Hades crashed backward. Her hair flailed around her eyes as she plunged, and so she could not be certain, but the glimpses of the figure that had pushed her unnerved Hades. She could have sworn it was herself... or at least someone who looked like her.

Accelerating through the whistling wind, Hades twisted to see the ground approaching fast. It beckoned for her flesh to break against it, but the black smoke vaulted from her body before hungry earth drew her closer to death. The tentacles ebbed and weaved, and she vanished only to crash down on the stone at the temple's entrance. She groaned as her back impacted, and Hades lay there heaving, sucking in all the air she could get as her spine exploded like sparks of searing embers.

"Hades!" Alkaios' voice boomed, followed by the sound of three sets of running footsteps. Hades forced her spasming back into a sitting position to see Alkaios, Zeus, and Poseidon barreling down upon her.

"Hades?" Alkaios plunged to his knees, uncaring that they skidded against the dirt like sandpaper. "What happened?"

"There was someone here," Hades answered, looking from her husband to Zeus and Poseidon and back. "Someone was here. It had to be one of them..." but her words died on her lips when she saw Alkaios' face. "What?"

"There was no one here," Alkaios said softly.

"Yes, there was," Hades demanded. "She was shrouded in mist, but she was here. She tried to kill me."

"Hades," Zeus interrupted. "We were watching you. We could see the whole mountain."

"I was covering the back of the temple when I saw you disappear into the clouds on that cliff side," Poseidon said, concern etched in his voice. "Hades, there was no one here... only you."

"THERE WAS someone up there with me," Hades repeated, turning to Alkaios who sat on the rubble next to her. Night was falling, but under the blackness of the sky, the setting sun was barely noticeable. Zeus and Poseidon had returned to Mount Olympus, but Hades remained at the temple, Alkaios faithfully beside her.

"You think I am crazy; that I am seeing things," Hades insisted, "but I was not alone up there."

"I want to believe you," Alkaios said sympathetically, wrapping an arm around her shoulders and pulling her into his side.

"But none of you saw anyone," Hades finished for him, exasperation in her voice.

"We were watching you," he said into her hair as he pressed his lips to her head. "No one moved on this mountain, save you."

"They have managed to hide from us these past days." Hades' tone rang bitter. "What is to say they cannot pass you unnoticed?"

Alkaios opened his mouth to answer but then snapped it shut. What could he say? She was right, and he was exhausted. He did not want to consider her words; that they possessed the ability to slip unseen before their eyes. So instead he stared off into space, clinging to his wife.

"I should get you home," Alkaios said after a long silence, turning his gaze to her still flat stomach. "You need rest."

"What does that matter?" Hades spat. She bolted to her feet, forcing his arm to fall from her shoulders. "I will be locked behind that door with them. What does it matter if I rest? This child will never see the light of the sun."

"Hades!" Alkaios jumped up in front of his wife, horror in his eyes.

"It is the truth!" Tentacles of wispy smoke seeped from Hades' skin as her anger simmered. "I do not see a way to save myself. The Old Ones may accept me as their own, but, Alkaios, what do you think they will do when they discover I carry a half-breed? They committed genocide. Slaughtered their families. They will rip our son from my womb, and what is worse, by that time I might not even care. Stop treating me as if I will survive this." Hades' voice caught in an anguished choke, and her lips fumbled as her speech faltered.

"Hades." Alkaios lunged for her, but she jerked from his grasp.

"I will never get to be a mother," she sobbed and disappeared in darkness. Alkaios closed his fist around the dark wisps of smoke, trying to hold onto it as if it would bring his wife back, but it drifted through his fingers and dissipated into the night air. He stood motionless in the waning light for a long moment and then faster than the crack of Zeus' lightning, had a piece of debris gripped in his fist. An unnerving roar broke from his lungs as he hurled the stone at the temple, and a cloud of rubble and dirt exploded on impact.

A feminine yelp came from behind the dissipating cloud of dust, and a wide-eyed Medusa peeked out from the sanctuary, her head inches from the collision. She said nothing, just stared at Alkaios through the settling cloud. Alkaios knew he should apologize for nearly decapitating her, but he could not open his mouth. Instead, he lowered his eyes, covering them with a broad and calloused hand, and stood in the dimming light. He took a long moment to regain himself, and when he finally managed to meet her gaze, all he saw was her sympathy, which only made it worse. His heart constricted, and Alkaios grabbed his chest as if to crack open his ribs and crush the agonized organ. He could not bear to have Medusa watch him crumble, so in a veil of inky black smoke, he vanished.

Alkaios appeared in his room in the Underworld a second later, and with all of his strength drained, he collapsed to the bed. He hunched over, head in his hands, and sat there destroyed.

Soft footsteps snapped him back from the rabbit hole of despair he was falling down. Alkaios would recognize the sound of that body moving anywhere. His eyes shifted to the door and saw Hades tentatively hovering just outside.

"I am sorry," she whispered. Alkaios rose from the mattress, and that was all the invitation she needed. Hades flew across the room and was in his arms in a heartbeat. Alkaios enveloped her smaller frame and pulled her as close as was physically possible. He wanted to cover her body with his and keep her safe, hidden from all who would harm her.

"I am sorry," Hades repeated into his chest, voice wavering as she clutched him. Her fingers dug into his broad back as if she was trying to claw a hold into him, and her ribs heaved against his in a warbled rhythm. "I am terrified." Her tears spread warm over his chest. Alkaios' heart shattered like fragile glass, and he tightened his grip on his wife. He buried his nose in Hades' hair and breathed in her scent before kissing her crown. His strong hand on the base of her head held fast as if he could hold together his own heart if only he clung to her tight enough.

"I do not want to do this," Hades sobbed uncontrollably. Her body collapsed into her husband's powerful arms, the only thing keeping her upright. "I know I have to, but I am terrified."

Alkaios tilted his head and buried his face in her hair, letting the soft tresses catch the tears that desperately escaped his eyes. His chest physically hurt as he clung to his wife, the only woman he had ever loved. Alkaios knew that this would kill him, and he was at peace with that because life without Hades was not worth living. He would welcome death over a lifetime of knowing this heinous fate befell the one and only woman he would ever love.

"I would trade places with you if I could," he cried into her hair, neither of them caring he was soaking it. "I would die if it meant you went free."

"I know." His massive chest muffled her soft voice. "But you cannot." Hades pulled back and shifted her swollen eyes to meet his. "I do not want to do this."

Alkaios grabbed Hades' face and swung his gaze to the ceiling. He could not look at her. It was killing him, and the tears running down his cheeks would not stop. He felt like he was choking or dying, drowning in excruciating sorrow. His breath came heavy as Alkaios stared heavenward. Refusing to look down and observe Hades' terrified features, he stood that way for a long moment, chest heaving as he cradled her face in his palms.

"I will find a way," Alkaios said, finally looking down, and her expression almost killed him. The fear in her eyes speared his soul.

"What if you cannot?" Hades asked with trembling lips.

"Then it will kill me," he answered, backing up and drawing her toward the bed. He crumpled to the sheets and took her down with him, wrapping his body around hers. "I refuse to live without you." Alkaios cradled Hades tight to his chest. "I do not think I can."

The whole of the earth slumbered, silent in the early morning hours, yet something startled the Oracle of Delphi out of a deep sleep. Blinking in the night, she listened for the sound that woke her but heard nothing save the breeze whispering through the windows. She rolled over and swung her feet off the bed. Something had woken her; she sensed it rather than heard it, and grabbing a shawl from the back of a chair, the Oracle wrapped it around her marked skin and wandered out of her chambers. Her eyes scanned left then right, but nothing out of the ordinary presented itself. The hallway was empty.

She was padding softly over the stone floors before she realized she was even walking. Something silently called to her, pulling her forward in the darkness, and it was not long before recognition dawned. Her feet were leading her to the room where her handmaid had found her, where she had carved an ancient prophecy in the floor with her own nails and blood.

Hesitantly, the Oracle reached out and pushed the door open. It swung with a soft creak, disturbing the silence, and she stepped inside, bare feet landing just in front of the scrawled prophecy. Her eyes searched the room but saw nothing. With a sigh, the Oracle made to leave when a shadow moved. She froze stiff. Alarm pricked its deadly needles into her neck as an ominous form took shape in the room's corner, and a woman of smoke appeared from the shadows.

Hades glided forward, irises black in the night. The Oracle wanted to run, to scream fleeing from this demon, but her feet were rooted to the tiles as the dark queen drifted closer.

"I have a prophecy for you," Hades growled into the midnight air, and the Oracle shivered at her voice. It was not the voice of the beautiful woman who had stood here just weeks before. She had little time to consider this though, for Hades lunged, closing the space between them with unnaturally swift grace and seized her skull. The moment Hades' palms pressed against the Oracle's temples, a shock jolted through the mortal woman's body, and white flashed through her vision before the world went black.

XIV

Charon could not be certain through the dense fog, but he swore he saw a huddled shadow lurking on the earth's shore of the River Styx. He had come from that direction moments before, ferrying the shades of a group of hunters who had left their village never to return. Their bodies decayed on earth while their souls had wandered the riverbed for days, unable to pass without coin, but their families must have found them and given them a proper burial, for in the early hours of the morning, their coins flew through the mist to his waiting palm. Charon could finally ferry them to their justice.

The moment the dead had stepped into his boat, he recognized something was wrong. Not with the men, but with their death. He was still a god, a resurrected Titan, and he sensed the change in the air as they climbed aboard. Their deaths reeked of darkness and evil, even greater than what was ever present in the Underworld. Charon's stomach had pitched the instant he felt them. Deep down, he knew what had killed them, but he could not bring himself to say it out loud. He would have to tell Alkaios, but the terror in his gut dreaded it.

So, as he pushed the ferry through the cold water back

toward earth's shore, Charon prayed the figure was not another hunter, a straggler he had missed. He had made a point to ferry them all at the same time. The cruelty wafting off them was sickening even to him, the dark ferryman of the Underworld, but the closer the boat drew, the more of the shadow he made out. Whatever it was lay crumpled in the sand. The fog weaved thicker around the shape, and he could not tell if it was a shade or a trick of the terrain.

Charon gave his pole one last hard shove, and the ferry plunged into the sandbank. Part of his deal with Hades was that he transport the shades from the land of the living to the land of the dead. As long as he remained in his boat and on the boathouse grown from a piece of this craft, he was protected from the Olympians. The new gods would kill him just as they had the rest of his kind if they realized a Titan still drew breath. Charon never left his ferry nor his home, save the few times Hades had commanded it, yet standing here inches away from the shore, something told him to move, to leave the boat.

Charon stepped over the edge and with a deep inhale, launched himself to the beach, careful not to touch the poison water. He moved cautiously toward the shape, and after a few steps, his toes landed on something that was not sand. He glanced down, and his heart lurched when he saw the black fabric strewn across the riverbank. He recognized who this was.

"Alkaios," Charon called, his deep voice echoing over the water. In a single stride, he was at the shadow and threw himself to his knees. There Hades lay, black hair and dress splayed over the bleak sand; eyes unopened, chest barely rising.

"Hades?" He scooped her limp form into his arms. She was cold to the touch, her skin pale and colorless. The air hissed behind him, and Charon snapped his head around to see Alkaios appear in dark tentacles. The King opened his mouth in a question, but the ferryman shifted his torso, revealing Hades' nearly lifeless figure.

"Hades?" Alkaios rushed forward. Charon stood, her body light in his strong arms, and passed Hades to her husband. Her head lolled sideways onto Alkaios' chest, her arm flopping down to hang in midair.

"What happened?" Alkaios clutched Hades as close to his heart as physically possible.

"I do not know," Charon answered, reaching out and lifting Hades' limp hand to place it on her stomach. "I just found her."

Alkaios said nothing, just stared at his friend. He did not have to speak. Charon already knew what was playing out behind the god's panicked eyes. Charon was terrified for Hades as well, but he knew it was worse for Alkaios. He was not sure he could bear this if it were Ioanna in harm's way, but he cast the thought aside with violent disgust. It was horrible enough this was happening to the woman who was his savior. Charon refused to let his mind wander to how it would be if it were his wife. It would kill him, and by the look in Alkaios' eyes, it was ravaging him.

"I should warm her up," Alkaios said after a moment and vanished with Hades, leaving Charon alone in the fog.

THE SUN HERALDED MORNING, and the city stirred with new life. A group of yawning women began to gather as they left their homes to draw fresh water from the well. One woman complained that her husband had kept her up half the night with his snoring. Not to be outdone, her friend lamented how her babe cried most of the night, leaving her exhausted and therefore to be pitied the most. A young newlywed stifled a yawn as the crowd traversed the sparse streets, and when all the women looked at her with knowing smiles, she blushed like a blooming rose at her reason for lack of sleep.

And so the journey to the well continued as a woman

complained about the aches in her body, and another gushed with pride over her son's first steps. Two women exchanged tips on the best way to roast lamb, while two younger girls giggled quietly about how handsome the blacksmith's son had become. A typical dawn, a daily chance to exchange their gossip as they started their day, but as they closed in on the well and found her, that changed. This morning was not normal, and perhaps no morning would ever be again.

For there, sitting in the dirt before the well, crouched the Oracle of Delphi. Dust streaked her light hair. Her subtly opaque shift revealed the marking on her skin and hung lopsided off her shoulder in filthy folds. The crowd froze as they filtered into the square, unable to bring themselves to move toward the water. They watched in horror as the Oracle, oblivious to their presence, drew unrecognizable symbols in the dirt with her fingers. The Oracle never traveled down from the temple. She served separate from the people; her access to the gods kept pure in her seclusion. Her handmaidens ventured into the market to make purchases for their lady, but the closest these women had ever come to seeing this strange yet divine woman was when she stood on her elevated balcony. Most who sought her council went into Delphi's sanctuary, but when the Olympians spoke through their prophet for all to hear, she would stand on that balcony and proclaim the words of the gods. Never did an Oracle descend into the city, yet here she huddled, squatting on the earth like the town drunkard.

The number of women slowly expanded as they all stood suspended in confusion, watching the Oracle mumble to herself as she scratched the dirt. Before long, the men, curious why their wives and daughters were not returning with water, began to appear. The city square grew more crowded; the onlookers alarmed by the Oracle's presence. Appalled by her disheveled appearance and terrified by her actions, no one moved save the sun, which would not halt its journey across the sky behind the darkened clouds.

"Oracle!" A frightened feminine voice shattered the silence. The entire crowd gave a collective jerk and stared as the Oracle's handmaid burst into the square. The girl skidded to a stop when she saw her lady crouched in the dirt, still mumbling and drawing in the dust as if nothing was happening around her.

"Mistress?" the handmaid whispered, creeping forward with her arm outstretched. Whether to protect herself or touch the Oracle, no one could tell. "Oracle?" But just as her fingers were upon her, the Oracle jerked her head upright, snapping her eyes to meet the handmaid's. The girl screeched and stumbled backward, for the Oracle's irises were rolled back into her skull, the whites flooding her sockets. Her unseeing eyes bore into her handmaid, and then slowly, they surveyed the crowd, noticing for the first time she was not alone.

"Olympus will burn in fire and agony," the Oracle said, sending a wave of cold through the throng, "and you will all kneel as you should have from the beginning before you die."

XV

Zeus was the only god absent their bed when the first shudder shook the mountain. Zeus had been unable to sleep. Uneasiness clutched his chest, so he had crawled out of bed not caring to be quiet as to not wake Hera. He had wandered out to the dark mountain and climbed down to the ledge that was solely his now that Hades was gone. Zeus had once loved that she had shared the solitude here, but in her absence, a cold woman he did not love warmed his bed. Zeus found himself here more often, in a space that was supposed to give him peace, but mostly it made him angry.

Yet here he sat, unmoving and uneasy when the mountain lurched. Zeus was on his feet faster than was possible for a man his size, and a moment later, he stood on the grass at the cliff's edge above his secret ledge. He froze, waiting and listening. Only once before had this mountain shook so. It was when Hades broke the seal to the Underworld, and Zeus' chest filled with dread at what the reason could be now.

With a whisper of wind, his thunderbolt flew into his hand, and Zeus gripped it tight. The sunrise that struggled to break through the thick clouds just moments before was strangled. Darkness was coming.

Without warning, Poseidon appeared next to his brother, trident grasped in his fist. He was not alone, for only seconds, later Athena, Ares, and Artemis emerged from nowhere brandishing their weapons fiercely. Artemis reached up to her quiver and removed one of the gold inlaid arrows and notched it. She turned to meet Zeus' eyes in the fading light. The clouds never blotted out the sun on this mountain unless Zeus pulled forth a storm. This darkness, this was not him. This was an ancient evil. The first had come.

"Olympians!" Zeus bellowed as the ridge shuddered again, and the gods answered the battle cry. Apollo materialized next to Artemis, notching his golden bow, ready to strike when she did. The mountain heaved, and the clouds thickened, blocking out all light. The Olympians stood frozen in the blackness, gripping their weapons in fear.

Cruelty and evil wafted on the breeze, and in this darkness, Zeus knew they were easy targets. He had to bring light to the peak, and so with a powerful thrust, he hoisted the thunderbolt into the air. An immense spark of lightning shot from the ancient, worn metal and pierced the clouds, lighting the field in an eerie white glow.

The sight that met him froze his heart. Inhuman creatures were crawling over the mountain's edge at an abnormally fast speed, even for a god. Zeus heard Hera gasp as she appeared beside him, but the sound barely registered; the sight was too appalling. Men with the heads of beasts, monsters so deformed they hardly resemble mankind poured onto the ledge. They charged toward the Olympians, their demonic black eyes hungry for blood. The Old Ones had finally shown themselves, and seeing them, Zeus knew this was the end. They could not win this.

Artemis and Apollo were first to move. In tandem, they

raised their bows and with expert aim, loosed them. Their aim true, the arrows shot with deadly purpose toward the onslaught of monsters. The Old Ones' speed did not slow as the arrows hurtled toward them, but as the tips prepared to shatter the hearts of the crazed gods, those in the way merely pitched sideways, causing the projectiles to hurtle by target-less. Artemis watched in horror as her arrow careened through the herd, striking not a single inch of flesh. Just as it arrived at the edge of the mountain where it would plummet through the sky toward earth, a monstrosity of a god with jet black scaled skin and rows upon rows of sharpened fangs housed in an imposing mouth leapt up from the rim of the cliff. His hulking body hovered in the air, jaw gaping wide, and with a powerful snap, his teeth crushed the arrow. The wood shattered into jagged splinters as the Old One landed heavily on the grass. He locked eyes with Artemis and struck his fist to the side, catching Apollo's arrow. He snapped it in half as if it were straw and dropped it, all the while staring down the goddess of the hunt. His immense clawed feet dug backward through the grass, tearing deep, gouging wounds in the dirt. Artemis swallowed and lifted her fingers, grasping another arrow from her never empty quiver, and slowly brought it to her bow. The moment it touched the string, the fanged god barreled onward. He was faster than the rest, and as the Old Ones vaulted across the open fields of Olympus, this hideousness aimed for her.

    A roar ripped through the huntress' lungs as she let another arrow fly. It flew true, but the fanged god surged head on to meet the projectile and at the last moment, hurtled to the left to miss it. His jaw whipped sideways and plucked it from the air with a sickening crack of wood.

    Poseidon unleashed a roar, and a cacophony of violence broke loose. The ruler of the seas charged, lifting his trident as he ran. All the mountain's water snaked its way over the grass, first in trickles then in small rivulets. Streams grew as they joined and built in speed and size until a wave as tall as a giant hurdled along the field behind him. Zeus shoved his thunderbolt heavenward, and a bolt of lightning shot into the clouds, setting off a chain reaction of electricity in the ash, the only light in the otherwise black sky. Jerking the bolt down, Zeus sent lightning hurtling at his brother's wave. The water crackled electric, sizzling dangerously. It hit the onslaught of Old Ones with such force, the gods on the front lines hurtled backward, their bodies electrocuted with a burning stench.

Seizing the opportunity, Athena chased the wave, unseen behind the wall of water. As the surge crashed, she dug her spear into the mud and vaulted herself over the foaming crest. She landed gracefully among the stumbling, wet gods and lashed out. The spear stuck a one-eyed beast square in the chest, and he grunted loudly as he stumbled in surprise. Poseidon barreled behind Athena just as the monster caught his footing and shoved the trident into the beast's breast. The god was not caught off guard this time and snatched the prongs in his meaty fists, halting the divine metal from piercing his flesh. Athena raised the spear high to strike when a violent blow to the base of her scalp sent her sprawling to the ground. Her vision blurred, and she heaved painfully, desperate to suck air into her lungs, but her chest refused to obey her will. Athena lay sprawled in the dirt, fingers searching for her weapon. Through clouded eyes, she found it and rolled on her back to see giant hooves poised above her head. Athena's lips parted in an attempted cry, but the pain in her ribs was too great, and the breath only wheezed out of her lungs. This was the end. She could never move in time, but just as the hooves were about to cave in her skull, Ares appeared out of nowhere, running full speed.

Ares collided with the beast with a sickening thud, and both of them hurtled through the air, plummeting to the ground hard as they rolled to a stop. Ares was back on his feet and at Athena's side in a heartbeat. He wrapped his mud-streaked arms around her waist and hauled her up with a powerful tug, and Athena saw for the first time who those massive hooves belonged to as the Old One raised himself from the gouged dirt. Taller than either of them, the creature was man only until his hips, his torso giving way to a dark brown horse.

Ares drew his sword and shoved Athena behind him as the half-breed monster pawed at the ground. Athena scanned the field frantically and saw Poseidon still grappling with the one-eyed god, but that was not the sight that stopped her heart. It was the dozens of gods closing in on them. She grasped her spear and shifted until her back pressed against Ares'. The gods of war would face death together.

Poseidon's wave did little to stop the onslaught of the deformed. As soon as the water cleared, Artemis lifted her bow again and let an arrow fly at the fanged god. The moment it whistled through the air, she notched a second. It, too, had barely escaped her grasp before she had another at the ready, a steady assault. Yet the fanged god merely leaned this way and that, easily avoiding all three. In seconds he would be upon her, and Artemis knew she would not survive him. With trembling fingers, she reached up and seized three more arrows, notching them together. Taking aim, she loosed them. They shot true, and for a moment she thought she had triumphed. If he pitched either left or right, their razor tips would impale him, yet he held her stare as he barreled forward without slowing. With an almost smirk in his dark eyes, he threw himself down and rolled under their flying arch, gracefully surging to his feet unharmed as his clawed feet ripped apart the ground as he ran.

A tear streaked down Artemis' face as she reached behind her and grabbed three more. She hoped her death would be quick and released the arrows. They shot with incredible force at the fanged Old One. Still holding her gaze, he launched himself into the air with the curl of his muscled thighs and soared over them. He landed on his palms and continued racing for her on all fours like a rabid beast. Artemis broke his glare and looked heavenward. It was morning now, though one could not tell with all the black clouds and raging lightning. But she knew where in the sky to look. She had spent many nights staring at the stars, memorizing Orion's pattern. Artemis took a depth breath and shut her eyes, picturing his constellation. She would join him soon.

"Artemis!" Zeus bellowed in horror as the fanged god closed in on her peaceful form. With all the power he possessed, he launched himself over the heads of the countless monsters rushing toward him. Zeus landed with a sickening thud behind them and dropped into a roll. He came out of it right in front of Artemis, and in a single swift movement was on his knees, his back to the goddess of the hunt. Gripping the bolt, Zeus shoved one end into the ground and aimed the other into the air ahead of him. At the speed the fanged god was coming, he could never stop in time. His own size and momentum would impale him on Zeus' bolt, and Zeus dug in hard knowing the impact of this monstrous body would be bone jarring.

The expression on the Old One's face shifted. It morphed from malicious confidence to a realization that no matter how he tried, he could not stop. His intestines would spill over this god of thunder, and he knew by the lightning sparking from the weapon that this was no ordinary god. This deity would not miss his mark.

Making a split second decision, the fanged deformity pushed harder, increasing his speed as he bore down on them. His eyes took on a wicked glint as he scowled, and Zeus' stomach dropped. He was speeding up. Why was he speeding up?

"Artemis, get down!" Zeus bellowed, and a wide-eyed Artemis flung herself behind her king's massive bulk. Zeus gritted his teeth and dug in, bracing for the painful blow. The fanged god's eyes flashed sinisterly, and just as he was upon them, his arm flew out and seized the closest Old One to him.

Jerking the much smaller creature to his chest, the fanged god gouged his clawed feet into the dirt and catapulted himself into the air. The god at his breast screamed as they hurtled through the wind, and with a sickening ripping of flesh, the smaller body collided with the tip of the thunderbolt. Together, they careened over Zeus, and both Zeus and Artemis cast their eyes down as his bolt gutted the god, breastbone to abdomen. The Old One's screams transformed into bloody garbles of agony as they soared over the Olympians to crash into the soil.

Finally clear of the deadly bolt, the fanged god unceremoniously dropped the exenterated carcass and rolled to his feet. He turned to Zeus, who leapt upright, wiping blood and entrails from his face. Zeus shoved Artemis behind him and gripped his weapon, but he could not tear his eyes away from the dying Old One on the grass. Behind him, Artemis gagged at the sight of the eviscerated body heaving and sputtering as his insides leaked onto the mountain.

As if to make the point that he would win even by sacrificing his own, the fanged god walked to his bleeding kinsman, his footsteps heavy and deliberate. With a clawed foot, he stepped on the god's shoulders, gouging rivets in his flesh. The dying Old One groaned, blood spurting from stained lips, and the fanged god responded by grasping his prostrated neck with his other taloned foot and snapping it.

Artemis yelped, and Zeus felt fresh panic inject itself into his heart. The Old One smirked, opening his massive mouth, showing off his rows of sharp teeth, and then he lunged.

Poseidon grappled with the one-eyed monster, watching the monstrous gods close in around Ares, Athena and himself out of the corner of his eye. They were not faring well; they had to get out of here, or it would not be long before they were dead. He could already see the Olympians, not blessed in the art of combat, fleeing for the protection of the stone city on the mountain. It would not save them, though. They would have to run much farther than that.

A scream from Artemis' lips jerked Poseidon's attention to his brother. The hulking fanged god was stalking Zeus, and Poseidon knew despite his brother's power, that Old One would eat him alive. The beast was almost double Zeus' massive size, so with all the strength he possessed, Poseidon shoved the cyclops and raised his palms into the air. Straining as if he lifted a heavy bucket, his fingers clenched as if they gripped invisible rocks. Water snaked through the trodden grass and wound up the one-eyed god's legs. Like ivy strangling a tree, the stream circled his body and pinned his arms down until the beast was unable to move. Poseidon roared and pulled back his trident. With a vicious strike, he slammed it into the Old Ones' face, the middle prong plunging into the single protruding eye. The bulbous eyeball ruptured, and death strangled the Old One's cry as the trident pierced his brain. Poseidon wrenched the weapon free, and the one-eyed monster collapsed to the ground. Not wasting a single moment, he spun on his heels and shot his hand forward. A current of electrified water exploded out and struck the half-horse god, knocking him away from the desperately fighting Ares and Athena.

"Go!" Poseidon bellowed above the din of violence. "Fall back! Take everyone with you!" And without waiting to see if they followed his command, Poseidon bolted into a frantic run. Halfway to his brother, he bent his legs, and with a powerful leap, hurled himself into the air. He crashed down to earth just as Zeus collided with the fanged god.

"Go!" Poseidon screamed at Artemis, and she did not hesitate, taking off full speed toward the buildings. "Use our home to your advantage!" Poseidon called to those who fled and then reared on the fanged god, well aware that the entire host of deformed Old Ones was closing in around the two greats.

Zeus drove at the Old One who merely batted him aside as if

he were a fly. Zeus cleaved a gouge in the dirt as his mass slid through the ground, but as he flew backward, his eyes met Poseidon's, and he thrust the thunderbolt forward. Lightning erupted from its tip, and knowing instantly what his brother meant, Poseidon forced his trident forward. Water flowed from the prongs to slam into the electricity. Seconds later, it crashed into the Old One, his body jerking from the electrified water. The creature stumbled, and Poseidon lunged. His trident hammered its metal into the fanged mouth, which caused the monster to stumble yet again as he spit shards of teeth and blood. That was all the time Zeus needed to recover, and he was there in a heartbeat. His thunderbolt jabbed at the monster's gut, but the fanged god grabbed hold of it before it could pierce his flesh. Lighting exploded into the Old One's stomach, and his black mass doubled over, losing his grip on the thunderbolt. Zeus wrenched it free and whipped it across the monster's grotesque face. A bloody red welt burst across the god's cheek as the weapon made contact, and he screamed. The howl was so loud the mountain shook, and the brothers lurched on the heaving ground. Hearing their brethren's pain, the army of Old Ones wailed a deafening response and charged.

"We have to go." Poseidon seized his brother's arm, wild panic permeating his voice. "We cannot hold them all!"

Zeus opened his mouth to argue, but a rumble, the likes of which Olympus had never felt before, drowned his protests. A whipping wind of power and cruelty rushed over the mountain, and Old Ones and Olympians alike stumbled at its strength. All the deformed gods froze in their assault on the brothers. Their eyes reverently turned to the mountain's ledge, waiting with bated breath for who was coming. Zeus and Poseidon realized in unison, bitter bile rising from their stomachs, that this onslaught was only the beginning; that this monstrous fanged god that seemed almost impossible to kill was merely the opening, the pawn before the king. They had been so foolish to think this Old One was the leader, was the demon that would be the hardest to defeat. No, he was simply part of the scouting party. Whoever came next, he was the true horror.

"We have to go!" Poseidon screamed, grasping his brother's bicep in an iron fist. "We cannot win this."

Zeus did not argue this time, and the two greats vanished just as a colossal shadow loomed onto the field.

XVI

The Underworld lurched, heaving violently like an ill stomach. Kerberos bolted upright without warning and with a vicious snarl, whipped his tail with savage accuracy at Alkaios' head. Alkaios grunted as he threw himself off the bed just in time to avoid being decapitated by the speared tip, and in one powerfully graceful lunge, Kerberos was on the mattress, hovering above the still unconscious Hades. His muscles tensed like a compressed coil, her small frame encased in the protective barrier of his powerful legs.

With vibrating panic, Chimera leapt through the doorway; body careening with such speed, he slammed into the doorframe with a harsh impact to his ribcage. His feline lungs let out a roar, but Kerberos growled a warning for the massive cat to be silent.

"It is them," panicked Keres as she and Hydra barreled into the room after the lion. Their eyes were wide, and Alkaios could hear the slamming of their hearts against their ribs.

"They are on Olympus." Alkaios' chest constricted. Deep in his soul, Alkaios felt the mountain of his people, and it screamed in pain within him.

"Stay here with her," he commanded Kerberos and Chimera, already knowing they would not leave Hades' side. He mostly voiced it just to say something, to delay the inevitability of his next words.

"I have to get to Olympus," Alkaios said, gravity in his voice. He grabbed the pitchfork and left the room, Keres and Hydra close on his heels.

"We are coming with you," Keres said.

"You will need help to save Olympus," Hydra added, determination flashing in her snake-like irises.

"No." Alkaios turned to them, eyes wide with horror. Both women opened their mouths to protest, to insist on lending their aid when he interrupted, "It is too late for that."

MOMENTS LATER, the three of them stood in Hades' old bedroom on Olympus. It was the only place on the mountain Alkaios could think of where their arrival would go unnoticed. The fields of Olympus were churning with the bodies of crazed gods, and the throne room and council chamber would be among the first they dominated. Alkaios figured it would be some time before the brutality ventured into the outer rings of the city, and he was right. The only sign of disturbance in her room was their own footprints in the thick film of dust. Alkaios tried to avoid observing the space beyond what was necessary. He did not care to see the place where his wife loved another man, the wife he was on the brink of losing, and so Alkaios hastened to the door and cracked it open to peer outside.

The acrid smell of smoke and death assaulted his nostrils, and Hydra coughed and gagged behind him. Fine ash drifted through the air to settle on the stone doorstep. The whole of the mountain burned, charred stains blackening the stone from where Zeus' lighting collided with the mountain. The scars birthed ravenous flames, which devoured the ransacked streets. Some of the homes were crumbling as if the fight had passed through their walls and left only dust and rubble in their wake. Alkaios looked up, watching the soot fall like a dark snow; the sky punctuated by Zeus' cloud-to-cloud lighting.

"Are they still alive?" Hydra asked, coming up and pushing the door out further so she, too, could see.

"Yes," Alkaios answered. He still felt their Olympian power running through him. "But who knows for how much longer? We have to get them out of here."

"Where are they?" Keres asked, scrunching her nose at the smell.

"Council chamber." Alkaios nodded his head toward the center of the mountain. In the beginning, when Zeus and Poseidon had first set foot on Olympus after the war that destroyed the Titans, it had shifted. Once only rolling grass and rocks under a perfect sky became a home for the gods. The peak had changed, growing beneath their feet until the city that stood today was complete. Not a single hammer or nail had created the residence of the gods. It had risen from the rock itself, offering its new masters perfection to solidify their reign with the council and the throne room at the center most point. The gods' dwellings surrounded them and circling out further, were the homes of the immortals all connected by beautiful pale grey stone hallways, their ceilings absent to reveal the crystal blue skies. On a typical day on Olympus, stepping out into the warm sun sparkling off of the stone must have been what Elysium was like, but as Alkaios stepped from the chamber that had housed Hades for decades, it was worse than hell. The ash fell and tangled with his hair, smearing on his bare shoulders. The red light from the burning mountain resembled the depths of the Underworld, a place he never set foot.

"The whole mountain will converge on that point," Keres said, doubt marring her features. "They laid waste here so quickly as if they were determined not to leave any of Olympus unscathed. I do not think we can make it there before they do."

"You do not have to come with me." Alkaios turned to the women, his wife's most trusted friends.

"Like hell we won't," Hydra said, the determination in her voice not quite reaching her eyes. She seized the door and pulled it wide. The ash melted against her limb, and a rippling chain reaction bubbled beneath her flesh. Within seconds, a vein on her back roiled violently, and the flesh tore open as the head of a small, midnight black snake burst forth in blood and skin. Leaving a bloody trail in its wake, it slithered over Hydra's shoulder and rounded her neck, increasing in size as it broke its tail free from his mother with a wet pop. Its head reared as its body thickened about her throat like a nightmarish necklace, and it licked the air with a forked tongue, tasting the scent of his prey. With eerie coal eyes, the snake twisted to meet Alkaios' gaze and held his king's stare for a moment. Then with a hissing scream, its ever-growing girth wrapped around Hydra's waist and down one leg, forming a massive moving barrier around her neck and torso. Cut the head off one and two more appear. The only way to kill Hydra was to take off the mother's head, and no blade would pierce her flesh.

Hydra roared an unearthly feminine howl and took off running as two more snakes ripped from her arms and fell to the ground. Alkaios and Keres bolted after her, passing her serpent-clad body, and into the fray, they plunged.

STREET BY STREET, they pushed onward, finding the stone of the mountain empty. The thickening smoke forced their pace to a crawl as they closed in on the ever-increasing clash of violence. It was not long before their eyes stung blindly from soot; their hands invisible even when held mere inches from their faces.

Alkaios froze, alarm tickling the back of his neck. The sneaking suspicion they were walking in circles nagged at his senses. He had never ventured out into the outer rings of Olympus, but the twists and turns he led Hydra and Keres around were beginning to look familiar. Alkaios paused for a moment to catch his bearings when the hair on his skin rose in gooseflesh. The air behind him, where Hydra and Keres were following, felt empty.

"By the gods," Alkaios cursed under his breath and whirled on his heels, coughing on bitter ash. The smoke was impenetrably black, blocking all but the shadows from sight, but he sensed it. They were gone, lost in the hellish labyrinth. He could not leave them to fend for themselves, not on this mountain. Not today.

Alkaios retraced his steps, but nothing looked familiar. The hallways all seemed rounded in the wrong directions, and after a few anxious minutes, he knew he would not find them by hunting blindly. Tentacles of power wove around his torso as his mind searched for the women. When Alkaios found them, he would drag them back to Hell where they belonged, where they would be safe, and then he...

Alkaios' brain did not finish that thought. His entire body froze, fear devouring his spine. The corridor before him suddenly cleared. The thick, acrid smoke hovered behind him as if it was terrified to venture further down the burning hall. Alkaios saw the monster only a fraction of a second before it sensed him, and Alkaios knew he should run, should use this miniscule head start to his advantage, but he could not move. He just stood there, feet rooted to the earth in nauseating terror.

There, hunched before him, was an Old One, his wife's people. Alkaios felt the overwhelming urge to vomit that this might be her fate. The grotesque god crouched on the ground, hovering over what must have once been the body of an immortal but now resembled a lump of bloody flesh. Unrecognizable as a human form, the heaped mass lay cradled in the monster's arms. Alkaios could not make out what it was doing to the corpse, but he did not care to find out. He should leave, run as far from this mutilation as possible, but the thought that this was the monster residing within his wife kept Alkaios frozen with nausea.

The creature stirred, realizing its feeding had a witness, and began to rise. Its head remained bent over the lump of broken and battered flesh. Its body caught the light of the fire, and Alkaios finally saw its actions clearly. He wished he had not. The Old One was long and lean, skin made up entirely of dark, greenish scales that ominously reflected the firelight. Alkaios gagged and stumbled backward at the realization that it was consuming the remains, sucking it down. Its entire face neither chewed, nor bit, but latched onto what little existed of the meat, absorbing it in suctioning inhales. How long had it consumed this poor immortal if this oozing mess was all that survived of what was once living?

Once it reached his full height, the Old One lowered his hands and released the globs of flesh, dropping them on the stone floor with wet smacks. Crimson dripped from his skin. Sharpened claws curled where fingers should have been, long enough to run a man through. They pulsed with murderous intent as the creature's head twisted to observe his new prey. The moment Alkaios saw the beast's face, he knew he had made a grave mistake. He should have fled the instant he saw this horrendous creature. The god of death was used to horrors, but nothing prepared Alkaios for this.

The scaled figure possessed no face. No eyes or nose adorned the scaly head, just a bloody slit from the top of its forehead to the base of its chin. The orifice split its head into two halves like a massive sideways mouth, the sight turning Alkaios' stomach to ash. Its mouth vibrated slightly as it faced Alkaios, anticipating the next meal his cavity would suck down. But before either one could take a single step, the Old One froze and shifted his eyeless face to Alkaios' hand, where the Olympian clutched the pitchfork.

For a pregnant moment, the monster stared unseeing at the bident, its talons clicking softly at his side. Alkaios prayed, to who he did not know, that the beast recognized his brethren's ancient weapon and would believe its welder was an ally, not a foe, but his hopes were short lived as the demon slowly turned its eyeless head back to Alkaios' face. The Old One's bloody sideways mouth quivered with a barbaric scream, and he lurched.

Snapping into action, Alkaios bolted from the fiery corridor, powerful legs propelling him down the hallway. Every fiber of his being pushed his body faster through the smog and flames. Alkaios could barely see, and the curves in the wall painfully herded him into a dead end, shoulders grazing the rough walls with punishing bruises. He was trapped by a collapsed section without a clue where he was. His heart thundered with every vibration of the Old One's heavy footfalls behind him. Alkaios' eyes stung with smoke as he spun to face his charging pursuer. The monster was almost upon him. Alkaios would have to fight, and after seeing what this ancient god did to flesh, he was terrified what losing meant.

"Get down!" screamed a feminine voice. Without thinking, Alkaios doubled over just in time to miss a wave of enormous black snakes hurtling through the air. He heard the impact as Hydra's snakes of Tartarus slammed into the Old One, their hungry mouths attempting to devour the monster's face, and Alkaios prayed out of sheer habit that these poisonous god-killers could melt the scales off this beast.

"Alkaios!" came Keres' desperate voice from above. She and Hydra stood on the roof adjacent to the collapsed wall, both beckoning wildly for him to join them. Alkaios spun on his heels and launched himself off the piled debris with a bend of his powerful legs. Keres reached down as Alkaios flew, and her iron fingers seized his forearm. The moment their limbs locked, she heaved, pulling him through the air. Alkaios' body collided with Keres as he landed, but his heels dug into the ashen roof as his biceps trapped her to his chest, halting their fall

"Are you both all right?" Alkaios set Keres firmly on her feet and gave her a once over before flicking his gaze to Hydra. They nodded, eyes wide and bloodshot, and Alkaios craned his neck over his shoulder to glimpse the Old One's struggle to free himself from the constricting snakes. "We have to keep moving," he said, urgently nudging them with insistent hands. They took off running, leaping from rooftop to rooftop above the burning and scorched ground, hoping none of the Old Ones had the same idea.

Careening over crumbling roofs and the burnt shells of what were once Olympian homes, they charged forward. Alkaios caught Hydra harshly by the arm as the charred roof beneath her feet gave way and jerked her along as the building opened wide to swallow her whole, a meal for its raging flames. He refused to slow as Hydra stumbled to regain her footing, pulling her at an unforgivable pace toward the council chambers. Its imposing size grew closer through the harsh smoke with each step they forced from their legs. They just had a little further to...

"Alkaios!" Keres screamed, but her voice was lost in an explosion of crumbling buildings. Their rooftop path exploded in flames as the blackened rocks caved in. Not slowing, Alkaios shot his free hand out and grasped Keres by her bicep's soft flesh as their foothold gave way to nothingness. They plunged into the scorching blaze, but black inky smoke twisted to ensnare their bodies, snatching them away almost a moment too late.

A fraction of a second later they were inside the council chamber. Alkaios barely materialized before something too fast to be anything natural careened for his skull. Instinctually, he jerked sideways and slammed a fist into the object, forcing its trajectory from his head and lodging it into the heavy door behind him with a thud.

"It's me!" Alkaios shouted, shifting to watch as the razor tip of Zeus' thunderbolt ripped free from where it was embedded. "Zeus!" Alkaios shoved the pitchfork forward just in time to catch the thunderbolt's second assault. "It's me!" he yelled into Zeus' bewildered eyes.

For a moment Zeus stood before him, crazed and aggressive, and then suddenly as if a veil had been drawn back, the force behind the thunderbolt slackened, a look of recognition dawning in his eyes.

"What took you so long?" Zeus asked, lowering his weapon. "We needed your help to defend the mountain, but now it is too late. It is overrun."

"We have to get out of here." Alkaios choose to ignore the question. He had come as soon as he felt the attack, but even if he had arrived sooner, it would have been of little consequence. Medusa had been right; they were no match for these monsters, even in their weakened form. "We cannot stay here."

"I will not leave our mountain," Zeus insisted, the dried blood covering his muscled body enhancing the crazed look in his eyes. "We must take it back."

"We cannot hold out against them," Alkaios said, urgency in his voice, "let alone drive them back. Olympus has fallen. We have to go now."

"We cannot leave," Zeus said adamantly.

"Zeus." Poseidon stepped forward with concern marring his beauty.

"Where would we go?" Zeus demanded. "Olympus is our home, an impregnable fortress of the gods. If they have breached it, then where can we go? Nowhere is safe." He stared at Alkaios; his perfectly smooth and chiseled features suddenly looking older. Alkaios swallowed uncomfortably and looked to Keres and Hydra before twisting back to face the Olympians.

"I have somewhere, but you will not like it."

Zeus studied Alkaios inquisitively, and when it dawned on him, his eyebrows shot up, mouth drawing into a firm, harsh line.

"Absolutely not. I will not trade one brand of monsters for another."

"What choice do you have?" Alkaios asked as a massive explosion of a crumbling building ripped through the air outside. "Between the poison of the river and the god-killers, we should be safer there."

"And what is to stop your god-killers from murdering us?" Zeus asked. "If we are to be torn to shreds by the unholy, we might as well stay here."

"I will keep all harm from you," Alkaios vowed, and all in the room believed him. For the first time, the gods saw Alkaios as one of their own and not as Hades' shadow. The strength emanating from his soot-streaked body gave them hope.

"Zeus," said Poseidon, "he is right. That river kills all it touches. If there is any place on this earth where they will not find us, it is behind those waters."

Zeus turned to meet his brother's eyes, desperation clouding his beauty. For a moment, he looked as if he would argue, but eventually, he sagged in resignation.

"Very well," Zeus said, "if we have your word?" Alkaios nodded in assurance of his promise and began to turn toward the door when Zeus' heavy hand landing on his shoulder stopped him. "We have to find the others first. We were separated from the other gods and immortals." He paused as if he did not want to finish the thought before letting out a deep breath. "Hera is one of them."

Alkaios looked around, taking the chamber in for the first time, and was appalled by how few were present. His stomach dropped.

"Take them to our throne room," Alkaios said to Keres and

Hydra. "Do not let Kerberos or Chimera near them until I return." Keres bowed her head in obedience, and the tentacles of black began to ooze from Alkaios' skin. "Zeus, Poseidon, and I will find the others."

"Wait!!" interrupted Ares' voice. "I am coming with you."

"As am I," said Apollo as he sidled up next to Ares. "You might need our help."

Alkaios nodded, and with a snap of his fingers, all in the room disappeared, leaving the five gods alone.

"Where are they?" Alkaios asked as he moved toward the double doors.

"I do not know," Zeus answered, falling in step beside the king of death. "I cannot see them... I think the Old Ones' power is blocking mine."

"Well then," Alkaios said, resting a massive palm on the door, wishing terribly Hades was here. His fierce wife was better equipped for this brand of chaos, and he felt her absence more now than ever. "We start at one end of the mountain and move to the other until we find them."

Together Alkaios and Zeus heaved the doors backward, opening the council chambers to the smoke-filled streets, and there he stood. The tall-scaled body hovered in their exit, ruptured face quivering. The Old One held a shredded snake in its talons, and Alkaios was thankful Hydra was not here to see the mangled carcass.

The monster let out a reverberating scream. Its split head opened wide, flaying its eyeless face. The unearthly screech echoed off the walls alerting all on the mountain of his find. The Olympians were rats in a maze, and this scaled god would bring all the Old Ones down on their heads like starving predators to prey.

Without hesitating, Alkaios leapt forward, swinging the pitchfork. It struck the god's flayed face with deadly precision, and the monster flew backward, digging its heels into the stone to stop from careening into a wall. The moment the metal contacted with the scaled flesh, a jolt shot up Alkaios' arm. He looked to his hand, feeling the weapon pulsing. It recognized one of its own. Suddenly Alkaios' mind cleared. The strength of the Old Ones' that had been blocking his sight vanished as if the power on the mountain accepted the pitchfork, welcoming it home.

"The pitchfork!" Zeus bellowed. "They are afraid of the pitchfork!"

Alkaios looked back to the scaled god and watched him eye the weapon warily. The Old One shifted its weight carefully between its feet, weighing his options. It stared at the bident, split face quivering, and Alkaios' racing mind registered that Zeus had said they. His gaze flicked to the rooftops filled with Old Ones, each more grotesque than the last. They were surrounded.

The scaled god paced erratically before them, its featureless face never leaving the pitchfork, but when it sensed Alkaios' movement, he looked up. He feared the weapon, but as his sightless scrutiny bore down on Alkaios, it was clear he was not afraid of the Olympian wielding it.

In a split second, the Old Ones moved, closing on the Olympians, but they were a breath too late. Alkaios had reached out with his inky black smoke, and all five vanished. Alkaios was not about to let these monsters get any closer, and that moment of clarity the pitchfork provided was all he needed. Alkaios knew where they had to go.

Seconds later, they stood before the mouth of a cave on the outskirts of the city, far from the fighting. Ares stepped forward to the dark opening, eyes searching warily for danger.

Whack! Something moving faster than light shot out and smashed his nose, sending him toppling to the grass. Ares cursed angrily, and the other four drew their weapons ready to cut down whoever emerged from the cave.

"Ares?" came a panicked feminine voice, and a second later Athena burst from the darkness. She looked wild, her hair tangled and face streaked with blood and soot. "I thought you were one of them!" Athena rushed to Ares and dropped to her knees. Her arms ensnared him, and a soft sob escaped her to be stifled against his neck.

"Hera!" Zeus called, lowering the thunderbolt and moving toward the cave. Her name had barely left his lips before Hera was in his embrace, small body flinging against his solid mass. Hera sobbed as she clung to him, and Zeus pulled her as close as he could manage without crushing her. Alkaios was surprised at the intimate reunion between husband and wife. He was under the impression they hated each other, but maybe he was wrong. Or perhaps after today, all sins between them were forgiven.

Slowly the rest of the gods and immortals emerged from the cave. Aphrodite shuffled out first, her beautiful face bedraggled, her dress torn in multiple places. An immortal man followed, bleeding profusely. A jolt of concern electrocuted Alkaios at the sight of the man's dangling wrist, the limb hanging on by a few sinewy threads of muscle.

"We have to leave," Alkaios said, resting a hand on Zeus' massive shoulder. "These people need help." Zeus extracted his face from his wife's hair and looked around with a bewildered horror.

"Is this all of them?" Zeus asked, turning to Alkaios. "I am still having trouble seeing through their power."

"This is all... all that are alive."

Zeus opened his mouth to speak when the mountain pitched, heaving violently. All eyes snapped back to the burning city that was so beautiful only hours before. The smoke was impossible to see through; the fires destroyed all as they raged. Nothing could be seen through the ash, yet there was a shadow. Something emerged from the darkness. Someone had arrived, and his image loomed, his dark presence greater than even that of the destruction.

All eyes watched in horror as the shadow grew, and Alkaios knew if they waited any longer, none of them would make it off this ridge. He clutched the pitchfork tight in his hand and drew upon his power. Inky black began to twist from his limbs, snaking around all the Olympians and immortals. The tentacles ebbed and flowed, growing and ensnaring by the minute, and when the last body was encircled, Alkaios pulled them to Hell, but not before something horrifying materialized in the smoke. Not before they all witnessed the shadow of a massive horned head.

XVII

Hades was not sure if it was sheer terror that woke her or the orchestra of panicked arguing ricocheting off the walls. Her eyelids shot open, sending her bolting upright only to crumple over, eyes searing with pain. She moaned like a drunkard waking without a bottle, brain fogged. The constant voices rattled off the bones of her skull, and she sat on the edge of the bed trying to recover from the torture scorching through her when a presence shifted the air.

Hades' eyes flicked up and found Kerberos' hulking frame shifting from one massive paw to another in the doorway, his expression that of an agitated child come to tattle to his mother. Hades squinted at the dog in confusion, wondering what bothered him, when the bellows of familiar voices barreled through the corridors. Hades shot to her feet despite the fire in her skull and on teetering steps rushed from the bedroom, nearly tripping over Chimera who crouched uncomfortably by the door.

Hastening toward the throne room, beasts on her heels, the voices grew louder. They were angry, full of fear and rage, and Hades knew why. She had the moment she woke. It was her fault; she had caused their horror and pain, and now they were trapped in a place that no one had willingly stepped foot into for centuries.

"Stop!" Hades screamed, bursting into the throne room. "Stop!" Her voice was drowned by hysterical gods and immortals. Normally it commanded great power, but the anguish in her head made it difficult for her to stand upright.

Hades' mouth opened to scream again when Chimera planted his feet firmly on the stone beside his mother and roared. His bellow so impressive, it shook the Underworld, the deep tone of his voice evil and terrorizing. Bloodied and battered faces and soot-covered bodies stilled impossibly motionless. All turned toward the noise and were met with the sight of the god of the dead. Despite Alkaios' power and claim to the Olympian title of King of the Underworld, here stood true death. Though disheveled, Hades with her long raven hair and flowing black dress, flanked by her hellhound and monstrous lion, was a terrifying vision to behold. More so now than ever before.

The crowd collectively sucked in their breath and almost leaned away from Hades as if to put distance between them without actually moving. For many, this was the first time they ever witnessed Kerberos, and his three vicious heads with mouths full of sharpened fangs shifted ever so slightly to observe the throng. Out of the frozen bodies, Alkaios emerged, defying Kerberos' warning. He covered the ground between them, both relief at seeing his wife and horror at the news he bore warring in his eyes.

"Olympus has fallen," Alkaios said gravely once he stood before her, pitchfork gripped tightly in his fist.

"I know," Hades answered, lifting a hand and resting it lovingly on his ash streaked face. "I prophesied it." Her fingers dropped from his cheek and slid down until they came to rest over his heart. "I can feel them... in my head." Hades lowered her wavering voice so only Alkaios could hear. "The pain... I feel their anger ripping through me."

Heartbroken, Alkaios placed his free hand over hers and clutched it to his chest, longing for a way to lift this burden from his wife. He was thankful Hades had not been on the mountain today. He knew what awaited her when their darkness finally consumed her mind, and it was almost too much for him to bear. Alkaios could not fathom how horribly it would weigh on her. But dwelling on it would only breed consuming dread, and so he withdrew his hand from hers and wrapped it around the base of her neck. He pulled his wife's forehead in close and kissed Hades with all the love he had within him.

Hades let Alkaios' lips press warm against her skin for a moment and then drew back to cast a look over his shoulder. Keres and Hydra had removed themselves from the crowd, and catching their eyes, she gestured them closer.

"Go to Charon," Hades instructed in a low voice. "Tell him to remain hidden. I do not trust Zeus to refrain from violence if he were to discover a living Titan."

The women nodded their understanding and left the throne room without a word as Hades dropped her hand from Alkaios' chest and began to make her way to the thrones. The sea of bodies parted as she and her unearthly pets passed, giving the monstrous god-killers a wide berth.

"We all should stay here for the foreseeable future," Hades said, collapsing on her throne and adjusting her feet so Kerberos could lie protectively before her. Alkaios followed suit and sat on the throne next to his wife. Chimera settled on the cold steps in front of him, but not as close as if it were Hades. The beasts usually flocked to their mother, but in the face of these strangers, the Underworld felt Alkaios was worth guarding.

"Between the Styx and the god-killers, we should be safe for now," Hades continued, noticing how uncomfortable Zeus was with the fact it was she on the throne and not him. "At least safer than Olympus I hope."

"But are we safe from you?" Hera spat, her brown hair

tangled atop her head. "How do we know we are safe from your monsters?"

"You don't," Hades answered truthfully and reached out her fingers to stroke Kerberos' closest nose as if to emphasize her point. "But where else will you go?"

"You have our word," Alkaios said, seeing that Hera, true to form, was about to spew more foul words. "The Underworld will do you no harm. Not to say it will not strike if provoked. It would be wise to be careful."

"There is no reason to leave the fortress," Hades interjected. "The Underworld was sealed long before we were born, and I am sure you are curious to lay your eyes on the beast called Hell. For those of you who wish to witness it for yourself, you may. But after today this offer is withdrawn, and you are to stay inside unless it is absolutely necessary you venture out. Hell is dangerous, even for gods."

"We will remain within these walls," Poseidon promised.

"That is all good and well," Zeus interrupted his brother. "But they took Olympus. It fell in minutes like a house of straw. That is our home, our holy mountain. Ever since the day Poseidon and I set foot on those peaks, an Olympian has always resided there, and now we are cast out, hiding in the darkness like cowering rodents. Stripped of our mountain, we are as good as dead."

"I am still here," Hades answered, voice carrying through the chamber. "They are not at full strength yet. Perhaps we can still trap them, and this time the god-killers will be with us."

As if on cue Kerberos reared all three monstrous heads, eyes and ears alert. The entire room jerked backward in fear, their breath sucked from their lungs. Zeus and Poseidon grabbed their weapons, but before they could brandish them, Hades lifted a hand, gesturing for all to hold still.

"Someone is here," she explained. "He is merely blocking their entrance." Hades flicked her wrist, and in a swirl of black smoke, Medusa materialized before the thrones in her human form, the braid of snakes weaving down her back the only hint at her true nature.

"Hades is right," the Gorgon said by way of greeting as if she had been part of the conversation from the beginning. "She has yet to join them, which means we still have time. We yet might trap them, and this time, we will use her dark monsters to help... including me."

Zeus wandered to the ancient door and paused at the cracked seal, running his fingers over the rough edges. Not that he wanted to see the Underworld, but he felt he had to. He needed to witness with his own eyes where he banished the woman he once loved and perhaps still did. Most of the immortals had ventured further into Titan fortress to find filthy, destroyed rooms to call home, but a few of the Olympians, under the watchful gaze of that monstrous lion, found it impossible to resist the chance to behold Hell.

With a steadying breath, Zeus stepped over the threshold and onto the dirt. The dark and barren terrain stretched out in a depressing wash of bleak colors. His eyes shifted to take it all in, but every time they returned to where they once rested, the land was different. It was solid, unchanging until you blinked. It was as if the earth itself writhed and altered while one's back was turned. The only constant was the fortress to his rear, the heavy distant fog to his front, and a crimson red burning in the depths to his right. Those never changed, and the king made note of that. Without those constants, a soul would be lost in this ever-changing beast.

Other gods filtered out, only to freeze in awe and horror, and Zeus moved away from the crowd, hiding his expression. How had he allowed Hera to convince him to send Hades here? He could have saved her from this darkness, kept her from bringing destruction on his holy mountain.

A shadow crossed his vision, jerking him out of his thoughts, and Zeus looked up to find a single vivid green tree with heavy, red fruit weighing down its branches growing alongside the fortress. The beauty of its vibrant colors starkly contrasted the bleak Underworld, and he would have ventured forward to caress the smooth, inviting skin of the plump, crimson spheres if his path had not been barred. Four furies hovered, protecting its roots. They peered at him with tilted heads and empty eyes, their talon fingers clicking together, hungry for flesh to rip. Zeus had seen these treacherous women before and took a step backward, putting a greater distance between him and the monsters.

"So that no one eats the fruit," came a deep voice. Zeus turned to watch the king of death settle beside him, pitchfork clutched in his still ash streaked fingers. "Once you eat of the pomegranate tree, you are bound to the Underworld," Alkaios explained. Without acknowledging his words, the blonde god spun on his heels and began to stride back toward the door.

"Zeus," Alkaios continued, pulling alongside him with powerful steps. "I am one of the three greats, but I am not your brother. You and Poseidon share blood, but not with me. Come, swear a blood pact with me; make me your brother. We have to let our past go and work together. If ever there was a time to unite, it is now. We lost Olympus; we cannot lose the Underworld. It is our only refuge."

"You will never be my brother," Zeus spat in a low controlled voice filled with malice. Here in the Underworld, he saw the darkness he condemned Hades to, and now he was forced to accept solace from the man she had chosen over him as the evil consumed his holy mountain. Anger coursed through him, white-hot under his skin, eating at his soul.

"I will never share blood with you, human," Zeus growled, hoping his petty attempt at an insult would wound Alkaios. "I am here only because I need you. I am only here until I can lock your wife behind that seal with the monsters who birthed her."

KERBEROS STOOD with all three heads hovered over the triplet's cradle. His six eyes gaped wide and careful as he stared at Charon's daughters. His middlemost nose pressed against the soft baby flesh to inhale her new scent. Fearless, the babe reached up with uncoordinated fists and seized his leathery lip flap causing Kerberos to sneeze and jerk back. The women watching him burst into laughter, and the dog arched his spine indignantly and curled up on the floor at the base of the girls' cradles.

Ioanna hesitantly bent over, and when the three-headed god-killer made no protest, she brushed her fingers over his middle skull.

"Watch over them for me," she whispered before standing and walking out onto the dock, keeping the open door in her sights. Hades, Hydra, and Keres stood watching her and the beast with wide grins spread across their lips.

"King of the beasts," Hydra smiled, "startled by the fist of a babe."

"As nasty as that dog can be," Keres said, "he seems to have a soft spot for your girls."

"We have come a long way," Ioanna said, settling against the railing with her friends. "No one used to even look at Kerberos, and now, by the gods I do not know why I allow it, he watches over my children. He loves Hades and tolerates the rest of us, but strange enough, he is drawn to my daughters."

"The Underworld is full of death," Hades interjected. "Chained above Tartarus, its stench was all he knew, but you brought new, beautiful life here to us. He wants to protect it."

"Soon Kerberos will have another new life to protect,"

Ioanna said, flashing a glimpse at Hades' still flat stomach. At her words, Hades' eyes glazed, her heart constricting in pain.

"Hades," Ioanna said, the commanding voice of a mother spilling over her lips and snapping the queen from her emotions before Hades could spiral out of control. "He will have another life to protect. Your son and my daughters will fill his days with mischief." She stepped forward and looped an arm around Hades' waist with a conspiratorial grin. "Now, which one is Hera?"

Hades smirked and raised a hand into the thick mist, swiping her fingers. The fog dissipated into a thin veil for them to peer through, revealing the fortress and the Olympians brave enough to venture into Hell.

"Is that her?" Ioanna asked, gesturing to a sooty covered beauty. "She is exquisite." She turned her eyes to Hades before adding, "Plain compared to you but lovely in an expected way."

"You only say that because I am standing right here," Hades huffed, but Ioanna only shrugged as if to say 'but it is the truth.'

"And no, that is Aphrodite, goddess of beauty and love. That," Hades said gesturing to the woman walking purposefully toward Zeus, "is Hera."

"Her?" Ioanna asked incredulously, and Hades, Keres, and Hydra all nodded in unison. "Zeus chose her over you?"

"She is Poseidon's sister," Hades said, "and at the time she commanded greater power than I did."

"Poseidon's sister? He married his sister?"

"Not exactly," Hades explained. "Cronus wed Rhea, goddess of motherhood and fertility. As an expression of her power, Rhea split her soul in half, inhabiting two identical bodies. Both versions of herself bore Cronus a son; Zeus his first-born and Poseidon his second. The version of herself that mothered Poseidon birthed Hera to another god."

"Still," Ioanna said, shaking her head, "Close enough."

"Perhaps it was for the best with all that is happening to me now."

Ioanna opened her mouth to reply when a soft thud landed on the end of the dock. The four women turned to watch Charon's body rise from the fog. Ioanna broke free from Hades' clasp and went to her husband, wrapping her arms around his neck.

"No one saw you?" she asked concern flooding her voice.

"No," Charon said against her lips as he pressed a kiss against them. "I ferried them across down a ways, far enough into the depths that none of the Olympians would see."

"The dead can wait," Hades said as the ferryman released his wife and strode toward her. "Go when all are sleeping and stay downriver. I will not risk your life for those who are already dead. Only go when you must."

"I will be fine," Charon answered and reaching out a calloused hand, grasped Hades' chin in his careful fingers. He peered into her eyes before twisting her face slightly to examine first one side then the other. "How do you feel? You frightened me when I found you on the riverbank."

"I am fine for now," Hades said, clutching his hand in hers and pulling it from her chin. "Do not change the subject. I am serious, Charon; be careful. I cannot lose or worry about you. There is already great chaos in my mind."

"Hades." Charon squeezed her hand roughly in his. "There is no need to concern yourself over me. I am still a god, and I will do as you ask. Zeus will never see me."

XVIII

Hades stood outside the crumbling temple, pitchfork strangled in her fist. She could hear the massive Gorgon slithering softly over the earth behind her, the scaled body lurking just out of sight. The wind gently tossed Hades' hair and fluttered her skirt as she stood stone still, the soft rise and fall of her chest the only hint of life. Under the cover of darkness, Alkaios, Zeus, Poseidon, Medusa, and Hades had spirited away to the ancient mountain and using their blood, carved markings into the ground. They had then gone to the broken seal and painted symbols, binding the land outside to the recently opened door. One step inside their ring of blood runes, anyone misfortunate enough would find themselves trapped behind this ancient seal, unable to stop themselves as the power of the Olympians transported their bodies in an instant.

Hades surveyed the surrounding rocks. The Olympians lay in wait for the Old Ones to show their faces, and the moment the first gods stepped within their runes, they would reveal their intent. They would surround them, forcing the deformed creatures into the trap, but the timing must be precise; move too soon, and the ambush would be sensed; too late and the Old

Ones would have Hades in their grasp, fleeing for Olympus. No, they had to be careful, strike at the opportune moment while mindful not to pass the carvings. All inside the blood markings would be forever trapped in the realm of the Old Ones, and as the bait, Hades would be transported with them. If this worked, this was her end. Her name would live on within the form of her husband, but this was Hades' demise. They had no plan to save her. The seal the Olympians would place on the door would only be breakable from the outside. Even if her son survived her pregnancy, he would be on the wrong side to release them. This was it; the last time Hades would be free to feel the sun on her face or smell the fresh air.

Hades shifted her eyes to where she knew Alkaios hid. It had taken excruciating convincing to force his hand in this plan, but there was no other choice. It was either Hades or all of them, and in the end, Hades had decided. It was her life that unleashed this new hell on earth, and it would be her death that would trap it. But now as she stood motionless and alone, the moment the Old Ones were encircled by runes, the Olympians would unleash the power of their blood soaking in the ground. All within the markings would instantly catapult behind the door, Hades included. It would be over quickly, and this was the last time she would see her beloved husband, the man she had sacrificed so much for to keep by her side. In the fray, the chances of glimpsing Alkaios' mud-blue eyes would be unlikely. As one of the three greats, his strength was needed more than the others, and he would have to act without hesitation. Hades shuddered imperceptibly knowing she had laid eyes on Alkaios for the final time. Her eternity would be separate from him, and that he would never meet his son broke her heart. Hades was not even sure she would ever experience the joy of enveloping her child in cradling arms. The Old Ones could very well carve the half-breed from her still swollen belly and destroy her only link to the man she loved.

PITCHFORK

After they had carved the marks in their blood, Zeus, Poseidon, and Medusa wandered into the shadows to wait, giving husband and wife their last moments together in peace. Neither of them said much. Instead, Hades clung to Alkaios, her body pressed as close to his as their skin would allow. They had remained entwined as one in the gloom, and none dared disturb them save the sun who cared not what her rays brought upon them. At her ever-growing presence, the darkness fled to give way to murky light, and Alkaios knew he had to leave his bride as bait. With pain scorching every fiber of his being, he pulled back, and Hades began to sob, repeating "no" over and over into his solid chest.

"I will love you always," Alkaios said as he caught her tears with his thumbs and kissed her; a kiss filled with passion and all the words he did not have time to speak. He kissed her fiercely, lips pressed against hers in a desperate hunger, and then with a roar, Alkaios tore his body away and spun on his heels. He fled into the darkness to take up his post, unable to turn around to look at Hades' broken face. Alkaios had felt how hard her chest convulsed. If he saw it, he would not have the strength to do what was necessary. He would let the Old Ones overthrow the world to stop his wife's heart from shattering.

Hades had stood convulsing in the new day's sun and watched Alkaios retreat into the shadows. The gods were watching her, but she could not bring herself to care. She just hovered before the temple's entrance. Sobs wracked her lungs until she was barely able to breathe, but eventually, the pain of her tears became too much, and Hades heaved air until she could no longer stand erect. It took long, painful moments, but she finally wiped her eyes and calmed her heart before taking up the pitchfork to stand as solid as the temple at her back.

The sun now stood overhead as Hades exhaled one last deep breath in the silence. Twisting the weapon in her fist, air rushed from her lungs in a steady wave. With her exhale, black smoke seeped from her skin. It ebbed and flowed, moving and stretching around her. The tentacles branched out and crept through the breeze like tongues tasting the day. They weaved and churned, growing vast around her body, and slowly Hades shut her eyes. They remained closed as her heart steadied, and then without warning, they snapped open. Gone were her intoxicating blue irises, and in their stead peered two onyx pits. They had found her. They were coming.

A weighted moment passed, tense as the Olympians crouched hidden, watching darkness seep from Hades' every pore. They waited with bated breath, daring to hope the Old Ones would heed the call of their long-lost daughter. Hades stood at the center of the trap, eyes black as death, body humming with power. She remained entirely motionless save the ebb and flow of her darkness, and just when it seemed her call would go unanswered, the mountain trembled.

Hades' gaze snapped to the sound, her head cocked in anticipation, and for the first time, her sight fell upon her own. A hoard of deformed gods rounded the bend, a tall, muscular monster with rows of razor teeth leading them. From their cover, Zeus and Poseidon exchanged a weighted glance as the huge, black muscles stalked Hades. She seemed not to notice or even fear him as they approached and allowed the fanged god to circle her like a lion stalking a lamb.

"The first have come," Hades said, her tone low and dark as it washed over the crowd.

"And we seek the last," came a haggard voice. All eyes turned to an elderly woman who separated herself from the hoard. Unlike her monstrous brethren, she was relatively normal save for the third eye that sprouted in the middle of her wrinkled forehead. Her grey hair was braided down her back, and she stood tall and upright despite her age.

"My child," she said, reaching out gnarled fingers to the

queen of the Underworld. "Come to me and let me look upon our salvation."

Hades, with an almost imperceptible flick of her eyes, looked to the blood runes but made no motion to move. Alkaios followed her gaze and knew that if Hades went to the woman, the carving in the ground would be useless. He held his breath, praying to who he did not know, that his wife would remain in control long enough to spring the trap.

The two women, one gray and haggard and the other an impossibly beautiful midnight, stood staring at each other, neither willing to move. In a sudden flash of unearthly speed, Hades shot out and slammed the fanged god with the pitchfork, terminating his prowl and hurtling him into the temple's wall. The stone erupted around his body, and he crashed to the ground with a thud. The Old Ones lunged forward but halted just as quickly as they had started before the blood runes, and Alkaios sucked in a harsh yet silent breath.

Unfazed, Hades shifted backward and settled on a boulder of debris, resting her bident across her legs. Her play for the upper hand was clear; unlike the Olympians, she would not be so easily defeated, and if the Old Ones wished to look upon her, they would have to come to her, come within the blood lines.

The elderly god stood for a silent moment staring down the raven-haired beauty whose smooth skin seeped black and chuckled.

"Much like your father, you are," she said and stepped to Hades. She was inside the trap, and the rest only had to follow.

ALKAIOS WATCHED with bated breath in the anxious stillness of his camouflage as one by one the deformed gods strode past the blood runes. The last only needed to toe the line, and the trap could ignite, yet as the Old Ones closed in on their bait, a thought nagged at Alkaios' brain. A voice whispered in his mind too faint to understand, but something about this scene unsettled him. Something was missing, and he dug deep searching for the reason that teased him. Silently, Alkaios shifted his weight to view the throng, the maimed gods blotting out his wife, and he studied their grotesque forms, grasping at the wisp of alarm seeping through his skull.

Suddenly as if Alkaios had been hit by Poseidon's storms, it dawned on him. The realization sent an icy jolt down his spine, and his eyes snapped to the crowd making their way within the trap. He searched each god and knew with a sinking gut, his initial reaction had rung true. Black inky tentacles seeped from his skin, and silently, Alkaios vanished.

A moment later, his body landed next to Zeus' hidden post, and before the king of the gods could grunt his alarm, Alkaios shot a calloused palm over Zeus' mouth to smother his surprise.

"The horned god," Alkaios whispered. "The one whose shadow we saw on Mount Olympus… he is not here." Slowly, Alkaios peeled his fingers from Zeus' lips, and Zeus flashed him a hostile glare before straining his neck to scan the crowd. After a moment, Zeus pulled back behind the stone, and a flicker of concern sprouted in his eyes.

"They are not all here," Alkaios continued in a hushed tone. "We cannot ignite the trap unless they are all here."

"Do not be foolish," Zeus snapped in a voice that reached only Alkaios' ears. "These gods are almost within the runes. We cannot let them escape our grasp."

"And if we trap them now, while there are others not on this mountain, our element of surprise will be gone. We can only use Hades as bait once. They will not fall for it again, and you witnessed the power of that horned beast on Olympus. If there is one god we need to take unaware, it is he. If we ambush his brethren, he will know we are coming, and I do not carry hope we can survive a direct onslaught from him."

"And how much longer will it be before your wife is not bait for them, but for us? We stick to the plan. We trap these gods, and then we worry about Olympus."

"Zeus," came a soft whisper, and both men jerked to attention to find Athena, her body huddled behind a mass of debris, but her eyes were not on them but transfixed on the spot ahead of her only just visible through the cracks. Alkaios followed her line of sight and therefore was completely unaware that Zeus had launched himself into the crowd with an ear-piercing roar until it was too late.

Hades let the three-eyed god take her cheeks in her gnarled hands. The elder turned her face side to side to study her flawless skin, and Hades felt the surge of familial power in the touch. She recognized this old woman; she had stumbled over her lifeless body in her visions. It was these fingers who had tied the Old Ones' lives to Hades. It was her prophecy that had resurrected her ancestors.

"So like your mother you are," the three-eyed god crooned softly, "impossibly beautiful, yet it is your father's strength you wield. We could not allow him to rise after his betrayal. His death was permanent, and it seems you inherited his power. Such greatness was in him, and now I sense it in you. It would seem he willed you more than his pitchfork." She looked down at the weapon draped across Hades' lap.

At her glance, Hades tightened her grip around the pitchfork and pulled her face from the gnarled grasp. Her eyes flicked to the edge of the clearing and saw the last Old One cross the blood lines. Her back stiffened ever so slightly, bracing for the power the trap would unleash, yet the stillness in the air held.

Desperate not to call attention to her movements, Hades stood and stepped backward, using the momentum to throw a subtle glance to where Alkaios hid. Why had he not moved? She knew he would hesitate, but this was taking too long.

"The king is most eager for you to return to the fold," the ancient goddess continued, and Hades shifted her gaze back to the older woman and froze. Behind her silver hair, an Old One, who was more monster than man, stooped over. His thumb gouged the dirt in front of the debris that concealed Zeus. Hades stiffened, and her fingers flinched, longing to lash out and stop him. He was brushing the soil where a blood rune had bled into the stain, and if he broke its shape, the trap would never hold.

"It's a…" the beast began, but before he could utter the rest of his warning, a roar of sheer power split the air, and Zeus launched from his concealment and slammed into the monster's chest.

"Now!" Zeus cried as they hurtled to the ground, muscled bodies carving dents in the rubble as they crashed. The Olympians wasted not a single moment, and in a heartbeat, they stood before their blood runes. Their weapons plummeted into the stained dirt, igniting a deafening hum in the air as power sprang from the earth.

"Do it now!" Zeus said as he rolled onto his feet, brandishing the thunderbolt. The deformed gods were closing in on him, but the trap would not contain them for long. "Poseidon!" he begged as he brought down his weapon in the head of an Old One.

"Hold!" Poseidon bellowed, stretching out his palm in a steadying motion. Zeus was within the runes, and Poseidon watched in horror as his brother was forced further and further from safe ground. "Brother, get out of there!"

All chaos broke loose. The Old Ones bore down on Zeus, and despite his power, he would not survive long. Hesitating for only a moment to contemplate if it was worth tipping her hand and revealing her true alliance, Hades stepped forward, but only made it a foot when the pitchfork violently wrenched from her grasp. Shocked, she looked up to see Alkaios rushing headlong after Zeus, fist outstretched. He shook his head 'no' as their eyes met, commanding her to remain neutral as the weapon flew into his palm, and with one mighty swing, crashed it into the skull of a monster closing in on Zeus.

Hades heard a hiss behind her, and from the darkness of the temple, Medusa erupted. Her massive tail whipped savagely as she dove into the fray. Well acquainted with her kind, the first gods barely flinched at her assault, beating her back with little effort, concentrating instead on the surrounded kings fighting for their lives.

Alkaios reached Zeus and spun, planting his back to the king and covering his flank. The Old Ones paused for a moment at the sight of the pitchfork in the hand of another god, and without questioning the small reprieve, Alkaios seized Zeus by the wrist and shoved black smoke from his body. The bident vibrated in his fingers, and he knew Hades was funneling power to him. With a roar and an explosion of a raw, dark force, they vanished to reappear outside the shimmering energy of the trap.

"Now!" bellowed Zeus as he met Hades' eyes. She stiffened and clenched her eyelids. Zeus' heart lurched in pain at her fear, but he slammed the thunderbolt into the ground above a blood rune and poured power out of his soul to unleash the ambush.

XIX

Nothing happened. The air fell still; all the power drained into oblivion. Hades and Zeus snapped their eyes open at the same time, their gazes landing on one another before searching for the reason the ambush failed. Standing with a gnarled hand raised above her head, the three-eyed god clenched her fist as if she were strangling the neck of an enemy. Hades watched the faint shimmer of power wane, strangled in her grip, and Hades knew this goddess had seized the trap in her hand and destroyed it. For a moment, both generations of gods stood frozen, and the bitter bile of fear ran up Hades' throat.

"Seize them," the three-eyed god commanded, and before the Olympians even thought to move, the Old Ones lunged forward and grasped them with savage power, forcing them to their knees. Alkaios, Zeus, and Poseidon struggled fiercely, and their combined force separated an Old One from the crowd. They offered him no mercy, and as Alkaios and Poseidon held him still, Zeus decapitated him.

A roar echoed off the mountain as the monster's lifeless body crumpled to the dirt, and a deformed god with a mallet larger than a man burst from the fray. He barreled down on the Olympians and swung his weapon at Poseidon's legs. With a crack, Poseidon's muscled limbs gave way, and the god of the seas collapsed with an agonizing explosion of pain. The beast wasted no time, and before either of the greats could react, the mallet smashed into Alkaios' ribcage.

The fracture of his ribs was so loud, Hades felt it in her chest. She stifled a cry, breath escaping her lungs in erratic pants. Tears flooded her eyes, and she blinked rapidly before her ancestors could see her weakness. Alkaios groaned in tortured agony, and Hades longed to go to him, to kill every last monster before her, but the tables had turned. The Olympians no longer had the upper hand. She had to remain silent. If Hades tipped her hand now, and they discovered she was merely bait, this ploy would never work again. Even as a third sickening thud rang through the air, and Zeus' strong voice screamed, she was not sure they would ever have another chance at catching these first gods unaware.

Hades' chest heaved as she witnessed the three greats of Olympus sprawled on the ground. Poseidon's legs jutted out beneath him at unnatural angles, and Alkaios clutched his side where blood seeped from concave bones. Hades gagged at the sight, and Alkaios caught her gaze, pain watering his eyes. Without realizing, she began to move toward her husband. Hades did not care. She would die with him rather than watch them torture him.

"Kill them," came the three-eyed god's voice, and Hades froze in her tracks. The elder commanded her ancestors with an evil that not even the Underworld knew. "Starting with her." The goddess gestured at Athena, whose bloody knees were digging into the dirt. "Save these brothers for last," she continued, narrowing her eyes in on Zeus, Poseidon, and Alkaios. "Let them watch the rest die and see what happens to those who oppose us."

A cry lodged itself in Hades' throat as two of the deformed gods seized Athena roughly by the biceps and hauled her to the debris Hades had perched atop moments ago.

"No!" Athena screamed, digging her heels into the dirt. They left bloody streaks on the ground as her feet scrambled for a foothold, but the dust gave way beneath her panic, offering no aid. "No! No!" Her arms flailed, and her torso bucked wildly as she struggled fruitlessly to free herself, but to no avail. The Old Ones simply dragged her panicked body to the rock, forcing her to kneel before it. The fanged god snuck up behind Athena and planting his foot on her back, shoved her head roughly against the boulder. The jagged edges bit into her soft flesh, blooming crimson against her skin. Tears streamed down Athena's cheeks as she writhed against his weight, but his heel held her prostrate. The beast wielding the mallet turned from the three greats and stalked toward Athena, and in that moment, all understood the fate that awaited the goddess.

"No! Please, no!" Athena screamed, squirming as the god closed in on her, mallet slung against his tremendous shoulders. "Zeus!" she shrieked in desperation, knowing full well he could not help. "No! Please, please, please!" Athena repeated her frantic begging over and over. Her breath hitched with sobbing hyperventilation. The Olympians knelt in the dirt in terror, tears running down many of their cheeks, yet the Old One took no notice of their distress and settled his hulking frame behind Athena. He lifted his mallet high in the air, lining up the blow that would crush the god of war's skull.

"Hades, please!" Athena sobbed, angling her head to meet Hades' eyes. Hysteria and fear colored her face as she shook on her knees, cheek pressed into the rock. "Please?"

The two women stared at each other for an endless moment. Horror and shocking disbelief passed between them, so strong the air iced over. Athena bucked and cried against her executioners. Her limbs and torso thrashed, fighting an unwinnable battle for freedom. There would be no escape for her, only death. Her skull would crack like an overripe fruit and paint the dirt with her brains, yet still, she struggled. Her voice grew more and more desperate; her words jumbled in incoherent terror, and Hades watched the entire horrifying scene as if she was no longer living in her own skin. Her eyes glazed as the monster raise the weapon. Her heart beat erratically slow within the confines of her chest. The vision before her blurred into a cacophony of confused madness, and with a numbing panic, Hades feared she would black out when the rush of the swinging mallet woke her with a stab of clarity.

In a flash, Hades' arm shot out, and the cracking of bone shattered Athena's sobs. Hades' fist viciously punched through the Old One's massive rib cage and closed around his heart. Hot blood ran down her forearm as the strong beat pounded against her palm. Every pair of eyes fell wide in shock, and not a soul moved. Hades stood stone still, a murderous rage blazing through her features, and then slowly she turned to the three-eyed god in an act of defiance and yanked. Her hand ripped from the back his chest, clutching a still pulsing heart. The monster spat bubbles of blood from parted lips as the mallet dropped harmlessly behind him, thudding to the ground only a second before his monstrous form did.

Holding the three-eyed god's gaze, Hades hoisted the heart for all to see and then squeezed. Blood spurt from the organ onto her face as her fist constricted until it was nothing more than a mangled pulp of flesh. Dropping it to the dirt beside the body, Hades lifted her bloody fingers and swept them through the air as if she were dismissing a soul from her court. Inky tentacles of black smoke sprung from Alkaios, enveloping all the Olympians and dragging them safely to Hell.

"So, you were bait," the three-eyed god murmured as the raven-haired beauty stared motionless at her, eyes cold and vicious. "It is no matter." The old woman walked to Hades and wiped a drop of blood from the younger woman's cheek. Her touch rippled beneath Hades' skin, forcing its evil on a lethal trajectory toward the beautiful woman's heart with only one goal, to blacken the still untainted soul.

"It will not be long before you are under our hold. I believed you to be already, but I was mistaken," the elder continued, surveying to the two dead bodies whose life seeped red into the mountain. "A mistake I paid for, and one I will not make again. But it is of little consequence. Your father's power runs strong through your veins, and it is far greater than what we lost today. That power, my child, I am willing to wait for. Soon... soon you will be one of us, and then nothing will stand in our way. Our reign will be absolute."

Without responding, Hades stepped backward and disappeared in a twisting mass of darkness.

"We had them!" Hades bellowed the moment her body materialized in the Underworld's throne room. "They were within the trap, and you hesitated!" She stormed toward Zeus, who stood clutching his mangled shoulder, but Hades did not care. She did not care that Hera cradled the sobbing Athena in the corner or that Poseidon sprawled crippled on the floor. "They could have been imprisoned behind that seal, but your hesitation cost us our surprise." Hades jabbed an accusatory finger into Zeus' pained face, her hand and forearm still soaked in blood. Black smoke twisted and curled around her, an extension of her rage, and her eyes shone almost blackened in her skull. The chamber fell silent, afraid to move for fear of the violence that rippled from Hades' skin.

"They were not all there," Zeus said in a placating tone, trying yet failing to raise his hand to halt her steps.

"Trapping half of them would still be better than none. Your stupidity has killed you all."

"Hades," a voice rumbled behind her.

"Silence!" Hades screamed, whirling around and shoving her dark power forward into the body of who interrupted her. Alkaios flew backward with a harsh snap of his neck and slammed into the stone with a cry of agony. He clutched his obliterated ribs as Hades' power sailed past him to collide with the ancient walls of the throne room, a resounding crack reverberating where it hit. Not a single person drew a breath, their bodies recoiling in fear and shock.

Hades heaved, chest bucking as she stared at her husband on the ground, and as quickly as her power had unleashed, it shrank back within her. Horror clouded her eyes as realization hit, and Hades rushed forward and scooped Alkaios' battered torso into her arms.

"I am sorry." Hades placed her fingers on his shattered side. Dark power seeped from her skin into Alkaios, and the bones cracked beneath her palm as they reformed, snapping back into position. Feeling the last rib knit together, Hades rested her forehead against her husband's and let the comfort his warmth ignited wash over her.

"I can feel them more and more," Hades whispered against his skin. "I do not know how much longer I have. I fear today may have been the last time I will ever help you. The old woman made it clear that they will only welcome me once the Hades I am is a forgotten dream. I doubt we will get another chance to trap them, and I am terrified of what our failure might have cost us."

"The horned god," Alkaios said, shifting to look her in the eyes. "The one from your visions. He was not there."

"Their king?"

"Yes. I was concerned what it would mean if we trapped his brethren behind our seal without him. With you locked away, we would have no chance of trapping him. It is my fault. I was worried that if we loosed our trap today, he would know you were bait. They would only fall for it once, and if we are to win, it is he who we must confine. It does not matter now. My hesitation cost us our upper hand."

Hades looked at Alkaios and without a word, bent forward and kissed him gently on the lips. Standing up, she turned to where Poseidon sprawled and placed her hand on his leg. The bones straightened and healed beneath her palm, and then Hades moved to Zeus and lay her fingers on his shoulder. The shattered socket reformed, and the bones and sinews knit together until no sign of damage remained. At least her greater power was worth something. Gods could not so easily heal the wounds inflicted by one another; Hades herself bore witness to the scares adorning her body from the Olympian's blades, but it seemed as the power leaked from her, Hades had conquered this failing. At least she could heal the gruesome wounds her ancestor inflicted before they slaughtered the Olympians.

"Thank you," Zeus whispered as Hades' fingers dropped from his broad shoulder, leaving sticky blood streaks painted over his skin.

"Do not thank me," Hades said bitterly, "I have done nothing but prolong your death."

THE UNDERWORLD WAS silent in the darkness, not even the pad of bare feet could be heard as Hades' toes slid over the cold stone. Unobserved, her graceful form crept through the dark like a lion stalking prey, the pitchfork gripped in her fingers. It had taken her seconds to leave the bed she shared with Alkaios and steal the pitchfork as he slept, and as Hades made her way to the throne room, her eyes glazed over, feet walking without direction. Her body moved absent of haste, the night consuming her as she passed the bedrooms of countless sleeping gods. Not a soul stirred. Their slumber made them oblivious to the death that roamed the halls.

Uninterrupted, the queen wandered into the cavernous chamber and halted before the twin thrones. Darkness began to ebb and flow around her, twisting like smoke snakes, and the pitchfork thrummed beneath her fingertips.

"Hades," came a strong, deep voice. The words echoed, bouncing off the cavernous walls, and for a moment, the night air held its breath. "Don't."

With a slowness that made her movements almost imperceptible, Hades twisted until she faced Alkaios whose hulking frame hovered in the entrance.

"Hades," he begged, seeing the glaze in her beautiful eyes. "Please." His voice broke. "Come back to me."

"The first have risen," Hades said in a voice that was not entirely hers. "We will rule again, and the blood of your race will be the holy sacrifice we resurrect our empire on."

"I will not let you have her," Alkaios said, staring through Hades' eyes as if he was speaking to the horned god himself, and with a powerful leap, he launched into the air. The ground beneath him cracked as his feet pushed off the stone, and his body propelled toward his wife. Arms outstretched, Alkaios' mass flew at Hades, colliding with her smaller frame with a thud that reverberated in the darkness. The two of them crashed to the floor in a tangle of flailing limbs, and with graceful force, Hades flipped him over onto his back, pinning his neck with her knee.

"You cannot win against us," Hades growled, angling the pitchfork for his throat, but Alkaios wasted not a single moment and thrust his hand out to seize her dress by the collar. With a harsh pull, he yanked her head forward and vaulted his forehead upward, colliding with her skull with a painful crack. Dazed, Hades teetered, which loosened her grip on the weapon. With a powerful strike, Alkaios slammed his wrist into the metal, sending the bident clattering across the stone. With a grunt of surprise, Hades flung herself after it, but Alkaios gripped her thighs and pulled her back. She landed with a thump astride her husband, thrusting her hands wildly for his neck. Alkaios flinched and caught her wrists, restraining her struggle, and yanked her down to hover her beautiful face over his.

"Let her go," Alkaios growled, anger spewing from his lips. "Return her to me!" At his words, Hades froze; her body suddenly rigid above him, and her dark eyes drifted to his in an icy glare.

"You will never get her back," Hades said with a coldness that stabbed Alkaios in the gut. "She is ours now," and with that declaration, Hades forced her hands to his throat. Alkaios caught her wrist, but her strength bent him to her will, her fingers clutching his neck with an iron grip. Alkaios coughed and gagged as her chokehold crushed his windpipe. He bucked and roiled beneath Hades' constricting thighs, but her grasp never wavered. The corner of his vision blurring to black, Alkaios released her wrists and with a massive swing, punched his wife in the ribs. Hades tumbled to the tile, gasping in pain, and Alkaios was unsure if the blow hurt her or him more. He did not want to do this. It was killing him, but Alkaios would not let them steal Hades from him.

"You cannot have my wife!" Alkaios bellowed into the darkness as she crawled over the floor toward the pitchfork.

"Fool!" Hades spat, whipping her head backward at an awkward angle to glare at him. "We already have her!" And in a flash like lightning, she vaulted across the stone to the weapon, fingers clawing to grab hold, but before her hand closed around the cold metal, Alkaios' heel crashed into the pitchfork. The force clattered it out of her reach.

Alkaios lunged to scoop the skidding bident into his palm, but it was barely within his grasp, when his wife barreled into him. Hades threw him ruthlessly across the room, and with a resounding thud, Alkaios' spine slammed into the wall before he crashed to the floor in a heap. Hades sprinted forward and plucked the weapon from the ground when a solid mass landed before her. A massive bicep struck out, colliding with her chest, and Hades flew back and landed hard on her tailbone. The wind knocked out of her, she gagged on her own breath as her eyes tilted up to see Zeus' towering hulk. Hades cocked her head as he loomed, and her lips curved in a wicked grin. With a flash of dark smoke, she vanished.

A moment later Hades was behind Zeus and with a vicious kick to the back of his kneecaps, sent Zeus plummeting to his knees. His head whiplashed as her fist slammed into his exposed neck, and Zeus' torso careened forward until his broad palms collided with the stone, harshly jolting his toppling weight.

"We have already won," Hades said without remorse as her body entwined with darkness. "Yield, and we will kill you quickly. Your deaths will be clean. Fight us… and you will suffer as no gods have suffered before," and with that she vanished, leaving only a thin tendril of smoke snaking through the air like a faded memory.

HADES STRODE through the burnt carcass of Olympus, a skeleton in ash. She took no precautions to remain hidden, walking out in the open instead. A victor among the ruins. All who saw her halted in their tracks as she walked past them, yet Hades spared them neither hesitation nor a glance. With great purpose, her feet carried her to the throne room doors, and with palms pressed to ancient heavy stone, Hades heaved and swung them wide.

A hush fell over the chamber, the only sound and movement the colossal doors crashing shut as Hades entered. All manner of deformed gods crowded the room, clamoring for a glimpse of the unnatural beauty invading their vanquished space, but Hades paid them no mind. She cared not for the small or the weak, but instead for who sat on Zeus' conquered throne. The true god returned.

Under the sea of eyes, Hades strode onward, darkness leaking from her skin, pitchfork striking the stone with heavy menace. The three-eyed elder of prophecy stepped forward to intercept her, but Hades brushed past the hag with indifferent strength and continued to the throne until her toes scraped the dais' steps. A host of spears greeted her, swinging down in challenge, but her body flinched not at their aggression. Her progress halted by tipped metal, Hades simply lowered her chin in respect, a bow that only extended to the necessary muscles required to bend her neck. Respect without prostration was all Hades intended to give, and her head remained bowed for a moment before her eyes slowly crept up until they met those of the King, the god almighty of her ancestors.

He was a monstrosity to behold, almost double Hades' build. His enormity was not entirely his mass, but his presence, as if his power consumed all of the space, a beast of unimaginable size. His colossal frame barely fit in Zeus' throne. His hulking muscles bulged, threatening to rip free from his dark, leathery hide. His body loosely resembled a man with legs, arms, and torso of immense power, but his head was that of a gigantic horned bull. Huge curved horns protruded grotesquely from his skull, dyed rust brown from the blood of those he skewered. His black eyes stared down at Hades with an animalistic hunger that would make a lesser god's skin crawl, yet Hades did not flinch as she held his oppressive gaze.

After a long moment, the monstrous horned god lifted a calloused hand that could crush a man's head with a single fist and waved it as he stood, looming to his full height. The spears rose, and his muscled thighs carried him down to settle before Hades. His frame towered over her with a menacing stature that dwarfed her lithe shape.

"My child," he said, voice harsh and demonic. "You have come to take your father's place." The King took Hades' chin roughly in his fingers and forced her face up to meet his gaze. Hades' spiteful glare matched his viciousness, which drove a small chuckle from his cruel lips. "Welcome home, god of death."

XX

THE WORLD BEGAN TO BURN. The skies turned to ash, and the seas churned dark and violent. The green of the land decayed, and crops blackened with rot. Even Alkaios' farm, which had been blessed to always bear fruit, faltered as the poison of the first gods seeped into everything that was once good and pure. Mountains erupted in lava, flooding the earth in hellfire and brimstone as if the earth itself was corrupted by the evil unleashed. Peasants and kings alike were swallowed whole as the tainted ground opened up beneath them. Cavernous gaping wounds ripped through the earth ravenous to swallow all in its path. Nothing was left untouched under the Old One's rule.

Alkaios, Zeus, and Poseidon stood at the edge of a burnt field, the smoke and raining ash the only remnants of what had once flourished. It had been days since Hades had abandoned the Underworld and returned to reign on the carcass of Olympus. Alkaios knew in his soul as he surveyed the scorched and violated earth she would not return to him. It was too late, and the world would pay for their mistake, their failure to stop the raging tyranny.

Overcome with a suffocating sense of despair, Alkaios

stepped forward to hide his face from the brothers. He wandered over the blistered ground, feet leaving indents in the ashen dirt. His toes dug the ravaged vegetation as he walked, searching for anything that resembled life, but it was a barren wasteland, irrevocable destruction. His eyes wandered over the bleak landscape landing on a stalk, though darkened by death, which was not the same brittle blackness the rest of the field had been reduced to. Alkaios moved toward it, his hands bending to capture it of their own accord. He rubbed it between his thumb and fingers, bruising the already damaged leaves. How many times had he examined the crops of his ailing fields like this worried they would die before harvest? Memories of his mortal farming days of fear and discouragement over his faltering crops were nothing compared to the obliterating carnage before him now. When Hades had come to him those years ago in a lie, her blessing had been on him and his land. Growth and prosperity had once flowed from her touch, but no longer. Death followed Hades, her destruction absolute.

"How long before the Underworld is no longer safe?" Zeus asked his brother once Alkaios was out of earshot. He stood solid and immovable, massive arms folded over his chest, thunderbolt clutched in an iron grip.

"Was it ever safe for us?" Poseidon's tall leaner frame mimicked Zeus' stance.

"No, but it is our only haven, the only place these demons have not come crashing down upon, but for how much longer? They took Olympus and are now taking the earth. How long before they cast their eyes to Hell? Hades will want her realm back."

"Technically, it is his realm now," Poseidon said, jerking his chin toward Alkaios.

"He may be the Olympian King of the Underworld," Zeus scoffed, "but we all know it is the mother of darkness those beasts follow. Alkaios holds great power, but it pales compared to hers. That is what I am afraid of." Zeus shifted his mass to look his brother in the eyes. "Those beasts are obedient to Alkaios because Hades asked it of them. They do not harm us because she demands it. It is all because of her. Alkaios is king, but Hades is the mother of death, and all children are loyal to their mothers. Right now, they are probably the only things keeping us from obliteration, but it was also in Hades' best interest to have them guard the Underworld. If it were not for her, Athena's brain would be painted across that stone, but now that she has abandoned us? What happens when Hades returns with a legion of mad gods? What happens when she requires entrance into her realm? The Underworld, the beasts... they will have to choose between her and her husband? Do you have any hope they will side with Alkaios? No. It will be our throats they rip out, not Hades'."

"Perhaps," Poseidon agreed, "but maybe not?"

"You truly believe they would refuse to bow to her?" Zeus asked incredulously, his perfectly sculpted eyebrows rising in disbelief.

"Her?" Poseidon continued, "I think they would, but bow to the Old Ones? Perhaps not. There is the chance they will do whatever their beloved Hades requires of them." He quickly held out a hand for Zeus to let him finish his thought before spewing his disagreement. "It is just the Old Ones have made no move toward the Underworld in any way. It could be because they are biding their time until they are at full strength, but perhaps there is another reason. When our father built the ancient fortress that is now our sanctuary, he raised it in-between Tartarus and Elysium. Our ancestors built their reign in-between heaven and hell, yet they only built the fortress. Hell predates even our father, the first and greatest Titan, which can only mean that it existed during the Old Ones' reign. Have you ever stopped to wonder why there are beasts in the depths vicious enough to slaughter the divine? How is it they possess such raw power, that they ripped a Titan to shreds before Cronus sealed the door? If we are the gods almighty, then how can that dog, that lion, and those snakes that live within Hydra end us? Those god-killers came into existence even before our Cronus did. What if this is why they are so savage? What if they were birthed to defy a whole different breed of gods?"

"You think they were created to guard the Underworld against the Old Ones?" Zeus asked.

"I believe it is a possibility. You have heard the stories Hades and Medusa told of them, how human lives were mere playthings to them. Perhaps that abomination Kerberos was put there to protect the souls of those who earned Elysium. The old gods are disfigured from the many times they performed the Touch of the Gods. Kill the body, the soul crosses the river to eternity; perform the Touch, and there is nothing left. Maybe the universe saw fit to defend the shades from the deformed deities. Perhaps they are still doing just that."

"And you are willing to bet our lives and the survival of earth on a theory that Hades' beasts were created to protect the Underworld and all who remain inside?" Zeus asked incredulously.

"It makes sense. Nothing has changed for them in centuries. They keep the unwanted out and the darkness in."

"Everything has changed. Their mother is one of those deformed gods now, and I cannot stake the lives of everyone I love on them rising against her when Hades finally comes for us."

"Whether you agree or not, brother," Poseidon said, nodding his head in Alkaios' direction alerting Zeus that the king of the Underworld was returning, "they seem to be the only thing that is standing between us and destruction."

"Well, I am not willing to take that gamble; that they will protect me from her," Zeus said, lowering his voice.

"Then what do you intend on doing?"

"Conceal my absence for me," Zeus answered, flicking his

eyes toward Alkaios. "We need the protection of someone whose loyalty does not lie with Hades, one Alkaios knows nothing about, and I aim to find such a creature."

"And where will you find such a beast?" Poseidon asked. Zeus shifted his gaze off into the distance, and Poseidon followed suit. Obscured by smoke, they could see nothing, but Poseidon knew what his brother looked toward. The snow-peaked mountain that loomed unseen in that direction.

"He will not help us," Poseidon said.

"Then I will make him," Zeus growled, deep venom in his voice.

ZEUS PAUSED at the base of the mountain, peering up despite that fact that even on a clear day where the sky was a crystal sea the snowcaps were invisible peaks in the heavens. But now as he stood, eyes stinging from the acrid smoke, he could barely make out crevasses to be used for finger holds for his immediate climb. Under ideal circumstances, this ascent was nearly impossible, as both god and man alike had to ascend hand over foot, clutching impossibly small cracks in the sheer rock. Forced to ascend as equals, all faced almost certain death on this mountain; the higher the rise, the further the plummet to earth. Zeus would have to scale miles of treachery with nothing but his iron will and brute strength to carry him heavenward, but it must be done. It was necessary he reach the top, and so with a heavy breath, he slung the thunderbolt across his back and dug his fingertips into the stone.

It was not long before Zeus' muscles burned with fatigue. The rock lacked anything more than insignificant footholds, and his legs cramped painfully. His fingers were raw from being shoved into crevasses too small for his large hands, and his biceps struggled to haul his tremendous weight skyward. His neck spasmed as he craned to see past the ash-littered clouds. He was not even halfway, yet Zeus felt he could go no further.

With a roar that shook the peak beneath him, Zeus bellowed heavenward and hoisted himself one more foot, clasping the rock with raw fingertips. Slick from blood, his grip slid from its hold, and he plummeted earthward with a stunning decline. Clawing at the stone, his massive body hurtled down as gravity fought to claim him, the crevasses too small to seize at this speed. Zeus twisted forcefully in the air and grasped the thunderbolt. He ripped it from his back and with all the strength left in his aching muscles, drove it into the mountain. His mass jerked to a joint-wrenching halt as sparks from the bolt's impact spit around his face. His chest heaved in an ashy breath, muscles fighting for control as he hung from the weapon. Zeus paused there, dangling for a long moment, gazing with frustration-clouded eyes at the distance this fall had lost him, the impossible climb made even longer. With a groan of pain, he shoved his fingers into a crack and wrenched the thunderbolt free. His coiled biceps bent and thrust. His thighs vaulted him high into the filthy wind where Zeus slammed the sharp tips of the bolt into the solid rock. It gave way under its sheer power, fissures sprouting in a web where the metal embedded itself. Zeus would not let this mountain beat him, not when the outcome of this brewing war might be decided by what waited in the heavens.

Zeus knew not how long he climbed. The hours slipped past in agony and determination. He lost track of the minutes ticking by for all he could focus on was putting aching, bloody fingers over weapon over foothold. Every time he pulled himself up by the thunderbolt with shaking muscles, Zeus convinced himself to move one more time. That was all he had to do, move once more, and so each time he ripped it from the stone and launched his weary body into the air, he caught himself by slamming the razor tip deep into the rocks. Zeus clung to his perch, hanging impossibly high in the clouds and breathing heavily, and told himself to climb one more step. If he moved just once, that was all he had to do, and when it seemed the peak would never be reached, that he would die on this mountain with sinews frozen solid in seizing cramps, his fingers grasped the corner of a ledge. With a bellow, Zeus shoved his hand further, palm pressing flush against the rock, and heaved. He hauled himself over the edge with a groan. His muscles scarlet with burning pain fought this final movement, yet Zeus managed to roll onto his back in safety. He lay there far above the earth, chest heaving frantically to suck in precious air. The rock beneath cooled his spine, soothing the burn of overexerted flesh. His eyes felt heavy with exhaustion, desperate for sleep. Zeus dare not give in to their desire though, not here with his weakened body so prone, and so he haltingly pushed himself to a seat.

The glinting sun caught his eye, and Zeus watched the golden rays crest the charred clouds. At this altitude, there was nothing but crystal blue and piercing sunlight. The ashen world was left far below in his climb, and as a result, this peak almost seemed untouched by the destruction as the new day's light crept higher from its slumber. It dawned on Zeus that he must have climbed through the night to reach his destination, and he rolled to his feet despite the soreness seizing hold of him. A fresh day had been birthed, and he had only just crested the mountain. There was no time to waste, so against his limb's protests, Zeus turned and surveyed the ledge.

It was sparse save a small bush that grew next to a boulder. Zeus moved toward it and discovered its greenery hid a narrow footpath that wound upward. Grateful for the ease that the path provided, the wearied king of the gods set his feet to the trail and continued the hike.

Refusing to give up so close to his journey's end, Zeus placed one foot in front of another. His lungs screamed for rest as they burned within his chest, but he ignored them with stubborn resolve, forcing his body to the breaking point until the footpath ended abruptly with a massive sheer cliff blocking all progress. Zeus looked for a way around, but the ledge offered no other option. It was either up the wall of stone or down the mountain in defeat, and so with a deep breath, Zeus lowered into a powerful crouch and launched heavenward.

    He could not clear the cliff in one leap, yet as his flight through the air slowed, his fingers grasped the edge. With a wrenching jolt, Zeus caught the ledge. He clung there, body suspended in midair, and let the pain of the jarring halt seep from his elbow and shoulder. When the sharpness of his nearly dislocated joints faded into dullness, he threw his free hand over the ridge with a wild swing and hauled himself up.

    His stomach and thighs scraped over the razor rim as he drew himself to his knees, and the sight of an incredible mass met him. Zeus sucked in a breath as he gazed upon a sight only a few were ever blessed or perhaps cursed enough to see. Slowly, he pushed himself to his feet and reached around to where the thunderbolt clung to his sweat-stained spine. Zeus saw no threat ahead of him, yet that didn't mean it would not come, for what lay before him was most likely guarded fiercely.

XXI

A NEST, the size of a warship, loomed before Zeus, a magnificent sight to behold. But that was not what caused his mouth to gape open nor his fingers to tighten around the thunderbolt. It was the fact that the nest was crafted from gold. Woven entirely of golden wood, priceless items were threaded throughout its walls as if the creator of this glinting monstrosity had found glittering treasures to embed into the tangled braids. Some articles were exquisite, treasure the kinds of which could have only been stolen from kings, yet others were ordinary, mundane objects like chairs or fruit made glorious by their shining surfaces.

"Few survive the ascent up my mountain," a deep voice rumbled. "Most are crushed by the fall when their bodies finally give out, but a few are smart enough to climb down to save themselves from such a fate… Almost none make it to the top."

Zeus gripped the thunderbolt tighter, eyes glancing left and right searching for whoever's low voice spoke, yet all that stood before him was the solitary nest.

"They come for the gold of course, but not a soul ever makes it down with any," it warned as the nest shook slightly. Zeus stepped back and watched in both awe and terror as a looming mass began to rise from the golden walls.

First to become visible were black feathers that branched out from the top of a monstrous skull. They were more horn than feather though as they protruded. Dark tar bound them to give them the appearance of solid horns angled backward. As they rose further into view, a pair of eyes crested the edge next, peering unblinkingly at their intruder. Pale gold irises surrounding vast coal pupils glared down at him with eagle precision, and they never broke Zeus' gaze as the beast continued to rise.

Zeus swallowed at the face that met his sight. Short dark fur matted its head, and the snout narrowed to a point. Small black plumes covered the beaked nose and jutted on an angle toward those unblinking bronzed irises, and although the features were that of a bird, this monstrosity was no eagle. An ode to the demonic, its pointed beak, tarred feathers, and thin fur formed a face that was more dragon in shape. Protruding fangs glinted in its mouth where some of the beak's smaller feathers had been ripped out.

"But you, king of the gods, do not seem to be someone who would brave my mountain just to steal my gold," the monster continued in a guttural and terrifying tone, and Zeus realized with alarm that the beaked horror was not speaking but communicating with him telepathically. Its mouth remained motionless as the ominous voice permeated Zeus' brain, unblinking eyes staring down as it rose, ever higher, ever larger.

Its thick neck broke the cover of the nest next with a girth of rippling muscles. The same dark fur that adorned its head traveled over the beast's throat, which eventually gave way to a massive protruding chest and shoulders. Zeus had to crane his neck to see the beast that emerged, for its colossal mass blotted out the sun.

The creature slowly lifted a giant leg and clearing the nest, stepped out onto the mountain. Zeus stumbled backward to avoid the treacherous clawed paw that shook the ground as it extracted itself from the confines of its golden abode. Zeus' pulse quickened at the sight of the creature's full frame. Impossibly huge, its front legs rose double the height of the blonde god. They were thickly muscled and wrapped in dark fur, and the claws on its paws grew razor sharp like swords. It was then as it stood finally in view, that Zeus realized the body was that of a monstrous lion, with a head deformed to appear as a demonic bird-like dragon, but that was not all the beast possessed. Folded against its back lay two massive wings covered in the same onyx feathers as its face except these were impressive, easily the length of a man's arm. As if for Zeus' benefit, the monster unfurled them to show the king of the gods their true enormity. It held Zeus' gaze the entire time as it recoiled his wings and flicked its tail forward to curl around its paws. At the tip where a tuft of hair would normally reside was an array of feathers, some broken or bald, a battle-worn tale of its viciousness. The creature was a sight to behold, a monstrosity in size, and Zeus had never felt so small or insignificant standing next to another living being.

"So tell me, Zeus of Olympus," the beast finally continued, its words echoing in Zeus' mind, "what brings you to brave my mountain?"

"Griffin," Zeus said, finding his voice as he addressed the legendary beast of the mountain. "Surely, you already know why I have come. Have you not seen the earth pale? The clouds fill with ash?"

"The first gods," the Griffin answered, and Zeus confirmed with the dip of his chin.

"So you, king of the Olympians, have sought me out to beg for my aid?" the Griffin finally asked after a long moment of studying his unannounced visitor. "The answer is no," he continued when Zeus nodded in affirmation.

"You will not help us?"

"I have not survived generations of gods by meddling in the affairs of earth," came the Griffin's cold response in his mind. "The wars that have come before and the wars that are yet to come are yours to fight, as is this one. I have never burdened myself with the dealings of gods or men, and your beseeching changes nothing. This war is not mine to wage. I will remain on this mountain as I always have."

"Do you think you are safe here?" Zeus asked, cold anger rising in his voice. "Is that why you refuse to help? Because you are protected by your peak? It is nearly impossible to climb, so the wars of humanity never breach your solitude, and you expect this time to be no different?" Zeus stepped forward, driven by purpose. "You are wrong. The Old Ones will not stop until there is nothing left. They will burn the earth, and once they are through, they will drain the seas and turn the skies to ash. You do not meddle in our affairs, but this is no longer just our war. It will come here, and it will cost you. Your mountain cannot save you, not from them. You believe because I, Zeus king of Olympus, struggled to defeat your elevation, they will as well? Their power is vast, and it only grows as the days pass. Eventually, they will scale it as if it were merely an anthill and swarm your nest in droves. This gold will not appease them. No, they will rip off your wings and cast you from this altitude, leaving you to plummet to the ground only to shatter into splinters of flesh and bone. Your fate will be that of all those who have tried to conquer this mountain and failed."

"Look, king of the gods," the Griffin spoke, interrupting Zeus' plea. Zeus bit his tongue and followed the Griffin's gaze. The sun had burned away some of the morning haze, and the earth was vaguely visible. Zeus walked to the mountain's edge and gazed down. At first the reason for the Griffin's warning was unclear, but as Zeus studied the land, drawing earth into focus until the miles counted for naught, the slaughter that plagued the land pricked his vision like the blooming of blood after a thorn's assault. Far below, the Old Ones were laying waste to a city, the horde nothing but swarming ants from this view. The screams of the dying and prayers for help bombarded his ears, and Zeus watched from the safety of this incredible height as one life after another was unceremoniously snuffed out. Among the mangled and deformed gods, one of bodily perfection stood out, dark dress churning as she killed, pitchfork dripping with mortal blood. The sight of Hades was a knife to his gut, and Zeus' hand shot to his mouth to trap the horrified cry. Witnessing her annihilate without remorse, even all these miles away, constricted his heart, and a single tear slid down Zeus' face as he observed what was becoming of the beautiful woman he had once loved.

Zeus did not have to watch long, for almost as quickly as the slaughter began, it ended. A hollow silence filled his mind where the prayers had been, and the land that had once been teeming with life was nothing but a blaze of scorching red flames. Zeus looked to the Griffin, hoping that this devastating sight would be the motivation the beast needed to aid them, but the creature only made his way back to the nest.

"The Old Ones are certain death," the Griffin spoke into Zeus' mind. "I cannot help you. I will take my chances with my mountain. It is not easily scaled, and that will be my defense."

"I hope you are right," Zeus said, sorrow and disappointment clouding his voice. "But I am afraid we are all doomed." With that, he started the long and treacherous trek down empty-handed, the pain in his body the only thing gained on this mountain.

XXII

Far below the treacherous mountain face where Zeus risked life and limb in his descent, Kerberos had escaped the bonds of the Underworld, released from the tether that chained him to Hell. Perhaps it was Hades' absence that allowed him to break through to earth's surface unaided, or perhaps it was her tasking him with protecting the entire race of Olympians, but either way, Kerberos stood alone and free on the grass. His journey to earth, though, was not that of escape. It was one of desperation. The Old Ones had descended Olympus bent on destruction and carnage, devastating every living thing in their path. The trail of blood left in their wake was thick and wide, its overpowering scent what the god-killer tracked.

It cut through the land and lives alike, and Kerberos followed, hunting the hunters. His three noses guided his steps toward that which he pursued. The aroma of power filled his snouts, but there was one strength he sought; one scent he hunted. Kerberos had come for Hades, and her dark power hung heavy in his nostrils. He was gaining on her, and when he found her, Kerberos would drag his mother back to Hell away from the evil that had such a deep-rooted hold on her.

Before long, his incredible sense of smell and powerful body caught up to the bloodthirsty war party. Kerberos stalked the Old Ones carefully, taking stock of every peril both they and the terrain presented. Not much in this world gave him pause, but the threat these old gods posed was unprecedented. It was no wonder the three greats of Olympus cowered in his Underworld. Not even the gods of the skies, seas, and the afterlife compared to those he hunted, which is why Kerberos tracked them alone. If there was one living that could withstand their crazed rule, it was he, the god-killer. He had slaughtered a Titan centuries ago. Perhaps these vile deformities would be ended with the same ease.

Lurking in the shadows, Kerberos bided his time for the perfect moment. The Old Ones were blind to his presence, a testament to the power churning through his hellish being. His crouched form readied to attack, coiled muscles burning with tension. Death and destruction surrounded this city, a cacophony of pain bombarding his ears, yet he waited. Kerberos remained as the ground bled red and the air choked with putrid smoke. He listened as the sound of annihilation rose to a pinnacle, waiting for it to mask any noise he would produce. Kerberos knew not how long he lingered, but time meant nothing. How many centuries had he been left to rot, chained above the Winding Staircase of Tartarus? He could bide his time now for the god he loved most.

As the carnage and chaos spread, Hades drifted closer to his concealment. The god-killer was deliberate in his positioning, choosing not to lie in wait where she was, but where she would be. And after countless lives lost and blood shed, Hades was before him, blocked from the Old One's sight by the burning building. The dog's muscles twitched in anticipation, and with a deadly, terrifying speed, Kerberos launched into the street, slamming into Hades with crushing force. Their figures hurtled into the thick smoke, severed from view.

They careened through the streets, tumbling limb over limb as his momentum drove them. Hades screamed in rage as they catapulted over the dirt, twisting desperately to free herself from the bonds of Kerberos' body, yet the dog's three heads and spiked tail caged her in, unrelenting in their hold.

Hades swung the pitchfork downward and pierced its base deep into the earth. With all the strength she possessed, she gripped the metal impossibly tight, forcing her body to remain where it was staked. Her joints popped and groaned as she was ripped from Kerberos' hold. His three fanged heads plummeted toward the dirt from the force of her departure, and he crashed, flipping over himself with a massive thud.

Growling in outrage, Kerberos' claws dug into the earth's flesh as he stood. With a three-throated snarl, he lunged for his mother, intent on claiming her once again, but Hades skillfully sidestepped his careening mass and swung the pitchfork. The ancient metal connected with his neck and sent him sprawling off balance. Infuriated, the god-killer locked his legs and skidded to a jarring halt, fangs bared in wicked anger. She wanted to do this the hard way. So be it.

Without warning, Kerberos shot forward. His six piercing eyes studied the pitchfork, and just when he was upon her, Hades swung it with deadly accuracy. Kerberos was prepared this time, and with a lightning whip of his tail, the vicious spikes at its end caught the metal with a resounding clang. The momentum careened him forward as the weapon ripped from Hades' fingers, and his solid chest barreled into his mother. Hades grunted as she flew backward through the air, but before her back could collide with the dirt, dark webs of smoke unfurled and engulfed her.

Hades re-appeared behind Kerberos an instant later, scrambling for the discarded weapon. Pebbled dust embedded itself beneath her nails with scraping insistency, but Hades ignored the filth, not halting until the pitchfork was within her grasp. She swung it around and plunged it toward the dog's ribs. Kerberos whipped his tail in a lagging response, but her aim was true. She would crush him. Kerberos' jaw desperately clamped down on the striking bident with a resounding clang and painfully wrenched it to a halt. Metal jarred his fangs and sliced into his soft gums, but he held fast, refusing to let it penetrate his body.

The ring of metal rattling against teeth hung in the air as Hades' free elbow crashed into Kerberos' eye socket. The dog howled in pain and recoiled. The pitchfork still clutched in his bite tore from her fist, and in one fell swing, he flung it far from her grasp. Hades launched herself after it, but barely made it past the god-killer, when she was shoved to the ground. Her chest slammed painfully into the dirt as Kerberos' paw pressed down atop her back. His razor-sharp claws burrowed into the soft flesh, and Hades' ribs groaned under the pressure. Her lungs lost their breath in ragged waves as she surged for freedom, but Kerberos's powerful body only crushed her to the earth.

Pain shot through Hades' skull, and as it seared her brain, an idea whispered in the back of her mind. Something buried deep begged to be freed. The pain prohibited her thoughts from taking a tangible form, but something was there, nagging… calling to her. Something forgotten pleaded to be remembered.

As Hades lay there, Kerberos bent and seized each of her shoulders with massive jaws, careful not to pierce the soft flesh with his fangs. He gently lifted Hades off the ground, and ebbing power began to circle them. He had captured his prey, and to Hell he would drag her.

Suddenly the door in Hades' mind swung closed, and whatever had been struggling to tunnel its way to the surface disappeared, the realization of the dog intentions locking it away behind the iron gate of madness. Survival overthrew her instincts, demanding escape from the deadly jaws, and Hades threw herself forward. Kerberos' teeth slashed through her flesh as she pulled free. His fangs tore her shoulders into fleshy ribbons. The carved wounds flooded red, and Hades gasped with blinding agony as fat droplets of blood poured over her perfect skin. Crimson seeped into the dirt like a fatal, blooming flower. The expanding blemishes distorted as her fingers scored the soil. Her soaked palms pushed her up with an unsteady pitch, and Hades brandished the pitchfork with a tooth-bared snarl.

Blood dripping from his jaws, Kerberos leapt for his mother at the same instant she flew at him. Their bodies collided with a force that shook the earth, sending him careening backward. The dog's spiked back struck the ground and carved a gouging wound as he skidded to a stop, and Hades was above him in a second. The pitchfork slashed across his middle head without warning, shredding two deep scourges in his leathered hide. His roar echoed through his chest with a reverberating tremor as his teeth closed around the weapon with a sickening clang.

Hades released the metal with one hand and crashed her fist into Kerberos' snout. The gouges on his cheek seared in pain as her knuckles connected, but his enraged growl was ripped from his tongue by a second relentless punch. His teeth loosed on the bident's staff, and it was all the opportunity Hades required. With ferocious speed, she pulled the pitchfork back before bringing it down hard to cleave more flesh from his face. Kerberos retaliated with a whip of his spiked tail lashed against her spine. It pained him to hurt her, but she had to be stopped. Blood spurted as his spikes flayed Hades wide, and Kerberos smashed her forehead with his unforgiving skull. The force sent her sprawling to the bloody mud, but the god of death was swift in her retaliation. Hades' heel slammed into his exposed throat as her hip collided with the earth and stole any victory his blow might have claimed.

The dog coughed, gagging at the choking sensation seizing his larynx. The pitchfork was at his throat in seconds, and in one fell swoop, Hades rolled to her feet, pinning him to the dirt. Prostrated before his god, Kerberos writhed trapped under the bident's uneven curve. He begged for air as Hades crushed his breath, yet her brutal strength denied him.

"We will crush all who oppose us beneath our heels," Hades said in a voice Kerberos had never heard from his beloved mother. "All will kneel, but you will die. I will rip your heads from your body." Kerberos froze unable to move. His six eyes opened wide in terror, not at her viciousness, but at her words... those words.

A snarl drifted over the city's dying sounds, and Kerberos snapped his side head around in horror to see the fanged god crawling through the ash on all fours. Kerberos growled in panic, body bucking, but Hades held firm. He could fight her, but not all of them, not at the same time. And as the Old One crept closer, massive tongue licking his razor rows of teeth, Kerberos knew his plan had failed. This fanged deformity would devour his flesh as Hades pinned him down as a sacrifice. Kerberos had come for his queen, not to destroy the host of madness that consumed the earth, and in that moment, he knew all was lost. He had failed her, the mother who had freed him, the god he pledged fealty to. Not even he, the mightiest of the god-killers, could bring Hades home.

The fanged god drew up to Kerberos salivating and crazed, and in one final act of retaliation, Kerberos shot his head out and seized hold of the monster's ankle. With a powerful snap of his jaws, Kerberos bit down, and hot blood spurted over his tongue in vile streams. The Old One screamed, bellowing for all his brothers to hear, yet the dog only sunk his teeth further into the leg's flesh until fangs crunched against bone. With a yank, Kerberos severed the fanged god's foot from his leg. All the while, the Old One howled, sacred blood pouring over the dirt, and Kerberos spit the depraved blood from his mouth and took one last look at his mother. He saw a shadow of a monstrous shape looming behind her and almost did not notice the pitchfork before it was too late. Hades brought the weapon down for the kill, for the annihilation of what she once loved so dearly. Hellhounds cannot cry; their eyes cannot shed tears of sorrow, yet as the queen Kerberos loved with an unholy fierceness prepared to snuff out his life, moisture blurred his vision. Kerberos' last sight of the mother he adored was obscured by his anguish and tarnished by her hatred, yet he paused to commit her face to memory. Then Kerberos vanished, his body sucked back to Hell.

Hades screamed, a visceral, savage rage bellowing deep from her belly. Slick crimson coated her arms and poured over her skin like blood spilled over an altar. The fanged god's blood bathed her feet as his severed limb pumped hot spurts from his veins. Birthed of terror and smoke, the horned god settled behind her. He slowly lifted a gargantuan palm to Hades' shredded shoulders and with a jolt of power, sent his life force into her. Cell by cell, her body knit back together until all traces of damage erased, unblemished once more. Only then did Minotaur bend and grasp the detached foot from the dirt. He unceremoniously shoved the jaggedly torn flesh against the lesser god's stump. In a matter of moments, he, too, was whole, the only sign of his turmoil being the red seeping into the earth.

In the Underworld, Kerberos crawled to a dark corner of sand and curled up to nurse his shredded face. He wanted nothing more than to lie on Hades' bed. The soft mattress would comfort his aching body. Her scent was still woven into the sheets, but Kerberos could not bear to be seen defeated, nor did he deserve such comfort after his failure. So, in the dirt he lay, panting in pain.

Kerberos was only alone for a few moments when the sound of padding feet drifted into his ears. He bared his teeth, resenting the intrusion, but the footsteps continued until Chimera rounded the boulder he huddled behind. The massive lion surveyed the dog, and a purring growl escaped his lips. Against his nature, Chimera sank to the sand, careful to avoid the razor spikes, and curved his body around the dog's back. With a lazy yawn, Chimera settled his monstrous head on the ground and shut his eyelids.

Kerberos stared at the lion for a long while, yet Chimera slept, rumbling snores escaping into the air. Weak and exhausted, Kerberos gave up fighting and lowered his heads next to the lion's and closed his eyes. Chimera's warmth encircled him, his power feeding Kerberos' healing, and the two god-killers rested at peace with one another for the first time in history and most likely for the last.

XXIII

Hades paced earth's bank of the River Styx, eyes boring through the impenetrable fog toward the realm that lay beyond. Not a shade was to be found on the bleak shore. Even the dead hid from her, subjecting themselves to endless wandering instead of being ferried across if only to evade the violence of the dark queen. Opposing pressure wafted over the water, pushing up against her power. Kerberos was blocking all entrances into the Underworld, just as she had tasked him to do, and standing here on the riverbank, Hades could feel his resistance brush against her skin in defiant waves. Normally his presence was a great comfort, but now with her irises glazed in rage and her pitchfork coated in blood, she wanted nothing more than to force past the hellhound's iron will and rip out his throats.

With a whoosh of air and a soft thud, a presence landed behind Hades, and her murderous stare shifted to the intruder. The monstrous horned god strode down the grey sand toward her, and after holding his gaze for a moment, she turned back toward the treacherous Styx.

"This is where the cowards are hiding," Hades said of the Olympians, "just beyond the water and fog."

"Then ferry us across, and we shall take them."

"No," Hades said, which caused the massive god to turn his eyes toward her, death in his glare.

"Can you not feel that?" Hades asked unfazed by his menace. She lifted a hand and pushed her bloody fingers through the smog. It drifted as if to clear a way for her, but almost as quickly as it dispersed, it folded back in on itself. "The Underworld resists anything that is not either dead or its own. It will deny us entrance, and while I can force its hand and bring us to the distant shores, there is a host of monstrosities there. There are god-killers beyond these waters, and the three greats of Olympus who will not be so easily defeated. You took Olympus in one fell swoop with little damage to your army. The Underworld will offer more of a challenge while we are still regaining our strength, but it will not be long until we are unstoppable. Now is not the time. It is too soon."

"I thought the monsters of the deep answered to you, god of death?"

"It is not me they will attack," Hades said, turning to glare icy eyes at her companion. "They will grant me passage willingly. It is you they will try to kill. They still answer to that imposter who sits on my throne, and they may stand with him if we invade. It is better to bide our time until I am strong enough to rip control from him. We want the beasts fighting on our side, not against us."

"We wait then," the horned god finally conceded. "Those imposters have nowhere to go. They will remain trapped here until we are ready; until it is too late for them, but the moment we are fully what we used to be, I expect you to ferry us… or I will use your body as a raft to bear me across this death."

At his words, Hades' eyes narrowed in contempt, and holding his gaze with an icy stare, she bent slowly to the river. The horned god shot out an arm, his large palm slamming into her chest to halt her descent, but Hades merely looked at him and continued reaching for the dark waters. Her dirty fingers plunged into the flowing current, and the Old One watched in amazement as she scrubbed the blood from her skin. Her flesh remained pure and unharmed submerged in the poison river, and all the while, Hades held his gaze in defiance, as if to prove his threats were hollow.

Once the water had carried away the last remnants of carnage, Hades rose, droplets falling back into the current. Shaking her hands of the excess water, she watched with a cold glare as a drop flung from her fingers and landed on the horned god's bare wrist. The circle of flesh bubbled and burned, marking a small trail of red and blistered skin as it rolled from his arm. He did not flinch in pain or utter a single syllable. He only held Hades' defiant stare as she gripped the pitchfork and turned to walk away. He may be the king of the almighty gods, but Hades was the god of death, and she had made it clear that he was not to forget that.

BATTERED, bruised, and aching in ways he did not know gods could ache, Zeus appeared on the banks of the River Styx and prepared to call to Alkaios to pull him from earth's shore to the Underworld's when a movement caught his eye. Turning his head, Zeus swore under his breath and hit the sand, flattening his massive form as if he could sink into the earth. The barren shore offered no coverage, and so he lay perfectly still in the sand and hoped the wafting fog would hide him.

Prostrate and frozen, he barely breathed as he watched Hades bend toward the river and plunge her hands into the poisoned water despite the giant god's attempt to stop her. Zeus held his breath, but neither of them seemed to notice him as he lay motionless on his back. He was at the water's edge, but his need to remain hidden outweighed the discomfort at being so close to the burning tide. He could not let them see him, not here alone on the earth's bank of the Styx. So instead, Zeus' body stilled, willed to be as stone.

He watched, out of the corner of his eye, the interaction between Hades and the Old One. Zeus had not seen their king so close before, and his stomach turned at the sight of the blood-drenched horns atop a monstrous hulk. The seemingly half man and half bull was larger than any god Zeus had witnessed. The horned monstrosity towered over Hades, a hulking giant not only in size but demeanor. His power permeated the air about him, consuming every inch of space and making him appear gargantuan, larger than he actually was, yet this did not seem to faze Hades. As best as Zeus could see from this distance, Hades appeared in control of their conversation, and despite himself, Zeus felt relieved at that. Regardless of her betrayal, he could not bear the thought of these vile gods inflicting their own cruel brand of torture on her.

After long moments without breath, Zeus' sore lungs burned hot, but as he watched in total stillness, Hades and her colossal companion turned and walked off, swallowed whole by the fog. With a pained gasp, Zeus pulled cool mist into his inflamed lungs and sat up, wiping sand from his skin. He called silently to Alkaios for entrance, and in a matter of seconds, black smoke crawled up the dismal sand and snatched him from the shore.

A moment later he stood in the Underworld just outside the fortress. The ever-shifting terrain was uninhabited, and Zeus turned to enter the citadel when Alkaios' broad figure came barreling out of the door.

"Where have you been?" Alkaios spat as he pushed Zeus further into the Underworld as not to be heard by any inside. "You have been gone for over a day, vanished without a trace."

"I do not answer to you," Zeus said, trying to sidestep Alkaios, but the king of the depths proved too fast. He lunged forward and settled himself before Zeus, blocking the path with his hulking frame.

"In this realm, you do. When my power and my beasts are the only reasons we remain, you will answer to me."

Zeus tried to elbow past again, but Alkaios simply reached out and shoved the god's chest with bruising harshness.

"Whether you like it or not, the three greats must act as one," Alkaios said, leaning threateningly into Zeus' face. "A unified front and the creatures of the deep are the only hopes we have at survival. When you disappear without a trace, you leave all of us to worry you are dead. If you die, if Poseidon or I die, any shred of hope we have disintegrates. If they take you, or your body is left somewhere unknown to bleed out, we cannot risk a rescue. The moment we step over the Styx's border, we are nothing but easy targets. So, while you are under my protection, I will know where you are. Now I ask you again, where were you?"

"He went to request help from the Griffin," came a voice when Zeus refused to answer. Both gods' heads snapped around to see Poseidon walking toward them.

"And you did not think to tell me this?" Alkaios growled at Poseidon, who only shrugged his shoulders as if to ask, 'what was I supposed to do?'

"The Griffin?" Alkaios turned back to Zeus with a flicker of hope. "Will he help us?"

"No," Zeus said in disgust.

"No?" Poseidon asked incredulously.

"It is not his fight."

"Not his fight?" Poseidon questioned, stepping forward. "Does he not see how the world burns? Does he think they cannot breach his mountain? Olympus was not safe; how much less so is his peak?"

"He has survived in solitude for centuries, far removed from the affairs of earth and its gods," Zeus said. "He sees no reason to become involved now." Alkaios opened his mouth to speak, but Zeus turned his harsh features toward him, cutting his words off before they could pass his lips.

"And as for your traitorous wife," Zeus said, tone bitter, "she brought an Old One to the River Styx's shore. How long before she breaches its waters and lays waste to this desolate realm? We should have let Medusa turn her to stone in the beginning and save us all from this certain doom." Zeus knew full well how his words would wound. He did not wish Hades to become a statue, but after the fruitless trek up the mountain, he was seething. Anger coursed through him, and he had no one to unleash his wrath on save the man who had stolen Hades from his life. "Perhaps we should have Medusa petrify her now," Zeus continued, driving the final blow home, "and be done with that…"

He never finished his sentence, for suddenly his head cracked sideways, a punishing impact igniting his jaw in pain. Zeus stumbled backward and glanced up in time to see Alkaios hurtling toward him. He barely was able to raise his hands before Alkaios' mass barreled into him, sending them both colliding with the dirt. Torso over limbs, they rolled until Alkaios shoved his heel into the ground and stopped himself on top of Zeus' crumpled body. He wasted not a moment and pulled back his fist, driving it hard into Zeus' nose. A crazed rage filled Alkaios' eyes as his knuckles connected, and he lifted his other hand and drove it down on the prone god's jaw. Alkaios could not bring himself to stop. He kept pounding, blood spitting to freckle his raging cheeks.

Alkaios was not sure how many punches he landed when he felt arms clutch his chest and haul him off. Vaguely, he heard Poseidon begging him to stop, but he was in such a blind rage, the pleading god barely registered. Alkaios roared, struggling to free himself from Poseidon's iron restraint when his face exploded in pain, and both men tumbled backward. Zeus recoiled his fist and launched himself forward again, but the king of the Underworld broke Poseidon's hold and thrust the heel of his palm at his attacker. The blow connected with Zeus' ribcage, and the punishing crack forced Zeus to choke on his own breath.

Alkaios seized the opening Zeus' incapacitation provided and delivered an elbow to Poseidon's ribs. The impact ruptured the blood vessels beneath the god of the seas' perfect skin, and he loosened his restraining hold. Alkaios bolted in temporary freedom only to be punched in the face. His head snapped backward, and his eyesight blurred for a moment, clearing in time to see Zeus' deadly aim closing in for a second punishment.

Alkaios roared, the agony of his sorrow bursting from his soul, and he caught Zeus' hand with brutal speed and crushed it. The trapped knuckles popped and groaned under the constricting pressure, and despite Zeus' thrashing attempts to wrench free, his hand was a prisoner to the inescapable grip. Spit flew from his lips as anger boiled in his veins. Zeus would have this insolent debauchery gutted for this, and in his rage, he never saw the fist aimed for his gut. The blow was so violent nausea overtook him instantly. Zeus heaved as Alkaios made contact. His stomach threatened to embarrass him and spill its meager contents, but he willed his body to obey his control. With a blind bellow and gasping breath, Zeus dove forward. The gods' foreheads cracked together with bone-jarring force, and both men stumbled backward dazed.

Zeus spat blood to the dirt and wiped his mouth. Anger boiled in his veins. Alkaios had publicly taken Hades' name but was nothing more than a born mortal, yet with the exception of Poseidon, he was stronger than any other Zeus had fought. It enraged him, and with all frustration and hopelessness pent up inside him, he was determined to put Alkaios in the ground.

Zeus flew forward, but Alkaios was faster, hurtling into Zeus' ribcage. Zeus grunted as his breath was shoved from his lungs and then again as his spine slammed to the earth. He ached from his climb up the Griffin's mountain, and the brutal impact crippled his muscles in cramping pain. Stunned, Zeus sputtered and writhed on the unforgiving terrain.

Long seconds of breathlessness rushed past, and when he finally regained control of his extremities, Zeus struck out without aim, hoping to connect with any part of his opponent's body. His fist cracked finely muscled ribs, and Alkaios roared in pain at the punishing blow. The agony did little to stop him though, and he prepared to strike the prone hulk called king.

But the punch never fell, for just as Alkaios was about to attack, the entire Underworld shook. The ground pitched violently, and both bloody gods froze. Their eyes shot to where the River Styx flowed hidden beneath the fog. They waited there, Zeus flat on his back; Alkaios' fist raised. For a moment, not a sound or a movement broke the peace, but then the thunderous boom convulsed again. This time it thundered more savagely than the first, almost deafening to the ears. Alkaios slowly twisted his head down and met Zeus' alarmed gaze. They held each other's panicked stare for a horrifying breath before Alkaios bolted to his feet, their quarrel instantly forgotten. They both looked to Poseidon as the rumble increased, who reached a helping hand down to his brother's prostrate form, and an echoing explosion ricocheted throughout Hell.

There was no peace after that earth-shattering violation. The shaking did not cease, and the echo of monsters desperate to fracture the gates of Hell, the determined banging of those clawing to break their way in, did not silence.

XXIV

Kerberos was the first to burst through the fortress' doorway, his spiked back raised in aggression. Power rippled off his body, an opposing force resisting the intruders at Hell's threshold. His three monstrous throats snarled with terrifying viciousness as he bolted through the trembling terrain with a roaring Chimera hard on his heels. The lion's paws slammed into the ground as he thundered after the god-killer, and both monsters disappeared into the fog.

Zeus shot a glance at Alkaios' concerned features, and as if by an unspoken agreement, they simultaneously launched into a run after the beasts.

"The Old Ones," Alkaios yelled over the quaking earth, "they are trying to force their way in." As if in answer to his words, the Underworld pitched, heaving like a retching stomach and causing him to lose his footing. Overtaking him, Poseidon lunged forward and seized Alkaios by the elbow and hauled him back to his unsteady feet.

"We have to aid Kerberos," Alkaios said, nodding in thanks as they barreled toward the river. "He may be the only thing that can keep them out."

"How do we know he is not rushing to his mother?" Zeus asked as the fog thickened around them.

"Hades freed him from the shackles that bound him above Tartarus," Alkaios said over the deafening thundering of the Old Ones. "He is not so eager to return to slavery, even if it is his mother who holds the chains."

The ground shook again, sending the three greats pitching forward, stumbling for solid footing. A snarl echoed over the banging at Hell's gates, and Alkaios angled toward the sound of the god-killer's voice. Through the mist, he careened, unable to see more than a few inches in front of him. It was as if the river itself was trying to block the first gods' entrance.

Blindly, Alkaios forced a path over the rocky terrain, unfurling his power to search for Kerberos. Black tentacles of smoke twisted through the air in dark contrast to the grey of the mist until they found their mark. The clawing fingers of death embodied encircled the dog, winding their way around his muscular body before plunging into his leathery hide. With a roar, Kerberos lunged forward, baring his protruding fangs. His claws dug deep into the drab riverbank and absorbed the strength Alkaios' darkness fed him. The force rippling off him hung tangible in the fog as he barred entrance to all who sought access to his sacred ground.

Alkaios skidded to a stop in the sand and without hesitation slammed his palm into Kerberos' side. Power jolted as their skin collided, and the god-killer's energy surged forward, pushing back the smog in a violent heave.

"Lay your hands upon him!" Alkaios bellowed at Zeus and Poseidon as the crashing across the river grew, all of Hell shaking at the fists of the almighty deformed gods banging at the gates.

"Do it!" Alkaios screamed when neither brother moved. "He needs to feed off us!" Both Zeus and Poseidon stared in terror at the massive beast planted at the river's edge.

"Now!" Rage and strength laced Alkaios' voice, and both gods lunged for the dog. With great trepidation, Zeus stretched out a hand and slid his fingers around one of Kerberos' spikes. The beast's back flinched at the contact, but his focus remained across the river, ignoring the violation of his space. Instantly, Zeus felt power rush through him and seep into the beast. Kerberos' hide twitched, and snarls rumbled deep in his throats.

Seeing his brother take hold of the god-killer without repercussion, Poseidon pressed his fingers to the dog's protruding hipbone. At his touch, Kerberos roared, unnatural energy flowing through him as he shielded the Underworld from their enemies. At his voice, the fog shuddered, pushed back by the waves of terrifying strength rippling off him, and for the first time since the Olympians had sought refuge in the Underworld, earth's shores were visible across the poisoned waters.

And there she stood in all her dark glory, the breeze tossing her hair about her gorgeous face. Malice in her eyes. Hades' cold expression met Alkaios' in a defiant stare as the fog began to roll back over the current, and his stomach knotted painfully at the sight. Kerberos flinched beneath his hand, and Alkaios knew the same knife that carved into his heart also plunged deep into the dog's. He wanted nothing more than to open his arms and call his wife home, to forgive all her bloody transgressions, but Kerberos sensed Alkaios' momentary weakness and forced a wave of resistance over the Styx. The mist folded in on itself, slowly obscuring Hades' withering gaze. The instant before she vanished from view, an imposing shadow shifted beside her, and through the thickening cloud, two massive horns pierced the air.

And the whole of the Underworld heaved at his deafening bellow.

THE BOATHOUSE PITCHED VIOLENTLY, the river clawing at its dock in hungry waves. Charon's boat reeled as the current fought against it, water vaulting over the sides in search of living flesh to burn. Charon lunged out of the water's vengeful path. The Styx had already claimed him in another lifetime, but too much was now at stake to allow it to reclaim him; too many people he refused to leave behind.

Charon threw himself to the rear of the ferry, pulling his feet from the sloshing water, but his weight landed heavy and tipped the boat dangerously in the bucking waves. He fumbled for balance in a desperate attempt to remain above water, but the Underworld boomed; a violent shaking that sent him careening at an alarming speed toward the dock. With a mighty lunge, Charon's fist seized the rough wood of his home, but his hand had barely closed, when the river lurched, wrenching the craft downriver. The ferryman roared as his body slammed into the dock's splintered edge. His feet hung precariously over the turbulent waves as the boat disappeared, racing down the Styx, but that did not matter. Alkaios could recall it if they survived the gods at their gate, and Charon was determined to survive the poison waters that clawed to consume him.

He flung his free hand over the dock's edge and dug his fingers into the wood's crevasses, grasping for even the smallest hold. His fingertips slipped as he heaved to keep his body from returning to a watery grave, but the roar of the Old Ones ripped through the air, jarring the trembling dock. Charon fumbled his precarious grip and plummeted deathward, losing what little ground he had gained. His fingernails tore where they clawed for a splinter of salvation. The damp wood fractured beneath his palms, descending him to his suffering finale when a hand clamped under his arm and jerked his weight to a halt. Charon's eyes shot up through the deafening air and landed on Ioanna crouched above him. Her knees burrowed into the dock as her small hands clutched his arms, face pinched with exertion.

"Climb!" Ioanna demanded over the crashing of the deformed gods. Charon groaned and hoisted himself up as his wife pulled with clutching fingers. His knee swung over the edge, and he scrambled over the wood until he was kneeling before the woman he loved with an excruciating fierceness. Charon wanted to envelop her in his arms, but the panicked look distorting Ioanna's face froze him to his bones. Charon reached out and grabbed hold of her bent thighs and opened his mouth to console her when he realized it was not him she fixated on. Ioanna's fixed gaze peered over his shoulder toward earth's shore, and slowly Charon twisted his head. The impenetrable smog had parted ever so slightly, splitting enough to see the shadowy masses on the distant bank. There, dark and immobile, her form almost obliterated by the thickening mist, stood Hades. Charon's stomach dropped at the sight of her hollow eyes as they stared piercingly upriver at her family turned enemies, and just as the fog swallowed the vision of her whole, horns speared the haze, cutting the fog into ribbons before disappearing.

Clotho, Lachesis, and Atropos' cries cut through the vibrating air. Their tiny lungs screamed their panic, and Ioanna caught Charon's gaze. Without a word, the parents scrambled to their feet and clamored inside. Charon cleared the doorway first and scooped up two of his infants, cradling his daughters in a muscled embrace. Ioanna bent behind him and snatched up their third babe. Her thin arms encircled her daughter, and Ioanna pressed her lips soothingly to the small forehead clutched to her breast.

"Mother is here," Ioanna cooed as their daughters' wails continued, and their terrified hysteria mixed with the unearthly crashing of those monstrosities banging at Hell's door. Ioanna clung to her daughter as she thrust herself against Charon in search of the strength that oozed from his warm body.

"I should go help Alkaios," Charon said, voice loud above

the writhing Underworld and the cries of his terrified children. "He will need all our aid to keep these old gods at bay."

"No!" Ioanna shifted to block their home's exit. "I forbid it." Her panic incited fresh screams from the child in her arms, the tiny cry rivaling the cacophony of the turmoil at Hells' gates. "That Olympian will see you killed."

"And if the Old One's breach our defense, they will see us all killed," Charon argued still clutching his daughters against his chest.

"I lost you all those years ago!" Ioanna leapt for her husband and pressed her body as close to his breast as she was able, their children the only barrier between them. "I will not lose you now if it gains us nothing. No, Charon, you will not leave this house. Not unless our king himself calls upon you."

At her words, the Underworld fell suddenly and eerily silent. Both Ioanna and Charon stared frozen and wide-eyed at one another, their ears ringing with silence. Even their daughters swallowed their cries as if waiting with bated breath for the crashing at the gates to resume, but it did not. The quiet held, and the ground stilled. The Titan sidestepped his wife and rushed out to the dock. The Styx resumed its normal flow toward the blazing depths, and even the oppressive fog lifted infinitesimally.

"What happened?" Ioanna asked hesitantly as she followed her husband out into the open. Charon's head twisted and met her gaze before he turned back to the rushing water.

"I believe," he said haltingly, tone uncertain, "they have left."

"WHY WOULD they leave with such sudden haste when they gave such little effort?" Zeus asked Alkaios incredulously. His fist still gripped Kerberos' spike. "They knocked at our threshold, but they failed to even attempt a crossing. Could the sight of the god-killer have deterred them so?"

"No," came Poseidon's shaken voice. The god of the seas cautiously lifted his hand from Kerberos's side and took a long step back from the beast. "This was a warning. They want us to know they have found us, and that they will come. They were sowing their last seeds of terror, showing us we have nowhere left to run, nowhere left to hide. We are trapped prey, and the hunters are coming."

XXV

THE SHORES of the Styx had barely silenced when an onslaught of screamed prayers ripped through the Olympians' minds. The fearful pleas of the dying washed over them in droves, begging the gods to save them from the massacre. The Old Ones had turned from Hell's doorstep and unleashed their fury on the unprotected. Humanity was being snuffed out life by life, and the Olympians were helpless to stop the genocide. Their only consolation was the knowledge that the dead would be ferried to the Underworld where Elysium's heavenly fields awaited them… but for how much longer? Once those deformed gods crossed the river and took for themselves the lives of every last god, what then would prevent the destruction of mankind's final resting place? The Old Ones had reduced Mount Olympus to rubble and ash. How long would it take them to burn Elysium to a hollow skeleton?

"I can't," Alkaios blurted, his panicked voice breaking the silence. "I can't." With eyes wild, he stumbled back from Kerberos as Zeus and Poseidon looked on with concerned expressions, but all he could force from his lips over and over was, "I can't." His body was shutting down, overwhelmed with panic and distress, and before anyone was able to stop him, he disappeared in tentacles of black inky smoke.

Seconds later, Alkaios emerged on earth and watched as the once thriving city was swallowed whole by blood and fire. The screaming prayers flooded his mind, but the longer he stood there helpless to offer aid, the quieter they faded as death overtook their voices. His stomach churned with nausea as his feet stumbled forward. The horribly mutilated dead lay strewn carelessly in the streets. Bodies were ripped apart; limbs separated viciously from torsos; flesh gnawed to the bone. Alkaios gagged and covered his mouth with a calloused palm as he picked his way through the carnage. This was not just genocide, this was demonic. The Old Ones were not slaughtering for power but for pleasure, and it seemed as if killing was not enough for them. They had to mutilate and desecrate as well, lay waste so completely that only ash and bones remained

Alkaios doubled over and clutched his knees fiercely as he sucked in acrid air. Hunched among the dead, his eyes clenched shut as he fought for control. His wife, the woman he loved more than himself, it was her hands that had helped to abolish these lives. Alkaios was no fool. He was well aware of the lives that had been destroyed at Hades' hands, but they were never like this. Never so desecrated. All the souls Hades had ended in her short reign were granted eternal bliss in Elysium in return for their sacrifice, but staring at the disfigured corpses, he knew they would not be granted such amnesty when she reclaimed the Underworld. Their violent end on earth would only be the beginning of the terror these souls would endure; their eternity sacrificed to the mad gods.

A sudden thud jerked Alkaios upright, and the sound of heavy footsteps drifted from behind him. Alkaios snapped his head around, searching for cover, but the footfalls carried the intruder too quickly for him to find refuge. Desperate for shelter, he dropped to the blood-soaked ground and seized the arm of a corpse, flinging it over his torso. Silently, Alkaios apologized to the soul as he further desecrated its flesh and shoved his fist into the gaping deathblow. Still warm blood oozed over his fingers, and Alkaios lifted them to his face and dragged them in rapid strokes down his skin just in time to force his body into deathlike stillness.

"We should have taken them," came a haggard female voice. Alkaios recognized the sound of the three-eyed goddess and kept his eyes motionless in a death gaze. The old woman's figure did not cross his eyesight, but a gargantuan shape filled his vision instead. It was all Alkaios could do not to flinch at the sight of the monstrous god. He had seen shadows of the Old Ones' king, but as he passed, nothing prepared Alkaios for the shock. The horned god was hulking, unnaturally large. His muscular body supported a bull's head, and deadly horns sprouted from his skull. Gore dripped from their peaks, displaying his recent kills. Watching this monstrosity pass sent alarm plunging through Alkaios' gut. How could the likes of Zeus ever compete with such massive power?

"In time," came another feminine voice, this one beautiful and strong. "We do not have long to wait before our reunion solidifies our full potential. Then we will crush their skulls beneath our heels."

Pain ripped into Alkaios' heart at his wife's words. He stared blankly, his eyes glazed over as Hades sidled up to the horned god and shoved the old woman aside. The three-eyed god glowered at Hades, but the king merely stepped sideways to accommodate the dark beauty. Alkaios watched with horrifying realization that Hades had not only been welcomed into their ranks but was exalted. She had thrust aside the woman who seemed to be the king's second and took her place with bloody resolve. This monster bent his ear to Hades' tongue, and she had risen to rule her ancestors. In that moment, Alkaios knew all was lost. All hope that simmered in his chest vanished, evaporating in despair as his wife and the king strode past side-by-side as equals, both covered in the blood of their slaughters. Hades was truly gone, mind taken by the homicidal madness of her people.

Alkaios' breath froze in his lungs, and he lay among the death unable to breathe. His heart struggled within the confines of his chest, erratic in its heaving pain. As if she sensed his thundering organ, Hades turned and looked at the pile of bodies he had buried himself beneath. Her once beautiful eyes were glazed, and she stared at his almost lifeless form, their eyes meeting. Alkaios' heart stopped, all functions of his body frozen in terror. She had seen him. Would he be the next flesh to be skewered upon those blood-soaked horns?

For an excruciating moment, Hades held his gaze, but when Alkaios was sure his life was forfeit, she angled back to her new king and continued through the city streets, disappearing from sight. Her eyes bore no recognition, but how had she not sensed him? Even if Hades no longer remembered the love she cherished so dearly, would she not at least have recognized him as Olympian? Why walk away when she had the chance to rid the world of one of the three greats?

Alkaios bolted upright; the body draped across him flung harshly to the ground. Hades had to have known he was there. Had she let him live? Allowed his survival? Perhaps she was not yet lost to him. Alkaios pulled himself to his feet. He had to follow them, to find and bring her home. He refused to accept this monster was all his wife would ever be.

Alkaios turned and vaulted up the structure behind him. Using the roof as cover, he stalked them from above. Careful to avoid the caving structures and hungry flames, Alkaios leapt from building to building, tracking the blood-soaked woman he loved, but the hulking horned god never left her side. Alkaios stood no chance against this king, but if he could just get Hades alone, perhaps he could stop her.

As if in response to his thoughts, a man flung open the door a house below and stumbled out, body painted in blood and soot. The mortal gulped the fresher air in relief, but it was short-lived. Without breaking stride, Hades hoisted the pitchfork and shoved it into the man's chest, sealing his fate. Blood spat from his lips as the twin prongs ripped free of his flesh, and Alkaios flinched involuntarily at the remorseless expression his wife bore. Blood dripped down the bident's shaft to her fingers, and yet Hades strode on, her glassy eyes harsh and soulless.

Alkaios went numb as he stared at Hades step over the carnage to regain her place beside the monstrous bull. Alkaios took a deep breath, shooting his eyes ahead. The cacophony of death was growing closer. If he did not act now, a whole host of bloodthirsty gods would be upon them, and he would stand no chance. His body aimed for Hades' form below. She was still marginally behind the king, and if Alkaios launched himself at her, he could drag her from here before the horned god stopped him. Alkaios offered up a desperate prayer, to whom he knew not, and vaulted into the air.

He barely made it two inches from the roof, when an arm thudded firmly against his chest. With a grunt, Alkaios was thrown harshly to his back where a small hand clasped over his mouth. With agile speed, a light body climbed atop him and pinned him down, her breast flush against him, desperate to hide. Alkaios struggled beneath the encasing human cage, rage boiling at the disruption to his plan, but the wiry limbs imprisoned him.

"Shhhhh!" came a sharp breath in his ear, and he stilled at the voice. Alkaios' eyes shifted and found Keres' face pushed into his neck. Her nose pressed against his skin, her panicked breathing washing hot over his flesh.

"Let me go." His whisper was demanding, but as Alkaios seized her wrists to cast her from him, a noise from streets below froze their struggle. The horned king's voice rumbled over the raging fire and bloodshed, but the chaos garbled his words.

Neither of them could make out what he said, although Keres was certain it was a response to Alkaios' grunt. She shifted slightly to look Alkaios in the eyes and shook her head no in desperation. They both lay in unblinking silence, frozen in fear that the demonic god below would find them, but after an agonizingly long moment, the sounds of his thudding footsteps receded into the anarchy.

The instant his steps disappeared, Alkaios shoved Keres harshly to the side and vaulted to his feet.

"What are you doing?" he demanded, anger lacing his deep voice.

"Stopping you!"

"Why? I almost had her. I could have brought her back!"

"No, you did not! Do you really think you could have taken her? Especially with that… thing with her? Hades would have killed you, and where would we be then? You are no good to her dead."

"What does it matter if she kills me?" Alkaios' lungs deflated in defeat. "We lost our opportunity to trap them, Olympus fell in minutes, and the Underworld is no longer a safe haven. In a matter of days, Hades will lead her ancestors to our gates, and they will not cease until the river flows red with our blood. We are living on borrowed time, so who cares if I die today trying to get her back? We are already dead."

"Do not say that," Keres begged, despair oozing from her lips. "You cannot give up hope. Not you. There must be something we can yet do?"

"Keres," Alkaios said softly, taking her head in his palms and tilting her face upward. "You know Hades. If she stands against us, we have no chance. We are out of options and out of time. All we have left is to die with dignity when they come. I will not submit to their victory without a fight, and perhaps I might take a few of them with me, but your stopping me today has not saved my life, just prolonged it." And with that, Alkaios turned from her, hands dropping from her cheeks. He walked to the edge of the roof and fell over the side, disappearing into the smoke.

"Alkaios!" Keres' voice wavered. "Alkaios!" she called as loud as she dared, but he did not answer, leaving her alone among the wreckage.

XXVI

The Old Ones had returned to the holy mountain, their lust for destruction satiated, and Hades strode through the ruins of Mount Olympus, the fallen stones of the once proud mountain crushed beneath her feet. The blood of the sacrificed bathed her skin, and she could feel it feeding her power. With each slaughtered soul, her blood pumped stronger within her veins. How much more so would it be when she cleaved the head of that great god of the Olympians from his neck? Hades craved the absolute power that would be hers once the Underworld ran red with the divine. It was only a matter of days now before the Old Ones reigned unopposed, supreme and almighty.

Her body wandered through the charred streets, feet guiding her path as if of their own volition. They twisted and turned through the carcasses of buildings until her journey came to an unexpected rest before a closed door. Hades' eyes marveled at the miraculously un-burnt wood, and a flash of recognition jolted through her brain. Without even realizing it, she was at the door, palm flush against the timber's grain. An overwhelming urge to see what lay on the other side forced her hand, and she pushed, flinging it wide.

Dust floated through the air and into her nostrils as Hades stepped over the threshold, and as her eyes grew accustomed to the dim light, a miraculously unblemished curtain hanging from the large window fluttered into her line of sight. Hades' eyes snapped to it, and that is when it happened. A sharp knife of a spasm ripped through her body emanating from her womb, spidering out through her limbs. Hades screamed and bent over, clutching her stomach as she gasped for breath. Her lungs heaved, sucking in gulps of air as she stood doubled over. The pain barely had time to pass before a second assault burned through her like scalding needles coursing through her arteries. Hades clawed at her stomach and gritted her teeth to stifle a scream. Tears burst into her eyes, and sweat beaded on her brow as she sobbed. The corners of the room began to fade, her vision blurring, and yet the suffering continued. Wave after wave it washed over her, her womb cramping in agony, but the pain ravaging her was nothing compared to the last jolt that seared through her bones like molten metal, absent of mercy. Unable to swallow her screams, Hades' voice cried out in torment as her fingers clutched her abdomen, and without warning, the world went black; her form crashing brutally to the floor.

HADES JERKED AWAKE AS IF ZEUS' lighting had electrocuted her. Alarm crushing her chest like the heel of an enemy, she tried to sit, but the aching in her head forced her back down. Hades clenched her eyes shut and breathed heavily until the pain passed, and when the ache was nothing more than a dull thud, she slowly peeled her eyelids back and looked around, realization hitting her. She was sprawled on the floor in her old room on Olympus, the window that Zeus used to stand at just before her.

Hades lifted a palm, grasping the familiar bed, and pulled

herself into a sitting position. A wave of nausea washed over her, and she lowered her head to the side of the dusty mattress to rest until it passed. How she had ended up on the floor she had no idea, nor why it felt as if someone had bashed in her skull, but she had to get up and find out what was going on. And so, with extraordinary effort, Hades pushed herself to her feet. Unconsciously, her fingers rested on her belly, holding her son's life beneath her fingertips. He was still too small to make a difference in her size, but she could discern his tiny life starting.

With a gasp, Hades' hand flew to her mouth, a broad smile spreading over her lips. She could feel him. Since learning she was carrying Alkaios' son, Hades had yet to sense the child within. She had accepted Medusa at her word, but now... now Hades knew. Joy spread through her heart and tears sprung to her eyes. Her fingers fluttered over her belly, and a small laugh whispered past her tongue. Alkaios, she had to tell him.

Hades rushed for the door when her gaze collided with the carcass of Olympus just beyond the window, and she froze, surveying the smoking ruins. An involuntary gasp burst from her mouth, and she dropped to the ground, pressing herself against the wall beneath the windowsill as if she could hide from the truth outside this room. It all came flooding back like a cresting swell of Poseidon's angered storms, horror replacing the joy she had moments ago. Hades remembered the bloodshed inflicted by her own hands... hands that were still painted red with the blood of the innocent. She recalled the evil of the Old Ones and her betrayal of the people she loved. She had been consumed by her ancestors, placed in a position of power in their ranks, and bile rose up her throat at the thought of what they yet planned.

Bending until her palms rested on the ground, Hades crawled toward the exit. She had to get out of here, had to warn Alkaios. She did not know how, but she would not let her family perish at her own hands.

Hades reached the door and inhaled a steadying breath. She

composed her features into a vile mask and flung her body out into the street. An Old One intoxicated with bloodlust crawled on all fours past the swinging door, canines exposed in a vicious growl at the startling intrusion to his prowl. Hades' first instinct was to recoil from his blood-drenched mouth, but she willed her face to remain impassive. Her ancestors believed her to be one of them, and she could not show weakness. It was her only chance at survival, so Hades turned terrifyingly cold eyes on the deformed god and bared her teeth. The Old One cowered in fear, and Hades calmly walked past him, darkness seeping from her skin. Despite the whispers of dread goading her ears, she drifted slowly until her steps bore her around the corner, but the instant the caved in hallways concealed her from any prying eyes, she bolted into a run, unable to control her uneasiness.

Hades ran through the city, using the smoke and debris as a shield until she came to the once rolling and lush fields. Her vision scanned the surrounding area with panicked speed, but not another soul was to be seen, only the wreckage of a beautiful home she had once cherished. Anxiety seized her brain and paralyzed her muscles, but there was no time for consuming weakness. If she stayed here, welded to this ashen field, she would never leave. The fear would entomb her.

"Move," Hades commanded her overwhelmed senses. Her voice released a ripple effect through her extremities, and bending her knees, she raced over the grass as fast as her thighs would carry her. In a few moments, Hades reached the edge and without slowing, stepped off. Her body plummeted, twisting midair, and Hades shot out a hand to grasp the side of the mountain. Her fingers dug deep into the dirt to slow her fall until her feet slammed into a ledge. Zeus' ledge, his secret only she knew of. The smoke and mist clouded the small ridge, obscuring it from view and rendering all who sought its refuge invisible.

Hades let out a desperate exhale, a breath she had not even known she was holding, and suddenly weak, she sunk to the rock. Her back collapsed against the mountain, struggling not to tremble, but fear, pain, and desperation ate at her muscles. All she could do was shake as tears overflowed her eyes.

Hades was not sure how long she sat there, but eventually the tears dried, and her body stilled. She shifted with a releasing sigh and crumbled forward to her hands and knees. She crawled with dejected fatigue to the edge and breathed deep the pungent air. Far below her perch, earth rested under the impenetrable ceiling of clouds, and as Hades stared into the thick smog of the Old One's ever-present destruction, her soul called out.

THE OLYMPIANS CROWDED the throne room. Their terrified bodies huddled together while the beasts of the Underworld stood watch. After the Old Ones had knocked at Hell's gates, all who sought refuge in the land of the dead had forgone the comforts of private bedrooms in favor of sleeping collectively on the floor of the vast throne room. Alkaios crouched in the far corner of the chamber shrouded in darkness, the flickering light of the torches casting dark shadows on his solitary figure. Keres and Hydra sat with Ioanna and her triplets on a makeshift bed near the thrones. Charon had forced his wife to take their children to the fortress where they would be protected, while he stayed behind on the boathouse far from Zeus' reach. Ioanna had protested at first, but her husband's insistence had been unwavering. Their daughters' lives were too precious to be without protection, for at least here among the Olympians, the three greats stood between the infants and any intruders.

The room was somber. No one dared to speak in tones above a whisper. Weapons were gripped in hands or placed close within reach, and for the first time since the gods sought refuge in the Underworld, no one recoiled when Kerberos or Chimera padded past.

It was impossible to tell the time of day, caged in the darkness, but by the exhaustion wafting throughout the throne room, it was well into the night. Few slept. Most sat, backs to the walls; hands clutching their neighbor's; eyes refusing to rest. The only ones sleeping peacefully were Ioanna's triplets, cradled protectively in Keres', Hydra's, and their mother's arms.

Hydra shifted uncomfortably, careful not to wake the babe resting with innocent peace. Her body felt wrong. At first, she had assumed it was because of the hard floor and the cramping of her muscles due to the child she held, but the longer she sat, the more restless she became. Hydra transferred her weight yet again and released a puff of air from grimaced lips which caught Ioanna's attention.

"Do you want me to take her?" Ioanna whispered as she moved the infant in her arms to her elbow, making space for her sister.

"I am all right. Just uncomfortable."

"If you need a break, I can...." But Ioanna's words were cut off by a sharp cry from Hydra. The crowd of gods and immortals shifted, looking to Hydra, whose face was flushed like a painful sunburn.

"Perhaps you should take her," Hydra panted, standing and walking the few steps to Ioanna. She bent and gently placed the babe in her mother's arms and stepped back as soon as she relinquished the child. Sweat beaded on her brow, a visible shine against her burning skin.

"Are you all right?" Keres studied the flashing white-blue eyes of her friend.

Hydra opened her mouth to respond, but instead of words, a harsh cry escaped.

"Hydra?" From the darkness, Alkaios emerged in long strides with concern thundering his steps, but Hydra's only response was a bellow bursting from her lungs. The whole room collectively jerked back as the woman of snakes began to convulse, her cries those of a body in pain. Alkaios rushed to Hydra and seized her shoulders, and at his touch, Hydra' snake-slit eyes flashed him a plea for help. Alkaios' sight ran over her body in a frantic search for what ailed her but found nothing, yet her voice continued to echo off the towering walls.

Within seconds Zeus and Poseidon were at her side, gripping their weapons.

"What is happening?" Zeus called above her cries.

"I'm not sure…"

"Alkaios," Keres interrupted, her strong tone piercing the chaos. The king of the Underworld shot his eyes to her, and Keres nodded toward Hydra's arm. Alkaios seized the god-killer's elbow and pulled her forearm out in front of him. There, writhing beneath Hydra's skin, was an engorged vein. It heaved and swayed confined in her flesh, and as he watched, it grew thick, rising like a mountain from her wrist.

Just when Alkaios feared it could grow no farther, the vein tore open, and a small black snake shot into existence. Its bloody slickness slapped to the floor with a wet thud while its tongue flicked in an enraged hiss. Zeus and Poseidon jumped backward, giving the snake a wide berth. They knew of these creatures, the punishers of Tartarus. They could not leave the Winding Staircase of Tartarus, yet Hades had unleashed them by binding them to the body of a shade cursed to suffer eternity in torture. These snakes were venomous to all, and they were what made Hydra the third god-killer of the Underworld.

Hydra collapsed, brow damp and breathing heavy. Alkaios clutched her to his chest, staring at the slowly growing serpent on the ground. Its whip-like tail painted streaks of Hydra's blood on the floor like a gory work of art.

"I did not release him," Hydra panted. "Something pulled him from me."

As if in answer to her declaration, black tendrils of smoke began to ebb and flow around the snake. The weaving tentacles engulfed its still growing body, and with a flash of its forked tongue, the animal vanished, the bloody stain on the floor all that was left of the monster.

"It was Hades," Hydra gasped, eyes wide with terror. "She pulled him from me, and I could not stop her."

Hades knelt on the edge of Zeus' hidden ledge, her blood-crusted palms pressed into the sharp rock. Her face peered patiently down the mountainside. The ashen clouds obstructed her vision, yet she waited, hovering over endless air motionless. If any eyes were to land on her, her rigidness would appear as nothing more than a protruding boulder.

The mountain stood sedentary, but far below the clouds' cover, a whisper of movement slithered its way through the vegetation. The higher it climbed, the larger it grew until its mass broke through the ash and surged toward Hades. Its onyx scales writhed over the rock as it reached Hades' outstretched fingers. Its tongue shot out to taste the air as it slid its large head over her skin. A menacing hiss escaped its mouth, and the snake twisted its solid form about her wrist. Snaking up his queen, weaving around her flesh until he intertwined her limbs, his head reared back so that his slit eyes could bore into hers. His tongue flicked out again, and then with a reverent dip of his head, the black scales pressed against Hades' forehead.

XXVII

"Are you all right?" Keres brushed Hydra's hair back from her damp forehead with tender concern.

"What is she doing with it?" Hydra ignored her friend. "Why would she pull the snake from me?"

"Are you sure it was Hades?" Zeus asked, stepping forward while maintaining a wary distance.

"There is no other who could rip a serpent from my veins."

Zeus opened his mouth to speak, but the crowd was shocked into silence when the air exploded. The tentacles of inky smoke permeated the throne room, and with a thud, the snake's immense body appeared from the blackness and plummeted to the floor. He was enormous compared to the small bloody snake that had torn free from Hydra moments before, and rearing as if to strike, his scaled body rose to half a man's height.

Zeus leapt back, but he barely made it a single step before the snake threw himself at his mother. The hiss that wrenched from the serpent's throat pierced the ears of all who watched as he shot through the air. Hydra scarcely had time to register the attack before he was at her breast, body hurtling toward her heart. A cry of alarm escaped her lips as Hydra braced for impact, but just as his scales collided with her skin, the snake turned to smoke and seeped into her flesh.

For a moment, the throne room was silent as all stared at Hydra's chest. All traces of the once venomous monster were gone, and Hydra stumbled on unsteady legs, the force of the dissolving snake knocking her off balance. Her alarmed eyes glanced from Keres' to Alkaios before they clenched shut, and a grimace marred her face. She remained frozen in place; teeth gritted in discomfort; breath heavy and shallow. For long seconds no one moved as Hydra shifted, uncomfortable in her own skin.

Then as suddenly as the snake's attack, her features softened and her eyes shot open, disbelief painted on her beautiful face.

"It's Hades." Hope colored Hydra's voice. "Our Hades," she continued when Alkaios raised his eyebrows. "She is awake."

"What do you mean awake?" Zeus asked.

"The fog of insanity has lifted. She remembers us, recalls who she really is. If she tried to tell us herself, we would have barred her entrance, which is why she pulled the snake from me. Hades lured him onto Olympus, tasking him with carrying a message. She wants to return home and make things right."

"How is this possible?" Alkaios asked as hope surged through him and threatened to overflow from his skin.

"Your son," Hydra stepped closer to her king. "Hades felt him within her. He reminded her of who she is, and she wishes to come here. She will arrive in the dead of night while the Old Ones lie sleeping and will wait to see if we allow her entrance. It is our decision to grant her safe passage to our realm or not, and Hades will respect our judgment."

"Of course, she is welcome!" Alkaios barely allowed Hydra's words to complete.

"Wait!" Zeus interrupted, the suspicious voice of reason.

"This could be a trap. How much easier would our destruction be if we greeted the bringer of death with open arms? I do not think we should allow her entrance. It could be a ploy."

"Hades is not lying," Hydra argued vehemently. "I can feel the truth. My snake touched her skin, and when he rejoined my flesh, there was no malice within him."

"Hades was born from a race of gods that far exceed our power," Zeus said, closing in menacingly on Hydra. How he missed the days of old, when defiance of his words would be crushed under his heel, but here on unfamiliar ground, these monsters held both his and his people's safety in their palms. "Do you think she could not mask her true intentions?"

"This is my wife we are talking about," Alkaios interjected, but neither Hydra nor Zeus batted an eyelid at him.

"You forget, Zeus," Hydra challenged, spitting his name into the air with irreverence, "that the snakes within my veins were birthed in Tartarus, poisonous enough to mute even your heart. I doubt their ancient evil could be so easily tricked."

"I still do not..."

"Stop!" Ioanna screamed, cutting Zeus off mid-sentence. The crowd flinched at the slight woman's outburst. The infants in her arms expanded their lungs and unleashed their tiny hellish fury, and by the rage coloring Zeus' face, those children were the only things keeping him from lashing out at this Underworlder.

"Just stop!" Ioanna placed herself between the arguers. "This division between us will be our downfall!" Zeus parted his lips to interrupt, but the mother only glowered at him before turning her attention to the crowd. "Hades at one time or another has helped each of us. Hydra, Keres, and I owe her everything for the lives that were returned to us. She saved Alkaios' soul from being shredded, and from what we understand of the Old Ones and the Touch of the Gods, she delivered every last one of you from a path of insanity with her sacrifice of power. And if that was not enough, Hades opened the Underworld to you as shelter. Yes, Alkaios is now the Olympian god of death, but we all know who truly rules here. Do you think for one second you would be allowed to live if Hades had not ensured Kerberos, Chimera, or the Styx itself leave you in peace? All in this room owe her our lives, some more than most, and I am one of them. We owe her this, to believe her when she says she comes to put things right. It was her son that woke her, and I know without a shadow of a doubt, that a mother would do anything for her child. If Hades swears on the life within that she is awake, then we will let her return home."

NOT ANOTHER WORD was uttered on the subject, much to the surprise of many, but the small mother who none of the Olympians had ever seen before had put an end to the arguing. So here they lingered, the darkest hours of the night creeping by as if they were allowing a snail to win a race. All were tired, yet not a single person slept, save the triplets whose little fists curled in slumber. Silence hovered over their shoulders, oppressive and ominous as they waited to see if Hades' return would be the trap that destroyed them.

And then the air shifted. A palpable shimmer rippled through it, and in wisps of smoke, Hades appeared. The tentacles began to dissipate, all the while clawing at her blood-crusted flesh, and a wave of absolute power crashed through the chamber. Her disheveled, violent appearance sent a jolt of alarm through the hearts of all who huddled in the throne room, and both Zeus and Poseidon stood with weapons at the ready.

For a moment, no one moved as the smoke diluted, and then with tentative movements, Alkaios broke from the crowd. His eyes pleaded with hope, and at the sight of him, Hades burst into tears. She bolted forward, heels pounding the ground in an urgent rhythm as she launched herself at her husband. Alkaios wanted nothing more than to race to her, but her feet carried her on a collision course with breathless speed, and so he braced himself for impact. In a flash Hades was upon him, her chest slamming his, and her arms were around his neck in a heartbeat like a boa constrictor about its prey. Alkaios enveloped her body in his powerful embrace and stumbled to regain his footing. Hades' strength had doubled, and the blow nearly stripped him of his breath, but it did not matter. Nothing mattered. Only the perfection of this, woman solid and warm in his arms.

Alkaios' strength held her feet dangling above the ground as Hades clung to him. Her violent sobs erupted on his neck as she buried her face against his skin, and the warmth of her tears spread over his throat and down his chest. His breath hitched despite his determination not to collapse into emotions before this judgmental audience. She smelled like rotted flesh and looked even worse, but she was his Hades. Alkaios could tell by the way her eyes shone and how her body felt pressed against his that this was his most beloved wife.

After an eternity passed between them in a single moment, Hades peeled her arms and chest from his, and Alkaios lowered her to the floor. She smiled softly, tears running anew, but his thumbs brushed them from her filthy cheeks in a heartbreakingly tender gesture.

"I am sorry," Hades whispered, but Alkaios hushed her with a needy kiss against her lips. He kissed her deep and long as tears ran down her cheeks and onto his. He could barely bring himself to release her, but he knew here among this anxious crowd he had to, and so he pulled back still holding her beautiful face.

And then Keres, Hydra, and Ioanna were upon them, clutching one another as if Hades had resurrected from the dead. Sobs from all four women flowed freely as they hugged.

None of them ever thought this reunion could be more than a reverie. Their fingers clutched their returned queen, needing to feel her warmth, to assure themselves that her kind and gentle caresses were not a cruel nightmare. All the while, Alkaios welded his palm to Hades' back and refused to part his skin from hers for fear that if he did, she would disappear.

After long heart-aching moments, Hades extracted herself from the loving arms of her family and turned to the crowd of gods, face streaked by tears and filth. To the surprise of all, she smiled and reached out to seize Zeus' palm. Zeus stood shocked still as Hades grasped it and watched with dazed confusion as she stretched her free hand out to Poseidon. Both brothers exchanged a wary glance before Poseidon folded it in his. His brother's action released Zeus' petrified muscles, and he curled his fist around Hades' expectant fingers. Warmth radiated from her dirty skin, but it was the sincerity in her eyes that thawed the barrier of ice surrounding his soul. Brightness glowed in her irises, masking a deep-rooted fear that lurked in hiding, but they were beautiful. Zeus had not seen Hades look at him with such genuine happiness in years, and his grip tightened involuntarily around hers.

"I did not think I would see any of you again," Hades' voice hitched. "Not like this. Not where I remembered all of you." She dropped Zeus' hand when she saw Hera's displeased scowl and with a small squeeze, relinquished Poseidon's in favor of grasping her husband's. She drew it close and pressed it flush against her still flat stomach. "Can you feel him?" she asked hopefully. "He is barely there... but there all the same."

Alkaios hovered, broad palm flattened against her womb for a long moment before he lifted his fingers to her chin. His eyes shone with pure joy as he tilted Hades' face up and pressed a kiss to her forehead.

"I feel him," Alkaios whispered. "Is this possible? Could our son return you from the brink of madness?"

"It did for her ancestors," Medusa answered. Her lingering figure weaved through the sea of bodies until she stood before Hades. "I did not consider this a possibility, but the innocence of an unborn child returned her forefather to his senses. Perhaps it is possible that the pure life within you, Hades, is strong enough to bring you back from the oblivion."

"How long do I have?" Hades asked. "Is this moment only a reprieve from their insanity, or am I fully myself?"

"I could not tell you," Medusa said apologetically. "We are in uncharted territory. Your ancestors did not have time on their side. The Old Ones slaughtered your father shortly after he sealed them in their realm, and they insured his death was final. Your mother was cast to earth where she became mortal in her separation from their dimension, as were all of her descendants until you. I have no answers, but I will say this," she hastily added when she saw the panic creeping through Hades' and Alkaios' eyes. "Your forefather performed the Touch of the Gods with his own hands, while you have not. Your madness was brought on by proximity, not as a punishment for your personal transgressions. You have never shredded a soul. In fact, you saved one when you gave your husband your Olympian power. I never considered this a possibility. I am no god, just a guardian, and am not all knowing, but your spirit is not tainted like theirs. Their evil is not within you, only surrounding you."

"So there is no way to know if I am truly delivered or if this is merely a remission?"

"Only time will tell," Medusa answered truthfully.

"Then we best make the most of the time we have," Hades said, turning from Medusa to the Olympians filling the throne room. "I am here to help. I cannot undo the evil I have unleashed, but I can help bring it to an end. We cannot kill them. They have grown far too strong for that. Not even with my aid could we put them all down, but I still think we can trap them. Any day now they intend to storm the Underworld. We cannot withstand that siege forever, and they must never cross this river."

"We tried that," Zeus interjected. "Athena almost lost her head."

"On Medusa's mountain, yes. They expect that, but I believe with my power, we can hold them in place until our portal opens to drag them back whence they came. They trust me. I can draw them out and deliver them into our ambush."

"You drew them out last time," Zeus said, "but not all came. We have to trap every one of them, especially that horned king of theirs. You say they trust you, but the question is, does he trust you?"

"Yes." Hades' eyes shifted uncomfortably from Zeus to Alkaios. "The horned god… his name is Minotaur, and I can bend his will." She paused and took a deep breath, steadying herself before uttering her next words. "He is my uncle."

"What?" Zeus, Alkaios, and Poseidon blurted at the same time. Keres' and Hydra's lips fell open, while Ioanna blinked rapidly as if an eyelash had violated her eye. Olympians and immortals alike burst into murmurs of surprise as they stared in confusion at the dark queen.

"The three-eyed hag, the woman who prophesied their second coming, she is the king's mother, but she also had a younger son… my father, the Old One who sealed the door with his dying bloodshed," Hades said softly. "They were once what Zeus and Poseidon are now, one a king and one a great. Minotaur ruled the realm of the Old Ones with an iron fist, but my father believed he was far too mighty to serve in his older brother's shadow. He left his brethren, creating for himself a new kingdom, a place that served and answered only to him." Hades paused and looked to Alkaios. The look in her eyes made him want to reach out and silence her. He did not wish to hear this confession. "My father was the first god of death," and at her words, the entire room went silent.

"We originally believed I opened the door to the Underworld because the universe saw me as a fit and just ruler. Medusa claimed I broke the seal because I was the last of the Old Ones, a race of gods whose power was unrivaled. Of course, the seal bent to me. That is not why," Hades said, turning and walking toward the thrones. Suddenly exhausted she had to sit, but instead of climbing to her throne, she sank to the topmost step and looked out at all who listened. Unwilling to be parted from her, Alkaios followed and settled his large frame next to hers.

"In the days when they reigned supreme, Minotaur was the king of the living." Hades reached out and grasped her husband's hand for support. "My father, the lord of death. The Alpha and the Omega. Because of my grandmother's prophecy, the Old Ones were never genuinely dead. They only slept in death until I found the pitchfork and woke them, returning them to their glory. All save my father. Despite being her son, she made sure he would never rise again. Of all of them, he is the only one truly to have perished, hence why the pitchfork passed down to me as well as his power. I took his place, the Old Ones' god of death. When I saved Alkaios, I gave him the Olympian within me, the part Zeus bestowed when he banished me here. That is why he is king of the Underworld, but I kept my father's reign over the Underworld and the dead. At my core, it is who I am."

"The Omega?" Medusa croaked. "That was who cast his pregnant wife from their realm?"

"You did not know it was him?" Hades asked, eyebrows raised.

"No! The Omega was hardly ever seen. He was feared almost as much as Minotaur and spent most of his time... here." She gestured to her surroundings and then in rushed movements, bowed low with reverent grace. "Your majesty."

"There is no need for that," Hades said, appalled that Medusa was bowing.

"Yes, there is." Medusa remained bent with respect. "You are the new Omega, the end and completion of life, and all Gorgons serve the Old Ones. I could not stand by what they became, but I can serve you, Omega. You are the second coming of death, and I swear my allegiance to you."

"Thank you," Hades said with a soft smile. "We will need your skills setting this trap."

"So that is why I always see you at his side?" Alkaios asked as his mind struggled to process the words escaping his wife's lips. "I went to earth, foolishly to retrieve you, and saw you push past your ancient grandmother to take your place next to the horned... Minotaur. You are second only to him?"

"As my father once was, I am now."

The room suddenly vibrated with a growl of three heads, severing all conversations. Hades bolted to her feet as her eyes searched for the owner of that rumbling voice and found Kerberos' hulking frame blocking the room's entrance. He had not been here when she first arrived, and she had feared he had chosen to patrol the Underworld rather than gaze upon her, yet here he stood, spiked back raised in menace.

Mother and dog locked gazes, tension and power radiating from their bodies, and when Hades could no longer contain herself, her feet pushed her from the floor, charging for the three-headed god-killer. As fast as Zeus' lightning, Hades was across the stone and with little consideration to her knees, fell before him. Eyes bursting with fresh tears, she seized Kerberos' massive neck, and her face burrowed into his warm hide where his comforting scent filled her nostrils. Her embrace threatened to strangle him it was so fierce. For a moment, Kerberos froze stiff, unsure of how to react, but after a long minute, he lowered his middle head until it rested on her hair. He wrapped his side heads around Hades to reciprocate her affection, his leathery body enveloping her.

"My darling," Hades sobbed against his throat, her tears dampening his hide. She remained on her knees and held him in a fervent hug, and finally, when she felt she could not breathe from his smothering embrace, she withdrew. Her fingers tentatively reached up and cupped Kerberos's middle head, and the beast rested his monstrous face lovingly against his mother. Peace flooded his veins, an impressive sight to behold. The hound of Hell consumed by forgiving love.

"My darling, I am so sorry," Hades whispered as Alkaios settled behind them. "You know he was not born with three heads," she said to her husband. "In the days of the first gods, he was not one hellhound but three brothers; the oldest being the largest and the most ferocious. They were my father's, raised by his hands from pups. They helped him guard the Underworld, for in the beginning none of this was here. Tartarus and Elysium have always been. Since the Universe began, there was a heaven and a hell, but the Underworld… my father created its terrain. As the lord of death, he wanted his own kingdom to rule, a place of his own far beyond the reach of his brother. He resented Minotaur's control, and so he built for himself a new domain, a home surrounding Tartarus and Elysium. He refused entrance to all save his wife, which is why his weapon was a pitchfork. It originally was something else, but he reshaped it in honor of her, of my mother. The two of them dwelled here with absolute dominion over the afterlife, but Minotaur grew angry with his brother for creating a realm of vast power. He tried to take it, but the Omega was prepared. He sealed his world from the earth with the River Styx. My father stood at the mouth of the river and slit his wrists. Blood flowed from his veins, birthing the poison waters, and all who touch the blood of the god of death would die. Only the dead can pass through the Styx. To this day, the Minotaur cannot break through his brother's defenses, which is why they so desperately need me, blood of my father's blood. The Omega created this all, and the three hellhounds defended it for him. Hounds bred to kill the divine. The largest hound guarded the Winding Staircase of Tartarus, the second watched over the River Styx, and the third at the gates of Elysium. They were loyal and fierce, but nothing could protect them from the madness the Old Ones cursed themselves with. Once obsessed with the Touch of the Gods, my father turned crazed and volatile. In a fit of rage, he lashed out at the beasts he loved most. He attacked the smaller dogs without mercy and tore their heads from their bodies. He was so enraged, he dragged their decapitated skulls to Tartarus, where he planned to murder the last. The fear and sorrow in the third's expression woke him from his madness, though, and he was ashamed of his actions. Overcome with guilt, he vowed to his final monstrosity of a dog that he would put things right, and so he grafted the two severed necks onto the living dog's body, creating a three-headed god-killer." Hades' fingers whispered over Kerberos's scarred skin as meaning dawned on all who listened, but she never took her eyes from his devilish stare soft with love. "But Kerberos, the largest of the three, eventually grew too strong and violent, and the Omega chained him above the staircase where he remained until I set him free."

Hades fell silent and gripped one of Kerberos' spines. He braced her as her cramping legs pushed to a stand, and she turned to find every eye filled with shocked horror. Both Keres' and Hydra's hands clutched their mouths as their eyes brimmed with tears. Even Alkaios was shaken, and after a steadying breath, he stepped forward and placed a palm on the dog's skull. Kerberos, sensing the importance of this occasion, remained motionless. He accepted Alkaios' touch without his normal aggression as he pressed his middle head against Hades' stomach. The god-killer understood that in this moment his life had come full circle. For, in the beginning, the cruelty of the first god of death had nearly destroyed him. That day, he was chained above the rotting shades, his soul condemned to shrivel and rot until he was no better than the deformed monster he called master. But now standing here, witnessed by a host of Olympians, he was freed by the kindness of the new gods of the afterlife. Fierce loyalty burned in Kerberos' heart for the dark queen who had become his world, a love that could not be severed. And because of Hades, his devotion extended to the King of the Underworld. Loyalty he would kill for, and if required, die for.

XXVIII

WHILE ALL MARVELED at the truth of Hades' origins, one Olympian found his feet fleeing the throne room. Quiet as to not alert any to his escape, Hephaestus crept from the fortress as fast and as silently as his crippled legs would carry him. He was shocked by Hades' ancestry, but a single part of her story caught his attention so thoroughly that the rest of her words were lost on him… the water of the poisoned River Styx was fatal to the gods of old. Those monsters of absolute power were unstoppable by all, yet the water, bled of a trusted brother, could end even that monstrous horned god, Minotaur.

The moment that fact burrowed into his brain like a worm escaping the paralyzing sun, Hephaestus could not halt the turning wheels of his thoughts. An elusive idea whispered through his mind, half-formed and unattainable, yet it was there somewhere deep like the faint wisps of a dying fire. All he knew as he hobbled unattended out of the fortress and into the Underworld was that he had to sample the water. Hephaestus imbued many powers into his holy metalwork and carried a blessed vial on his belt at all times for such a time as this; such a time when that which must be contained was greater than his blacksmith's palms could withstand.

Bursting through the fog, his feet sunk into the murky sand as Hephaestus bent over the current, vial in hand, but before he plunged it through the river's surface, a hiss broke through the mist. Frozen by fear, Hephaestus slowly twisted his head, remembering Hades' warning never to venture into the Underworld alone. In his desperate haste, all he could think about was the nagging of a solution brewing in the depths of his mind, casting all caution to the wind. The warning came rushing back tenfold now though, and the blacksmith of the gods crouched suspended over the water as a dark shape took form in the ominous fog.

Through the mist, the fury staggered, her stringy hair, blank stare, and gnashing fangs sending icy terror through his veins. Hephaestus had heard of these women, curses of vengeance, and knew that the long claws on her hands were meant for the sole purpose of cleaving flesh from bone.

"Please?" he begged softly, voice drifting over the Styx's steady current. "Please let me have this, and I will leave." Hephaestus gestured at his still empty vial.

The fury looked at him with hollow eyes and then glanced to the water and back. Her limping gait did not slow as she pulled her deformed legs along, claws beginning to stretch forward in bloody hunger.

"Please," Hephaestus pleaded. "This might help us." At that, the fury halted with a jolting pitch. Her thin arms dropped limply to her sides, and the smith seized her hesitation and plunged the vial into the river. Despite his best attempts to keep the poison waters from his skin, a small droplet dribbled onto his thumb as he corked the glass. The scream of agony that ripped from his lips shook the air, and the startled fury screamed, voice shrill and deafening. She launched at the blacksmith, but Hephaestus had what he came for and was gone from the Underworld and back in his forge before the hellish creature was upon him.

"If we draw them out into the open, we will not risk the Underworld, and using the blood runes, we can create a portal to their realm," Hades said, sitting on her throne, Alkaios beside her. Kerberos lay a guardian at their feet, and Chimera sat between the gods of the dead, his knotted mane tangled in Hades' fingers. "We pick the place, somewhere visible so they cannot ambush you, and the moment they set foot within our enchantments, they will be shoved behind that once sealed door. But I will not be the bait this time, you will. They crave Olympian deaths and refuse to rest until they are the only remaining deities. If the Old Ones discover you on earth, unprotected by my father's domain, they will seize the opportunity, and I shall encourage them."

"I do not like this," Alkaios interjected. "I do not want you going back to Olympus. If they recognize you have returned to your true self, they will try to kill you."

"What choice do we have?" Hades asked. "This is our best chance. If I return, the reincarnation of the Omega, Minotaur will have no reason to suspect a trap. He believes we both crave death to befall the Olympians. If I am there beside him, I can whisper our desires in his ear. His stroked ego will not allow you to go unchallenged."

"With such almighty power, they still might ignore our beckoning." Zeus leaned on his thigh as his foot rested on the steps to the thrones.

"That is why you need me to return to Olympus. I will plant ideas of triumph and glory in Minotaur's head. Like overgrown weeds, I will crowd out all other thoughts until only my words consume his mind."

"It is our only option," Medusa interjected from her perch on the stairs. Keres, Hydra, and Ioanna sat beside her all nodding their agreement. "If she can convince Minotaur to take the bait, it could be our last real chance at survival."

"We do it Hades' way," Zeus said decidedly. "But we must find the perfect advantage."

"Then it is settled," Hades said before Alkaios protested. "Choose a place and mark it with the blood runes with haste. When you are ready, send word, and I will deliver them to you." She stood then, her toes extracting themselves from beneath Kerberos' comforting yet oppressive weight. "I must return before I am found missing." Hades turned to Alkaios, palm outstretched. Her husband captured it, and she pulled him into her arms and held him with all the strength her body possessed. Hades clung to Alkaios for a long moment; chest pressed against his, fingers clutching at his warm skin. She could not bear to tear herself free, and so she released her power while encircled in his embrace. The inky black tentacles twisted around them, weaving in and out until she was obscured in darkness. When it cleared, Hades was gone, and Alkaios' limbs fell empty to his sides.

"I would not get your hopes up," Zeus said bitterly into the echoing silence. Seeing Hades in Alkaios' arms sent stinging pangs of jealousy through his heart. Hera was little comfort to his loss of Hades, and the canyon in his soul tore ever wider at the sight of love not intended for him. "She remembers who she is now, but we know not how long this will last. We may not be able to save Hades. We may yet have to lock her up."

"Alkaios," Ioanna's voice interrupted. Alkaios' gaze shifted to her, relieved for the reprieve. He was seconds away from launching himself at Zeus. Consequences be damned, if Zeus did not return to the mountain soon, Alkaios would kill him.

"You are needed at the river," Ioanna continued with a look he recognized as Charon requesting his presence.

"Thank you," Alkaios sighed in relief at this chance to escape and brushing his fingers over the soft hair of the child in Ioanna's arms, fled the room.

When he arrived at the boathouse, the mist was thicker than he had ever remembered seeing over the river. If he outstretched his palm, even his divine eyes could not see it. Alkaios knew the way by heart though, and with a flick of his wrist, the wooden tree that had woven itself into a home grew outward until it settled on the shore. Climbing up the ramp, Alkaios peaked his head inside but finding it empty, rounded the house to the dock out back. It stretched over the angry, churning waters of the Styx, and shrouded in fog stood Charon, arms folded across his broad chest.

"How are my wife and daughters?" he asked by way of greeting.

"As well as can be expected," Alkaios said. "Do you know what happened?"

"Yes." Charon shifted to face his king. "Ioanna opened her memories so I could witness it. It is how I told her I needed to speak with you." Graveness filled Charon's eyes. "I heard Zeus suggest that we may yet have to lock Hades behind that seal. We know not if her madness is cured or if only temporarily suspended; nor do we understand these first gods. Even Hades, with all her might, may not be able to resist their pull, and even if she can, what is to say your son will be able to? The boy still poses a threat. We cannot predict if your child will be born pure or with the delusion of his ancestors. Any blood seal, Olympian or Old One, he could break."

Alkaios looked at his friend, dumbfounded. These words had gutted him coming from Zeus, but from Charon? They struck deeper, the pain and desperation filling him to overflowing.

Alkaios opened his mouth to speak, not knowing what sounds to let fall from his lips.

"I mean not to burden you with what already weighs you down," Charon said. "I requested your presence to present a solution." Alkaios' eyes shot wide as he looked at his friend, but the ferryman only raised a hand in a halting gesture. "First… promise me something?"

"You are my brother. I will grant you whatever you ask for as long as it is within my power to give."

"No one must know of what I am about to say," Charon said gravely. "Not Hades and especially not Ioanna. This remains between you and me."

"Of course, but why?"

"Because," Charon said, turning to the shrouded water, "what I am about to tell you will most likely result in Zeus ending my life."

Hades paced on Zeus' hidden ledge, anxiety coursing through her veins. She begged the universe that she would remain in control of her own mind, but the anxiety over her madness was second only to that caused by waiting. They had formed a plan, and now she must wait. Wait for the Olympians to find a plot of land that suited their needs, to create the blood runes in the dirt that would portal the Old Ones behind the door. The deformed gods were growing restless, clamoring to break down the gates of Hell and take what was hers for themselves. If the Olympians did not hurry, their trap would be too late.

So here, Hades paced. She had fled to this hidden ledge to await the signal, but as time wore on and none came, she would have to return to the mountain, to her ancestors. Being forced to live among them as herself was excruciating. She was no longer blind to their madness, their irreverence for life, and the smell of blood sickened her. Hades' stomach turned just thinking about it. She longed to wash the days' old filth from her skin but it would raise an alarm. While in Minotaur's presence, she remained bloodthirsty and cruel, but the butchery dripping from his horns only served to remind her of the atrocities she had committed. Hatred of herself bubbled within like sulfuric tar, and Hades almost wished for the insanity to relapse so she might forget her sins.

    A sudden sound wrenched her from her tormented mind, and Hades jerked to see a black snake slither onto the ledge. Its dark mass slid over the rocks to her ankle, curling itself around the limb. As it rose up her body, it slowed over her stomach as if feeling what lay inside before it continued traversing her torso and coming to a rest across her shoulders. The trap was set. Time to send these demons back whence they came.

XXIX

Alkaios carried a toddler on each hip as he fled the hovel. Their mother ran behind him, struggling to keep in step with his superior speed, a wailing infant clinging to her breast. Her husband and their eldest son brought up the rear, clutching every necessity hastily seized from their home, and the family followed the god at a breathless pace as Alkaios lead them toward the seaside cave. He was not the only Olympian tasked with evacuating the modest fishing village by the sea. Ahead, Hera pulled two young girls by their small hands as their parents dragged goats and all their earthly possessions. To their left, Apollo and Artemis helped a widower and his four sons carry the elderly residents over the field.

Alkaios, satisfied they had escorted the last of the villagers, charged over the land to where Zeus and Poseidon stood guard over the mouth of the cave. Sweat poured over his brow as he placed the toddlers on the ground and ushered them inside the dark, gaping entrance. The toddler's parents rushed to join their children, and Alkaios turned to watch the slower elders cross the threshold. It was crammed full, bursting at the seams, every inch of space occupied by either man, beast, or supply. This seaside cavern had not been there this morning, but Zeus, Poseidon, and Alkaios had forced the stone to give way, creating a safe haven for the people whose homes were about to be destroyed in a deadly clash between the gods.

"Is that all of them?" Zeus asked, and Alkaios nodded in affirmation. "I hope they witnessed this."

"She will make sure they did."

Alkaios stepped from the cave's mouth, and the rest of the Olympians followed his lead. They had selected this village for a reason. The huts were small, offering no cover. They could not hide, but neither could their enemies, and with the sea at their back, Poseidon would protect their flank. This is where they had chosen to make their stand, the blood runes marked in the dead of night as not to be noticed. The evacuation of the villagers was performed under the full light of day, though. They were part of the bait. The Olympians hoped the Old Ones were watching from atop the mountain and would see their attempt to save those mortals left. They hoped this would enrage the deformed gods into attacking, that their presence would be too much of a temptation. Behind the protection of the Styx, Minotaur would be forced to combat a power birthed into this world by his own brother, but here on earth, the Olympians were nothing more than wounded, helpless prey to be devoured.

Zeus hoisted his thunderbolt into the air. Lighting tore free from the sky and plummeted to meet the metal. Upon impact, he thrust it toward the cave. The flash of light hurtled into the rock, breaking it apart at the crown. Boulders and debris caved in sealing the villagers inside, buried alive.

"If we do not make it out of this," Zeus said, turning to Aphrodite, "release them so they might flee." The goddess of beauty nodded and drifted backward, folding herself among the rubble until her form blended in with seamless camouflage. "Although if we do not survive today," Zeus muttered under his breath, "it would be kinder for them to suffocate within the earth than to perish at the hands of the Old Ones."

"What do they think they are doing?" the three-eyed goddess asked no one in particular as she peered off of Olympus to the distant sea. She stood directly atop Zeus' secret ledge, but thank the gods, the clouds shrouded it in mystery. Still, Hades felt anxious at her proximity and forced herself not to even glance down least she was being watched.

"They are attempting to save the mortals of the earth from our sacrificial blades," Minotaur answered with disgust.

"We should take them now while they present themselves," the fanged god said, seething with a need for vengeance. Hades flicked her eyes to the monstrous mouth and sighed in relief, thankful he stole the words from her lips. Better the call to attack fall from another's tongue and not her own, least her eagerness reveal her truth.

"The Underworld does present difficulty," Hades offered when Minotaur remained silent. She could not come across impatient, but they had to snap at the bait. "Perhaps he has a point." She gestured to the fanged god. "Taking them on earth works to our advantage, but I doubt they will remain so unprotected for long. If you wish to take them, command us now before we forfeit the upper hand."

Minotaur shifted his mass and gazed down at his new Omega. She had proven herself as bloodthirsty as he was. He approved of his brother's daughter far greater than he did of his brother. Hades was vicious and cruel, bent on domination for her people. He would place her on the throne beside him once his conquest was over, and they would rule in chaos together. The beginning and the end.

Minotaur gave a nod of his horned head, and Hades smiled,

wickedness curving her lips in a beautifully dark masterpiece. The gods behind them roared a battle cry that shook the mountain, a death rumble that reached the ears of the Olympians below despite their distance, and the Old Ones dove off Olympus in a wave of chaos, hell-bent on bloodshed.

THE OLYMPIANS HEARD the thundering of the horde before they saw them. The Old Ones pounded over the earth, shaking it to its core. Alkaios crouched closer to Kerberos. They were hopefully far enough from the small village to be passed unnoticed by the death march. As soon as the final deformed god crossed their blood runes, Alkaios would ignite their power. The Old Ones had to be trapped together at the same moment, and not one by one as they entered the runes' circle. If there was a single iota of time between the foremost gods' entrapment and the lasts', not even Hades could stop their skulls from being crushed beneath that monstrous hammer. No, these monsters had to be captured simultaneously, and the burden of timing weighed on Alkaios' weaponless shoulders. The dog's hidden mass lay flat in the tall grass; their last line of defense if all else should fail. No matter who perished or how much hope was slaughtered in the mud, Kerberos was to stand his ground until the end, to hold the ancient gods until Alkaios bound them once again in darkness.

Body tensed for battle, back against a fisherman's home, Zeus gripped the thunderbolt, extending it slightly, ready to swing at a moment's notice. His eyes shifted to the shore where his brother stood calf-deep in the waves. Zeus dipped his head, and Poseidon nodded in return before turning to face the never-ending horizon of water. Reaching up, Poseidon slid a hand over the razor tips of his trident, slitting his palm. Blood sprung from the wound, dripping to the cerulean ripples and staining it with blooming petals of red. Instantly the sea lurched, heaving and churning around its god's ankles, forcing the stained water out where it painted itself into runes. From their power, a wall of water rose high into the sky, impenetrable and solid. No god would be able to penetrate it to flank them, but it also served as a cage. The Olympians could not elude it either. There would be no escape for them once the Old Ones came. They were trapped by a barricade of water at their backs and monsters at their front. And as the thundering of chaos pounded closer, Poseidon hoped they could hold out against the deformed long enough for Alkaios to ignite the portal, otherwise this ocean barrier meant to save them would be their end.

Turning back to Zeus, trident poised to kill, Poseidon watched as the terrifying site of countless gods descended upon them. Flying over the land at a speed not even he could outrun, Poseidon balked as the Old One's crashed through the rune barrier and destroyed any hopes the Olympians had of victory in one vicious swoop.

ALKAIOS WAS HIDDEN in the grass one second and flipping head over heels through the air the next, disoriented as distorted images and sounds accosted him. Just seconds before, Poseidon had raised the sea's wall barely in time for the Old Ones' approach, all poised for impact, yet now as his back hit the ground with a painful thud, Alkaios understood their folly. There was no hope against these first gods. The Olympians' defeat would be swift and merciless.

Head spinning, Alkaios scrambled to his feet as fast as the pain would allow. How the Old Ones had found him, he did not know, and as they charged, he stood no chance of fighting them without a weapon. They bore down on him, a barricade of chiseled flesh. Alkaios would never make it through their onslaught alive to ignite the runes at their flanks.

Suddenly he was hauled off the ground again, body hurtling to the side. He landed harshly, his attacker crashing atop him. Alkaios kicked violently, desperate to free himself from the mad god, but the grunt that rattled his eardrum at his kick was all too familiar.

"Go!" Zeus shoved Alkaios out from under him. "Get to the runes!" And then Zeus was gone, barreling back out into the open. "Olympians!" his voice echoed. "Hold them!" They answered his call with screams, wild like banshees, and brandished weapons. A crack of icy lighting hurtled from the sky and collided with his thunderbolt, igniting the grass just as the colossal bodies clashed.

Alkaios scrambled to his feet. The pit of his stomach knotted in constricting gnarls as he watched the wave of Old Ones crash upon the Olympians like a devastating storm upon the shore. The plan had been to remain hidden, their hope resting on his ability to ignite the portal before any combat was necessary, but their plan had failed. They had found him before they even crossed the runes' threshold, and with a heavy heart, Alkaios knew what Zeus faced. He was buying Alkaios time to return to the runes, but it meant almost certain death. By giving themselves over to a head-on assault, they were sacrificing themselves to give him precious moments. Alkaios would not let them die in vain, and so he ran, forcing his legs as fast as they could go, silently praying to Hades to keep the fighting from him.

Whack! Alkaios rounded the last village hut only to slam headlong into a solid mass. He crashed in a heap of excruciating pain, eyesight blurring from the impact. A massive, unfocused shape bent over and hauled him into the air, hurling him across the field before Alkaios could even register what had happened. His body slammed to the earth for the second time in seconds, and the force jarred his spine with such intensity he felt as if his skeleton had shattered to dust. Groaning in agony, Alkaios flipped onto his stomach, his bones unable to support his weight, and crawled at an agonizingly slow pace in the direction he thought the runes were. He was not sure where they had been bled into the dirt, the searing in his head dimming his sight, but he had to move. His finger clawed the earth, grating his torso over the rough soil. Sharp knives of breath stabbed his ribs as his lung wheezed within his chest, but he barely made it a few feet when an iron hand seized his ankle and yanked. Alkaios flew backward, fingers clinging to the grass for purchase, but it was in vain. He was hoisted into the air and dangled upside down high above the ground. The unbreakable grip choked his skin. The bones in his ankle threatened to shatter like fragile glass as Alkaios swung. The blood rushed to his brain, flushing his cheeks hot, and his skull swelled with exploding pressure. His unfocused eyes watched with hazy clarity as blurred shapes clashed against one another, the Old Ones beating back the Olympians with savage ferocity. Despite Alkaios' distorted vision, it was clear the Olympians faltered against the imposing show of force. Their strength waned from their inferior bodies; a sight not even Alkaios' impaired eyesight could deny.

A roar above him snapped Alkaios' attention from Zeus' failing defense to the giant who dangled him upside down. The pain in his ankle pulsed excruciatingly from the monster's grip, and when Alkaios saw the bloodstained horns cast their dark shadows, fear ripped through him in paralyzing waves. Minotaur's head was plummeting, and despite Alkaios' savage struggle, the horned god meant to slice him in two with his razor horns. Alkaios pitched wildly, but it was no use. He could not free himself, and this would be his end. The Alpha would rip him into ribboned halves, split skull to thighs.

Suddenly, a brutal roar shattered his fear, and Alkaios plummeted. His neck snapped as his crown connected with the grass, and through tumbling vision, he glimpsed three heads sink their fangs into Minotaur's torso. The earth shook as the king and dog fell, their bodies a whirlwind of limbs and teeth, spikes and horns. They hit the ground with earthquake force, gouging the dirt as they clashed, but Kerberos deftly rolled off Minotaur before the god's hulking size crushed him. He landed on massive paws with heavy grace and loosed an ear-shattering growl that reverberated through three angered throats. His knees bent, ready to attack as Minotaur scrambled to his feet, but as the dog flew through the air, intent on ripping flesh from the deformed king's bones, a dark, beautiful figure crashed into his chest and slammed him earthbound. Hades landed harshly atop her god-killer. A demonic scream howled from her throat, and as the dog's spikes gouged the soil, she flung her gaze back to the bleeding Minotaur.

"He is mine!" Hades bellowed, voice terrifyingly powerful, and Minotaur settled onto his heels, pleased at the sight.

"Kill him, my child." Minotaur's cruelty echoed over the horrific din of battle. "Your father created that beast to defy me. It is fitting that the new Omega destroy him!"

Hades smiled at Minotaur's words, wicked beauty turning her lips, and Alkaios' heart lurched at her smile, so ruthless and bloodthirsty as she pinned Kerberos. Had she forgotten herself so quickly? But just as she tore her eyes from the horned king, they flitted across Alkaios' gaze. It was imperceptible to all but him, for he knew his wife well. In the millisecond that their gazes brushed, Alkaios recognized her plea. Hades was buying him time, distracting Minotaur if only for a few precious seconds. She wanted him to run, to complete the task at hand, and so without wasting a single second, Alkaios vaulted to his feet and bolted through the grass. His dark power snaked around him, and in an instant, he disappeared, appearing by the line of runes a fraction of a moment later. He froze in horror when he saw the dirt. Some runes were whole, but most were broken, the soil beneath the gods' spilled blood splayed wide.

Panic flooding his veins in icy waves, Alkaios' eyes shot to the battle waging. He could see, even from this distance, that Athena was bathed in carnage, and her arm could barely raise her spear in defense. Artemis had loosed all her arrows save one and was using it as a dagger with little effectiveness. Ares and Zeus stood back to back, their weapons swinging wildly in frenzied attempts to cut through the masses surrounding Poseidon. The god of the seas was vastly outnumbered, fiercely fighting off the onslaught converging on his front only to be carved into bloody ribbons of flesh by the assault at his back. The Olympians were battered and bruised, oppressed on all sides, and it would be a matter of minutes before the first of his kind fell never to rise again. Alkaios was not sure he could redraw the runes in time, but his wife, their dog, and the gods who had once reigned on Mount Olympus were about to sacrifice their lives to buy him time. Alkaios would not let them down, and so with gritted teeth, his nails dug into his wrist and tore. His flesh peeled back, deep crimson flooding the wound and spilling out onto the ground. With haste, Alkaios plunged his fingers into the fountain of his lifeblood and bent to rebuild the first of many destroyed runes.

ONE LOOK AND KERBEROS UNDERSTOOD HADES' plan. By attacking him, she was both buying Alkaios time and saving him from Minotaur's savagery. Kerberos saw in her eyes that this fight between them would not be the same as the last time they had clashed. She meant to put on a show, sparing his life by assaulting him, and roaring with savage blood-thirst, Kerberos thanked his mother by shoving her from his body and vaulting to his paws.

With violent grace, Kerberos whipped his spiked tail at Hades, which her pitchfork blocked with a resounding clang. Not missing a beat, Kerberos lashed out and seizing his mother's arm in his mouth, yanked. Hades flew sideways, legs ripped savagely from beneath her only for her shoulder to connect with the ground a moment later with bruising force. Agilely, she rolled and thrust her heels against the earth. They launched her upward to a readied stance, and Hades did not have to glance down to know that Kerberos, despite his utter strength, had not pierced her skin. She smiled, lips curved in taunting violence, but the grin was for Minotaur. Her eyes... her eyes were for the godkiller, and they were filled with thanks and encouragement. Kerberos growled his reply and flung himself at his mother, his massive bulk colliding into her with terrifying force.

ATHENA FARED WORSE than the rest. The Old Ones had identified the Olympians with the greatest combat threat and attacked them first, pounding them with relentless viciousness. Her skin was split open in more places than she could count, and her left eye was so bruised and swollen, she no longer saw out of it. Her breath labored, lungs on fire with the exertion, and she barely possessed the strength to raise her arms, let alone continue to stand. Athena stumbled as waves of deformed gods crashed against her battered body, and despite her stoic and ruthless nature, tears streamed from her single good eye. This was her end, and this time, Athena knew Hades would not save her like on Medusa's mountain. Their only hope was Hades remaining the traitor in their enemy's midst. Although, from the looks of it, she had forgotten her true self in her savage struggle to slaughter Kerberos.

A bloodcurdling scream jerked Athena from her mind in time to see the three-eyed goddess fly at her. The force with which the old hag collided into her frame caused a bone in Athena's forearm to splinter with an audible crack. Eyes blurring with tears, Athena howled and reeled back with such aggression, falling hard on her tailbone. Arm shattered, she dropped her spear, the pain rendering it impossible to grip the weapon, and before she could even consider capturing it with her good hand, the hag had it clutched in her boney fingers. The three-eyed god loosed a screeching war cry as she shoved the spear into the air, the first spoil of battle. The Old Ones joined in her revelry, their voices drowning out all other sounds, and Athena thrashed in terror as four deformed gods bent and hoisted her above their heads.

Their fingers clawed at her flesh. Their hands tugged her body, and Athena realized with terrifying clarity that they intended to rip her apart limb from limb. The scream that escaped her raw throat froze the hearts of her brethren, her panicking terror shards of ice in their veins.

"Athena!" Ares screamed, dread shooting strength into his exhausted legs. He bolted through the throng, leaving Zeus' flank unprotected as he elbowed his way through the fight toward his partner. What was the god of war without the god of warfare?

"Ares!" Came Athena's strangled plea. "Ares!"

"Athena!" Her name was cut short by a grunt as a tremendous hammer bludgeoned his stomach. The pain flung Ares backward, and vomit spat involuntarily from his mouth as he stumbled. Hades had killed the behemoth who bore this weapon on the mountain, but another had risen to take its place. He was massive, his hulking power raising the hammer again, preparing to deliver its crash into Ares' skull.

Hades spat a ruby stain onto the ground. Kerberos' forehead had slammed so aggressively into her mouth that her lip had split, and her teeth bit down on her tongue. Blood flooded her mouth again with its oozing metallic tang, but she did not have time to rid herself of it as Kerberos charged at her. Throwing herself to the side, Hades caught his necks with the pitchfork's curve, forcing a gurgle to ripple up his throat as he fell. With panicking haste, her eyes flicked to the battle. The Old Ones had Zeus and Poseidon surrounded while others had Athena raised like a trophy above their heads. Any moment someone would die, and it would be on her head. This had been her idea, and if Hades showed her hand, allowed Minotaur to see her true allegiance, they would all be dead. Hiding among her ancestors was their only chance at saving the world from madness. If the Olympians had the upper hand, revealing her loyalty might work in their favor, but now it would only end them. Minotaur would be unforgiving in his vengeance, and with the Olympians so close to death, they would be vanquished before Hades could even touch the horned king.

Hades flicked her eyes to her husband, willing Alkaios to move faster, knowing he could not. The blood runes had to be drawn with perfection and care, and with only him bleeding to repair those her ancestors disrupted, he was fighting a losing battle.

"Enough of this!" Came Minotaur's bellow, and Hades' head jerked back to her uncle. His hulk was striding toward the dog, and before she could move, he was behind the god-killer. With a massive hand, Minotaur grabbed Kerberos' middle neck and hoisted him into the air. A cry of pain escaped the dog's lips as Minotaur flung him harshly to the dirt, and Hades' heart constricted in torment. She longed to scream, to fly at Minotaur and skewer him like the animal he was. She wanted to slit him navel to collar and watch his innards litter the grass, and without realizing it, Hades was moving. Her feet carried her toward her ancient ancestor, pitchfork poised for the kill.

Kerberos struggled to stand, and one look at his mother told him all he needed to know. Hades was coming to save him, and he knew it would not end well. Not for any of them, especially for the Olympians who were seconds away from slaughter. With a growl and gnashing of his jaws, he launched himself at Minotaur. The king simply reached his hands out and caught the dog by his rib cage. Kerberos was created to defy this god though, and with a flick of his tail, he slammed its spikes across Minotaur's face. The king howled in pain, a bloody slash ripped through his eye. He dropped the hellhound as if he were burning coals, and Kerberos lashed out again, this time slashing at the god's ankles. Blood spurted from Minotaur's legs as he collapsed, and Kerberos was atop the monster before he even hit the ground. The hound's massive side mouths dove for the horned god, and with fatal precision, his fangs dug into Minotaur's shoulders. His teeth cut deep, slicing through the soft flesh until they carved against bone, yet the horned demon did not scream nor cry out. Minotaur only reared his head back and crashed it against the dog's middle forehead. Kerberos reeled, still clutching the severed muscles in his fangs, mouth filling with foul blood. Minotaur continued unfazed and brought his brutish arms hurtling down on Kerberos' skull. A crack shattered the air, and the god-killer fell limp, chest heaving.

Hades stifled a scream and threw her gaze to her husband. Alkaios stared at the panic on her face before looking down. The runes were incomplete. He had but two remaining, but as he glanced up, he knew they had lost; there was no time. Minotaur had pulled his mass to his feet and had a foot raised over Kerberos' ribcage, preparing to crack it open like a brittle egg. Behind the horned god, the battle faltered. Athena was hoisted above the Old One's heads as they positioned themselves to rip her limbs from her torso. Ares was moments away from having his head caved in. Hera kicked and wailed on the dirt as three monstrosities pinned her down while a fourth carved etchings into her flesh with a knife. Zeus and Poseidon were surrounded, and for every strike they doled out, they received sevenfold. Artemis screamed as her shoulder was violently dislocated, and Apollo lay unconscious as gods trampled him in their fighting. They were seconds from death, and as Alkaios looked on, he caught his wife's desperate eyes. Hades shook her head slightly at him, her beautiful, dark blue irises pleading.

Alkaios nodded, his eyes trying to convey his apology and his love for her. Hades understood. A flash of the same flitted through her features, and then Alkaios stood to his full height. His arms rose from his sides, fingers still dripping with blood, and from them smoke erupted. Like ink diving into water, the black tentacles shot over the field with urgent panic. Their tendrils wrapped suffocatingly around the suffering gods, and with a snap of his almighty fingers, Alkaios dragged Kerberos and the host of Olympians back to Hell, robbing the victorious Old Ones of their kills.

XXX

Hades skidded to a sudden halt, heels gouging the dirt as her body jolted still. Her eyes were wide with panic, her breathing manic, yet she forced herself to stop dead in her tracks least someone see her intended treachery. Hades had been seconds away from assaulting Minotaur, a sin they would have crucified her for if any had seen. Thankfully, the Old Ones had been too preoccupied with the destruction of the Olympians.

Minotaur brought his heel down with earth-shattering force, and Hades flinched at the power. If Alkaios had been but seconds later, Kerberos' ribcage would have been nothing but a tangled web of fragmented bone and blood.

"Cowards!" Minotaur whirled on Hades, who barely had enough time to rearrange her distraught features into those of rage and malice. "They hide behind the walls of my brother's infernal creation."

"It is no matter," Hades said coldly with all the disdain she could muster, the bile at her own words threatening to spill past her lips. "We will take the Underworld, and then they will have nowhere left to cower. The ancient sands of the Styx will never be washed clean of their blood."

"You will make sure of that," Minotaur said, taking Hades' chin in his filth-stained fingers and tilting it up at a craning angle to meet his towering gaze. Her skin crawled at the contact, but her face betrayed nothing, a perfect picture of a loyal servant so blessed to be caressed. "You have the power of the Omega, and you must control your realm. When we take the Underworld, you will bind them within your father's domain. There can be no escape for them."

"It will be as you command," Hades said with a reverent lowering of her eyes, all the while panic swarming her veins. Her flesh recoiled where he clutched her chin, yet she held still, refusing to be the one to break the contact.

"Good, my child." Minotaur's fingers pried from her jaw, and Hades' head fell back to its normal stance. "You are a treasure to your race, unlike your father." Brushing past her, Minotaur descended upon his brethren. "Now where are these villagers?" he asked. "Find them for me and slaughter them. There is a price that must be paid when you align yourself with the wrong gods."

The Old Ones let loose a collective roar that struck fear in the hearts of all for miles around. Eager for bloodshed, they charged the cave where the mortals hid as vulnerable offerings, where their fate had been sealed along with their bodies. If the deformed could not have the Olympians, they would settle for human blood.

Hades twitched, desperate to stop them. She could not bear any more butchery, not now that she was awake and aware of the sins they committed, but as Minotaur's eyes bore into her, she swallowed the rage and desperation and stood stone still in defiance. She was still trusted, the last chance they had at collapsing the reign of madness, and Hades refused to tip the scales against herself with a revealing slip of emotions. So she remained motionless and harsh, ears ringing with every death scream as the Old Ones slaughtered the innocent. Hades forced herself to watch and listen, to witness their sacrifices, to see them through to their ends. Their prayers crashed like waves upon her mind, praying for Hades to deliver them. Earth had not forgotten those bloody days in which the god of the Underworld had loosed Hell's monsters, making it known only the god of death could save them. Hades knew that they meant the pleas to fall on her husband, but that did not matter. Alkaios was god in name and king alongside her, but she was the true Hades. It was her name they screamed, and although she hovered feet from their begging lips, she was helpless to rescue them. Hades witnessed them die, her only consultation that they would pass on to the eternal fields of Elysium. Not that Elysium would be safe for much longer. Not a single pure would be left if she allowed Minotaur to cross the poison river.

The villagers were dead in a matter of minutes. Not even the young spared. The rage at being robbed of their divine victims spurred the Old Ones into a frenzy. They did not take their time, savagely cutting down all who had breath to give. Hades was grateful the mortals were not tortured, their ends thankfully swift, but as the breeze carried the scent of their blood, her stomach lurched, threatening to heave itself onto the grass. Hades clamped her full lips shut, desperate not to vomit, but just the slight shudder was all Minotaur required to pull his attention from the bloodbath. He looked at Hades long and hard, his nose sniffing the surrounding air. Hades froze, and fear rippled through her veins like razor shards of ice. She held her breath and commanded herself to remain motionless as his gaze lingered on her abdomen. She was barely showing, and the dress bloomed around her waist to hide the life inside, but Hades knew Minotaur need not see to understand.

Long seconds passed, and Hades felt the prick of tears sting her eyes. He had found out, smelled the half-breed growing within her womb. He may not kill her, but Minotaur would rip Alkaios' offspring from her body while the child was still infinitely small. Hades longed to place a protective hand over her belly, a warning to Minotaur not to take her son, yet after a moment, the horned king simply raised his eyes to her face and grunted.

"I grow tired of this." Minotaur turned his back on the slain. "Come, my child." He extended a bulging bicep, and demanding her hand not to shake, Hades slid a small palm around his blood-soaked arm. Together they vanished from earth, leaving the rest of the deformed gods to revel in their recent kills.

HADES SCRAMBLED OVER THE EDGE, hardly able to flee fast enough. Dirt and rocks showered down about her head as she fell more than climbed down the mountain face to Zeus' hidden ledge. She could barely breathe, the panic and terror clogging her throat. She could not disappear soon enough, careless in her descent until her feet crashed against a solid foothold.

Concealed by smoke and fog, Hades' breaths came out in ragged gasps, soft cries escaping her lips. Tears pricked her eyes as she blindly rushed to the end of the ledge and thrust her face over the edge, the contents of her stomach threatening to heave up from her throat and down to earth. Hades felt uncontrollable sorrow and terror, and it had been all she could do to keep her emotions in check. The Old Ones had returned to the mountain where they feasted on the village's stolen harvest, and worse, the villagers' roasted flesh. The scent had turned her stomach so violently that Hades had paled with nausea, and as the night wore on and the more intoxicated the gods became, the more she struggled to blend into the background. Her place of honor was beside Minotaur's seat, and every time a tray of meat passed her, and she did not partake, the more their eyes had appraised her with wariness.

It had taken all the strength within her to remain next to the horned king, but as soon as the last of them had drifted into a drunken slumber, Hades had flung herself from the room, gasping for what little fresh air remained on the charred mountain. Here on Zeus' hidden refuge, all the fear, sorrow, and horror rushed out in waves. She sobbed, choking. Her breathing irregular, body shaking. With careful tenderness, Hades laced a hand over her small womb to convince herself the child was still there, still alive.

A slight movement caught her attention, and as fast as she had plummeted to this ledge, Hades was at the ready. Pitchfork aimed for death.

"Hades!" A strong and familiar voice broke through the ashen clouds.

"Zeus?" Hades cried out as the hulking god emerged from the shadows with hands raised in surrender. For a split second, she chided herself for being so reckless. If this had been an Old One, lurking in wait on her small slice of sanctuary on this mountain, she could very well have been brought to a swift end. Her panic only lasted a moment before an overwhelming sense of crippling relief replaced it, and without thinking, as if a hidden impulse and old memories took over, Hades launched herself at Zeus. The pitchfork hit the ground with a soft thud an instant before she collided with his solid frame. Tears burst from her eyes in an uncontrollable torrent, and she clung to his familiar figure with an iron grip.

"I got you," Zeus soothed, enveloping Hades in his powerful embrace and letting his warmth seep into her cold skin. He held her close as she cried, running a large palm over her matted, dark hair. It was a long while before Hades' sobs slowed and her breathing returned to normal, and when she finally stopped hyperventilating, Zeus released her. Backing away from the king of Olympus, Hades wiped her eyes, desperate to remove the tears and mucus from her red and puffy face.

"I hoped you would come here eventually," Zeus said. "The

Underworld is in chaos, too many injured. Alkaios had to remain there with the others." Hades nodded in understanding and then lifted her eyes to the man she once loved as if to question his presence.

"I had to make sure he had not killed you," Zeus said in answer to her silent query. "I saw you go for Minotaur when he tried to kill Kerberos. I was afraid they would crucify you for that."

"They did not see, but they massacred the villagers... and then ate them." Her voice hitched as fresh tears watered her cheeks. Zeus ran a trembling hand over his blonde hair and turned his eyes away from Hades. She watched as he heaved air into his lungs, trying to steady himself before angling back to her.

"Alkaios told us they died," Zeus said, "but we did not know about..." his voice trailed off, unable to finish the sentence. His body sagged in defeat, and he sank to a seat, legs hanging over the ledge. Hades slowly slumped beside him, remembering all the times in their decades together she had seen him sit so.

"Their deaths are on our heads," Zeus said, sorrow choking him. "We killed them."

"No." Hades took his hand in hers. "They killed them. We are trying to stop this, and if we die, earth has no hope. Elysium greeted the villagers in the end. I assured it as did Alkaios, but if the Old Ones kill us, they will ensure there is no afterlife. Who then will stop them?"

"I know." Zeus squeezed her fingers, holding on to them as if they were his only lifeline. "I never truly stopped to consider the havoc us gods can wreak on earth. I swear by my throne, if we live through this, I will be better. I promise you."

Hades nodded and gave him a small smile before lowering her head to his shoulder. They sat in quiet reflection for a long moment, comforting one another in the stillness, before Hades finally broke the silence.

"I thought Minotaur found out about the baby."

"What?" Zeus looked down at her resting against him.

"He stared at me like he knew," she whispered, afraid to utter the words any louder lest they be heard. "The past hours have been excruciating, waiting for him to rip me open and take my son. I do not think Minotaur knows, not yet at least. But in that moment, when he looked at me, it was as if he smelled something he could not quite place. It will not be long now before he figures it out, and when he does…"

"Do not say it," Zeus interrupted, wrapping a large arm around her shoulders. "Do not go there. I know you, and you will not let that happen. You are stronger than you realize. You are the Omega to his Alpha, and if there is one thing I have learned about Alkaios, despite my feelings for him, is that he is my equal. He will die before he lets that fate befall you."

"But we tried to stop them, and we failed miserably."

"We cannot win against them, but you might. You have to draw them out into the trap, and you have to face them."

"If I do that, we only have one shot," Hades said, lifting her head to gaze at Zeus. "The moment they find out I have turned against them, they will make it their mission to slaughter me just as they did my father. They will never accept me back into their fold after that betrayal."

"But with you," Zeus said with all the conviction he still carried within him, "we only need one shot."

ZEUS AND HADES appeared in the Underworld, and instantly, the severity of the injuries her ancestors had inflicted struck Hades in the gut. Gods lay sprawled about the fortress, blood and pain seeping from their bodies. She should stop and make sure each and every god was cared for, but in that moment, Hades could only bring herself to search for one. Her gaze flitted wildly about until it rested on the broad shoulders bent over in care of her dog.

"Alkaios," Hades whispered through the din, yet it was all he needed. Jerking upright, he whirled around to see her standing across the room, and before she could move, he was in front of her. In a blink of an eye, Alkaios had her in his arms, and a fresh wave of tears burst from her as he kissed her again and again. He enveloped her, refusing to part from her body, and slowly his fingers drifted down to her belly. Hades clamped her hand over his, and Alkaios tore his lips from hers and bent to kiss the growing child before he pulled her back into his embrace, suffocating in his hold. Hades did not care. She did not need to breathe, not as long as her husband's life pulsed against her own.

"I am sorry," Alkaios said, pulling away just enough to look into her beautiful eyes. Eyes he missed excruciatingly. "I could not…"

"It was not your fault," Hades cut him off, palms pressing against his firm chest. "They are stronger than you. They are better than you, and I was a fool to think you could take them." Alkaios flinched, hurt washing over his features at his wife's insult. "What I mean to say," she hastened, "is that I am the only one who can truly face them as an equal. I am Minotaur's Omega. Despite what he has become, as Alpha, he was the god of life, and as the reincarnated Omega, I am the god of death. I may be his second, but as we all know, death always wins in the end. All who live must die. There is no escaping it. This time, it will be me they stand against."

"Hades," Alkaios said in panic, eyes wide as he stepped away from her. "If you do this, this is our last chance. Once they discover your betrayal, the whole host of ancients will descend upon you. If we do not trap them once and for all, you cannot go back. We surrender the upper hand of your infiltration, and we could very well lose you."

"It does not matter," Hades whispered, lifting a palm to rest against Alkaios' cheek. "They are coming for the Underworld, and they have tasked me with binding you all here. There will be no escape, no Hell to retreat to when they come. We have little choice. We either die fighting, or we die here like caged rats."

"I have an idea that might help," came Hephaestus' voice from behind them. Hades, Alkaios, and Zeus all turned around to find a battered and bruised crowd closing in on them.

"In the beginning, your father slit open his wrist, and the River Styx flowed from it," Hephaestus continued, hobbling forward. "The god of death's blood was poison to all, even his brethren. It would fall to reason that as his heir, your blood inherited his power. They destroyed the trap created from our Olympian runes, but I would wager they cannot destroy yours with such ease."

"He may have a point," Medusa interjected, settling next to the mason of the gods. "We have been trying to fight and trap them the Olympian way. It was the Omega's blood that sealed them the first time. I believe it shall fall upon the shoulders of the Omega once again."

"Then I will draw the runes," Hades said, "but we have to hurry. After today, they will not bide their time. They are at full strength and will take the Underworld with or without my help. Minotaur cares not how many he must sacrifice to cross the river as long as you are all dead in the end."

"You may not have to do this alone." Hephaestus held up a small vial of clear liquid. "Water from the Styx," he said in response to Hades' raised eyebrows. "The three greats of Olympus, they are powerful. I have been testing the poison waters." He offered his burned hands as proof for all to see. "I believe that mixed with the blood of Zeus, Poseidon, and Alkaios, it can hold the Old Ones just as yours will. With luck, the four of you can set it fast enough that Hades will not be missed upon the mountain."

"After seeing what they are truly capable of, are we certain any seal we carve into their gate will bind the Old Ones?" Hera interrupted, but unlike the other times she had challenged Hades' plans, her words were softened by fear and genuine concern. Hades opened her mouth to speak, but Medusa's voice answered for her.

"Blood magic is powerful. It cannot be broken save by he who it was intended for. It is why, despite his superior power, Minotaur could not sever the Omega's hold over the door after their resurrection. Only Hades, his blood reincarnated, could release its bond."

"And if that is not enough, I will bathe the gate in the waters of the River Styx," Hades said with unusual softness toward Hera. "May it burn the flesh from the bones of any soul foolish enough to touch that door."

"Then I say we leave now." Poseidon hoisted his blood-crusted trident. "They will not wait for us to heal and will attack while we are still weak... unless we strike first."

"Agreed," Alkaios nodded.

"But far from people," Hades insisted. "I cannot..." her words drifted off as she swallowed the bile fast rising in her throat. "We choose a place wide and open, away from anyone living." The entire crowd murmured their agreement, and Hades exhaled. "They will know it is a trap after today. They may not take the bait so easily."

"Witness how badly they beat us," Zeus argued, gesturing to the battered crowd. Hades shifted her eyes, her gaze landing on Athena's broken arm. The goddess cradled the swollen limb close to her chest, and the bone twisted at an unnatural angle. "They will take it if only to finish us."

"Especially if I confront Minotaur," Alkaios added somberly. "I will challenge him for you." He gripped Hades' hand. "And when you encourage him to kill me, to sever your connection to us, you will prove your loyalty to your ancestors. What better way to cement your position beside the horned god than to spur him to execute the man you once loved? He will do this to separate you completely from the Olympians. Minotaur will see you as one with the first gods, and so he will not be looking behind him when you stab him in the back."

"So be it." Hades left her husband's side and crossed the floor to Athena. Grasping her battered arm, Hades yanked it forward, and the bone gave a sickening pop. Athena cried out, her voice echoing off the walls, but as her cry faded down the hallways, so did the swelling. The color returned to its normal healthy shade, and Athena stretched it out experimentally. Not a single ounce of pain resided in her bones, and with a thankful tear, she looked up at Hades. The dark god lifted her finger and swiped the escaped droplet before it could roll from Athena's cheek, and then with a sweep of her hand, darkened tentacles of power burst through the room. Their smoke fingers clawed and weaved through the wounded until all broken bones were reformed and split skin knit back together. What the Olympians could not heal, Hades healed for them, but it was only temporary. What was to come could kill them all.

With a heavy heart and exhausted body, Hades rejoined Alkaios. Her fingers reached out to clutch his with desperation. Like ink dropped in water, black smoke began to twist from her to encircle the three greats.

"Hades!" Medusa called as the darkness swirled. "I will stand watch over the door and turn all who attempt to leave to stone. Once you ignite the portal, I will close it behind them and wait for you to seal it." Hades nodded in agreement, but Medusa stepped forward to clutch her arm. "I do not want to enclose you with them. You are the Omega, the end of all ends, and as a Gorgon, it is my duty to serve the first gods. All of them are unworthy save you, and I do not wish to sacrifice you and your child to an eternity of brimstone and the gnashing of teeth. I know not if your insanity will return or if your son will be born mad. I do not know if you will ever break open the gate to their realm again, but while you are still worthy of my service, I refuse to cage you. Perhaps once the Old Ones are sealed in their dimension and unable to touch us, we can find a way to ensure you are saved."

"Thank you." Hades smiled, squeezing the Gorgon's hand.

"But Hades," Medusa continued, a warning in her tone, "your blood runes will be strong; strong enough to trap you should you be within the portal when it ignites. Once all the Old Ones are inside the markings, we must act. The portal will be instant with no escape. We are relying on you to ensure that they take the bait, but whatever you do, do not get caught with them. Then there will be no saving you. Once the Old Ones are behind that door, we cannot open it for anyone, not even you. I do not wish to seal you with them, but I will if I have to. So by the gods, do not be within the blood when the last of them cross the threshold."

"I won't."

And with that, Hades, Alkaios, Zeus, and Poseidon vanished from the Underworld.

In the premature hours of the morning, while the world was still bathed in darkness, Hades drew the runes in the dirt with her blood. They had found a wide-open field at the base of a mountain, and they hoped the peaks would aid in trapping the deformed gods within their portal. After carving their runes into the gate on Medusa's mountain, each god had taken a quarter of the circle and bled onto the earth. From time to time she heard Zeus or Poseidon curse, a result of the water searing their hands, but Alkaios never uttered a word, her immunity having passed to him.

With the exception of the muttered expletives, they worked in utter silence, the gravity of their actions weighing heavy on their shoulders. If this last desperate act did not save them, this was the end. Earth would descend into madness, and Hades had already made up her mind. If they failed, and the Olympians perished, she would end her own life. There was no living with the Old Ones if they won. She refused to be part of their cruelty as they annihilated every living and dead soul until nothing remained of the world. No, it was better to join Alkaios in death than live beside the mad.

It took some time, but eventually, the massive field had been covered in holy blood and poisoned water. The four gods traveled to the center of the trap, their faces grim.

"We will be on the mountains," Zeus said, breaking the silence. "All of us. We will not retreat this time. I swear it. We will contain them for as long as our lives hold out, and we will either stand victorious, or the age of the Olympians will end."

"We stand with you." Poseidon clapped Alkaios on the shoulder with one hand and gripped Hades fingers with his other. "May favor fall upon us," and he turned and left, disappearing into the mountain.

"May favor fall upon us," Alkaios repeated to Poseidon's retreating form before shifting his eyes to Zeus. When he neither spoke nor moved, Alkaios reached his arm out into the air between them. Zeus slowly raised his hand and grasped Alkaios' forearm in an iron grip, and together they stood locked in solidarity before Zeus severed the contact. Without a word, he turned to Hades and slipping a palm behind her head, tilted it down. He bent and placed a reverent kiss on her raven hair, and then Zeus, too, was gone.

"I wish I could leave the pitchfork with you," Hades said in the early morning stillness once they were alone, two solitary figures amidst the wavering grass.

"They would know you had given it to me," Alkaios answered softly. "We cannot risk their suspicion before we have even begun."

"Do not die on me," Hades blurted, tears bursting from her eyes. In a heartbeat, Alkaios closed the distance between them and scooped her into his arms. He clung to her with all his strength, absorbing all the love and pain pouring from his wife's body.

"I love you," Hades sobbed into his chest, warmth from her tears spreading over his skin. "I will love you until I die."

"No." Alkaios smoothed her dark hair with a calloused palm. "Our love is infinite and cannot end. I will love you long after my days have ended. Not even death can steal you from me." He pulled back and grabbed her face in his hands. Tenderness poured from his skin to heat her cheeks. "I love you, Hades - my wife and my heart. I loved you when you were merely a lost woman named Persephone."

"To some, I still am Persephone, my lord Hades," she said, smiling through her tears, and Alkaios smirked at her words.

"To the world, we are Hades and Persephone, King and Queen of the Underworld, but to me, we will always be Hades and Alkaios. A destiny that cannot be broken brought us together, and despite the path it has taken us down, I would never trade it for another. If I die today, I will still have lived a better life than most men because of you."

And with that, Alkaios kissed Hades. A kiss to end all kisses.

XXXI

"Minotaur!" Alkaios bellowed into the early morning. The sky was beginning its transition from black to grey, and the King of the Underworld stood a tall and solitary figure amid the billowing grass. "Minotaur!" he screamed heavenward. "I have nothing left. You took everything from me. You destroyed our holy Olympus, you killed our devout followers, and now you have taken my wife. You are a monster worthy of neither the throne nor my queen. Stop hiding upon our mountain and come face me. I challenge you for my wife!"

High above the clouds, Minotaur and the Old Ones looked down on the earth and the raging god. Alkaios was a mere ant at this elevation, and Minotaur wanted nothing more than to squash these pitiful gods like the insects they were.

"This could be another trap," the three-eyed god said to her son. "They baited us yesterday."

"But to what end?" Hades spat, malice coating her words. "Their traps cannot hold us. They are weak. No, this one wants to die. After yesterday, he realizes they stand no chance. He wishes to die a quick death instead of enduring the agony we have in store for them when we invade the Underworld, and what better way to ensure your death than by challenging the king of all kings."

"How do you know this?" the three-eyed god spat, her old, worn eyes boring into Hades.

"Because." Hades met her grandmother's gaze with her own wall of icy disdain. "That one is my husband. I made him what he is, and without me, he is weak. He cannot survive in my absence. The coward hopes you kill him quickly to end his misery."

"I still think this is a trap," the old hag started to say.

"Silence!" Minotaur backhanded his mother with an echoing slap of flesh. The three-eyed god's head snapped backward, but she made no sound or cry, instead only taking the blow in stride before returning to her rigid stance. "You know these cowards," Minotaur addressed Hades. "Tell me, is this a trap?"

"Perhaps." Hades shrugged in nonchalance, willing her palms not to sweat. "But I carry little concern for any traps the likes of them can conceive. If it is, this is a final desperate act effort to save their skin, and after the defeat they faced yesterday, they are exhausted and sorely beaten. Their weakened bodies could never withstand us. No, this is a suicide. He is hoping you end him quickly."

"Should I grant his request?" Minotaur asked her. "Or are you going to beg I spare him?"

"Why would I beg for that?" Hades asked coldly. "He means nothing to me. He is a weak man and not worthy of breathing the same air as you, my King. He has been sitting on the throne of the Underworld in my stead, calling himself king of what is mine by birthright. His death brings us closer to victory."

"Then come, my child." Minotaur grinned, extending his arm for her to take. "Watch as I flay your imposter. I will slaughter him for you, but I will not make it swift. He will regret challenging me." Hades swallowed the revulsion rising in her throat and slipped a small hand around Minotaur's bicep. Out of the corner of her eye, she saw the three-eyed god's mouth flapping open in attempted protest.

"But we best heed your mother's warning," Hades said before the old woman could speak. "If they foolishly attempt an attack, perhaps we all should descend to earth. If they all lie in wait, it will work to our advantage. It will be as if they are serving themselves up to us on a feasting platter."

"Until they descend to Hell, making a fool of us," the three-eyed god muttered under her breath.

"No," Hades said unfurling her dark power around her body, "Not this time." And with a sinister glint in her eyes, she dropped from the mountain.

The web of dark power writhed through the air to encircle the field, and as Hades stood stoic before her husband, she saw Alkaios understood. Her power was as much a trap for the Olympians as the blood runes were for Minotaur and his foul brethren. This day would end with the destruction of a race of gods, although which had yet to be determined.

Not a soul moved in the morning light. The host of Old Ones hovered just beyond the snare's reach, the Olympians concealed within the protection of the mountain. Alkaios stood tense in the grass, the sacrificial bait, and with one last glance at the woman he loved beyond words, he pounded his fist against his chest and roared.

"What are you waiting for?" Alkaios bellowed, his voice ricocheting off the mountain.

"I will revel in the sound his bones make when they crack," Minotaur menaced low for only Hades' ears as if he knew the bile that rose within her throat. Hades forced her features to remain motionless, desperate not to show a single sign of vulnerability. "I will flay the flesh from his skeleton while he yet lives." Minotaur looked down at Hades, eyes boring like blistering worms into her skin. "This is my sacrifice to you, my Omega. Then you will be free of his weakness." And at his words, Minotaur strode forward.

Hades held her breath as his feet crossed the runes' threshold. She knew he would take his time with Alkaios, torturing him until he begged for death. She prayed to the universe her husband would be able to withstand Minotaur's viciousness and beseeched for her own resolve. What was at stake was more significant than them, and she could not break... not even as Alkaios' body did.

A raging bellow ripped the air wide with its flaying lash, and Hades flinched as Alkaios launched himself across the grass. His voice snarled, powerful legs hurtling him forward, and as his form leapt through the air on a collision course with the horned god, Minotaur raised his fist. The blow landed on Alkaios' jaw, sending a spew of dark blood flying from his mouth, and Alkaios' body plummeted backward. The dirt gave way beneath him as he skidded to a limp halt, and Hades bit her tongue to keep from screaming.

Not waiting for him to recover, Minotaur stalked forward and hoisted Alkaios' drooped mass above his head. With a savage crack, he brought Alkaios down hard upon his knee, and all who heard the snap knew Alkaios' spine had been severed.

"I will not be free of his weakness until they are all dead," Hades said to the Old Ones beside her, forcing her panic down her throat. She had to get her remaining ancestors to step within the rune, and she looked upon the three-eyed god's face. "The rest lie in wait on the mountain." The old hag gazed back at her, justified her concerns were valid, but also as if she suspected Hades of treachery. Desperate to control the situation despite her consuming fear at the scene of torture before her, Hades lifted the pitchfork and shot a bolt of inky smoke from its prongs. The blackness hurtled for the ridge, colliding with the stone in a cacophony of destruction, and the face of the mountain crumbled in an avalanche of dirt.

With a battle cry that shook the world, Zeus and Poseidon launched themselves through the cloud of settling dust, their muscled forms plummeting with the collapsing mountain to earth. The skies rained Olympians as each and every one fell to the field with brandished weapons, unsettling screams upon their lips. Both Hydra and Keres strode from the crumbling debris. Snakes as giant as a man entwined Hydra's torso and limbs and cascaded behind her like a magnificently embroidered train. Chimera followed, a host of furies at his flank, and at the sight of them, Minotaur halted his battering of Alkaios' broken body. He observed the charging gods with disinterest before returning to his prey.

"Kill them," the three-eyed god ordered, her wrist flicking in a command. It was all the encouragement her vicious brethren needed as they barreled into the fray led by the gnashing teeth of the fanged god, and just as Hades was about to breathe a sigh of relief, her grandmother raised her gnarled hands once more. The Old Ones still behind her ground to a halt, sending the icy grip of dread groping down Hades' spine.

"No need for all of us to step within their ambush," the hag cooed as the waves of gods crashed together, and Hades' stomach turned. Flicking her eyes to Alkaios, she knew he was not long for this world. His mottled flesh seeped his life's blood in spewing rivers onto the dirt, and judging by the screams of pain, the Olympians were not far behind him in their departure of this life. Hydra's snakes lay scattered in bloody tangles about the battlefield, her skin unable to birth them as rapidly as they died. Chimera and Keres fought back to back; the lion's jaw unhinged as his fangs shredded flesh, and Keres' bloodlust feeding the frenzied furies. Hades could see by the grotesque angle of Chimera's rear paw, that the bones were shattered. The battle had barely begun, and already the Olympians outnumbered ranks were faltering.

Lighting erupted from the heavens, slamming with fire and smoke upon the blood-riddled field. Through the blinding light Zeus stepped, brandishing his bloody thunderbolt. The sky reeked of burnt flesh as he crushed the singed bodies beneath him until he settled over Alkaios' destroyed body. His weapon lifted to challenge Minotaur, and the monstrous horned god abandoned the dying king of death for a greater prey. He bellowed as he bolted for Zeus, and with speed unnatural for such a hulking size, Minotaur bent his head and slammed his horn into Zeus' thunderbolt. The metal wrenched itself free of its master's grasp, and before Zeus could even bring his brain to acknowledge its absence, Minotaur shifted his horn and rammed it through Zeus' chest. Blood burst from Zeus' mouth as his ribs shattered under the piercing blow, and Minotaur rose to his full height, hoisting the skewered god into the air; his gore painted horn protruding from Zeus' muscled back.

Hades froze, mind numb. Her lungs rejected every breath she tried to suck down. Her throat constricted in horror as Zeus' blood ran in torrents down the horn and into Minotaur's eyes. Her brain began to spin, her stomach in upheaval. Hades thought she could hear the gratuitous cheers of the Old Ones beside her, but she could not be certain. Her ears blocked out all noise. Her heart refused to beat, and before she knew what she was doing, Hades opened her mouth and roared.

Her voice shattered the field with her anguish, a bellow that frightened even the Old Ones. Her scream ripped through her in terrifying desperation, the sound a raw pain, and when her breath finally ran dry, and her lips fell silent, Hades lifted the pitchfork and swung.

The head of the Old One closest to her rolled across the grass, blood spewing from severed arteries in stark contrast to the dull green. Hades lowered her gore-streaked weapon and turned her venomous stare to the three-eyed god. The old woman seethed a startled hiss, but that was all the response Hades allowed before she barreled into her. The women collapsed, and Hades forced herself atop her cursed grandmother. She lifted a fist and pounded it so harshly into the hag's forehead, the third eye popped like overripe fruit. The Old One screamed in fury, clawing at Hades' cheeks, nails gouging her soft flesh, but she was no match for the rage of the Omega. His mother's screams drew Minotaur's attention, yet Hades paid his blood-soaked shock no mind as she grabbed the woman's head and slammed it into the ground. Over and over again, she smashed it, and when the fight had left the hag's body, Hades gripped her face and pushed. Her two remaining eyes were the first to give way and then her skull. As the king's mother lay seeping into the earth, Hades stood up and pointed her pitchfork at Minotaur. Wrath emanated from him as he dropped the sputtering Zeus from his horn. Outrage at his mother's slaughter welcomed Hades' challenge. His incense at her betrayal fueled his anger as he stared down the field to the tips of her bident.

Hades opened her lips and loosed a bone-chilling scream as she bolted across the trodden sod. Her feet pounded the earth with a jarring force as she bore down on the horned god. She would kill every last one of them with her bare hands if she had to, and lowering her shoulders, she braced for impact. Her smaller frame barreled into Minotaur's chest, but unlike all the Olympians before her, her blow sent him crashing backward. His hulk burrowed into the ground as he fell, yet Hades did not delay. Landing gracefully in the trampled grass, she pulled back her arm and let the pitchfork fly. True to aim, its twin prongs buried themselves into her uncle's thigh as he struggled to stand, the demand behind her strike sending him sprawling once more.

Hades knew she had a split second before Minotaur wrenched the weapon free from his thick muscle, and her heart screamed to go to Alkaios, whose crumbled body barely resembled a man, yet Zeus' heaving form lay only steps from her feet. Desperately, Hades whirled on her heels and dove for the blonde god and slammed her palms against his gaping wound. Power poured from her, and the dark tentacles plunged into his flesh. Instantly Zeus' tissues began to knit together cell by sinew, staunching the river of blood.

"Hades!" Zeus warned weakly below her. The hairs on the back of her neck bristled, and Hades ducked. Her own weapon grazed the top of her head as her forehead slammed into Zeus' crimson-soaked chest, and as soon as the blow swept past, she shot her hand out. Hades grasped the pitchfork and rolled over the Olympian king in one graceful move before she bolted to her feet out of Minotaur's reach. Zeus' blood dripped from her fingers and face, a sacrifice for his people and their world across her skin's altar.

"Get out of the way!" Hades screamed, but Zeus was already moving, his feet scrambling beneath his almost fully restored chest.

"A traitor just as your father," Minotaur growled as Zeus lurched across the terrain toward the pulverized Alkaios. The whole field momentarily froze save Zeus' fleeing form as they watched the Alpha and Omega hover on the precipice of bloodshed.

"Better than a mad king," Hades spat, twirling her weapon, and as Zeus lifted her husband out of harm's way, she leapt. Their bodies crashed together with a resounding clang that shook the earth's plates. Their blows fell with vicious brutality, Hades a glorious match for the deformed Alpha. She blocked Minotaur's every move, countered his every blow, and as if terrified by their clash of power, the Old Ones began to drift outward, driving the Olympians back from the trap.

"Hold them!" Hades heard Poseidon bellow as she threw herself to the dirt and slid beneath Minotaur's thighs. The pitchfork's sharpened prongs sliced his thick flesh, and his howl rang painfully in her ears. Hades' eyes flicked to the god of the seas despite Minotaur's rage ringing in her skull. A fresh wave of terror washed over her as she watched the horde slowly seeping from the trap's circle. The Olympians tried to force their enemies back within, but it was no use. Blow by blow the Old Ones bled through the runes. Poseidon's face was a mangled disarray as he desperately fought. Athena and Ares could barely lift their broken limbs. Dead snakes littered the ground, and Chimera's mane had been all but ripped from his massive neck.

Hades watched in desperation as the Olympians wavered on the verge of falling, the Old Ones escaping their trap. She had shown her hand, betrayed her true allegiance for nothing. Hardly any remained within the blood runes, and the chance of driving them back was lost.

With a sudden crack, Hades' head exploded in pain, sending her sprawling. Minotaur hovered above her prostrate form. Wickedness spread across his lips as he bent and captured the front of her dress, hoisting her into the air. She coiled her arm for a devastating blow, determined not to be skewered like a hunted boar upon his horns, but before her fist could fall, a roar unlike anything she had ever witnessed shook the sky. Its sheer power thundered through the earth, and Hades tilted her sight heavenward and swore. What fresh hell was this monster?

XXXII

Minotaur dropped Hades at the sight of the beast descending upon them. Its wingspan stretched so wide it blotted out the sun, and its elongated tail swept below it in search of prey to feed his sword length claws. It shrieked into the air, its voice a cross between a lion and an eagle, and all who heard it were struck with terror.

As it closed in on them, the beast angled its wings as if to herd the Old Ones against the mountain, and at that same moment, the tall grass of the field beyond quaked. Hades knew who it was before she saw, and with the snarl of massive throats, Kerberos leapt from the grass. His razor fangs lowered as he sailed over the Old Ones instructed to remain steadfast and removed from the conflict by the three-eyed goddess. With a snap of his jaws, he separated three heads from their bodies. Their decapitated forms fell in a tangled heap, yet the dog charged onward, blood streaming down his chest as he followed the winged beast into the fray.

"Fall back!" Zeus bellowed as the Old Ones barreled past to escape the monster. "Fall back!" And with sudden realization, Hades understood. The beast had come to corral the deformed gods into the trap, her god-killer following him to punish those who did not heed Griffin's warning.

"Get out!" Hades screamed, arms gesturing wildly for the Olympians to flee as the Griffin swooped down and seized an Old One in his beaked mouth. With an incredible force, he bit down, splitting the body into two and letting the cleaved parts plummet to the grass. "Get out!" Hades pushed her legs as fast as she could, frantic to escape the onslaught of Old Ones barreling against her.

The Griffin soared overhead, doubling back to renew his attack, and Hades' eyes landed on Zeus desperately trying to pull both Alkaios' and Artemis' limp forms from the runes trap. She surged forward, forcing crazed gods from her path, and snatched Alkaios from the king's hands, refusing to slow. Hades poured her power into her husband, willing life to return to his destroyed flesh as she flung him over her shoulder. Kerberos caught her eyes among the sea of thrashing bodies and bolted for her, howling into the air with a vengeance. Chimera answered the dog's call, and together they flanked their queen as she ran through the oncoming throng.

Minotaur swung his gaze heavenward as the Griffin circled for another assault, the wind beaten beneath his wings. Minotaur stood motionless among the chaos as the beast bore down upon his brethren; claws and fangs poised for a massacre. Minotaur's eyes tracked the heavy beating of the wings, the feathered mass dipping low to the ground, yet still the horned god held. Feet pounded behind him as the gods scattered, but he remained a statue, listening to one whispered footfall that sharply contrasted the stampede.

The Griffin's beak parted in a macabre display, and Minotaur bolted into action. He twisted and shot out a brutal fist just as the master of those soft footsteps raced past. Athena coughed a strangled gasp as his blow cracked her ribs. Her body collapsed to the carnage-soaked grass, her grip on her weapon a lost cause as her shattered bones struggled to allow breath into her collapsing lungs. Minotaur plucked Athena's falling spear from the air and turned from her struggling form, abandoning her choke to death as she crawled to escape him, her ribcage trampled by the fleeing masses.

The Griffin's tail dove for the earth and carved a furrow into the soil. Minotaur grimaced as the beast hurtled for his next kills and spun on his heels. Athena's spear flew from his hands, its momentum hurtling its blow for the creature's exposed chest. With blinding speed, the holy weapon vaulted through the air. The Griffin's breast would be splayed out before he even saw his death coming.

"Below!" Athena's garbled voice rang out. Blood bubbled on her lips as she yelled, her words made unintelligible by her punctured lungs, but her alarm was all the warning the Griffin needed. His eyes shot forward and widened at the spear driving for his chest. Pitching violently, the beast heaved sideways. His claws snagged the ground as he moved, but the warning had come too late to save him from all harm. The spear ripped through the flesh at his shoulder and embedded itself deep into his muscles. The Griffin's shrieks shook the sky as his wings bore him heavenward, and his blood rained upon the battlefield like a crimson thunderstorm.

The fanged god licked his lips at a chance to sink his teeth into the reeling giant above, the torn wound his invitation to victory; an opportunity to taste such legendary flesh. The Old One angled his racing legs and launched himself off the shoulders of a lesser god. His dark mass flew into the air, rows of teeth bared for the kill as he crashed into the winged beast. His fangs sank into the Griffin's soft throat and ripped, and the Griffin screamed, his flight faltering. For a moment all below feared they would fall from the sky atop them, but with a shriek of anger, the Griffin lowered its jaw and plucked the deformed figure from his chest. Holding the black-scaled body firm in his mouth, the Griffin picked up speed as he careened toward the mountainside. The fanged god writhed and pitched, but the Griffin held fast and slammed the Old One between his beak and the rock, leaving nothing but a sinewy stain upon the stone.

The winged beast loosed a scream so colossal even the dead in Tartarus felt the vibrations through their torture. The Griffin beat his wings, igniting a gale force to sweep across the field as his body rose. The blackened clouds of the Old Ones' destruction welcomed the Griffin into their camouflaged ranks, and the winged beast vanished from sight as he prepared to strike again. Just as the sky swallowed him whole, his dark eyes locked with Zeus'. Their onyx gleam flashed at the King, and Zeus dipped his chin. No words passed between their minds, but none were needed. Zeus understood. The Griffin had seen the great god of Olympus nearly forfeit his life to stop an unstoppable evil, and that sacrifice could not be ignored. The Griffin did not meddle in the affairs of men, but when Zeus, lord of thunder, gave of himself, the Griffin finally recognized a reason worth fighting. This was his world, and no monstrosity would ever rule his golden nest save him. The Griffin tossed his head at Zeus, and then he was gone, silently soaring above the battle as the mad gods below clamored to predict where his mighty wings would attack again.

Minotaur bellowed as the red blemish of his brethren dripped down the mountain's face. In three long strides, he was at Athena's back. With his punishing weight, he stepped a heavy heel on the goddess' spine and sank into her. Her agony sputtered out in wet gurgles, but before he could extinguish her life, a figure hurtled to the ground before him. Pain exploded through Minotaur's muscles as a battered Hera drove a dagger into his foot. She growled with bared teeth as she twisted the blade with one hand and gripped the barely breathing Athena to her breast with the other.

"You cannot have her," Hera snarled, "Hades will ensure the

suffering you have inflicted upon our heads will be returned sevenfold." Her words of solidarity about her former enemy rang like a prophecy over the anarchy, and with Hera's defiance, the goddesses vanished from his grasp.

Minotaur wiped the blood from his foot. A wave of excruciating anger washed his soul, and with renewed vigor, he leapt after the retreating Hades. He was behind her in seconds, crushing the bodies of the fleeing Old Ones beneath his raging mass as he hunted her down. As Hades fled with her healing husband flung over her back, Minotaur shot out a massive hand and grabbed her ankle. A cry escaped Hades' throat as they plummeted to the ground, rolling over one another in a heap of tangled limbs, but before they came to a halt, Minotaur was above her, plucking her from Alkaios' crumpled figure.

"Save him!" Hades screamed at Kerberos, who bent his three heads in obedience and shoved them beneath Alkaios. He tossed his king over Chimera's back and turned to his mother. "Go! Get out!" Hades willed her dog to escape the trap. All others had cleared the runes, save them, and Hades knew as her uncle's unforgiving fingers clawed her body that her fate was tied to the Old Ones. She would not bind Kerberos' destiny to hers.

"Go!" she cried as Minotaur flung her to the ground. The dog pressed a wet nose to her fingers, but Hades slapped him aside as her bloodied form crawled through the grass. He had to leave. She needed him to live, and Kerberos backed away from her with hesitant steps. He withdrew as the Griffin above raged against their enemy, forcing the horde into the trap with his sheer, monstrous size. The Olympians formed an encompassing barrier around the battlefield, aiding the creature in the sky with his vicious assault, yet Kerberos continued to walk backward, eyes never parting from the one person he loved in this world. He would watch Hades until the end.

Hades' brain dizzied from the blow, and her palm instinctively went to her small belly. Minotaur paused at her protective gesture, and realizing what she had done, Hades snapped her hand back. She scrambled to her feet and brandished the pitchfork. She shot her eyes to where the Olympians stood as she bent her knees to attack. Zeus and Poseidon had their weapons pressed into runes, and Hades' saw their flicker of hesitation. They wanted her to move, to escape the runes, but there was no time. Minotaur was upon her, and only the Omega could contain his strength. With a shuddering breath, Hades locked gazes with Zeus and nodded with gritted teeth before slamming into the Alpha. With an excruciatingly heartbroken cry that ripped through the hearts of the Olympians, Zeus slammed the base of his weapon into the bloody symbol, and with a jolt of electricity from the thunderbolt, the trap ignited.

Wind began to howl about them, its ferocity clawing at all who remained within the trap's grasp. Desperate to free themselves, the Old Ones clawed their way through the grass toward safety, but it was no use. The blood of the Omega and the poison of the River Styx kept them bound, Hades' dark tentacles of smoke barred any escape, and the floodgates opened, sucking them in.

Minotaur threw himself into a crouch, fighting against the wind as his brethren began to disappear into midair, the portal drinking them down, but Hades drove the pitchfork into the ground as an anchor. She clung to it for dear life, yet it was not survival in her eyes but a goodbye. Across the field, Alkaios had recovered from his brutal assault enough to stand, and Kerberos and Chimera supported his weakened body as he rose. Keres and Hydra settled behind them, and the people who loved Hades the most watched as their salvation clawed at Hades, desperate to rip her away to an eternity of fear. Hades met each of their gazes, pausing to witness the love and sorrow in their eyes, and then she turned her features upon Alkaios. Among the chaos and screams, the couple stood solemn and stoic as if they were alone. Hades' knuckles drained of color as she gripped her weapon, but her gaze did not falter. A savage wind pummeled her body, and her legs staggered with its force. Alkaios' breath caught in his throat, yet still her gaze did not falter. Tears pooled in their eyes, and Alkaios slowly lifted a palm to his heart. He clutched his chest as if he could carve the organ out and send it into the madness with his wife, and Hades bit her lip to keep from shattering. Despite their hopes for salvation, it was not meant to be. This was the last time Hades would look upon Alkaios, and her heart broke. It shattered like glass against the rocks, yet still her gaze did not falter. They were in this together, husband and wife, refusing to part until the end.

Minotaur clawed through the howling gale toward his Omega as his race disappeared. He would snap her neck while an anguished husband watched, and then he would claw his way forward and fracture the so-called three greats' spines. Yet as he moved amidst the wailing wind, no one noticed his crouched crawl through the chaos, their focus instead on the raven-haired woman they were about to lose.

Hades' footing stumbled as the portal grew in strength, and Zeus knew she could not hold out much longer. His eyes flicked to Alkaios' distraught face only to be distracted by a movement out of the corner of his eye. A tearful Artemis, with the support of Apollo and Aphrodite, had lifted herself into a seat. Her bow was raised, its aim for Hades' heart. The promise Zeus made her swear rung in his brain, and with sudden clarity, Zeus knew that although death would be a better end than being trapped with these monsters, he could not allow that to happen. Watching Hades standing within her fate, resolved to suffer for their freedom, emotion overwhelmed him. He hated Alkaios for capturing her love, but with him, she was happy. Hades was her true self, a woman about to be blessed with motherhood. Zeus could endure Alkaios' stealing her, but he could not bear the knowledge of what losing her to these demons would mean for Hades. With all the power he possessed, Zeus hoisted his thunderbolt heavenward.

"What are you doing?" Poseidon bellowed over the roaring wind, forcing his trident harder into the blood marks.

"What needs to be done," Zeus said. An electrical current charged the air, surrounding the battered bodies of his brethren, and he cast the Olympians from where they lay collapsed in exhausted heaps. Medusa would need their help to hold the door firm until they trapped the mad gods inside, sealed away for all eternity, and Zeus sent the gods to her aid. At their disappearance, Zeus drew a bolt of lightning from the sky and whipped it at Hades who had finally succumbed to the trap's power. The pitchfork had ripped free from the dirt's hold, and Hades' body gave in to the whipping wind. Like a lasso, the crackling light ensnared her as she hurtled through the air, and as the last of the Old Ones vanished, Zeus pulled with all his might. Hades flew forward and disappeared with a boom of thunder as the wind of the portal died.

The field before him fell still. Its scorched and bloody grass stood empty, all within the trap shoved violently back into their own realm save Hades who Zeus had sent away… and Minotaur, who at that last moment realized Zeus meant to spare his Omega and grasped her heel just as she vanished.

XXXIII

"Hold!" Poseidon hurled his frame against the gate as the door pitched, sending a ripple through the Olympians as they clambered to regain their pressure. They only had to survive until Zeus joined them, and then with the shedding of blood, the king of the gods would bind those hellish monsters in their realm of chaos. The door heaved again, and both Poseidon and Alkaios threw their mass against it, a snarl seeping through Alkaios' gritted teeth as the Olympians shoved their weight into his back. He welcomed their brutal demand against his spine, the pain drowning out the nausea churning his gut at the thought of Hades' final moments. Suddenly the power in the room shifted, and with a rush of air, Zeus was beside them, broad palms slamming against the gate in resistance.

"Seal it!" Poseidon bellowed over the deafening anger on the opposite side of the stone.

"I can't!" Zeus strained against the door.

"What do you mean?"

"Minotaur escaped the trap. He is not behind this."

"What!" Alkaios jerked back to look at Zeus. Without his

strength, the door lurched under the Old One's pressure, and the Olympians dove forward, scrambling to shove it into place.

"I was trying to save Hades!" Zeus strained, his skin flushing red with exertion. "Alkaios, you were right. I was too selfish and arrogant to see it, but you were right. She does not deserve an eternity of madness locked behind this seal. I could not condemn her to this horror, so I sent her away. I will not let one of us suffer, and despite her lineage, Hades is one of us, my brother's wife." At his words, Zeus sliced his hand over the tip of the thunderbolt and extended it to a gaped-mouth Alkaios. "Become my brother in blood, King of the Underworld," Zeus continued, shoulder pressed against the door as he waited. "We will never be great if we allow hatred to fester. Both the Old Ones and the Titans allowed pride and rage to be their downfall. Let us not follow in their footsteps. The Olympians will be the last and final race of gods."

Alkaios slammed his mouth closed, though shock and relief still lingered in his eyes as he twisted against the heaving door and pressed his spine against it. He reached past Poseidon and dragged his palm over the thunderbolt, blood springing dark from his flesh.

"I stand with you." Alkaios seized Zeus' hand. With a wordless nod, Zeus turned from the King of the Underworld to the lord of the seas. His eyebrows rose in a question, and Poseidon shifted so that he might reach the thunderbolt.

"Always, brother." In a flash, Poseidon sliced his skin on the tip and placed his bloody flesh atop Alkaios and Zeus' joined fists. The instant the greats connected, wind whipped through the room and silenced even the raging Old Ones for the briefest moment. The electric power singed the air at their pact, and as their hands parted, two brothers became three.

"How did saving Hades allow Minotaur to escape?" Poseidon asked as the door resumed its violent pitching.

"He saw I meant to pull her from the trap. He grabbed hold of her as I freed her."

"You what?" Medusa screamed suddenly beside them, her snaking hair writhing about her body.

"I will not condemn her..." Zeus started.

"This is not about Hades!" Medusa's human shape trembled. "She was willing to sacrifice herself for our salvation, but by selfishly saving her to appease your guilt, you have allowed him to be free... the one we cannot afford to let live among us."

"You, Gorgon, do not command me..."

"You destroyed our last chance at survival," she screamed in desperation as her body began to shimmer, and all watched in horror as she shifted to her true self.

"Eyes down!" Alkaios bellowed as Medusa launched herself at Zeus.

In the split second before the Gorgon slammed into him, Zeus saw the blood that oozed from her scales and the bald patches atop her skull where patched of the snakes had been ripped out. He understood the pain she had endured to keep the door closed before the Olympians had arrived and the unending, lonely torture she had survived to stand guard over this seal after the Old Ones' fall. As Zeus thudded to the stone and his eyes clenched shut, he knew her anger was not waged over Hades' escape but over the burden she had been forced to bear for centuries.

"Medusa!" Zeus shouted as he fought blindly against her clawing fingers.

"You have killed us all!" Medusa screamed over his voice, her body pressing him into the cold floor. "For an eternity I guarded this temple! I was all that stood between mankind and annihilation before Hades unleashed their poison upon the world. We had one last chance to put this right, and you ruined it with your foolishness!"

Hearing the escalation in her voice, Alkaios dared to flick his eyes in their direction. A sigh of relief rushed through him when he saw her back, and with all the strength within him, Alkaios bolted forward. He flew across the stone, Ares and Apollo surging to hold the door in his stead as the rest pressed in behind them. With a jarring crash, Alkaios' large frame barreled into Medusa and wrenched her from atop Zeus. The Gorgon's scream split the air as she thrashed her massive serpentine body, yet Alkaios held firm, his arms restraining her in a prison of his flesh.

"Get the door!" Alkaios ordered Zeus who had already scrambled to his feet, but he had barely moved across the floor when the gate heaved. It threw the straining Olympians backward, and with clawing fingers, the faceless Old One forced it wide to release his grotesque form. The howl that ripped from his split and featureless face shattered the air, and the serpents about Medusa's head hissed, their small voices echoing her anguish. The snakes turned their fangs upon Alkaios and plunged them into his flesh. His breath sucked past his teeth as the pain involuntarily loosened his grip. Medusa bucked free and in a heartbeat, was upright, slithering with alarming speed. The snakes atop her crown surged about her neck, and with a blood-curdling scream, she leveled her gaze on the rogue Old One.

The effect was instant. The deformed god's green-scaled muscles hardened until his blood-warmed skin was cold, solid stone and his clawing talons froze in their hunt for flesh. Zeus and Alkaios balked with slackened jaws, momentarily forgetting to avert their eyes. They followed in awe as Medusa's thick, coiling tail flicked forward and collided with the petrified statue, shattering him into a thousand fragments of rubble. A shock of violent rage and pain jolted through the realm on the opposing side of the door at the loss of their brethren, and Zeus barely threw himself against the entrance in time to push it back into its frame as the Old Ones clambered to regain access to the world.

"You have doomed us!" Medusa started again, anguish and

dread consuming her. "With both Hades and Minotaur free, they will re-break this seal!" Her voice escalated in panicked waves as she dove for Zeus, and his sight dropped to the floor to keep from meeting the same horrific fate as the shattered wreckage at his feet.

"Medusa, stop!" Alkaios bolted for her. Fear was devouring her, her mind overrun, but even as he flew through the air, eyes clenched, Medusa coiled her immense, scaled body and struck. Her tail slammed into Alkaios' core and hurled him into the temple wall. The stone cracked against his spine as his collision punched an indent into its ancient surface. His breath left him in sputtering coughs as he toppled to the floor. Alkaios had to quell Medusa's panic before she destroyed any hopes they had at trapping the Old Ones, yet as he struggled to his feet, a hellish snarl ripped through the halls.

Alkaios' eyes snapped up in time to see Kerberos's hulking mass crash into Medusa's Gorgon shape. His brutal strength drove her to the ground, and with a growl, he pinned her head with his spiked tail. Medusa flailed, yet she was no match for the hellhound's might, and after long struggling moments, she collapsed in defeat. Sobs ripped from her mouth as she shook beneath the dog, all the fight evaporated from her muscles.

"You have doomed us!" The Gorgon cried. "All my years for nothing. You destroyed it with your selfishness."

"Not necessarily," came a deep voice, and the power in the atmosphere shifted. Something the Olympians had not felt in centuries.

XXXIV

Hades groaned, her lungs expelling air in ragged pants. Her back ached as she lay sprawled in the grass, the force of the impact wreaking havoc on her body. Her skin crawled with the electric jolt of Zeus' thunderbolt, and her fingers clung to her womb protectively as if the lightning had burned her son.

A sudden shift beside her was all the warning Hades received before a heavy hand was atop her stomach, clawing at the fabric of her dress. Frantically, Hades scrambled back, palms and heels gouging the dirt as she crawled, but Minotaur already had a hold of the cloth. With violence, he cleaved the front of her garment in two, revealing the subtle swelling of the child within her. Instantly his face darkened, evil seeping from every pore on his blood bathed skin. Hades vaulted backward, snatching the pitchfork as she found her footing before the Alpha.

"I will kill you for your treachery," Minotaur snarled, his tone so low and deep it rumbled through her chest, "and feast upon the abomination within you."

"You will never have my son," Hades spoke, her voice a calm terror, and twirling the pitchfork in her deft hands, she attacked.

AN EXCRUCIATING STILLNESS fell over the temple, the Olympians' shock denying them their movement. For a weighted breath, all was quiet, and then with painful slowness, Zeus turned to the powerful intruder.

"I killed your kind," Zeus growled, low and menacing. "Wiped every one from existence. So how is it a Titan yet draws breath?" All eyes fell upon the trespasser as his hulking form pushed through the frozen crowd, the only sound his soft footfalls and the rage beyond the door.

"You destroyed all but one," Charon answered, weaving through the bodies. "It was the Styx who claimed me, and therefore, I belong to Hades."

"Then I will remedy that!" Zeus gripped his thunderbolt as he lunged.

"No!" Alkaios bellowed, vaulting between them, arms outstretched. His palms slammed into both Charon's and Zeus' chests, forcing them to remain separated. "You will not touch him!"

"How long have you been harboring a Titan?" Zeus' anger reverberated through his chest. "The sins of the Titans demand his death. I cannot allow him to live, not when the evil of the first gods is still upon us. His kind wants nothing save our downfall," and at his words, Zeus forced his body forward. Alkaios stumbled, gritting his teeth, and with equally powerful resistance, slammed Zeus across the room.

"How dare you stand in my way," Zeus said, regaining his footing.

"You will not touch him." Alkaios settled his frame before Charon's in defiance, his heels grinding into the stone.

"Now is not the time for this!" Poseidon said as both he and Ares hurtled themselves against the lurching door, the weary efforts of the gods waning as fatigue chewed through their muscles.

"Get out of my way," Zeus growled, ignoring the pleas of his brother.

"Stop," Charon's deep voice commanded as he sidestepped Alkaios' protective stance. "Do with me what you will, but only once this is over, for I have come to help." Zeus' eyebrows pinched in confusion, but when he failed to move, Charon continued, "I am Charon, ferryman of the Underworld and the last living Titan. I owe my life and my family to Hades, and I am here to repay that debt. Zeus, if you, Hades, and I band together to create this blood seal, then only one born of all three generations of gods can break it. Alkaios and I have already sworn a blood oath to ensure that should any of our descendants wed, no children will be birthed from their union, assuring the door forever remains welded shut."

"Listen to him," Alkaios pleaded. "This will save Hades and my son. Even if the madness consumes her again, both she and our child will be helpless against this seal."

"Will this work?" Zeus asked, looking to Medusa who had shifted back into her disheveled human form.

"It might," she breathed as Kerberos lifted his pressure from her chest. "But you need to confine Minotaur before we can bind them."

"Go." Charon clapped Alkaios on the shoulder as he strode to the door and heaved his weight against it. "We will hold them for as long as possible," and as if to prove the urgency, the Old Ones crashed against the stone at his touch. Charon braced himself, and both he and Poseidon forced it back, the Olympians' gathering to lend their power.

"Dispatch me to where you sent her," Alkaios asked Zeus, and his eyes flicked to the Titan with hesitation.

"I swear to you, I will not harm a hair on his head while this door remains unsealed," Zeus promised.

"We will hold you to that," Keres' voice drifted from a dim hallway, and Keres, Hydra, and Chimera padded through the darkness to join the gods in their resistance. As he passed the King of Olympus, the lion loosed a soft menace, his protruding fangs bared, fur stained with the blood of his battle victims.

"We will remain as long as we can," Zeus said as Kerberos settled beside Alkaios. He wrapped his spiked tail around the god's waist, making it clear he intended to aid in the retrieval of his mother. "But I beg you to make haste, we cannot withstand them forever," and with that Zeus reached out his palm and placed it against Alkaios' chest. With a flash of light, the room surged with static power, and Alkaios and the god-killer disappeared.

HADES SCREAMED A BLOODCURDLING battle cry and collided with Minotaur's back. With terrifying grace, she curled her thighs around his neck, latching on tight as she lifted the pitchfork. Hand gripping his bloody horn for leverage, Hades drove the weapon's twin points down toward his skull, but at her moment of triumph, Minotaur seized her ankle and yanked. Her frame jerked sideways as she clung to his horn with all her strength, her torso hanging halfway down his body, but before Hades could regain her seat, he pulled again. With a violent pop of her ankle, Hades careened to the dirt and landed in a heap with pain on her lips. She groaned in agony, desperate to rest, to lie in the grass and cradle her bleeding body, but she felt Minotaur settle his mass over her. With a roar, Hades dragged herself forward, struggling to recover her footing, yet the horned god was hard on her heels.

The air shifted as Minotaur's fist hurtled toward her spine, but before he connected, Hades twisted on the grass and swung the pitchfork. The ancient metal cracked Minotaur's wrist with such force, the monstrous god howled and withdrew his arm to cradle the bent bones. Hades smirked. Her tongue flicked out to lick the blood from her split lip, and she leapt, refusing him time to recover. The tips of her bident drove deep into his thigh. Sacred blood burst from Minotaur's flesh, and with a bellow, he seized Hades by the throat and wrenched her off the ground. His hand closed around her windpipes as he drew her up to his eyes and squeezed. Hades gagged, her skin paling to blue as her body was deprived of oxygen. Her fingers clawed at his fist, frantic to free herself from his iron grip. She kicked with ruthless accuracy, but Minotaur simply held her away from his frame, her legs thrashing the empty air far from their target. Her vision began to blur, and Hades recoiled her leg and aimed for the weapon protruding from his muscles.

With a forceful kick, Hades drove the pitchfork further into his leg. A grunt of pain escaped Minotaur's normally stoic lips, and he hurled her across the field. Hades hit the dirt with an agonizing thud. Her lungs burned as oxygen rushed past her bruised throat. Coughs wracked her chest, and as her vision cleared, she watched Minotaur wrench the pitchfork from his thigh and take aim. Hades realized, with terrifying clarity, that its trajectory was intended for her skull, and the dark tentacles of smoke engulfed her as quickly as she could conjure them. She vanished only to reappear seconds later beside the flying bident. Her fist plucked it from the air, and using its momentum to swing her body around to face her uncle, Hades brandished the weapon. Vicious hatred painted his features at her effortless escape. She was not so easily killed.

Urgency renewed, Minotaur broke into a thundering run, and Hades launched herself forward in retaliation. As he neared, she threw herself to the ground. The force propelled her over the grass and through Minotaur's racing legs. As she hurtled beneath him, Hades swung the pitchfork and gouged the bloody points through his leg. The flesh severed with a wet tear, the metal slicing a jagged wound until its prongs struck solid bone, but instead of faltering as Hades hoped, Minotaur's foot lashed out and pummeled her head as her momentum slowed. Hades tumbled across the field with bruising speed. Her mind fogged at the impact, and when she rolled to a stop, her muscles begged for relief. Her spine ignited. Her ribs threatened to shatter with every shuddering breath she gulped. As she struggled to her knees, Minotaur turned, his detached calf causing his gait to hobble an uneven limp. He was upon her in a heartbeat, and capturing her scalp, he hoisted Hades' battered face to meet his gaze.

"You cannot win against me, Omega," Minotaur snarled as he crushed pressure against her skull. Hades loosed a vicious scream from her bloodied lips and shifted to attack when a dark movement behind the horned god caught her eye. She froze as the force on her brain built and lifted her eyes to greet the Alpha's. Hades smirked, a haughty expression flashing through her features, a secret only she could see. For a moment, her uncle faltered, confused by the look on her face, and that was all the pause Kerberos needed as his hulking body careened through the air and collided with Minotaur.

XXXV

Minotaur plummeted to the ground with such force the plates of the earth shifted, but before he registered the attack, Kerberos was atop him, crazed fangs gnashing at his throat. Minotaur's muscular arms heaved and shoved against the hound, yet the dog did not give way, his aggression intensifying in viciousness. His claws gouged the soft flesh of the god under him, blood bursting forth to bathe his paws as his three heads assaulted Minotaur from every direction.

"Get up," a deep voice commanded as rough hands seized Hades' arms and hauled her to her feet - calloused palms she would know anywhere.

"Did it work?" The words tumbled from Hades' lips as she twisted to face Alkaios, fists clutching his skin.

"All save him." He swung his eyes to Minotaur before shifting them back with concern to the shredded fabric of Hades' dress that exposed her stomach.

"Our son is fine," Hades said before Alkaios could ask. "We have to get…" but the whistle of rushing wind silenced her words. Both gods stumbled apart just in time to avoid Kerberos's soaring figure. The dog flew past, limbs and tail flailing in the air as he collapsed to the ground and scored the dirt with his spiked spine.

Earth rumbling beneath their feet, Hades shot her eyes to her husband, who gave her a slight nod as he shoved his legs into a run. Hades swung the pitchfork and caught the barreling Minotaur in the stomach with a stunning blow. The monstrous god roared as a red welt swelled his flesh. He turned his murderous intent upon Hades, all thoughts of Kerberos forgotten, but as he reached for her, the pitchfork evaporated in black tentacles.

Alkaios careened through the air. Smoke became metal as he soared, the pitchfork re-solidifying in his waiting grasp. Weapon clenched firmly in hand, he drove it into Minotaur's back. The beast howled. His arms desperately clawed behind him to wrench Alkaios from his back, but Alkaios held firm, driving the prongs deeper.

"Kerberos!" Alkaios called as his body pitched violently, but the dog was already moving. Powerful legs propelled him forward, and the god-killer plowed into Minotaur's exposed chest and sunk his middle fangs deep into the soft flesh of Minotaur's throat, his side heads latching onto his broad shoulders. Both god and beast careened backward, and Alkaios barely had time to tug the pitchfork clear before the falling monster crushed him. But free it he did, and as he rolled from harm's way, Alkaios hurled it through the air.

Hades deftly captured the weapon as it soared and bolted into a run. Her exhausted legs protested as she bent her knees and hurdled over the grass, her aim for his skull true, but Minotaur's speed was unmatchable. With the ease of one flicking away a fly, the horned god flung the hellhound from his chest with a sickening tear of his own flesh that was caught in the dog's teeth and lifted a thunderous thigh. Hades' eyes widened with fear as she hurtled down upon him. Minotaur's foot aimed for her womb, a blow meant not for her but her son. Contorting midair, Hades twisted barely in time for impact. Her voice ripped from her throat as his heel impacted her spine and sent her slamming to the earth.

Hades thought she heard Alkaios screaming behind her, but the world felt muted as her brain fought for control. Her limbs shook beneath her. Her breath sliced her chest like knives to her lungs, and Hades barely registered the movement above her as Alkaios skidded to a halt. His figure cast a shadow about her heaving body as he snatched the pitchfork from her weak grasp, and with not a moment to spare, he anchored the weapon's base in the dirt.

The impact jarred the air around them as Minotaur's chest slammed into the uneven prongs. Minotaur's mouth loosed no scream of pain as his flesh poured fresh crimson. Minotaur's only mission was to shred the traitorous Omega before him, and not even the weak King of the Underworld she called husband would stand in his way. Minotaur leaned forward, forcing the metal both further into his rib cage and into the ground where it was imbedded, and watched for the moment Alkaios realized he was trapped. The Olympian heaved against the pitchfork, but it was no use. The metal was locked in place, and with a satisfied snarl, Minotaur plucked the lesser god from the dirt and hurled Alkaios across the field. The crunch his bones made against the far-off stone was sickly satisfying to the horned king, and as Alkaios' body crumbled, Minotaur turned his attention to his true prey.

Suddenly he was on his stomach, prostrate before Hades in a cloud of dust. Bewildered, Minotaur struggled. His fingers clawed the trodden soil, but Kerberos had both of his ankles in his mouth and was hauling him from his mother. Hades ripped the pitchfork from the dirt with unsteady limbs and whipped a blow across his horned skull. The crack of metal striking god was deafening, and a small fracture fissured through one of his horns as Kerberos hauled Minotaur bleeding through the grass.

"Get your husband," a sudden voice urged in Hades' ear.

She jerked in terrified surprise and swung her weapon for the throat of the interrupter but froze when she saw Hephaestus stride past her. The limping god carried a bloodied stone in one fist. Blood she recognized the scent of. It was hers. In the other, he gripped a vial, and Hades noticed angry, pus-filled blisters about his hands and wrists. With a horrifying realization, her eyes focused in on the glass. It contained water from her River Styx. Water Hephaestus had paid dearly to possess.

"Go to the door," the mason of the gods ordered as he bent, lowering himself to the ground, and with arms honed powerful by the pounding of metal, he shoved his fists into the dirt. Immediately, the earth began to quake. The soil rippled out over the vast field, and slowly as a plant pushes up toward the sun, stone grew. Haphazard at first, its pale visage forced higher, spreading from Hephaestus' clenched fist.

"The cage I built for you, altered for such a time as this when all hope of sealing Minotaur in his ancient realm was lost," Hephaestus called over the thundering of rising stone. "An ever-shifting maze designed for a god, it boasts an entrance yet no exit; all ensnared within its changing walls will be trapped for eternity, never able to find an escape while its prisoner survives. The stone is a blend of the Titan fortress and the Olympian mountain; rocks blessed by two generations of gods, cursed by the blood of the true god of death, and forged by a hammer washed in your blood, our end of all ends. The water is from your poison river, the Omega's greatest defense against the Alpha. Imbued with the waters of the Styx and the power of his brother's heir, Minotaur will never break free from its bonds, lest he wish his skin to be burned and flayed from his bones."

Hades gripped the pitchfork and watched the stone grow and evolve, a massive circular maze beginning to take shape. At the center stood Kerberos and Minotaur locked in combat, and a sickening fear rose in her throat.

"Kerberos…"

"I will pull him from the trap if I can." Hephaestus groaned and strained against the earth, "but I need him here to contain the god. The labyrinth needs time to grow. Minotaur must not leave this spot. If he escapes, we lose our last chance of containing him."

"Then I will stay."

"No." Hephaestus' command halted her in her tracks. "The Olympians cannot hold that door much longer. They need you to seal it. Please, Hades, go before it is too late."

"Do not let him die."

"I swear it by all that is holy, I will do all I can to save your god-killer."

Hades stood frozen for a moment staring as Kerberos attacked Minotaur with vicious assaults only to be beaten back by the Alpha's brute strength. She knew she had to move her feet, yet she lingered, rooted to the ground, watching her beloved companion struggle until the walls of the maze grew too tall for her to see past. Her eyes moistened with tears, and with a silent plea to whoever might be listening that her dog would survive, she turned and bolted for Alkaios. Hades had him in her arms in seconds, and together they vanished from the grass in a twisting upheaval of smoke.

XXXVI

Hades landed on the temple stone with a graceful thud and lowered Alkaios to his feet. The sight before her jolted urgency through her veins. The Olympians and the beasts of the Underworld strained against the pitching door, their waning strength faltering as her ancestors clawed for release, but it was her ferryman wedged between Zeus and Poseidon that caused Hades to bolt into a run.

"Charon!" Hades elbowed her way through the crowd. Charon's sweat-stained face turned at her voice, and with a welcoming arm, he seized her smaller frame and drew her to his side.

"What are you doing here?" Hades' eyes flew wildly between him and Zeus.

"Helping bind the gate," Charon answered, guiding her between himself and the King of Olympus. Poseidon slipped back to allow Hades room, and all three generations of gods held palms against the stone.

"If we seal the door," Zeus explained over the thundering beyond, "only he whose veins flow with the blood of all three generations can break it. Not you, not your son."

"Where is Minotaur?" Medusa interrupted, her voice a frayed nerve.

"A trial for another day," Alkaios answered as he settled behind Hades. Medusa opened her mouth in protest, but something about the look in his eyes silenced her, and Medusa drifted back to be swallowed by the crowding Olympians.

"Are you ready?" Zeus asked, extending his hand to Hades. Blood still flowed from the slice he had carved with his brothers, and Hades studied it curiously for a moment before lifting her sight to his haggard face. With a solemn nod, Hades lifted her hand to the tip of the pitchfork and sliced the soft flesh of her palm with its broken prong. Charon followed her lead, and with a deep breath, Hades, Zeus, and Charon placed their bloodied skin against the ancient door.

Alkaios raised his arms and encircled his fingers about his wife's shoulders, forcing all of his dark energy into Hades. Smoke snaked from their bodies, encircling both husband and wife until raging power consumed them. The tentacles twisted and churned, ensnaring Hades' wrists before diving into the stone. Behind him, Alkaios felt the hands of Keres and Hydra rest upon him, lending their support, and one by one the Olympians followed suit. Together they formed a web of limbs, each and every god linked in unity. Strength flowed from one body to the next until all connected with the three gods at the gate, and as soon as the last hand joined, a shock ripped through the room.

Power raged through them. The air pulsed with palpable waves, and the door vibrated with rattling tension. It bucked beneath their palms, opposing their force, but the gods did not give way. They forced their blood into the stone, their solidarity driving it deep, and slowly, the grain began to seal itself. The rock knit together to reform a solid surface, devoid of any cracks and blemishes.

The gate flared hot against Hades' flesh, the Old Ones

resisting the gate's healing with all their strength, and Hades loosed a scream. Her limbs trembled as she urged her power further into the temple stone. Her hands burned. Her skin begged for reprieve, yet Hades refused to back down. Beside her, Charon's breath labored, and Zeus' roar tore through the temple with raw, visceral pain. Together, their anguish and struggle mixed with the anger that oppressed them on the opposing side. Their bodies shook. Their vision blurred, yet still, they held, the rock knitting closed at a sluggish pace.

Knowing they could not hold on for much longer, Hades peeled her hand from the door and grasped her father's weapon tight in her bloody palms. It had been his power that sealed the gate those centuries ago. It had been the Omega who had ended it. She was now the Omega reborn, her father's heir, and once again it fell to her to be the end. With trembling, exhausted limbs, Hades lifted the pitchfork and with astonishing force, slammed the twin prongs into the stone with a lung-piercing scream.

The jolt that rioted through the temple shook the mountain to its core, a charge so intense it ripped through all who stood joined to the Omega. As power vacated her veins and flowed through the ancient weapon, Hades' eyes went dark. Her hearing muffled, and her limbs numbed. She fought against the pain. Her voice screamed in rage, refusing to yield, and with a violent groan and heave from the earth beneath her feet, Hades collapsed into darkness.

HIS VOICE WAS the first she heard - the voice she loved with a fierce devotion. Hades' eyelids peeled apart. Her head shrieked in agony at the dim light, and her lids clenched shut, returning her to the blackness.

"Hades?" It came again low and laced with concern. His

calloused palms cupped her cheeks, and when she did not open her eyes, he scooped her against his chest.

"Is it done?" Hades breathed, her lungs stinging. A collective sigh rippled through the room, and Hades finally forced herself to look up when she felt Alkaios' fingertips press against the swell of her belly.

"It is done." Alkaios studied this woman his soul craved, love seeping from his skin into hers, and Hades lifted her bloody fingers to his stubbled, handsome face. That was all the encouragement Alkaios needed. Within a breath, he closed the space between them and covered her mouth with his. He kissed her deeply, enveloping Hades in his arms as if he meant to never let her go.

Eventually, Alkaios released her lips, much to her heart's protest, and Hades gulped air breathlessly as her fingers left his face to find his hand. She flipped it over and studied the slice on his skin that mirrored the one on Zeus'. Her mind retraced time and realized Zeus' blood had already been spilled when she had arrived. Hades' gaze searched the host of disheveled gods, and Poseidon anticipated her searching and twisted his palm, revealing he, too, bore a matching wound.

"A blood oath?" Hades asked, scrutinizing Alkaios' face. He answered with a smile and unable to release her, pressed a kiss to her forehead.

"I witnessed firsthand what hatred did to the Titans." Zeus stepped forward. "I thought the evils of my father poisoned them, but look what hate and greed did to the first gods. How long before that becomes us? We are now brothers in blood and in name. Since humanity knows your husband as Hades, god of the Underworld, let it be known that Zeus, Poseidon, and Hades are the three greats of Olympus, brothers who will stand together from this day until the end of our days. Our predecessors perished by violence, and we cannot allow our sins and pettiness to destroy us. Let us give our children no reason to slaughter their parents to save the world." At his words, Zeus knelt beside Hades and rested his palm against her belly, feeling the strong life growing within her.

"Thank you," Hades whispered through cracked lips. Her fingers found his bloodied hand and clenched it weakly. Zeus flashed a quick glance at Alkaios to ensure he was not overstepping and then planted a kiss atop Hades' head.

"While the world may recognize you only as Persephone, Queen of the Underworld," Zeus continued, "You will always be our Hades. The Omega - the end of all ends and the true god of death. Know this, when we rebuild our holy mountain, a seat on our council is yours. A throne will rise from the stone beside your husband's at my left hand. Hades and Persephone rule together, both in the Underworld and on Olympus." Zeus' voice fell silent, and he shifted toward Alkaios. The dark king nodded his head, and Zeus clapped him on the shoulder respectfully before returning to his feet.

"Hades." Poseidon stepped forward. He bent and grasped her hand in his and lifting it to his lips, pressed a kiss to her knuckles. "Do not go opening any more doors."

At his words, the tension dissipated, and a few voices released laughter into the room. A smile brightened Hades' face, and Poseidon's handsome eyes winked playfully as he clapped Alkaios on the back.

"I will see you soon, brother," Poseidon promised Alkaios. "Now what do you say we go and repair our mountain," he continued as he joined Zeus. "The Underworld might have been our salvation, but I am looking forward to a home that is not dead, even if it is in ruins."

"I could not agree more," Zeus smiled and reached his hand out to a disheveled Hera. His wife rushed to him, clinging to him beneath the protective pressure of his arm. Their bodies began to vibrate as they prepared for their departure, and Hades lifted shaking fingers into the air. With a shuddered breath, she released all the strength she had left. Dark tendrils licked and devoured the wounds of the suffering Olympians, and together in tumultuous smoke, they vanished from the temple for their holy mountain.

As soon as they were alone, Keres and Hydra flew to Hades. They enveloped her in their warm embrace, and even Chimera limped forward and laid his heavy weight across her legs. Keres smothered Hades' filthy face with kisses while Hydra clutched her hands and cried. Chimera's rumbling purrs reverberated throughout his mother's chest, and all the while, Alkaios refused to release his wife from his hold.

"Your son?" Keres asked through her sobs.

"Strong," Hades whispered.

"Like his mother," Alkaios said and pressed his lips to the back of Hades' head when the air cracked with a violent wave of wind. The ground thundered, and in a heartbeat, Chimera bolted to a stand and settled his battered mass before the huddled group. A protective snarl seeped past his fangs, and for a terrifying moment, all froze in fear of the worst.

Without warning, Hades leapt to her feet and raced into the darkness. Alkaios and Keres exchanged bewildered looks and scrambled after her, Hydra and the lion hard on their heels. They tore through the temple at a breakneck pace and burst out into the open.

"Hades?" Alkaios called as the fresh air caressed his cheeks. The ashen sky was slowly clearing above them, allowing slivers of sunlight to pierce the ground as Hades raced through the rubble. She ignored her husband's question and searched frantically through the debris. Her eyes peered behind every boulder until they landed on a shredded ribcage panting with fragmented gasps. Plummeting to her knees, Hades scooped one of Kerberos' bloodied and bruised faces into her arms. She gathered his head close to her breast, tracing his flayed flesh with delicate fingers. Tentacles of inky power drifted from her skin to seep into his, trying to heal his battered body. Kerberos was so utterly broken that for long moments she waited with bated breath for the dog to breathe his last breath, yet struggle as he might, Kerberos drew one ragged inhale after another.

"You cannot leave me," Hades whispered into her god-killer's ear. "I need you, my darling. I love you." Tears rolled down her stained face and onto his leathery hide, and as she sobbed bent over his ribs, the dog stirred. Slowly at first, his side head lifted and with a weak slobbery tongue, he licked the tears from her cheeks. Hades jerked back in surprise and watched in awe as he raised his three heads and pressed them against her womb.

A smile broke Hades' sobs, and her arms snaked around his thick neck. This was not the great hellhound's end. It was a new beginning, for as Kerberos' beloved mother clung to him, Alkaios settled beside his three heads. He wrapped one arm lovingly around his wife and rested his other on the hound's side. Chimera was next to join them, lowering his body to the dirt at Kerberos' belly. His warm back insulted the dog's healing abdomen. Lastly, Keres and Hydra knelt beside their raven-haired queen, their tentative hands resting lightly on the god-killer's three heads.

Kerberos had been both created and destroyed by the first Omega, but as he lay there battered and bruised, his ears listening to his mother's thudding heartbeat, he was granted a new life. This Omega was his, and she loved him. She loved them all, and as they clung together among the rubble of the ruined temple, the proof of Hades' love radiated from the tiny soul growing in her womb beneath Kerberos' head.

EPILOGUE

Hermes strolled through the sunshine, enjoying the warmth on his face. Between their retreat to the Underworld and the grueling months it had taken for the dark ash to clear from their mountain, he had despaired he would never see the light of day again. Yet here he was, the brightness blinding his eyes. It was a long and seemingly endless task to restore Olympus to its former glory. Hades' son had already seen two summers in the time it took to scour the blood from their defiled home, but true to his word, Zeus slaved tirelessly to rebuild what was holy and to ensure both Hades and Alkaios claimed a seat on the council. Hera still hated that fact, even after these past years, but Zeus had made the right decision. Both the gods and the earth had not known peace like this in decades, and as the world healed from Minotaur's genocide, so did Olympus.

Hermes turned down a side street and trudged his way lazily through the residences of the immortals. Many of them had perished in the Old One's attack, but Hades and Alkaios personally delivered them to the great fields of Elysium. These dwellings stood mostly empty now, which is why he relished the peace felt wandering through them. With only the sun as his companion, Hermes reveled in these stolen moments of solitude. He was gloriously alone with his thoughts in these minutes where the endless tasks of restoring the mountain and the earth disappeared from his mind.

A sudden freezing wind ripped him from his reveries, and Hermes' face jerked down, lamenting the loss of heat on his cheeks. The icy blast whipped again, the cold air swarming his ankles, and he dropped his gaze to the clean stone on which he stood. Wisps of pure snow fluttered around his feet and melted against his sun-heated skin, the tiny crystals like needles as they assaulted his flesh.

Alarm seized his spine. Panic froze his veins. His legs followed the fluttering ice before Hermes knew he was moving despite the pit gnawing at his gut. Its frozen beauty led him down the stone to a familiar door where the snowflakes seeped under its crack and out into the openness of the sun-soaked corridor. Hermes' stomach knotted uncomfortably as he registered two things. The first was that this had been Hades' old room when she was a mere immortal, and the second was that it did not snow atop this sacred mountain.

Never in all their centuries had ice cursed Olympus' perfection, yet there was no denying the snow that whispered from beyond the door, freezing Hermes' skin.

HADES RETURNS IN PANDORA

IF YOU ENJOYED THIS BOOK & FEEL COMFORTABLE LEAVING AN AMAZON REVIEW, I WOULD GREATLY APPRECIATE IT. THANK YOU FOR READING PITCHFORK!

SIGNUP FOR FOR MY MONTHLY NEWSLETTER TO RECEIVE WRITING UPDATES AND MY NOVELLA

'OF MOMS, MUTTS, & MURDER.'

SUBSCRIBEPAGE.IO/NICOLESCARANONEWSLETTER

ALSO BY NICOLE SCARANO

Autopsy of a Fairytale
Murder Mysteries Inspired by Fairytales

Autopsy of a Fairytale

Forensics of a Fable

Kidnapping of a Myth

Criminology of a Character

Evidence of a Folktale (Coming March 2025)

The Scattered Bones
A Dark Fantasy Romance

The Pomegranate Series
A Gender-Swapped Hades & Persephone Reimagining

Pomegranate

Pitchfork

Pandora

The Competition Archives
A Horror Dystopian

There Are Only Four

There Was Only One

There Will Be None

We Are Not Blood (Coming 2025)
A Found Family Post Apocalyptic

Season's Readings
Holiday Romances

*As N.R. Scarano

Wreck The Halls

X Marks the O's

Tryst or Treat

Happy Hunting (Coming Easter 2025)

Married & Bright

The Expanse Between Us
*As N.R. Scarano

An Enemies to Lovers Sci-fi romance

A Loyal Betrayal
*As N.R. Scarano

A Camelot Reimagining Age Gap Romance

ABOUT THE AUTHOR

Nicole Scarano *The Mood Writer for the Mood Reader* is a Multi Genre Author who writes Romantic Crime Thrillers/Police Procedurals with twists, Fantasy romances, and Sci-Fi romances because it makes her brain happy. She doesn't like to box herself into one genre, but no matter the book, they all have action, true love, found family, a dog when she can fit it into the plot, swoon-worthy men & absolutely feral females.

In her free time, Nicole is a dog mom to her rescued pitbull, a movie/tv show enthusiast, a film score lover, and sunshine obsessive. She loves to write outside, and she adores pole dancing fitness classes.

For more information & to sign up for her newsletter visit: nicolescarano.com

Made in the USA
Columbia, SC
10 April 2025